Dear Reader,

Over the years I have written a number of Christmas novels and novellas, all of them love stories, all of them as full of sheer romance as I can possibly make them. They vary, too. I try my best never to write the same story or create the same character more than once. I aim for originality. However, all my Christmas stories have something else in common apart from the romance. They all have three main characters—the hero, the heroine, and Christmas itself!

Christmas is never incidental to my stories; they are never love stories that just happen to occur over the Christmas season. Christmas is central to all of them. None of them could happen quite as they do at any other time of the year. Christmas has so many meanings. There is the religious, of course, and, yes, that sometimes appears in my stories. More than that, though, Christmas represents all that is finest in the human experience. It represents family and warmth and kindness and joy and peace and second chances and a whole host of other desirable things.

Give me a pair of star-crossed lovers, I have always said, and Christmas, and preferably a child or two, and watch me go! In *A Christmas Bride*, Edgar Downes falls in love with the wrong woman, Lady Helena Stapleton, who is carrying around with her a great deal of baggage from her guilty past. Aware that he cannot be happy with her, he nevertheless marries her. But when he takes his bride home for Christmas, the magic of the season contrives to bring her pardon and peace, and to bless the two of them abundantly. In *Christmas Beau*, Judith Easton, who had once jilted the Marquess of Denbigh for another man, finds that he is pursuing her relentlessly again now that she is a widow with two small children, and he invites her to a Christmas house party in the country. His motive is revenge—but he has chosen the wrong season, foolish man, for such a negative plan!

I hope these two classic stories from the 1990s will help warm your hearts over the Christmas season and beyond.

Mary Balogh

"One of [Balogh's] best books to date."
—A Romance Review

AT LAST COMES LOVE

"Sparkling with sharp wit, lively repartee, and delicious sensuality, the emotionally rewarding *At Last Comes Love* metes out both justice and compassion; totally satisfying." —*Library Journal*

"*At Last Comes Love* is the epitome of what any great romance should be. . . . This novel will leave you crying, laughing, cheering, and ready to fight for two characters that any reader will most definitely fall in love with!" —Coffee Time Romance

THEN COMES SEDUCTION

"Exquisite sexual chemistry permeates this charmingly complex story." —*Library Journal*

"Balogh delivers another smartly fashioned love story that will dazzle readers with its captivating combination of nuanced characters, exquisitely sensual romance, and elegant wit." —*Booklist*

"Mary Balogh succeeds shockingly well."
—Rock Hill *Herald*

FIRST COMES MARRIAGE

"Intriguing and romantic . . . Readers are rewarded with passages they'll be tempted to dog-ear so they can read them over and over." —McAllen *Monitor*

"Wonderful characterization [and a] riveting plot . . . I highly recommend you read *First Comes Marriage*."
—Romance Reviews Today

"Peppered with brilliant banter, laced with laughter . . . and tingling with sexual tension, this story of two seemingly mismatched people struggling to make their marriage work tugs at a few heartstrings and skillfully paves the way for the stories to come."
—*Library Journal*

"The incomparable Balogh delivers a masterful first in a new trilogy. . . . Always fresh, intelligent, emotional and sensual, Balogh's stories reach out to readers, touching heart and mind with their warmth and wit. Prepare for a joyous read." —*Romantic Times*

SIMPLY PERFECT

"A warm-hearted and feel-good story . . . Readers will want to add this wonderful story to their collection. *Simply Perfect* is another must-read from this talented author, and a Perfect Ten." —Romance Reviews Today

"With her signature exquisite sense of characterization and subtle wit, Balogh brings her sweetly sensual, thoroughly romantic Simply quartet to a truly triumphant conclusion." —*Booklist*

SIMPLY MAGIC

"Absorbing and appealing. This is an unusually subtle approach in a romance, and it works to great effect."
—*Publishers Weekly*

"Balogh has once again crafted a sensuous tale of two very real people finding love and making each other's lives whole and beautiful. Readers will be delighted."
—*Booklist*

SIMPLY UNFORGETTABLE

"When an author has created a series as beloved to readers as Balogh's Bedwyn saga, it is hard to believe that she can surpass the delights with the first install-ment in a new quartet. But Balogh has done just that."
—*Booklist*

"A memorable cast . . . refresh[es] a classic Regency plot with humor, wit, and the sizzling romantic chemis-try that one expects from Balogh. Well-written and emotionally complex." —*Library Journal*

SIMPLY LOVE

"One of the things that make Ms. Balogh's books so memorable is the emotion she pours into her stories. The writing is superb, with realistic dialogue, sexual tension, and a wonderful heart-wrenching story. *Simply Love* is a book to savor, and to read again. It is a Perfect Ten. Romance doesn't get any better than this."
—Romance Reviews Today

"With more than her usual panache, Balogh returns to Regency England for a satisfying adult love story."
—*Publishers Weekly*

SLIGHTLY DANGEROUS

"*Slightly Dangerous* is the culmination of Balogh's wonderfully entertaining Bedwyn series. . . . Balogh, famous for her believable characters and finely crafted Regency-era settings, forges a relationship that leaps off the page and into the hearts of her readers."
—*Booklist*

"With this series, Balogh has created a wonderfully romantic world of Regency culture and society. Readers will miss the honorable Bedwyns and their mates; ending the series with Wulfric's story is icing on the cake. Highly recommended." —*Library Journal*

SLIGHTLY SINFUL

"Smart, playful, and deliciously satisfying . . . Balogh once again delivers a clean, sprightly tale rich in both plot and character. . . . With its irrepressible characters and deft plotting, this polished romance is an ideal summer read." —*Publishers Weekly* (starred review)

SLIGHTLY TEMPTED

"Once again, Balogh has penned an entrancing, unconventional yarn that should expand her following." —*Publishers Weekly*

"Balogh is a gifted writer. . . . *Slightly Tempted* invites reflection, a fine quality in romance, and Morgan and Gervase are memorable characters."
—*Contra Costa Times*

SLIGHTLY SCANDALOUS

"With its impeccable plotting and memorable characters, Balogh's book raises the bar for Regency romances." —*Publishers Weekly* (starred review)

"The sexual tension fairly crackles between this pair of beautifully matched protagonists. . . . This delightful and exceptionally well-done title nicely demonstrates [Balogh's] matchless style." —*Library Journal*

"This third book in the Bedwyn series is . . . highly enjoyable as part of the series or on its own merits." —*Old Book Barn Gazette*

SLIGHTLY WICKED

"Sympathetic characters and scalding sexual tension make the second installment [in the Slightly series] a truly engrossing read. . . . Balogh's sure-footed story possesses an abundance of character and class." —*Publishers Weekly*

SLIGHTLY MARRIED

"*Slightly Married* is a masterpiece! Mary Balogh has an unparalleled gift for creating complex, compelling characters who come alive on the pages. . . . A Perfect Ten." —Romance Reviews Today

A Christmas Bride
Bride

Christmas Beau

MARY BALOGH

DELL

NEW YORK

2012 Dell Mass Market Edition

A Christmas Bride copyright © 1997 by Mary Balogh
Christmas Beau copyright © 1991 by Mary Balogh
Epilogue for *A Christmas Bride* copyright © 1997 by Mary Balogh
Excerpt from *The Proposal* by Mary Balogh copyright © 2012 by Mary Balogh

Published in the United States by Dell, an imprint of The Random House Publishing Group, a division of Random House, Inc., New York.

DELL is a registered trademark of Random House, Inc., and the colophon is a trademark of Random House, Inc.

A Christmas Bride was originally published in paperback in the United States by Signet, an imprint of Dutton Signet, a division of Penguin Books USA Inc., in 1997.

Christmas Beau was originally published in paperback in the United States by Signet, an imprint of Dutton Signet, a division of Penguin Books USA Inc., in 1991.

The epilogue for *A Christmas Bride* originally appeared on the author's website.

ISBN: 978-0-440-24546-9
eBook ISBN: 978-0-345-53579-5

Cover design: Lynn Andreozzi
Cover photograph: © Herman Estevez

Printed in the United States of America

www.bantamdell.com

9 8 7 6 5 4 3 2 1

Dell mass market edition: December 2012

A Christmas Bride

1

$\mathcal{M}$R. EDGAR DOWNES HAD DECIDED TO TAKE A bride.

Doubtless he should have made up his mind to do so long before he did, since he was six-and-thirty years old and had both a high respect for matrimony and a fondness for family life. But the truth was that he had procrastinated. He had felt caught between two worlds. He was not a gentleman. He was the son of a Bristol merchant who had grown enormously wealthy over the years and had eventually purchased and renovated a grand mansion and estate near Bristol and retired to live there like a gentleman. Edgar had been educated at the best schools, had become a respected and successful lawyer, and then had taken over his father's business.

He was hugely wealthy in his own right. He had received a gentleman's education. He spoke and dressed as a gentleman. He would inherit Mobley Abbey on his father's death. He was extremely eligible. But he was not a gentleman by birth, and in certain circles that fact made all the difference in the world.

He had thought about marrying someone of his own kind. At various points during his adulthood he had even singled out a few daughters or sisters of his middle-class acquaintances as possible wives. But he had never felt that he quite belonged in their world—not when it came to something as personal and intimate as marriage. He would have been hard put to it to explain exactly why that was so. There were certain almost puritanical attitudes in the class, perhaps, or a certain vulgar preoccupation with money and possessions for their own sake. Though neither explanation quite accounted for his discomfort.

He had thought of marrying a lady. But there had been obvious arguments against that. And they all narrowed down to one simple fact—he was not a gentleman. It was true that Cora, his sister and only sibling, had married a younger son of a duke seven years before and had become Lady Francis Kneller as a result. It was true, too, that Edgar got along remarkably well with his exceedingly elegant brother-in-law and with those of their aristocratic friends he had met. But though Cora's marriage appeared to be bowling along very nicely indeed and had produced four bouncing children, Lord Francis would not in the normal course of events have wed her. It was her disastrous tendency to play heroine without pausing for one hundredth part of a second to consider the wisdom of her actions that had forced him on more than one occasion to her rescue and to compromising circumstances at the same time. Finally, poor fellow, he had had no choice—as a *gentleman*—but to take on a leg shackle and Cora all at the same time.

Lord Francis Kneller and his friends—the Earl of Thornhill, for example, or the Marquess of Carew or the Duke of Bridgwater—might be quite prepared to treat Mr. Edgar Downes, Lady Francis's brother, as a friendly acquaintance. But would they be happy to watch him woo and wed their sisters or cousins if he so chose, and if there were any such females available? It was a question Edgar could not answer with any certainty since he had never posed it to any of the gentlemen concerned, but he could make an educated guess.

Some lesser gentleman with a daughter difficult to fire off in a more acceptable manner—due to impoverishment or lack of beauty or a shrewish nature, perhaps—might be very willing to ally her to a cit, to a lawyer-turned-merchant who also happened to be as wealthy as all but a few of the bluest-blooded lords in the land and with as much more wealth again to inherit on the death of his father. That lesser gentleman, however, would believe in his heart—and all the genteel world would believe with him—that he had stooped low indeed for the mere satisfaction of seeing his daughter wed.

But at the age of six-and-thirty Edgar Downes had decided to take a bride. A bride of good birth. A lady, no less. And he was going to do it soon. By Christmastime he would either be betrothed or have fixed his choice firmly and confidently enough that he would invite the woman and her family to Mobley Abbey for the holiday and a celebration of the betrothal. It was a promise he had made his father, and he always kept his promises.

The elder Mr. Downes celebrated his sixtieth birthday at the beginning of September. And though it would be difficult to find a healthier, more robust, more mentally agile man of his age anywhere in the kingdom, he had chosen on that occasion to remember his mortality and to declare himself an old man. An old man with a dying wish. Cora had shrieked when he had put it thus, doubtless imagining all sorts of hidden and deadly ailments, and Lord Francis had pursed his lips. Edgar had rocked back on his chair. The dying wish was to see his son wed. Perhaps he would even be spared long enough to see a son of his son in the nursery . . . a man longed for an heir to his heir.

And since Mr. Downes had achieved almost every goal that any man could possibly set himself in the course of his lifetime—including a lamentably short but blissfully happy marriage, the birth and survival of the best son and daughter a man ever had, not to mention a challenging and successful career and the acquisition of the abbey—he had only one more thing to wish for, apart from the marriage of his son, of course, and that was the birth of a son to his son. He could wish that his son would marry well, that he would finally ally the Downes name to one of undoubted gentility.

"You are a gentleman, my son," he said, nodding his head in Edgar's direction, his eyes beaming with pride and affection. "Your dear mother was a lady in every sense that mattered to me. But for my son I want a lady by birth. You have deserved such a wife."

Edgar felt embarrassed, especially since these words had been spoken in the presence of Lord Francis Kneller. He also felt suspiciously damp-eyed. His father meant more to him than almost anyone else in this world.

"And it is high time you married, Edgar," Cora said. "It is all very well for the children to have an uncle who spoils them dreadfully every time he crosses paths with them, but cousins would be of more practical value to them. And an aunt."

Lord Francis chuckled. "You must confess, Edgar," he said, "you have had a good run of it. You are six-and-thirty and only now is your family laying siege to your single state."

"That is quite unfair, Francis," Cora said. "You know that every time Edgar has come to Sidley since our marriage I have thrown the most eligible young ladies in his way. You know that I have tried my very best."

Lord Francis chuckled again. "You are as successful as a matchmaker, my love," he said, "as you are at your swimming lessons."

"Well," she said crossly, "whoever says that the human person—*my* human person anyway—is not heavier than water and will not sink like a stone when laid out on top of it must have windmills in his head and that is all I have to say."

"For which mercy may the Lord be praised," Edgar said, provoking outright laughter from his brother-in-law and a glare followed by a rueful chuckle from his sister.

But his father was not to be diverted from what he had clearly planned as the mission of his sixtieth birthday. Edgar was to marry and to marry a lady. A duke's daughter could not be too good for his son, he remarked.

"What a pity it is that Francis's sisters are married," Cora commented. "Is it not, Francis?"

"Quite so, my love," he agreed.

But any lady of breeding would do nicely, Mr. Downes continued after the interruption. Provided Edgar could like and respect her—and feel an affection for her. That, it seemed, was of greater importance than almost anything else.

"She does not have to be a lady of fortune, my boy," Mr. Downes said. "She can come to you penniless, provided she has the birth and breeding and can love you."

A penniless lady of *ton* would probably love his money a great deal, Edgar thought cynically. But he could not argue with his father, who looked as if he would live until the age of one hundred with all his energies and faculties intact, but who was, when all was said and done, sixty and aging. It was understandable that his father should need the assurance that all he had worked for through his life would descend to more than just an unmarried son.

And so Edgar found himself agreeing that it was indeed time he took it upon himself to find a bride and that if it would please his father he would choose one who had some distinction of birth. And there was nothing to be served by delaying, he suggested without waiting to be prompted by his father. He had some business in London, a city he hated and avoided whenever it was possible to do so. He had a few connections there who would effect some introductions. He would undertake to choose himself a bride, perhaps even to be affianced to her by Christmas. He would bring her down to Mobley Abbey for Christmas—or at least invite her parents to bring her. By his father's sixty-first birthday he would be married and be in a fair way to getting his first child into the nursery.

Cora shrieked and clasped her hands to her bosom.

"You are conceiving an idea, my love?" Lord Francis asked, sounding amused. He was frequently amused, having decided long ago, it seemed, that it would be far more comfortable to laugh his way through life with Cora than to grimace his way through all her excesses and disasters. Wise man.

"Francis was not able to have his month in London during the Season this year," she said. "First we were in the north with Jennifer and Gabriel and then we went with them to Stephanie and Alistair's, and we were all having such a marvelous time and so were the children— were they not, Francis?—and Stephanie has the most *adorable* baby, Papa. He even had me dreaming of number five, but Francis insists in that most odious voice he uses when he wants to pretend to be lord and master that four is quite enough, thank you very much. What was it I set out to say?"

"That since I was not obliged to spend a month of the Season in town," Lord Francis said, "I should be encouraged to take you and the children there for the autumn. I do believe that was where your verbal destination lay, my love."

She favored him with a dazzling smile. "What a splendid idea, Francis," she said. "Jennifer and Gabriel and Samantha and Hartley were talking about going there for a month or so after the heat of the summer was over.

We could have a wonderful time. And we could take Edgar about with us and see to it that he meets the right people."

"With all due respect, my love," Lord Francis said, "I do not believe Edgar is a puppy who needs our patronage. But certainly we will give him the comfort of having some familiar faces to greet at whatever entertainments are to be found during the autumn. And you will stay with us if you please, Edgar. The Pulteney Hotel may close its doors and go into a permanent decline when they discover that they are not to have your business, but we can offer some rowdy nephews and a niece for your entertainment. Who could possibly resist?"

"Edgar will spoil them and make them quite unmanageable," Cora said.

"Their maternal grandfather has spoiled them for the past two weeks as well as their uncle. *We* spoil them, my love," her husband said. "Yet we manage them perfectly well when it is necessary that they be managed. Their rowdiness and exuberance do not denote lack of all manners and discipline."

Between them they sealed Edgar's fate. He was to go to town by the end of September, it seemed, and stay at his brother-in-law's town house. He was to involve himself in the social life of the capital as it was lived in the autumn. There would not be all the balls and huge squeezes for which the spring Season was so renowned, but there would be enough people in residence in the grand houses of Mayfair to allow for a fair sprinkling of social entertainments. Lord Francis would see to it that Edgar was invited to a goodly number of them, and Cora would undertake to introduce him to some likely matrimonial prospects.

He needed their help. Despite the courteous tact of his brother-in-law's words, Edgar felt no doubt about that. He might have managed it himself, but with far more

effort than would be needed if he simply relied upon the
fact that Francis was a member of the upper echelons of
the *ton*. Edgar was resigned to forcing his way into
ranks from which his birth would normally exclude
him. He was prepared for some coolness, even some rejection. But he knew enough about the world to believe
that his wealth and his prospects would open a number
of doors to him, especially those of people who felt
themselves in need of sharing in his wealth.

He did not doubt that it was within his power to win
himself a bride by Christmas. Someone of birth and
breeding. Someone who would not look upon his own
origins with contempt or condescension. Someone pretty
and personable. Someone of whom he could be fond, it
was to be hoped. He came from a family that set much
store by that elusive something called love. He loved his
father and his sister and was loved by them in return.
His parents had enjoyed a love match. So did Cora and
Francis, though the marriage had not appeared too
promising at the start. Edgar rather thought that he
would like to make a love match, too, or at least a match
of affection.

He had until Christmas. Three months.

He was going to choose himself a bride. He traveled
up to London at the end of the month, a little chilled by
the thought, a little exhilarated by it.

After all, he was enough his father's son to find a challenge stimulating.

LORD FRANCIS KNELLER'S friends were indeed in
London. The Earl and Countess of Thornhill and the
Marquess and Marchioness of Carew had come down
together from Yorkshire with their six children for the
purpose of shopping and seeing the sights and socializing
at a somewhat less frantic pace than the Season would

have allowed. Even the Duke and Duchess of Bridgwater had come up with their new son, mainly because their other friends were to be there. The duke's sister and Cora's special friend, the Countess of Greenwald, was also in residence with her husband and family. And they all decided to be kind to Cora's brother and to take him under their collective wing.

It was all somewhat daunting. And rather embarrassing. And not a little humbling to a man who was accustomed to commanding other men and to thinking himself very much master of his own life and affairs. His first social invitation, to what was termed an intimate soirée, came from the Countess of Greenwald. The affair was termed "intimate," Edgar guessed, to excuse its lack of numbers in comparison with what might have been expected during the Season.

But when his sister informed him that quite one hundred people had been invited and that surely all but a very few would make an appearance, Edgar felt absurdly nervous. He had never forgotten how the other boys at school had made him suffer for his birth. He had never complained to his father, or to any of the masters, who had undoubtedly shared the sentiments of the bulk of their pupils anyway. He had learned how to use his fists and his tongue, too, with blistering effect. He had learned endurance and pride and self-respect. He had learned that there was an invisible barrier between those men—and boys—who were gentlemen and those who were not. He had vowed to himself that he would never try to cross that barrier.

As a very young man he had scorned even to want to cross it. He had been proud of who he was and of what he had made of himself and what his father had made of *him*self. But Cora had married Francis. And the bridge had been set in place. And then his father had expressed his dying wish—surely thirty years before he was likely to die.

Edgar dressed carefully for the soirée. He wore a plain blue evening coat with gray knee breeches and white linen. He directed his valet to tie his neckcloth in a simple knot rather than fashion one of the more elaborate and artistic creations his man favored. His only jewelry was a diamond pin in the folds of the neckcloth. His clothes were expensive and expertly tailored. He would allow the tailoring to speak for itself. He would not try to put on any show of wealth. He certainly would not wear anything that might suggest dandyism. The very thought made him shudder.

Cora and her friends would doubtless introduce him to some young ladies. Indeed, he had been quite aware of them going into a huddle after dinner at the Carews' the evening before. He had been painfully aware from the enthusiastic tone of their murmurings and the occasional furtive and interested glance thrown his way by one and another of them that he had been the subject of their conversation.

He hoped they would not introduce him to very young ladies. He was thirty-six. It would be most unfair to expect a young girl straight from the schoolroom to take him on. And he did not believe he would find appealing a girl almost young enough to be his daughter. He should have told Cora that he wanted someone significantly past the age of one-and-twenty. Such ladies were deemed to be on the shelf, of course. There had to be something wrong with them if they had not snared a husband by the age of twenty. And perhaps it really was so. How would he know?

"I would lead you in the direction of a congenial game of cards, old chap," Lord Francis said to him as they arrived at the Greenwalds' town house. He clapped a hand on his brother-in-law's shoulder and grinned. "But Cora would have my head and your purpose in coming to town would not be served. I shall allow her to go to work as soon as she emerges from the ladies' room. But no, you will not have to wait that long. Here comes our hostess herself, and from the look in her eye, Edgar, I would guess she means business."

And sure enough, after greeting them both with a gracious smile, Lady Greenwald linked one arm through Edgar's and bore him off to introduce him to a few people he might find interesting.

"Everyone is starved for the sight of a new face and the sound of new conversation, Mr. Downes," she said, "especially at this time of year when there are so few people in town."

It seemed to Edgar that there was a vast number of people in Lady Greenwald's drawing room, but the fact that almost all of them were strangers might have contributed to the impression.

He was introduced to a number of people and conversed briefly with them about the weather and other such general topics until Lady Greenwald finally led him to where he guessed she had been leading him from the start. Sir Webster Grainger shook him heartily by the hand instead of merely bowing, and laughed just as heartily for no apparent reason. Lady Grainger swept him a curtsy that looked deferential enough to have been made in the queen's drawing room. And Miss Fanny Grainger, small, slight of figure, fair of hair, rather pretty, blushed rosily and directed her gaze at the floor somewhere in the vicinity of Edgar's shoes.

It had been planned, he thought. As both an experienced lawyer and a businessman he was canny at interpreting tone and atmosphere and the language of the body. Words were not always necessary for the assessment of a situation. It was very clear to him from the first moment that Sir Webster Grainger and his lady were in search of a husband for their daughter, that they had heard of his availability, and that they had determined to fix his interest. He did not doubt that Lady Greenwald would have done her job well. The Graingers would be well aware of his social status.

"You are familiar with Bristol, I understand, Mr. Downes," Sir Webster said as Lady Greenwald excused herself to greet some new arrival at the drawing room door.

"I live there and conduct my business there, sir," Edgar said very deliberately. Let there be no possible mistake.

"We invariably spend a day in Bristol whenever we go to Bath for Lady Grainger to take the waters," Sir Webster said. "She has an aunt living there. At Bristol, that is."

"It is an agreeable place in which to have one's residence," Edgar said. Good Lord, the girl could be no more than eighteen. He must have been her present age when she was born. Her mother must be of an age with him.

"Fanny always particularly enjoys the days we spend in Bristol," Lady Grainger said. "You must tell Mr. Downes what you like best about Bristol, Fanny, to see if he agrees with you."

There could have been no suggestion better calculated to tie the girl's tongue in knots, Edgar could see. She lifted her eyes to his chest, tried to raise them higher, failed, and blushed again. Poor child.

"Whenever I have been to London and return home," he said, "I am invariably asked what I liked best about town. I am never able to answer. I could, I suppose, describe the Tower of London or Hyde Park or a dozen other places, but I can never think of a single one when

confronted. In my experience, one either likes a place or
not. Do you like Bristol, Miss Grainger?"

She shot him a brief and grateful glance. She had fine
gray eyes in a rather thin face. "I like it very well, sir,"
she said. "Because my great-aunt lives there, I believe,
and I like her."

It was not a profound answer, but it was an endear-
ingly honest one.

"It is the best reason of all for liking a place," he said.
"I grew up in Bristol with a father and a sister whom I
loved and still love, and so for me Bristol will always be
a more pleasant place than London."

The child had almost relaxed. She even smiled briefly.
"Is your mother d— Is she not living, sir?"

"She died giving birth to my sister," he said. "But I
remember her as a loving presence in my life."

"And your sister is Lady Francis Kneller, Mr. Downes,"
Sir Webster announced, just as if Edgar did not know it
for himself. He rubbed his hands together. "A fine lady.
I remember the time—it was before her marriage, I do
believe—when she saved Lady Kellington's poodles
from being trampled in Hyde Park."

"Ah, yes." Edgar smiled. "My sister has a habit of
rushing to the rescue."

"She saved some dogs from being *trampled*?" Miss
Grainger's eyes were directed full at him now.

It needed Francis to tell the story in all its mock-heroic
glory. But Edgar did his best. It appeared, though, as if
he failed to convey the humor of Cora's heroism in en-
dangering her life to save some dogs who had been in no
danger except from her rescue. Miss Grainger looked
earnestly at him, her mouth forming a little O of concern. A very kissable little mouth—in rather the way
that Cora's children's mouths were kissable when they
lifted them to him on his visits to the nursery.

He must be getting old, he thought. Too old to be in search of a bride.

And then he glanced across to the doorway, where another new arrival stood. A woman alone, dressed fashionably and elegantly in a high-waisted, low-bosomed dress of pure scarlet silk. A woman whose magnificent bosom more than did justice to the gown. Her whole figure, in fact, was generous. It might even be described as voluptuous more than slender. But then it was a mature woman's figure. She was not a young woman, but well past her thirtieth year if Edgar's guess was correct. Her dark hair was piled high and dressed in smooth curls rather than in more youthful ringlets. She looked about her with bold eyes in a handsome face, a half smile on her lips, which might denote confidence or contempt or mere mocking irony. It was difficult to tell which.

Before Edgar could realize that he was staring and proving himself to be indeed less than a gentleman—Sir Webster was saying something complimentary about Cora—the woman's eyes alit on him, held his own for a moment, and then moved deliberately down his body and back up again. She lifted one mocking eyebrow as her eyes met his once more and pursed her lips into something like the O that had just made Miss Grainger's lips look kissable. Except that there was nothing this time to remind him of his niece and nephews. He felt heated, as if there had been a hot hand at the end of her eyebeams that had scorched its way down the length of his body and back up again.

If he had not been standing in the Earl of Greenwald's drawing room, he would have been convinced that he was surely in the presence of one of London's more experienced and celebrated courtesans.

"Ah, yes, indeed," he said to Sir Webster, feeling that

it was the correct response to what had just been said, though he was not at all sure.

Sir Webster seemed satisfied with his answer. Lady Grainger smiled and Miss Grainger lowered her gaze to the floor again.

The scarlet lady had moved into the room and was being greeted by the Earl of Greenwald, who was bowing over her hand.

2

ELENA STAPLETON WAS INVITED EVERYWHERE. She was quite respectable, even though the general feeling seemed to be that she was only just so. She had been a widow for ten years, yet apart from the first four of those years, when she had gone to stay with cousins in Scotland, she had adopted neither of the two courses that were expected of widows. She had not retired to live quietly as a dowager on the estate of her dead husband's son, and she had not shown any interest in remarrying.

She had gone traveling. Her husband, more than thirty years her senior, had been besotted with her and had left her a very generous legacy. This she had conserved and increased through careful investments. She traveled to every corner of the British Isles and to every country of Europe, the wars being long over. She had even been to Greece and to Egypt, though she would tell anyone who cared to ask that she thought too highly of her creature comforts to repeat either of those two experiences. Sometimes she rested from her travels and took up temporary residence in London, where she proceeded to amuse herself with whatever entertainments were available. This was one of those occasions. She almost always avoided the crush of the spring Season.

She was always careful to travel with companions,

with congenial female acquaintances and with gentlemen to serve as escorts. She always set up house in
London with a female companion, usually an aunt,
whom she sent into the country to visit a nephew and a
brood of great-nephews and great-nieces as soon as respectability had been established. And so she almost always arrived alone at entertainments, making her aunt's
excuses to her hosts. There never had been such a sickly
aunt.

Ladies—even those of six-and-thirty with independent means—were not expected to move about town or
about *ton* parties alone, even when they had the misfortune to have female companions who were always
catching chills or suffering from headaches. And ladies
of six-and-thirty were not expected to dress as they
pleased, unless it pleased them to wear such colors as
purple or mulberry and to cover their hair with large
turbans decked out with waving plumes. They were certainly not expected to favor scarlet gowns or emerald
green or sunshine-yellow ones—or to go bareheaded
into society.

Lady Stapleton did all that a lady of six-and-thirty
was not expected to do. But there was a confidence and
a self-assurance about her that seemed excuse enough
for the absence of escorts or companions. And she had a
beauty and arrogance of bearing, coupled with an impeccable taste for design and elegance, that made one
hesitate about describing her appearance as vulgar or
even inappropriate to her age.

She had few, if any, close friends. There was an air of
aloofness, even of mystery, about her, even though she
conversed quite freely about her travels and experiences.
Everyone knew who she was—the daughter of a respectable but impoverished Scottish gentleman, the widow of
Sir Christian Stapleton of Brookhurst. She was amiable,
charming, sociable—and yet she gave the impression

that there was a great deal more to be known about her than she had ever revealed.

She was invited everywhere. Gentlemen found her fascinating despite the fact that she was long past her youth. Ladies were secretly envious of her, though her age protected her from their jealousy. Yet the feeling was—though no one could quite explain it—that she hovered dangerously close to the edge of respectability.

She knew it. And cared not the snap of two fingers. She had decided long ago—six years ago, to be precise—that life was to be lived and enjoyed, and live it and enjoy it she would. She had earned her enjoyment. She had been snatched from the love of her life—or so she had thought with the foolish sensibilities to which very young people were so prone—at the age of nineteen in order to be forced into marriage with the wealthy, fifty-four-year-old Sir Christian Stapleton. She had lived through seven years of marriage to him with bright smiles and determined affection and feigned eagerness in the marriage bed. She had lived through—but she would not remember what else she had lived through during those years. She had punished herself after her husband's death for her widowhood and her youth and her human frailties by retiring to a quiet life in Scotland, where she had seen her former love himself married with five children and an eagerness to begin an affair with her. Although she had longed to give in, she had resisted and had in general become a dull and abject creature, as if she believed that she deserved no better.

She deserved better. She deserved to live. Everyone deserved to live. No one owed anyone else anything. She owed no one anything. And if she did, then she had more than paid with eleven years of her life—seven with Christian and four after his death.

At the age of thirty—perhaps it was the nasty shock of that particular number—she had thrown off the shackles. And though she was always careful to cling to the semblance of respectability, she did not care that she hovered close to its edge. Indeed, she rather enjoyed the feeling of being almost, but not quite, notorious.

HELENA ARRIVED RATHER late at Lady Greenwald's soirée, as was customary with her. She liked to arrive after everyone else so that she could look about her and choose the group to which she wished to attach herself. She hated to be caught among people who had no conversation beyond the weather and the state of their health. She liked to be with interesting people.

She was acquainted with most of the people, she saw, standing in the doorway, looking about her. But then one usually was at *ton* events in London. And it was even more true of events outside of the Season. There were not a great many families in residence at this time of the year. Inevitably, all who were, were invited everywhere. Equally inevitably, all who were invited attended every function.

The Marquess of Carew was there, she saw, in the midst of a group of his particular friends. She had met the marquess for the first time just the week before. She had not sought out the introduction since he was a very ordinary-looking man with a slightly crippled hand and foot and a smiling placidity of manner that usually denoted dullness. He had spoken to her about his passion, landscape gardening, a dull topic indeed. And unexpectedly he had held her fascinated attention. The extremely elegant, almost foppish Lord Francis Kneller was part of the same group. Whenever she saw him, Helena felt regret that he was a married man. He had married a cit's daughter, who went with him almost wherever he went. She was with him now, laughing with quite ungenteel amusement at something someone had said. What a waste of a perfectly lovely man.

And then her eyes, moving on to another group, alit on a man whom she did not know—and paused on him. At first she looked only because he presented the novelty of being a stranger. And then she looked because he looked back and she would not glance away hastily and in apparent confusion. Though in reality there was more reason to look at him than stubbornness. He was a very tall and very large gentleman. Large not in the sense of fatness. She doubted that there was one spare ounce of fat on his frame. But he was certainly not a slender man. It was a perfectly proportioned frame—she looked it down and up again in leisurely fashion, noting at the same time the simple yet very expensive elegance of his clothing. And he had a head and face worthy of such a body. His brown hair was short but expertly styled. His face was strikingly handsome. He gave an impression of strength and power, she thought. Not just physical power. He looked like a man who knew exactly who he was and what he was and was well satisfied with both. Like a man who knew his own mind and was comfortable with his own decisions and would not be easily moved by anyone who opposed him.

She felt a wave of pure lust before he looked away to pay attention to the Graingers, with whom he stood, and the Earl of Greenwald arrived almost simultaneously to greet her. She explained that her aunt had been persuaded to stay at home to nurse a persistent cough.

Who was he? she wondered. She would not ask, of course. It was not her way to signal so direct an interest in a man. But she set about maneuvering matters slowly—there was no hurry—so that she would find out. And not only find out who he was. She was going to meet him. It was quite soon obvious to her that the man was not married, even though he must be very close to her own age. There was no strange lady in the Green-walds' drawing room. And it was unlikely that he had a wife who was absent. The Graingers took much of his time, and it was an open secret that they had brought their daughter to town in the hope of finding her a husband before Christmas. They were not wealthy. They could not afford to bring their daughter to town during the Season, when there would be the exorbitant expenses of a court dress and innumerable ball and party gowns. And so they had come now, hoping that there would be a single gentleman of sufficient means to be snared. The girl was twenty and perilously close to being on the shelf.

The unknown gentleman must be both single and rich. He certainly *looked* rich—wealthy and self-assured enough not to have to make an obvious display of his wealth. He was not bedecked with jewels and fobs and lace. But his tailor doubtless charged him a minor fortune to fashion coats such as the one he wore tonight.

She talked with Lord Carew and Lord Francis Kneller and their wives for a while, and then sat with elderly Lord Holmes during a musical presentation. She told Mr. and Mrs. Prothero and a growing gathering of other people about some of her more uncomfortable experiences in Egypt while they all refreshed themselves with a drink together afterward and then accepted Sir Eric Mumford's invitation to join him at the supper table. He did not even realize that she led him rather than submitting to being led once they were inside the dining room. She seated herself beside the still-unknown gentleman, but turned her head immediately away from him to speak with her partner.

She was an expert at maneuvering matters to her own liking. Especially where men were concerned. Men were so easily manipulated. She laughed with amusement at something Sir Eric said.

* * *

HER LOW LAUGH shivered down his spine. It came straight from the bedchamber, even though she was sitting in a crowded dining room beneath brightly lighted chandeliers.

She had seated herself in the empty chair beside his and was reacting to something her supper companion had said to her. She was totally unaware of him, of course, Edgar thought, as she had been all evening after that first assessing glance. She had not once looked his way after that. She was Lady Stapleton, widow of Sir Christian Stapleton of Brookhurst. Brookhurst was not so very far from Mobley Abbey—not above twenty-five or thirty miles. But she did not live there now. Sir Gerald Stapleton, the present owner, was only her stepson.

Edgar had been introduced to three marriageable ladies during the course of the evening, all of whose parents had clearly been informed of his own possible interest and had acquiesced in allowing their daughters to be presented to a man whose immense wealth would perhaps compensate for the fact that he was not a gentleman. All three ladies were amiable, genteel, pretty. All three knew that he was a prospective bridegroom and they appeared docile and accepting. His sister and her cohorts had done a superlative job in so short a time, he thought. They had gone about things in the correct way, choosing with care, preparing the way with care, and leaving him choices.

There was only one problem—well, two actually, but the second was not in the nature of a real problem, only of an annoyance. The problem was that all three ladies appeared impossibly young to him. It struck him that any one of them would be a perfect choice for just that reason. All three had any number of breeding years ahead, and breeding was one of his main inducements to marry. But they seemed alarmingly young to him. Or rather, perhaps, he felt alarmingly old. Did he want a wife only so that he might breed her? He wanted more than that, of course. Far more.

And the problem that was not a problem was his constant awareness—an uncomfortable, purely physical awareness—of the lady in scarlet. Lady Stapleton. His mouth had turned dry as soon as she seated herself beside him and he smelled her perfume—something subtle and feminine and obviously very expensive.

And then she turned his way, leaned forward slightly, ignored him completely, and spoke to the young lady at his other side.

"How do you do, Miss Grainger?" she said. "Allow me to tell you how pretty you look in blue. It is your color."

Her bosom brushed the top of the table as she spoke. And her voice was pure warm velvet. Edgar could see now that he was close that the red highlights he had noticed in her dark hair were no reflection of her gown. They were real. He could not make up his mind whether her eyes were hazel or green. They had elements of both colors.

"Why, thank you," Miss Grainger said, blushing and gratified. "It is my favorite color. But I sometimes wish I could wear vivid colors as you do."

Again that low bedroom laugh.

"Oh," Miss Grainger said, "may I present Mr. Downes? Lady Stapleton, sir."

Her eyes came to his. She did not move back, even though she was still leaning forward and was very close to him. He resisted the urge to move back himself. She looked very directly at him, a faint mockery or amusement or both in the depths of her glance.

"Ma'am," he said, inclining his head.

"Mr. Downes." She gazed at him. "Ah, now I remember. Lady Francis Kneller was a Downes before her marriage, was she not?"

"She is my sister," he said.

"Ah." She made no immediate attempt to say anything else. He could almost sense her remembering that Cora was the daughter of a Bristol merchant and realizing that he was no gentleman. That half smile deepened for a moment. "You are from the west country, sir?"

"From Bristol, ma'am," he said. And lest she was not quite clear on the matter, "I have lived there all my life and have worked there all my adult life, first as a lawyer and more recently as a merchant."

"How fascinating," she murmured, her eyes moving to his lips for a disconcerting moment. He was not sure if it was sincerity or mockery he heard in her voice. "Pardon me. I am neglecting Sir Eric quite shamefully."

She turned back to her companion. Obviously it had been mockery. Lady Stapleton had found herself seated beside a cit and conversing with him before realizing who he was. She would not repeat the mistake.

He set himself to making Miss Grainger feel comfortable again. He felt quite protective of her. She so clearly knew why she was in London, why she was here tonight, and why she was spending a significant portion of the evening in his company. The Graingers, he guessed, were going to be more persistent in their attentions to him than either of the other two couples. Miss Grainger's pretty blue gown, he noticed, was neither new nor costly. Nor was it in the first stare of fashion.

HELENA SAT WITH Mr. Hendy and a few other guests after supper. The others mainly listened while the two of them exchanged stories and opinions about the land-crossing from Switzerland to Italy. They both agreed that they were fortunate indeed to have lived to tell of it.

"I admire mountains," Mr. Hendy said, "but more as a spectator than as a traveler crawling along a narrow icy track directly above a sheer precipice at least a mile high."

"I do believe I could endure crawling with some equanimity," Helena said. "It is riding on the back of one of those infernal mountain donkeys that had me gabbling my prayers with pious fervency."

Their audience laughed.

Mr. Downes had left his group in order to cross to a sideboard to replenish the contents of his glass. There was no one else there. Helena got to her feet and excused herself. She strolled toward the sideboard, her own empty glass in hand.

"Mr. Downes," she said when she was close, "do fill my glass with whatever is in that decanter, if you please. One becomes mortally sick of drinking ratafia merely because one is female. I would prefer even the lemonade at Almack's."

"Madeira, ma'am?" He looked uncertainly at the decanter and then at her with raised eyebrows.

"Madeira, sir," she said, holding out her glass. "I suppose you do not know about the lemonade at Almack's."

"I have never been there, ma'am," he said.

"You have not missed anything," she told him. "It is an insipid place and the balls there are insipid occasions and the lemonade served there is insipid fare. Yet people would kill or do worse to acquire vouchers during the Season."

He half filled her glass and looked into her eyes. She had the distinct feeling that if she ordered him to fill her glass he would refuse. She did not issue the order. He was a lawyer and a merchant. He had freely admitted as much. A prosperous merchant if her guess was correct.

But a cit for all that. If his sister had not had the good fortune to snare Lord Francis Kneller, he would never have gained entry to such a place as the Earl of Greenwald's drawing room. But she understood now the aura of confidence and power he exuded. He was a wealthy, powerful, self-made man. She found the idea infinitely exciting. She found *him* exciting.

Sexually exciting.

"I am tired of this party, Mr. Downes," she said. "But I am a single woman alone, alas. My aunt, my usual companion, is indisposed, my manservant and maid walked home rather than stay in the kitchen with my coachman, and will not return for another hour at the earliest. Yet I will be scolded by aunt and servants alike if I return unaccompanied."

He was not sure he understood her. His eyes shrewdly regarding her told her that. She raised her eyebrows, half smiled at him, and sipped her madeira. It was a vast improvement on ratafia.

"I would offer my escort, ma'am, if I thought it would be welcomed," he said.

"How kind you are, Mr. Downes," she said, mocking him with her eyes. "It would be accepted."

"Shall I have your carriage called around, then?" he asked. "Shall I have a maid accompany us?"

She allowed herself to laugh softly. "That will be quite unnecessary, Mr. Downes," she said, "unless you are afraid of me. We are both adults."

He inclined his head to her without removing his eyes from hers, set down his glass, and slipped quietly from the room.

She found flirtations exhilarating, Helena admitted to herself as she sipped from her glass and looked about the room without making any attempt to rejoin any group. She indulged in them whenever she felt so inclined—always in private. She scorned the appearance of propriety for its own sake, but how could one conduct a satisfactory flirtation in the sight of others? She did not care if people noticed her disappearing alone with a certain gentleman and thought her promiscuous.

She was not. She had never desired the distastefulness of full physical intimacy—she had endured enough of that during her seven-year marriage. Though of course there had been a time during that marriage . . . no! She shuddered inwardly. She would not think of that now—or ever if she could help it.

She had never sought to enliven her widowhood with affairs—or even with *an* affair. But then she had rarely met a man with as great a physical appeal as Mr. Downes.

She would take him home and lure him up to her drawing room. She would find out more about him. She suspected that he might be a fascinating man—perhaps he could fascinate her for an hour or more of the night. Nights were always interminably long. She would flirt with him. Perhaps she would even allow him to steal a kiss—there was definite appeal in the thought, though she normally avoided even kisses.

Perhaps he would not be satisfied with a mere kiss. But she was not afraid. She had never found herself unable to deal with amorous men, though she had known her fair share.

She smiled as her eyes found the Countess of Greenwald.

She set her glass down in order to go bid her hostess a good night.

And perhaps *she* would not be satisfied with a mere kiss, she thought a few minutes later as she allowed Mr. Downes to hand her into her carriage and climb in beside her.

She had never felt quite so tempted.

How would it feel *with him?* she wondered, turning her head to smile half scornfully at her companion, though he was not necessarily the object of her scorn. With a handsome, virile, powerful, doubtless very experienced man.

She felt a twinge of alarm at the direction her thoughts had taken. And more than a twinge of desire.

She would talk sense into herself before she arrived home, she told herself. She might even dismiss him on the pavement outside her door and send him back to the soirée.

But she knew she would not do that.

Sometimes loneliness was almost a tangible thing.

3

EDGAR WAS NOT REALLY SURE HE UNDERSTOOD THE situation. Or believed her story. Why would two servants have walked home after accompanying her to the Greenwalds'? And she did not seem the sort of person to tire early when she was at a party. She had been the center of attention in every group gathered about her all evening.

And why him?

He sat beside her as close to his side of her carriage as he could so that she would not think he was taking advantage of the situation. She sat with her back half across the corner at her side, looking at him in the near-darkness, talking easily and quite without malice about the people who had attended the party. She spoke in that low, velvety voice, the half smile of mockery or something else on her lips every time a street lamp lit her face.

He would help her to alight at her door, he thought, see her safely inside her home, and then walk back to Greenwald's house. It was not very far. He would refuse the offer—if she made it—of a ride back in her carriage. He would go back to the soirée rather than straight home. He had not told Cora he was leaving.

But when the lady had stepped down from the carriage to the pavement and had removed her hand from his, she did not lift her skirt with it the more easily to ascend the four steps to the front door. She slipped it through his arm.

"You must come inside, Mr. Downes," she told him, "and have a drink before returning."

Presumably the aunt she had mentioned was inside the house. But was it likely that an ailing lady would be out of her bed at this time of night—it must be well past midnight—and sitting in the drawing room with her embroidery on the chance that she would be called upon to play chaperone? He was not being naive. He was merely unwilling to accept the evidence of his own reasoning powers.

A manservant had opened the front door even before the steps of the carriage had been set down. He took Edgar's hat and cloak from him, after favoring him with a level, measuring look—he was as tall as Edgar and even broader, and as bald as a polished egg. He looked more like a pugilist than a butler, an impression enhanced by his crooked, flattened nose.

"You need not wait up, Hobbes," Lady Stapleton said, taking Edgar's arm and turning him in the direction of the stairs.

"Very well, my lady," the servant said in a voice one might expect a man to use if he had a handful of gravel lodged in his throat.

The lady paused on the first landing as if in thought, appeared to come to some decision, and climbed on to the second. Edgar would have had to be an innocent indeed if he had expected to find a drawing room beyond the door at which she stopped, indicating with an inclination of the head that he might open it. This was not the living floor of the house. Even so it was something of a shock to find himself entering a very cozy bedchamber. There was a soft carpet underfoot. The curtains were looped back from the large canopied bed. The bedcovers were neatly turned back. There were lit candles on the dressing table and bedside table. A fire burned in the hearth.

Edgar closed the door behind his back and stayed where he was. It was a very feminine room, warm and comfortable and clean. That subtle perfume she wore clung to it. It was, he thought, the room of a very expensive courtesan. He found himself wondering if he would be presented later with a quite exorbitant bill. He did not much care.

"Well, Mr. Downes." She had walked into the room and turned to him now, one hand resting on the dressing table. There was a look almost of defiance on her face. She raised one mocking eyebrow. "Shall I ring for tea?"

"That seems hardly necessary." He walked toward her until he was a foot away from her. But why him? he wondered. Because of her discovery that he was not a gentleman? Would a gentleman have offered his escort? Would he have come inside the house with her? Ascended that second flight of stairs with her?

To hell with what gentlemen would have done or would do. She had made her choice. She would live with it for tonight. He set his hands on either side of her waist—not a slender waist, but an undeniably shapely one. He drew her against him, angled his head to one side, parted his lips, closed his eyes, and kissed her.

And felt that he had landed in the very midst of a fireworks display—not as a spectator but as one of the fireworks.

She moved against him. Not just to bring herself closer to him but to—move against him. He became hotly aware of everything—her warm and shapely thighs, her generous hips, her abdomen rubbing against his almost instant erection, her breasts, her shoulders. One of her arms had come about his waist, beneath his coat. The fingers of the other hand twined themselves in his hair. Her mouth opened beneath his own and moved against it. He found himself doing what he had not done since his youth, having found it distasteful then. He pressed his tongue deep into her mouth.

And then she withdrew and he withdrew and they stood gazing at each other, still touching from the waist down, their breathing labored. That strange smile lingered about her lips. But her eyes were heavy with passion and excitement.

"I do hope you live up to early promise, Mr. Downes," she said.

"I shall do my very best, ma'am," he said.

And then she turned and presented him with a row of tiny pearl buttons down the back of her gown. He undid them one at a time while she lifted her arms and withdrew the pins from her hair. She held it up until he was finished and then let it fall, long and dark and wavy, with its enticing reddish tints. He nudged the gown off her shoulders with the straps of her shift and she let them fall to the floor before turning and removing her undergarments and her stockings while he watched.

She had a mature figure—firm, ample, voluptuous. She was incredibly beautiful. He felt his mouth go dry again as he shrugged out of his coat and reached for the button of his waistcoat.

"Ah, no," she said, brushing his hands aside and laughing at him with that throaty laugh that now seemed to be in its proper setting. "You have had the pleasure of unclothing me, Mr. Downes. You will not deny me the pleasure of doing the like for you."

She undressed him while he listened to his heartbeat hammering against his eardrums and concentrated on controlling and mastering the urge to tumble her back onto the bed so that he might the sooner explode into ease. She took her time. She was in no hurry at all.

Not until they were finally on the bed. Then she became passion unleashed. There was no shyness, no shrinking, no ladylike modesty, no taboos. Her hands explored him with frank interest and wild demand while his did the like to her. Her mouth participated in the exploration, moving over him, kissing, licking, sucking, biting. He devoured her with his own mouth, tasting perfume and sweat and woman.

He had never been a man for rough sex. Perhaps because of his size he had always been careful to leash his passions, to touch gently, to mount slowly, to pump with control. But he had never before been with a woman whose passion could equal his own—and perhaps even outstrip it. When he rolled her nipples between his thumbs and the bases of his forefingers, she spoke to him.

"Harder," she begged him. "Harder."

And when he squeezed and she gasped with pain and he would have desisted, her hands came up to cover his, to press his thumbs and forefingers together again. She gasped with pain once more.

"Come to me," she was saying then, her body in frenzied motion. "Give it to me. Give it to me."

He moved between her thighs, felt her legs lift to twine about his, felt her hands spread hard over his buttocks, positioned himself, and thrust hard and deep. She cried out. He settled his weight on her—his full weight. He knew what she wanted and what he wanted. Neither of them would have it if he allowed her to buck and gyrate beneath him. And he was very aware that she had led the way thus far. It was not in his nature to allow a woman to dictate his every action and reaction.

She urged him on with frenzied words and clawing hands and with the muscles of her thighs and the muscles inside, where he worked. But he took her without frenzy, with deep, methodical, rhythmic strokes. His heart felt as if it must burst. With every inward thrust he felt as if he must surely explode into release. But he would not let a woman master him.

She was pleading with him. She was swearing at him, he realized in some surprise. And then she lost her own control and came shuddering and shattering about him. He continued to stroke her while it happened and then, when she began to relax, he drove to his own release, growling out his pleasure into her hair.

He was not quite sure he was going to survive, he thought foolishly, relaxing downward onto her damp and heated flesh. He felt her legs untwine themselves from about his and somehow found the energy to lift himself off her and draw her against him before closing his eyes and sinking into sleep.

SHE DID NOT sleep. She lay relaxed against the heat of his body. She tried to summon the energy to wake him and dismiss him. She would have to dismiss him. She needed to be alone.

She needed to digest what had just happened—what *she* had caused to happen. She had not even taken him as far as the drawing room. She had scarcely even paused on the first landing.

She had seemed to be led by a power quite beyond her will to control. A ridiculous notion—*though it had happened before. She* had chosen to bring him to her bed, just as she had chosen that other time. . . .

She breathed in slowly—a mistake. She breathed in the smells of his sweat and his cologne, of his maleness.

Her earlier curiosity at least had been satisfied. She knew now how it felt with him.

It had felt frightening. The pleasure—oh, yes, there had been an overabundance of that—had got far beyond her control. It had been in his control and he had held it from her—quite deliberately, she would swear—

with his weight holding her immobile and with his insistence on setting the pace himself. Having made the decision she had made, she had at least wanted to command the situation. She had wanted to protect something of herself. He had not allowed it.

She had been frightened. All she had was herself.

He had the most magnificent body she could ever have imagined. It seemed all massive, solid muscle. And that part of him . . . She closed her eyes and inhaled slowly. She had been stretched and filled. For one foolish moment she had felt the terror of a virgin that there could not possibly be room. She rather believed she had screamed.

He was a man who expected and got his own way. He was a businessman. Clearly a very successful and wealthy one. A man did not achieve success in the business world unless he was firm and controlled and even ruthless, unless he was well able to make himself undisputed master of any situation. She had sensed that on her first sight of him, of course. It was not his looks alone that had prompted that rush of lust and the growing temptation. And then she had had her intuition confirmed at supper when he had told her, a look of cool defiance on his face, that he had been a lawyer and was a merchant. Lustful words. She wondered if he had realized that she found them so.

She should not have chosen to break her own—and society's—rules with him of all people.

She wanted him again, she thought after a while. She could feel her breasts, her womb, her inner thighs begin to throb with need. She wanted his weight, his mastery. No, she did not. She wanted to be on top. She wanted to master him. She wanted to ride him at her own speed, to drive him mad with desire, to have him shatter past climax so that she could feel she had avenged what he had done to her.

She wondered if she would be able to master this man if she woke him and aroused him and got on top of him. Would she win this time? Or would he merely resume that alarmingly controlled stroking and endure long enough to send her headlong again into release and happiness—and weakness? It would be humiliating to have that happen twice.

And wonderful beyond belief.

She did not want anything wonderful beyond belief.

And then, while she was still at war with herself, the decision was taken out of her hands. She had not noticed that he was awake again. And aroused again. He turned her onto her back and came on top of her. She found herself opening her legs to him, lifting to him, letting her breath out on a sighing moan as he came, hard and thick and long, sliding into her wetness. And she found that she had his full and not inconsiderable weight on her again and that she did not fight either it or him. She lay under him rather as she had always lain beneath Christian— but no, there was no comparison. None whatsoever.

She observed their coupling almost like a spectator. Almost. There was, of course, the throbbing desire she had felt even while he still slept, and the crescendo of desire that built *there*, where he stroked relentlessly, and spread upward in waves, through her womb, up into her breasts, into her throat, and even behind her nose. He found her mouth with his and she opened to his tongue and did not even try to fight the total invasion of her body—or even the frightening sensation that it was her whole person that was being invaded.

She was, she thought a moment before she burst past control to another of those intense moments of something that felt deceptively like happiness, though it was not that at all—she was a little frightened of Mr. Downes, Bristol merchant and cit. And that was perhaps a large part of the attraction. She had never felt frightened of any other man. His own climax came a few moments after hers, as it had the first time. He was, then, in perfect control of himself, even in bed.

She had made a mistake. *Of course* she had made a mistake.

They lay beside each other, panting, waiting for their heartbeats to return to normal. The backs of their hands touched damply between them. She wondered if he had set out to make a fool of her, or if mastery came so naturally to him that he did not even think of her as a worthy adversary. She hated him in that moment, quite as intensely as she had earlier lusted after him.

She got off the bed, crossed the room unhurriedly on legs that shook slightly—the candles, though low, were still burning—picked up her night robe, which her maid had set out over the back of a chair, and drew it about her as she went to stand at the window, looking out on the deserted street below. She drew a deep, silent breath and released it slowly.

"Thank you, Mr. Downes," she said. "You are superlatively good. A master of the art, one might say. But I daresay you know that."

"I can hardly be expected to reply to such a compliment," he said.

She looked over her shoulder at him. He was lying on the bed, the covers up to his waist, his hands clasped behind his head. Even now, sated as she was, he looked magnificent.

"It is time for you to leave, sir," she said.

"Past time, I believe," he said, throwing back the covers and coming off the bed with remarkable grace for such a big man. "It would not do for me to be seen slinking from your house at dawn, wearing evening clothes."

"No, indeed," she agreed. And she stood watching him dress. She had never thought of any other man as beautiful—*oh, yes, she had*. Yes she had. She clenched her hands unconsciously at her sides. But he had been youthful, slender, sweet. . . .

She turned back to the window.

She shrugged her shoulders when his hands came to rest there, and he removed them.

"Thank you," he said. "It was a great pleasure."

"I daresay you can see yourself out, Mr. Downes," she said. "Good night."

"Good night, ma'am," he said.

She heard the door of her bedchamber open and close again quietly. A minute or so later she watched him emerge from the front door and turn right to walk with long, firm strides along the street. She watched him until he was out of sight, a man quite unafraid of the dark, empty streets of London. But then he had probably known a great deal worse in Bristol if his work took him near the dock area. She would pity the poor footpad who decided to accost Mr. Downes.

What was his first name? she wondered. But she did not want to know.

She stood at the window, staring down into the empty street. Now, she thought, her degradation was complete. She had brought home a total stranger, had taken him to her bed, and had had her pleasure of him. She had given in to lust, to loneliness, to the illusion that there was happiness somewhere in this life to be grasped and to be drawn into herself.

And she was to be justly punished. She already knew it. Her bedchamber already seemed unnaturally quiet and empty. She could still smell him and guessed that the enticing, erotic smell, imaginary though it doubtless was, would linger accusingly for as long as she remained in this house.

Now she was truly promiscuous. As she always had been, though she had never lain with any man except Christian—until tonight. Now her true nature had shown itself. She closed her eyes and rested her forehead against the cold glass of the window.

And she had enjoyed it. Oh, how she had enjoyed it! Sex with a stranger. She heard herself moan and clamped her teeth hard together.

She was awash with the familiar feeling, though it was stronger, rawer than usual—self-loathing. And then hatred, the dull aching hatred of the one man who might have allowed her to redeem herself and to have avoided this. For years she had waited patiently—and impatiently—for him to release her from the terrible burden of her own guilt. But finally, just a year ago, he had plunged her into an inescapable, eternal hell. She felt hatred of a man who had done nothing—ever—to deserve her hatred or anyone else's.

A hatred that turned outward because she had saturated herself with self-hatred.

She could feel the rawness in her throat that sought release through tears. But she scorned to weep. She would not give herself that release, that comfort.

She hated Mr. Downes. Why had he come to London? Why had he come to Lady Greenwald's soirée? He had no business there, even if his sister was married to a member of the *ton*, even if he was something of a nabob. He was not a gentleman. He had stepped out of his own world, upsetting hers.

But how unfair it was to hate him. None of what had happened had been his fault. She had seduced him. His only fault had been to allow himself to be seduced.

For one moment—no, for two separate moments— the loneliness had been pushed back. Now it was with her again, redoubled in force, like a physical weight bowing down her shoulders.

She must never again—not even by mild flirtation— try to dislodge it. She must never again so much as see Mr. Downes.

* * *

EDGAR FELT SHAKEN. What had just happened had been a thoroughly physical and erotic thing, quite outside his normal experience. He had been caught up entirely in mindless passion.

Lady Stapleton. He did not know her first name. It somehow disturbed him that he did not even know that much about her. And yet he knew every inch of her body and the inner, secret parts of her with great intimacy.

He had had women down the years. But except for his very early youth, he had never been led to them from lust alone. There had always been some sort of a relationship. He had always known their first names. He had always bedded women with the knowledge that the act would bring him more pleasure than it brought them. He had always tried to be gentle and considerate, to make it up to them in other ways.

He had never known a truly passionate woman, he realized—until tonight. He was not sure he wanted to know another—or this one again. There had been no doubt about her consent, but still he felt vaguely guilty at the way in which he had used her. He had not been gentle. Indeed, he had been decidedly rough.

He felt distaste at what he had done. He felt dislike of her. She had clearly set out to lure him to her bed. If there was a seducer in tonight's business, it was she. He did not like the idea that he had been seduced. If she had had her way she would have dictated every move of that first encounter, including, he did not doubt, the moment and manner of his climax.

He had come to London, he had gone to that soirée, in order to find himself a bride. And he had been presented with three quite eligible prospects. He would perhaps choose to pay court to one of them. He would betroth himself to her before Christmas or perhaps at

Mobley Abbey during Christmas. He would wed the girl soon after and in all probability have her with child before spring had turned into summer. He had promised his father, and it was high time, even without the promise.

And yet on the very evening he had met those three young ladies, he had allowed himself to be drawn into a scene of sordid passion with a stranger, with a woman whose first name he did not know.

She was a lady, not a courtesan. A beautiful lady, who was accepted by the *ton*. Obviously tonight's behavior was not typical of her. If it were, she would be unable to keep it hidden well enough to escape the sharp eyes and gossiping tongues of the beau monde. Clearly, then, he was partly to blame for what had happened. He had stared at her when she had first appeared, and she had caught him at it. He had freely admitted his origins and present way of life to her at supper and had thus revealed to her that he was a man outside her own world.

Somehow he had tempted her. He understood that young widows—and perhaps those who were not so young, too—could feel loneliness and sexual frustration. One of his longer-lasting mistresses had been the widow of a colleague of his. He might eventually have married her himself if she had not suddenly announced to him one day that she was to marry a sea captain and take to the sea with him.

He had done Lady Stapleton a great wrong. It would not be repeated. He wondered if he owed her an apology. Perhaps not, but he owed her something. A visit tomorrow. Some sort of an explanation. He must make her aware that he did not hold her in contempt for what she had allowed tonight.

He did not look forward to the visit.

* * *

LORD FRANCIS CAME out of his library as Edgar let himself into the house. He lifted the cup he held in one hand. "The chocolate is still warm in the pot," he said. "Come and have some."

Edgar had hoped everyone would be safely in bed. "Waiting up for me, Francis?" he asked, entering the library reluctantly and pouring himself a cup of chocolate.

"Not exactly," Francis said. "Waiting for Cora, actually. Annabelle woke up when we tiptoed into the nursery to kiss the children, and Cora lay down with her. I daresay she has fallen asleep. It would not be the first time. Once Andrew came to *me* for comfort and climbed into bed beside me because his mama was in his own bed fast asleep and there was no room left for him."

"That sounds like Cora," her brother said. He felt some explanation was necessary. "I escorted Lady Stapleton home because she had no other escort. And then I decided to walk about Mayfair and get some fresh air rather than return to Greenwald's. A few hours at such entertainments are enough for me."

"Quite so," Francis said. "Firm up the story for Cora by breakfast time, old chap. She will wish to know about every post and blade of grass you passed in your nocturnal rambles. You do not owe me any explanation. She is a woman extraordinarily, ah, well-endowed with charms."

"Lady Stapleton?" Edgar said carelessly, as if the idea were new to him. "Yes, I suppose she is."

Lord Francis chuckled. "Well," he said, "I am for my lonely bed. You look as if you are ready for yours, too, Edgar. Good night."

"Good night," Edgar said.

Damnation! Francis knew all right. But then he would have to be incredibly dim-witted to believe that story about the walk and fresh air.

4

*H*ELENA WAS USUALLY FROM HOME IN THE MORN-
ings. She liked mornings. She loved to walk in the
park early, when she was unlikely to meet anyone except
a few tradesmen hurrying toward their daily jobs or a
few maids running early errands or walking their
owners' dogs. Her own long-suffering maid trotting
along behind her or, more often, the menacing figure of
Hobbes, the one servant who traveled everywhere with
her, made all proper. She liked to go shopping on Oxford Street or Bond Street or to the library to look at the
papers or borrow a book. She also liked to visit the galleries.

Mornings were the best times. The world was fresh
and new each morning, and she was newly released
from the restlessness and bad dreams that oppressed her
nights. Sometimes in the mornings she could fill her
lungs with air and her body with energy and pretend
that life was worth living.

But on the morning after Lady Greenwald's soirée, she
was at home. She had not found the energy nor the will
to go out. The clouds were low and heavy, she noticed.
It might rain at any moment. And it looked chilly and
raw. In reality, of course, she rarely allowed weather of
any type to divert her when she wished to go abroad.

This morning she was tired and listless and looking for excuses.

She would send for her aunt, she decided. Aunt Letty liked town better than the country anyway, and would be quite happy to be summoned. She was, in fact, more like a friend than an aging relative—and therein, perhaps, lay the problem. Helena had numerous friendly acquaintances and could turn several of them into close friends if she wished. She did not wish. Friends, by their very nature, knew one intimately. Friends were to be confided in. She preferred to keep her acquaintances at some distance. She certainly did not need a friend in residence. But, paradoxically, her friendless state sometimes became unbearable.

She procrastinated, however, even about writing the letter that would bring her aunt home. She stood listlessly at the drawing room window, gazing down on the gray, windblown street. She was standing there when she saw him coming, walking with confident strides toward the house just as he had walked away from it last night. He wore a greatcoat and beaver hat and Hessian boots. He looked well-groomed enough, arrogant enough, to be a duke. But that firm stride belonged to a man who had all the pride of knowing that he had made his own way in his own world and was successful enough, rich enough, confident enough to encroach upon hers.

She hated him. Because seeing him again, she felt a deep stabbing of longing in her womb. What she had allowed last night—what she had initiated—was not so easily shrugged off this morning. Her hands curled into fists at her sides as she saw him turn to approach her front door. She stepped back only just in time to avoid being seen as he glanced upward.

So he thought he had acquired himself a mistress from the beau monde, did he? As a final feather in his cap? She supposed that a mistress from her class might be more satisfactory even than a wife, though perhaps he thought to acquire both. The Graingers would not have shown such interest in him last evening if they had not heard somewhere that he was both eligible and available.

He thought that because he had given her undeniable pleasure last night she would become his willing slave so that she could have more. She swallowed when she remembered the pleasure. How humiliating!

The door of the drawing room opened to admit her butler. There was a card on the silver tray he carried. She picked it up and looked at it, though it seemed an unnecessary gesture.

Mr. Edgar Downes. *Edgar.* She had not wanted to know. She thought of Viking warriors and medieval knights. *Edgar.*

"He is waiting below?" she asked. It was too much to hope, perhaps, that he had left his card as a courtesy and taken himself off.

"He is, my lady," her butler told her. "But I did inform him that I was not sure you were at home. Shall I say you are not?"

It was tempting. It was what she wished him to say, what she intended to instruct him to say until she opened her mouth and spoke. But it was not to be as simple as that, it seemed. She was on new ground. She had done more than flirt with this man.

"Show him up," she said.

She looked down at the card in her hand as she waited. Edgar. Mr. Edgar Downes.

She felt very frightened suddenly—again. What was she doing? She had resolved both last night and this morning never to see him again. He posed far too great a threat to the precarious equilibrium of her life. She had spent six years building independence and self-assurance, convincing herself that they were enough.

Last night the glass house she had constructed had come smashing and tinkling down about her head. It would take a great deal of rebuilding.

Mr. Edgar Downes could not help. Not in any way at all.

She could no longer possibly deny that she wanted him. Her body was humming with the ache of emptiness. She wanted his weight, his mastery, the smell of him, his penetration. She wanted him to make her forget.

But she knew—she had discovered last night if she had been in any doubt before that—that there was no forgetting. That the more she tried to drown everything out with self-gratification, the worse she made things for herself. She should not have told Hobbes to send him up. What could she have been thinking of? She must leave the room before they came upstairs.

But the door opened again before she could take a single step toward it. She stood where she was and smiled.

AT EACH OF his professions in turn Edgar had learned that there were certain unpleasant tasks that must be performed and that there was little to be gained by trying to avoid them or put them off until a later date. He had trained himself to do promptly and firmly what must be done.

It was a little harder to do in his personal life. On this particular morning he would have preferred to go anywhere and do anything rather than return to Lady Stapleton's house. But his training stood him in good stead. It must be done, and therefore it might as well be done without delay. Though he did find himself hoping as he approached the house that she would be from home. A foolish hope—if she was out this morning, he would have to return some other time, and doubtless it would seem even harder then.

He knew that she was at home when he turned to climb the steps to her door and looked up and caught a glimpse of her at a window, ducking hastily from sight. She would not, of course, wish to appear overeager to see him again. His irrational hopes rose once more when that pugilist of a manservant who answered the door informed him that he thought Lady Stapleton might be from home. Perhaps she would refuse to see him—that was something he had not considered on his way here.

But she was at home and she did not refuse to see him. He drew deep breaths as he climbed the stairs behind the servant and tried to remember his rehearsed speech. He should know as a lawyer that rehearsed speeches scarcely ever served him when it came time actually to speak.

She looked even more beautiful this morning, dressed in a pale green morning gown. The color brought out the reddish hue of her hair. It made her look younger. She was standing a little distance from the door, smiling at him—that rather mocking half smile he remembered from the evening before. The events of the night seemed unreal.

"Good morning, Mr. Downes." She was holding his card in one hand. She looked beyond his shoulder. "Thank you, Hobbes. That will be all."

The door closed quietly. There was no sign of the aunt or of any other chaperone—an absurd thing to notice after last night. He was glad there was no one else present, necessitating a conversation about the weather or the social pages of the morning papers.

"Good morning, ma'am." He bowed to her. He would get straight to the point. She was probably as embarrassed as he. "I believe I owe you an apology."

"Indeed?" Her eyebrows shot up. "An apology, sir?"

"I treated you with—discourtesy last evening," he said. Even in his rehearsed speech he had been unable to think of a more appropriate, less lame word to describe how he had treated her.

"With discourtesy?" She looked amused. "*Discourtesy*, Mr. Downes? Are there rules of etiquette, then, in your world for—ah, for what happens between a man and a woman in bed? Ought you to have said please and did not? You are forgiven, sir."

She was laughing at him. It had been a foolish thing to say. He felt mortified.

"I took advantage of you," he said. "It was unpardonable."

She actually did laugh then, that low, throaty laugh he had heard before. "Mr. Downes," she said, "are you as naive as your words would have you appear? Do you not know when you have been seduced?"

He jerked his head back, rather as if she had hit him on the chin. Was she not going to allow him even to pretend to be a gentleman?

"I was very ready to take advantage of the situation," he said. "I regret it now. It will not be repeated."

"Do you?" Neither of them had moved since he had stepped inside the room. She moved now—she took one step toward him. Her eyes had grown languid, her smile a little more enticing. "And will it not? I could have you repeat it within the next five minutes, Mr. Downes—if I so choose."

He was angry then. Angry with her because despite her birth and position and title she was no lady. Angry with her because she was treating him with contempt. Angry with himself because what she said was near to truth. He wanted her. Yet he scorned to want what he could not respect.

"I think not, ma'am," he said curtly. "I thank you again for your generosity last night. I apologize again for any distress or even bodily pain I may have caused you. I must beg you to believe that whenever we meet again, as we are like to do over the next few weeks if you plan to remain in town, I shall treat you with all the formal courtesy I owe a lady of your rank." There. He had used part of his speech after all.

She took him by surprise. She closed the gap between them, took his arm with both of hers, and drew him toward the fireplace, in which a fire crackled invitingly. "You are being tiresome, sir," she said. "Do come and sit down and allow me to ring for coffee. I am ready for a cup myself. What a dreary morning it is. Talk to me, Mr. Downes. I have been in the mopes because there is no one here to whom to talk. My aunt is on an extended visit in the country and will not be back for a couple of days at the earliest. Tell me why a Bristol merchant is in London for a few weeks. Is it for business, or is it for pleasure?"

He found himself seated in a comfortable chair to one side of the fire, watching her tug on the bell pull. He had intended to stay for only a couple of minutes. He was feeling a bit out of his depth. It was not a feeling he relished.

"It is a little of both, ma'am," he said.

"Tell me about the business reasons first," she said. "I hear so little that is of interest to me, Mr. Downes. Interest me. What *is* your business? Why does it bring you to London?"

He had to wait while she gave her instructions to the crooked-nosed servant, but then she looked back at him with inquiring eyes. They were not rhetorical questions she had asked.

He told her what she wished to know and answered the numerous other questions she asked—intelligent, probing questions. The coffee was brought and poured while he talked.

"How satisfying it must be," she said at last, "to have a purpose in life, to know that one has accomplished something. Do you feel that you have vanquished life, Mr. Downes? That it has been worth living so far? That it is worth continuing with?"

Strange questions. He had not given much thought to any of them. The answers seemed, perhaps, self-evident.

"Life is a constant challenge," he said. "But one never feels that one has accomplished all that can be done. One can never arrive. The journey is everything. How dull it would be finally to arrive and to have nothing else for which to aim."

"Some people would call it heaven," she said. "Not being on the journey at all, Mr. Downes, is hell. It surely is, is it not?"

"A self-imposed hell," he said. "One that no one need encounter for any length of time. It is laziness never to reach beyond oneself for something more."

"Or realism," she said. "You must grant that, Mr. Downes. Or are you so grounded in the practicalities of a business life that you have not realized that life is ultimately not worth living at all? Realism—or despair."

He had been enjoying their lively discussion. He had almost forgotten with whom he spoke—or at least he had almost forgotten that she was last night's lover, to whom he had come this morning in some embarrassment. But he was jolted by her words. The smile on her lips, he noticed now, was tinged with bitterness. Was she talking theoretically? Or was she talking about herself?

She gave him no chance to answer. She took a sip from her cup and her expression lightened. "But you came to town for pleasure, too," she said. "Tell me about that, Mr. Downes. For what sort of pleasure did you hope when you came here?" Her smile was once more pure mockery.

To his mortification Edgar felt himself flush. "My

sister and brother-in-law were to be here the same time as me," he said. "They have insisted upon taking me about with them."

"How old are you, Mr. Downes?" she asked.

She had a knack for throwing him off balance. He answered before he could consider not doing so. "I am six-and-thirty, ma'am," he said.

"Ah, the same age as me," she said. "But we will not compare birthdays. I was married at the age of nineteen, Mr. Downes, to a man of fifty-four. I was married to him for seven years. I have no wish to repeat the experience. I have earned my freedom. But it is an experience everyone should be required to have at least once in a lifetime. You have come to London in search of a wife?"

He stared at her, speechless. Did she really expect him to answer?

She laughed. "It is hardly even an educated guess," she said. "Sir Webster Grainger and his lady were determinedly courting you last evening. They are in desperate search of a wealthy husband for poor Miss Grainger. I daresay you are very rich indeed. Are you?"

He ignored the question. "*Poor* Miss Grainger?" he said. He was feeling decidedly irritable again. How dare she probe into his personal life like this? Would she be doing so if he were a gentleman? "You believe she would be pitied if she married me, ma'am?"

"Very much so," she said. "You are sixteen years her senior, sir. That may not seem a huge gap in age to you and me—we both know that you are vigorous and in your prime. But it would appear an enormous age difference to a very young lady, Mr. Downes. Especially one who has a prior attachment—but a quite ineligible one, of course."

He frowned. Was she deliberately goading him? He could not quite believe he was having this conversation with her. But was it true? Did Miss Grainger have an attachment to someone else?

"You need not look so stricken, Mr. Downes," she said. "It is a common thing, you know. Young ladies of *ton* are merely commodities, you see. Sometimes people make the mistake of thinking that they are persons, but they are not. They are commodities their fathers may use to enhance or repair their fortunes. Unfortunately, young ladies have feelings and an alarming tendency to fall in love without sparing a single thought to the state of their fathers' fortunes. They soon learn. That is one thing women are good at."

This, he thought, was a bitter woman indeed. And doubtless an intelligent woman. Too intelligent for her own good, perhaps.

"Is that what happened to you?" he asked. "You loved another man?"

She smiled. "He is married now with five children," she said. "He was kind enough to offer me the position of mistress after I was widowed. I declined. I will be no man's mistress." Her eyes mocked and challenged him.

He got to his feet. "I have taken too much of your time, ma'am," he said. "I thank you for the coffee. I—"

"If you are going to apologize again for your discourtesy in bedding me without saying 'please,' Mr. Downes," she said, "I beg you to desist. I should then feel obliged to apologize for seducing you and that would be tiresome since I do not feel sorry. But you need not fear that I will do it again. I never seduce the same man twice. It is a rule I have. Besides, in my experience no man is worth a second seduction."

"Ah," he said, suddenly more amused than angry, "you will have the last word after all, will you? It was a magnificent set-down."

"I thought so, too," she said. "You are a superior lover, Mr. Downes. Take it from someone who has had some experience of lovers. But I do not want a lover, even a very good one. Especially perhaps a very good one."

He despised himself for the satisfaction her words gave him.

"I would prefer a friend," she said.

"A friend?" He looked at her.

"Life can be tedious," she said, "for a widow who chooses not to burden her relatives with the demand for a home and who chooses not to burden herself with another husband. You are an interesting man. You have more to talk of than health and the weather and horses. Many men have no knowledge of anything beyond their horses and their guns and their hunting. Do you kill, Mr. Downes?"

"I have never been involved in gentlemanly sports," he said.

She smiled. "Then you will never be properly accepted in my world, sir," she said. "Let us be friends. Shall we be? You will alleviate my tedium and I will ease you into my world. Do you enjoy wandering around galleries, admiring the paintings? Or around the British Museum, absorbing history?"

"I am, I believe, a tolerably well-educated man, ma'am," he said.

She looked at him measuringly. "You are not perfect after all, are you?" she said. "You are sensitive about your origins. I did not imply that you are a clod, sir. But you do not know London well?"

"Not well," he admitted.

"Take me somewhere tomorrow," she said. "I shall decide where between now and then. Let me have someone intelligent with whom to share my observations."

He was tempted. How was he to say no? He must say no.

"You are afraid of ruining your matrimonial chances,"

she said, reading his hesitation aright. "How provincial, Mr. Downes. And how bourgeois. In my world it is no matter for raised eyebrows if a gentleman escorts a lady about who is not his wife or his betrothed or his intended, even when there is such another person in existence. And no one is scandalized when a woman allows a man to escort her who is not her husband or her father or her brother—even when she is married. In my world it is considered somewhat bad *ton* to be seen exclusively in the company of one's spouse."

"I daresay, then," he said, "that my sister is bad *ton*. And Lord Francis Kneller, too."

"Oh, those two." She waved a dismissive hand as she got to her feet. "I do believe they still fancy themselves in love, sir, though they have been married forever. There are other such oddities in the beau monde, but they are in the minority, I do assure you."

"You were right," he said. "I came to London in search of a bride. I promised my father that I would make my choice by Christmas. I rather think I should concentrate upon that task."

"My offer of friendship is rejected, then?" she said. "My *plea* for friendship? How very lowering. You are no gentleman, sir."

"No," he said with slow clarity, "I am not, ma'am. In my world a man does not cultivate a friendship with one woman while courting another."

"Especially with a woman whom he has bedded," she said.

"Yes," he agreed. "Especially with such a woman."

Her smile this time was one of pure contempt. "And you were right a minute or two ago, Mr. Downes," she said. "You have stayed overlong. I tire of your bourgeois mentality. I would not find your friendship as satisfying as I found your lovemaking. And I do not desire lovemaking. I use men for my pleasure occasionally, but only very occasionally. And never the same man twice. Men are necessary for certain functions, sir, but essentially they are a bore."

Her words, her looks, her manner were all meant to insult. He knew that and felt insulted. At the same time he sensed that he had hurt her somehow. She had asked for his friendship and he had refused. He had refused because he would not be seduced again and knew beyond a doubt that any friendship with Lady Stapleton would inevitably lead eventually back to bed. She must surely know it, too.

He did not want a thirty-six-year-old mistress. *Rationally* he did not want her. Irrationally, of course, he wanted her very much indeed. He was a rational being. He chose to want a wife who was below the age of thirty, a wife who would give him children for his contentment, a son for Mobley Abbey.

"I am sorry," he said.

"Get out, Mr. Downes," she said. "I shall be from home if you call again, as I would have been today if I had had any sense. But I daresay you will not call again."

"No," he said, "I will not call again, ma'am."

She turned away from him and crossed the room to the window. She stood looking out of it while he let himself out of the room, as she had looked from the window of her bedchamber the night before.

She was a strange woman, he thought as he left the house and made his way along the street, thankful for the chilliness of the air. Confident, independent, unconventional, she appeared to be a woman who made happiness and her own gratification her business. Other women must envy her her freedom and her wealth and her beauty. Yet there was a deep-seated bitterness in her that suggested anything but happiness.

She must have had a bad marriage, he thought, one

that had soured her and made her believe that all men were as her husband had been.

He had, it seemed, been one of a long string of lovers, all of whom had been used and never reused. It was a lowering and a distasteful thought. She made no secret of her promiscuity. She even seemed proud of it. His brief involvement with her was an experience he would not easily forget. It was an experience he was very glad was in the past. He was relieved that he had found the strength to reject her offer of friendship—he had certainly been tempted.

She was not a pleasant woman. A beautiful temptress of a woman, but not a pleasant one. He did not like her.

And yet he found himself regretting that he would not see her again, or if he did, that he must view her from afar. She could have been an interesting and an intelligent friend if there had never been anything else between them.

5

*H*ELENA SUMMONED HER AUNT FROM THE COUNTRY and felt guilty when she arrived for having encouraged her to leave just a few weeks before. She was uncomfortably aware that her aunt was not a person who deserved to be used.

"How very thoughtful you are, Helena, my dear," Mrs. Cross said as she stood in the hallway, surrounded by her rather meager baggage. "You know that I find life with Clarence and his family trying, and you have invited me back here, where I am always happy. Have you been enjoying yourself?"

"When do I not?" Helena said, hugging her and linking her arm through her aunt's to draw her toward the stairs. "Hobbes will have your bags attended to. Come to the drawing room and drink some tea. There is a fire there."

She let her aunt talk about her journey, about her stay in the country, about the snippets of news and gossip she had learned there. Sometimes, she thought, it felt good to have a companion, someone who was family, someone who loved one unconditionally. Often it was annoying, confining. But sometimes it felt good. Today it felt good.

"But here I am going on and on about myself," her

aunt said eventually. "What about you, Helena? Are you looking pale, or is it my imagination?"

"The wind has not stopped blowing and the sun has not once peeped through the clouds for days," Helena said. "I have stayed indoors. I *feel* pale." She smiled. "Now that you are here, I shall go out again. We will go shopping tomorrow morning. I noticed when you arrived that there was a hole in the palm of your glove. I daresay there were no shops of note in the village close to Clarence's where you might have bought new ones. I am glad of it. Now I have an excuse to buy them for you as a gift. I was still in Switzerland at the time of your birthday, was I not?"

"Oh, Helena." Her aunt was flustered. "You do not need to be buying me presents. I wore those old gloves because they are comfortable and no one would see them in the carriage."

Helena smiled. Mrs. Letitia Cross was a widow, like herself. But Mr. Cross had not left her with an independence. Her meager stipend barely enabled her to keep herself decently clothed. She had to rely on various relatives to house her and feed her and convey her from place to place.

"I need gloves, too," Helena said, "and perhaps a muff. I need a warm cloak and warm dresses for a British winter. Ugh! It seems to be upon us already. Why can no one seem to build up the fires decently in this house?" She got up and jerked on the bell pull.

"But Helena, my dear." Her aunt laughed. "It is a magnificent fire. One would need a quizzing glass to be able to detect the fires in Clarence's hearths, I do declare. Though I must not complain. They were kind to me. The children and the governess were not allowed fires in their bedchambers either."

"I shall have one built half up your chimney tonight," Helena said. And then she turned to speak irritably to

Hobbes, who looked expressionlessly at the roaring fire and said he would send someone immediately with more coals.

"I think I may go to Italy for Christmas," Helena said, throwing herself restlessly back onto her chair. "It will be warmer there. And the celebrations will be less cloying, less purely hypocritical than they are here. The Povises will be going at the end of November, I daresay, and there is always a party with them. I shall make one of their number. And you will make another. You will like Italy."

"I will not put you to so much expense," Mrs. Cross said with quiet dignity. "Besides, I do not have the wardrobe for it. And I am too old to be jauntering around foreign parts."

Helena clucked her tongue. "How old *are* you?" she asked. "You speak as if you are an octogenarian."

"I am fifty-eight," her aunt replied. "I thought you planned to stay here for the winter, Helena. And for the spring. You said you longed to see an English spring again."

Helena got restlessly to her feet and walked over to the window, although it was far from the fire, which a maid had just built up. "I am bored with England," she said. "The sun never shines here. What is the point of an English spring, Aunt, and English daffodils and snowdrops and bluebells when the sun never shines on them?"

"Has something happened?" her aunt asked her. "Are you unhappy about something, Helena?"

Her niece laughed. "Of course something has happened," she said. "Many things. I have been to dinners and dances and soirées and private concerts and have seen the same faces wherever I go. Pleasant faces. People with pleasant conversation. How dull it is, Letty, to see the same faces and listen to the same conversation wherever one goes. And no one has been obliging enough to do anything even slightly scandalous to give us all something more lively to discuss. How respectable the world has become!"

"There is no special gentleman?" her aunt asked. It was always her opinion that Helena should search for another husband, though she had never done so herself in twenty years of widowhood.

Helena did not turn from the window. "There is no special gentleman, Aunt," she said. "There never will be. I have no wish for there to be. I value my freedom far too much."

The street outside was quite busy, she noticed, but there was no tall, broad gentleman striding along it as if he owned the world. It was only as the thought became conscious that she realized she had spent a good number of hours during the past five days standing just here watching for him, waiting for him to return to apologize again. Had she really been doing that without even realizing it? She was horrified.

"And yet, my dear," Mrs. Cross said, "all husbands must not be condemned because yours made you unhappy."

Helena whirled around, her eyes blazing, her heart thumping with fury. "It was *not* an unhappy marriage," she said so loudly that her aunt grimaced. "Or if it was, the fault was mine. Entirely mine. Christian was the best of husbands. He adored me. He lavished gifts and affection on me. He made me feel beautiful and charming and—and lovable. I will not hear one word against him. Do you hear me? Not one word."

"Oh, Helena." Her aunt was on her feet, looking deeply distressed. "I am so sorry. Do forgive me. What I said was unpardonable."

Helena closed her eyes and drew a deep breath. "No," she said. "The fault was mine. I did not love him, Letty, but he was good to me. Come, let me take you up to your room. It should be warm by now. I am in the mopes because I have not been out in five days." She laughed. "That must be something of a record. Can you imagine me not going out for five whole days?"

"Frankly no, dear," her aunt said. "Have there been no invitations? It is hard to believe, even if this is October."

"I have refused them," she said. "I have been suffering from a persistent chill—or so I have claimed. I do believe it is time I recovered my health. Do you fancy an informal dance at the Earl of Thornhill's tomorrow evening?"

"I always find both the earl and the countess charming," Mrs. Cross said. "They do not ignore one merely because one is past the age of forty and is wearing a gown one has worn for the past three years and more."

Helena squeezed her arm. "We are going shopping tomorrow morning," she said. "I feel extravagant. And I feel so full of energy again that I do not know quite what to do with it." She stopped at the top of the stairs and hugged her aunt impulsively. "Oh, Letty, you do not know how good it is to have you here again." She was surprised to find that she had to blink her eyes in order to clear her vision.

"And *you* do not know," Mrs. Cross said, "how good it is to be here, Helena. Ah, the room really is warm. How kind you are to me. I feel quite like a person again, I do declare. And how ungrateful that sounds to Clarence. He really was very good to me."

"Clarence," Helena said, "is a sanctimonious, parsimonious bore and I am very glad he is not *my* relative. There. I have put it into words for you so that they will not be upon your conscience. I am going to leave you to rest for a while. There is nothing more tiring than a lengthy journey."

"Thank you, dear," her aunt said with a grateful sigh. Had she really not been out for five days? Helena thought as she made her way back downstairs. Had she really convinced herself that the weather was just too inclement? And that the company of those of the beau monde who were at present in London was too tedious to be borne?

Her lip curled with self-mockery. Was she afraid to face him? Because he had rejected her? Because he had refused her offer of friendship and declined her invitation to escort her to one of the galleries? Was she so humiliated that she could not look him in the eye?

She *was* humiliated. She was unaccustomed to rejection. No man had ever rejected her before—oh! Her stomach lurched uncomfortably. Oh, that was not true. She realized something else suddenly about the past five days. She had hardly eaten.

To have been rejected by a cit! To have been rejected by any man—but by a man who was not even a gentleman. And a man to whom she had *given* herself. She had offered to make him better acquainted with London. She had offered her—patronage, she supposed was the word she was looking for. And he had said no for the purely bourgeois reason that he was about to pay court to some young girl.

How dared he reject her! And how petulant that thought sounded—and was.

She should, of course, never have asked for his friendship. She wanted no one's friendship, especially not any man's. Most especially not his. She could not imagine what she had been thinking of. She should not even have received him. And he had not even come to beg for further favors, but to apologize for his lack of *courtesy*. If it were not so lowering, it would be funny. Hilarious.

She certainly was not going to avoid him. Or show him that his rejection had meant anything to her. The very idea that she should mope and hide away just

because he had refused to give her his escort on an afternoon's outing! She wished him joy of his young girl.

She was going to the Earl of Thornhill's informal ball
tomorrow evening and she was going to dance and be
merry. She was going to be the belle of the ball despite
her age or perhaps because of it. She was going to wear
her bronze satin gown. She had never worn it in England
before, having judged it far too risque for stodgy English
tastes. But tomorrow night she was going to wear it.

She was going to have Mr. Edgar Downes salivating
over her—if he was there. And she was going to ignore
him completely.

She hoped he would be there.

EDGAR WAS UNCOMFORTABLE with Fanny Grainger's
age. It seemed that she was twenty, at least two years
older than she looked. But even so she seemed a child to
him. Lady Stapleton had been wrong when she had said
that the age gap must appear nothing to him, that it
would be apparent only to the girl herself. He was uncomfortably aware that he was well past his youth,
while she seemed to be just embarking upon hers.

The other two young ladies he had met at the Earl of
Greenwald's appeared equally young. And less appealing in other ways. Miss Turner, whom he had met two
evenings later, was noticeably older—closer to thirty
than twenty at a guess—but she was dull and lethargic
and totally lacking in conversation. And she had a constant dry sniff, an annoying habit that grated on his
nerves when he sat beside her for half an hour.

Miss Grainger, he rather suspected, was going to be
the one. He had imagined when he came to London that
he would be able to look about him at his leisure for
several weeks before beginning a serious courtship of
any lady in particular, almost as if he had thought he

would be invisible and his intentions undiscernible. Such was not the case, of course. And Sir Webster Grainger and his lady had begun to court him. They were quite determined, it seemed, to net Edgar Downes for their daughter.

She was sweet and charming in a thoroughly youthful way. If he had been ten years younger, he might have tumbled head over ears in love with her. At his age he did not. He kept remembering Lady Stapleton's saying that the girl had a previous, ineligible attachment. He did not know how she had learned that. Perhaps— probably—she had merely been trying to make him uncomfortable. She had succeeded. The thought of coming between a young lady and her lover merely because he happened to be almost indecently rich was not a pleasant one.

He wondered if the girl disliked him, was repulsed by him. Whenever he spoke with her—and her parents made sure that he often did, always in their presence— she was polite and sweet, her deeper feelings, if she had any, quite hidden from view.

Cora was pleased. "She is a pleasant young lady, Edgar," she announced at the breakfast table one morning, "and will doubtless be a good companion once she has recovered from her shyness, poor girl, and her awe at your very masterful bearing. You could try to soften your manner, you know, but then it comes naturally enough to you and soon she will realize that behind it all you are just Edgar."

"You do not think I am too old for her, Corey?" he asked, unconsciously using the old nickname he had tried to drop since her marriage.

"Oh, she will not think so when she comes to love you," his fond sister assured him. "And that is bound to happen very soon. Is it not, Francis?"

"Oh, quite so, my love," Lord Francis said. "Edgar is eminently lovable."

Which remark sent Cora off into peals of laughter and left Edgar quite unreassured.

The promise he had made to his father seemed rash in retrospect. Perhaps at the Thornhills' ball, he thought, he would dance with the girl and have a chance to converse with her beyond the close chaperonage of her parents. Perhaps he would be able to discover the answers to some of his questions and find out if Cora was right. Could Miss Grainger be a good companion?

Was there something in his bearing that other people, particularly young ladies who were facing his courtship, found daunting, even overbearing? Lady Stapleton had not been daunted. But he did not particularly wish to think of Lady Stapleton. He had not seen her since that ghastly morning visit. He hoped that she had left town.

He realized she had not when he was dancing with Miss Turner, feeling thankful that the intricate patterns of the dance took away the necessity of trying to hold a conversation with her. It was not a great squeeze of a ball. Lady Thornhill had been laughingly apologetic about it and had insisted on calling it a small informal dance rather than a ball. To him the ballroom seemed crowded enough, but it was true that it was possible to see almost all the guests at once when he looked about him. He looked about him—and there she was standing in the doorway.

He did not even notice the older lady standing beside her. He saw only her and found himself swallowing convulsively. She wore a gown that might have appeared indecent even in a boudoir. It was a bronze-colored sheath that shimmered in the light from the chandeliers. To say that it was cut low at the bosom was seriously to understate the case. It barely skimmed the peaks of her nipples and dipped low into her decolletage. The gown was not tightly fitted and yet it settled about her body like a second skin, revealing every shapely and generous curve. It left little if anything to the imagination. It made Edgar remember with unwilling clarity exactly how that body had looked and felt—and tasted—beyond the thin barrier of the bronze satin.

She stood proudly, looking about her with languid eyes and slightly mocking smile, apparently quite unaware of any impropriety in her appearance. But then she somehow looked too haughty to be improper. She looked plainly magnificent.

The lady beside her must be the aunt, Edgar decided, noticing the woman when she turned her head to address some remark to Lady Stapleton. She was grayhaired and pleasant looking and dressed with neat propriety.

Edgar returned his attention to the steps of the dance.

She had been late to the Greenwalds' soirée, too, he remembered. Clearly she liked entrances. But then she had the looks and the presence to bring them off brilliantly. Thornhill was hurrying toward her.

Edgar returned his partner to her mother's side at the end of the set, bowed to them both, and made his way in the direction of his sister. There was to be a waltz next. He would dance it with Cora, who was closer to him in height than almost any other lady present. He felt uncomfortable waltzing with tiny females. But the Countess of Thornhill, one of Cora's close friends, hailed him as he passed and he turned toward her with a sinking heart.

"Mr. Downes." She was smiling at him. "Have you met Lady Stapleton?" It was a rhetorical question, of course. She did not pause to allow him to say that, yes, he had met the lady at Lady Greenwald's soirée the week before and had escorted her home and stayed to bed her two separate times.

"And Mrs. Cross, her aunt," Lady Thornhill continued. "Mr. Edgar Downes, ladies. He is Lady Francis Kneller's brother from Bristol."

Edgar bowed.

"I am pleased to make your acquaintance, Mr. Downes," Mrs. Cross said.

"How do you do, Mr. Downes?" He had forgotten how that velvet voice could send shivers down his spine.

"Lady Francis is a very pleasant lady," Mrs. Cross said. "She is always very jolly."

Yes, it was an apt description of Cora.

"And quite fearless," Mrs. Cross continued. "I remember the year the Duchess of Bridgwater—the dowager duchess now, of course—brought her out. The year she married Lord Francis."

"Ah, yes, ma'am," he said. "The duchess was kind enough to give my sister a Season."

"The next dance is a waltz," the Countess of Thornhill said. "I have promised to dance it with Gabriel, though it is perhaps vulgar to dance with one's own husband at one's own ball. But then this is not a real ball but merely an informal dance among friends."

"I think one need make no excuses for dancing with one's husband," Mrs. Cross said kindly.

Edgar could feel Lady Stapleton's eyes on him, even though he looked intently at her aunt. He could feel that faint and characteristic scorn of her smile like a physical touch.

"Ma'am." He turned his head to look at her. "Will you do me the honor of dancing with me?"

"A waltz, Mr. Downes?" She raised her eyebrows. "I believe I will." She reached out one hand, though there was no necessity of taking to the floor just yet, and he took it in his.

"Mrs. Cross," the countess was saying as Edgar led his partner onto the floor, "do let me find you a glass of lemonade and some congenial company. May my husband and I have the pleasure of your company at the supper table when the waltz is at an end?"

Edgar's senses were being assaulted by the heady mixture of a familiar and subtle perfume and raw femininity.

"WELL, MR. DOWNES," she said, turning to face him, waiting for the music to begin, "in your school for budding merchants, did they teach you how to waltz?"

"Well enough to keep me from treading on your toes, I hope, ma'am," he said. "I was educated in a gentleman's school. They allowed me in after I had promised on my honor never, under any circumstances, to drop my aitches or wipe my nose on my cuff."

"One can only hope," she said, "that you kept your promises."

She was alarmed by her reaction to him. She felt short of breath. There was fluttering in her stomach, or perhaps lower than her stomach, and a weakness in her knees. She had vowed, of course, to ignore him completely tonight. But then she had not planned that very awkward introduction Lady Thornhill had chosen to make. Strange, that. It was just the sort of thing she would normally maneuver herself. But not tonight. She had not wanted to be this close to him again. He was wearing the same cologne. Though it seemed to be the smell of the very essence of him rather than any identifiable cologne. She had fancied even as recently as last night that there was a trace of it on the pillow next to her own.

He danced well. Of course. She might have expected it. He probably did everything well, from making love on down—or up.

"Are congratulations in order yet, Mr. Downes?" she asked to take her mind off her fluttering nerves—and to shake his cool air of command. "Have you affianced yourself to a suitably genteel and fertile young lady? Or married her? Special licenses are available, as you must know."

"Not yet, ma'am," he said, looking at her steadily. He had been looking into her face since the music began. Was he afraid to look lower? But then he had seen all there was to see on a previous occasion. "It is not like purchasing cattle, you know."

"Oh, far from it," she agreed, laughing, "if by *cattle* you mean horses, Mr. Downes. I would not have asked you so soon if I must congratulate you if it were a horse you were choosing. I would know that the choice must be made with great care over an extended period of time."

He stared at her for so long that she became uncomfortable. But she scorned to look away from him.

"Who hurt you?" he asked her, jolting her with surprise and even shock. "Was it your husband?"

The same assumption in two days by two different people. Poor Christian. She smiled at Edgar. "My husband treated me as if I were a queen, Mr. Downes," she said. "Or to be more accurate, as if I were a porcelain doll. I am merely a realist, sir. Are your riches not sufficient to lure a genteel bride?"

"I believe my financial status and my personal life are none of your concern, ma'am," he said with such icy civility that she felt a delicious shiver along her spine.

"You do that remarkably well," she said. "Did all opposing counsel crumble before you in court? Were you a very successful lawyer? No, I will not make that a question but a statement. I have no doubt you were successful. Do all your employees quiver like jelly before your every glance? I would wager they do."

"I treat my employees well and with respect," he said.

"But I will wager you demand total obedience from

them," she said, "and require an explanation when you do not get it."

"Of course," he said. "How could I run a successful business otherwise?"

"And are you the same in your personal relations, Mr. Downes?" she asked. "Am I to pity your wife when you have married her—after congratulating you, of course?" With her eyes she laughed at him. Her body was horribly aroused. She had no idea why. She had never craved any man's mastery. Quite the opposite.

"You need feel nothing for my wife, ma'am," he said. "Or for me. We will be none of your concern."

She sighed audibly. "You are naive, Mr. Downes," she said. "When you marry into the *ton*, you will become the concern of the *ton*. What else do we have to talk about but one another? Where can we look for the most fascinating scandals but to those among us who have recently wed? Especially when the match is something of a misalliance. Yours will be, you know. We will all look for tyranny and vulgarity in you—and will hope that there will not be only bourgeois dullness instead. We will all look for rebellion and infidelity in her—and will be vastly disappointed if she turns out to be a docile and obedient wife. Will you insist upon docility and obedience?"

"That will be for me to decide," he said, "and the woman I will marry."

She sighed again and then laughed. "How tiresome you are, Mr. Downes," she said. "Do you not know when a quarrel is being picked with you? I wish to quarrel with you, but I cannot quarrel alone."

For the first time she saw a gleam of something that might be amusement in his eyes—for the merest moment. "But I have no wish to quarrel with you," he said softly, twirling her about one corner of the ballroom. "We are not adversaries, ma'am."

"And we are not friends either," she said. "Or lovers. Are we nothing, then? Nothing at all to each other?"

He gave her another of those long stares—even longer this time. He opened his mouth and drew breath at one moment, but said nothing. He half smiled at last— he looked younger, more human when he smiled. "We are nothing," he said. "We cannot be. Because there was that night."

She almost lost her knees. She was looking back into his eyes and unexpectedly had a shockingly vivid memory of that night—of his face this close, above hers. . . .

"Do you understand the etiquette of such sets as this, Mr. Downes?" she asked. "It is the supper dance. It would be unmannerly indeed if you did not take me in to supper and seat yourself beside me and converse with me. What shall we converse about? Let me see. Some safe topic on which people who are nothing to each other can natter quite happily. Shall I tell you about my dreadful experiences in Greece? I am an amusing story-teller, or so my listeners always assure me."

"I believe I would like that," he said gravely.

She almost believed him. And she almost wanted to cry. How absurd! She felt like crying.

She never cried.

6

$\mathcal{I}$T WAS AMAZING HOW FEW CHOICES COULD BE LEFT one sometimes, Edgar discovered even more forcefully over the following month. He tried very hard not to fix his choice with any finality, simply because he did not meet that one certain lady of whom he could feel confident of saying in his heart that, yes, she was one he wished to have as his life's companion, as his lover, as the mother of his children.

Miss Turner was of a suitable age, but he found her dull and physically unappealing. Miss Warrington was also of suitable age, and she was livelier and prettier. But her conversation centered almost entirely upon horses, a topic that was of no particular interest to him. Miss Crawley was very young—she even lisped like a child— and had a tendency to giggle at almost any remark uttered in her hearing. Miss Avery-Hill was equally young and very pretty and appealingly vivacious. She made very clear to Edgar that she would accept his courtship. She made equally clear the fact that it would be a major condescension on her part if she stooped to marry him.

That left Miss Grainger—and the Grainger parents. He liked the girl. She was pretty, modest, quiet without being mute, pleasant-natured. She was biddable. She would doubtless be a good wife. She would surely be a good mother. She would be a good enough companion.

She would be attractive enough in bed. Cora liked her. His father would, too.

There was something missing. Not love, although that was definitely missing. He did not worry about it. If he chose a bride with care, affection would grow and even love, given time. He was not sure quite what it was that was missing with Miss Grainger. Actually there was nothing missing except fortune, and that certainly was of no concern to him. He did not need a wealthy wife. If there was something wrong, it was in himself. He was too old to be choosing a wife, perhaps. He was too set in his ways.

Perhaps he would even have considered reneging on his promise to his father if matters had not appeared to have moved beyond his control. He found that at every entertainment he attended—and they were almost daily—he was paired with Miss Grainger for at least a part of the time. At dinners and suppers he found himself seated next to her more often than not. He escorted her and her mother to the library one day because Sir Webster was to be busy at something else. He went driving in the park with the three of them on two separate occasions. He was invited one evening to dinner at the Graingers', followed by some informal musical entertainment. There were only four other guests, all of them from a generation slightly older than his own.

Cora spoke often of Christmas and began to assume that the Graingers would be coming to Mobley. She was working on persuading all her particular friends—hers and Francis's—to spend the holiday there, too.

"Papa will be delighted," she said at breakfast one morning after the topic had been introduced. "Will he not, Edgar?" Francis had just suggested to her that she write to her father before issuing myriad invitations in his name.

"He will," Edgar agreed. "But it might be a good idea

to fire off a note to warn him, Cora. He might consider it somewhat disconcerting to find a whole gaggle of guests and their milling offspring descending upon him and demanding a portion of a lone Christmas goose."

Lord Francis chuckled.

"Well, of *course* I intend to inform Papa," Cora said. "The very idea that I might neglect to do so, Edgar. Do you think me quite addle-brained?"

Lord Francis was unwise enough to chuckle again.

"And everyone knows that my main function in life is to provide you with amusement, Francis," she said crossly.

"Quite so, my love," he agreed, eliciting a short bark of inelegant laughter from his spouse.

"And I daresay Miss Grainger will be more comfortable with Jennifer and Samantha and Stephanie there as well as me," Cora said. "She is familiar with them and they with her. But she *is* rather shy and may find the combination of you and Papa together rather formidable, Edgar."

"Nonsense," her brother said.

"I did, Edgar," Lord Francis said. "When I dashed down to Mobley that time to ask if I might pay my addresses to Cora, I took one look at your father and one look at you and had vivid mental images of my bones all mashed to powder. You had me shaking in my Hessians. You might have noticed the tassels swaying if you had glanced down."

"And what gives you the idea," Edgar asked his sister, "that Miss Grainger will be at Mobley for Christmas? Have I missed something? Have you *invited* her?" He had a horrid suspicion for one moment that perhaps she had and had forced his hand quite irretrievably.

"Of course I have not," she said. "I would never do such a thing. That is for you to do, Edgar. But you will do it, will you not? She is your favorite and eligible in every way. I love her quite like a sister already. And you did promise Papa."

"And it is Edgar's life, my love," Lord Francis said, getting to his feet. "We had better go up and rescue Nurse from our offspring. They are doubtless chafing at the bit and impatiently awaiting their daily energy-letting in the park. Is it Andrew's turn to ride on my shoulders or Paul's?"

"Annabelle's," she said as they left the room.

But Cora came very close that very evening to doing what she had said she would never do. They were at a party in which she made up a group with the Graingers; Edgar; Stephanie, Duchess of Bridgwater; and the Marquess of Carew. The duchess had commented on the fact that the shops on Oxford Street and Bond Street were filled with Christmas wares already despite the fact that December had not even arrived. The marquess had added that he and his wife had been shopping for gifts that very day in the hope of avoiding any last-minute panic. Cora mentioned Mobley and hoped there would be some snow for Christmas. All their children, she declared—if she could persuade her friends to come—would be ecstatic if they could skate and ride the sleighs and engage in snowball fights.

"There are skates of all sizes," she said, "and the sleighs are large enough for adults as well as children. Do you like snow, Miss Grainger?"

Edgar felt a twinge of alarm and looked pointedly at his sister. But she was too well launched on enthusiasm to notice.

"Good," Cora said when the girl had replied that indeed she did. "Then you will have a marvelous time." She reacted quite in character when she realized that she had opened her mouth and stuffed her rather large slipper inside, Edgar noticed, wishing rather uncharitably that she might choke on it. She blushed and talked and laughed. "That is, if it snows. If it snows where you happen to be spending Christmas, that is. That is, if . . . Oh dear. Hartley, do tell me what I am trying to say."

"You are hoping there will be snow to make Christmas a more festive occasion, Cora," the Marquess of Carew said kindly. "And that it will fall all over England for everyone's delight."

"Yes," she said. "Thank you. That is exactly what I meant. How warm it is in here." She opened her fan and plied it vigorously before her face.

Sir Webster and Lady Grainger, Edgar saw, were looking very smug indeed.

AND THEN AT the very end of November, when the noose seemed to have settled quite firmly about his neck, he discovered the existence of the ineligible lover—the one Lady Stapleton had mentioned.

Edgar was walking along Oxford Street, huddled inside his heavy greatcoat, avoiding the puddles left by the rain that had just stopped, wondering if the sun would ever shine again and if he would ever find suitable gifts for everyone on his list—he had expected London to make for easier shopping than Bristol—when he ran almost headlong into Miss Grainger, who was standing quite still in the middle of the pavement, impeding pedestrian traffic.

"I do beg your pardon," he said, his hand going to the brim of his hat even before he recognized her. "Ah, Miss Grainger. Your servant." He made her a slight bow and realized two things. Neither of her parents was with her—but a young man was.

She did not behave with any wisdom. Her eyes grew wide with horror, she opened her mouth and held it open before snapping it shut again. Then she smiled broadly, though she forgot to adjust her eyes accordingly, and proceeded to chatter.

"Mr. Downes," she said. "Oh, good morning. Fancy meeting you here. Is it not a beautiful morning? I have come to change my book at the library. Mama could not come with me, but I have brought my maid—you see?" She gestured behind her with one hand to the young person standing a short distance away. "How lovely it is to see you. By a very strange coincidence I have run into another acquaintance, too. Mr. Sperling. May I present you? Mr. Sperling, sir. Jack, this is Mr. Downes. I-I m-mean *Mr. Sperling*, this is Mr. Downes."

Edgar inclined his head to the slender, good-looking, very young man, who was looking back coldly. "Sperling?" he said.

A few things were clear. This particular spot on Oxford Street was not between the Grainger lodgings and the library. The doorway to a coffee shop that sported high-backed seats and secluded booths was just to their right. The maid was not doing a very good job as watchdog. Jack Sperling was more than a chance acquaintance and the meeting between him and Miss Grainger was no coincidence. Sperling knew who he was and would put a dagger through his heart if he dared—and if he had one about his person. Miss Grainger herself was terrified. And he, Edgar, felt at least a century old.

He would have moved on and left his prospective bride to her clandestine half hour or so—he doubted they would allow themselves longer—with the slight acquaintance she happened to call by his first name. But she forestalled him.

"Jack," she said. She was still flustered. "I m-mean *Mr. Sperling*, it was pleasant to meet you. G-good morning."

And Jack Sperling, pale and murderous of countenance, had no choice but to bow, touch the brim of his hat, bid them a good morning, and continue on his way down the street as if he had never so much as heard of coffee shops.

Fanny Grainger smiled dazzlingly at Edgar—with terrified eyes. "Was not that a happy chance?" she said. "He is a neighbor of ours. I have not seen him for years." Edgar guessed that beneath the rosy glow the cold had whipped into her cheeks she was blushing just as rosily.

"May I offer my escort?" he asked her. "Are you on your way to or from the library?"

"Oh," she said. "To." She indicated her maid, who held a book clasped against her bosom. "Y-yes, please, Mr. Downes, if it is not too much trouble."

He felt like apologizing to her. But of course he could not do so. He should be feeling sternly disapproving. He should be feeling injured proprietorship. He felt—still—a century old. She took his arm.

"Mr. Downes," she said before he had decided upon a topic of conversation, "p-please, will you—? That is, could I ask you please— Please, sir—"

He wanted to set a reassuring hand over hers. He wanted to pat it. He wanted to tell her that it was nothing to him if she chose to arrange clandestine meetings with her lover. But of course it *was* something to him. There was one month to Christmas and he had every intention—he had thought it through finally just last evening and had come to a firm decision—of inviting her and her parents to Mobley Abbey for the holiday, though he had thought he would not make his offer until they had all been there for a few days and he could be quite sure before taking the final step.

"I believe, my dear," he said, and then wished he had not called her that, as if she were a favored niece, "my size and demeanor and—age sometimes inspire awe or even fear in those who do not know me well. At least, I

have been told as much by those who do know me. I
have no wish either to hurt or distress you. What is it?"

He noticed that she closed her eyes briefly before answering. "Please," she said, "will you refrain from men-
tioning to Mama and Papa that I ran into Mr. Sperling
by chance this morning? They do not like him, you see,
and perhaps would scold me for not giving him the cut
direct. I could not do that. Or at least I did not think of
doing it until it was too late."

"Of course," he said. "I have already forgotten the
young man's name and indeed his very existence."

"Thank you." Some of the terror had waned from her
eyes when she looked up at him. "Though I w-wish I
had done so. It was disagreeable to have to acknowledge
him. I was very relieved when you came along."

"It is a quite impossible situation?" he found himself
asking when he should have been content to play along
with her game.

There was fright in her eyes again. She bit her lip and
tears sprang to her eyes. "I am sorry," she whispered.
"Please do not be angry with me. It was the last time.
That is— It will not happen again. Oh, please do not be
angry with me. I am so frightened of you." And then the
fright escalated to terror once more when she realized
what she had said, what she had admitted, both about
him and about Jack Sperling.

This time he did set his hand over hers—quite firmly.
"That at least you need not be," he said. "What is the
objection? Lack of fortune?"

But she was biting hard on her upper lip and fighting
both tears and terror—despite his words. The library
was before them.

"I shall leave you to your maid's chaperonage," he
said, stopping on the pavement outside it and relinquishing her arm. "We will forget about this morning,
Miss Grainger. It never happened."

But she did not immediately scurry away, as he rather expected she would. She looked earnestly into his face. "I have always been obedient to Mama and Papa," she said, "except in very little things. I will be obedient—I would be obedient to a husband, sir. I would never need to be beaten. I—Good morning." And she turned to hurry into the library, her maid behind her.

Good Lord! Did she imagine—? Did he look that formidable? And what a coil, he thought. He could not possibly marry her now, of course. But perhaps it would appear that he had gone rather too far to retreat without good cause. There was excellent cause, but nothing he could express to another living soul. He could not marry a young lady who loved another man. Or one who feared him so much that she imagined he would be a wife-beater.

Whatever was he going to do?

But he was not fated to think of an answer while he stood there on the pavement, staring at the library doors. They opened and Lady Stapleton stepped out with Mrs. Cross.

He forgot about his problem—the one that concerned Miss Grainger, anyway. He always forgot about everything and everyone whenever his eyes alighted on Lady Stapleton. They had avoided each other for the past month. They attended almost all the same social events and it was frequently necessary to be part of the same group and even to exchange a few words. But they had not been alone together since that evening when they had waltzed and then taken supper together. The evening when he had told her they could be nothing to each other because there had been that night.

That night. It stayed stubbornly in his memory, it wove itself into his dreams as none other like it had ever done. Not that there had been another night like that. Perhaps, he thought sometimes, he would forget it sooner if he tried less hard to do so. He did not want to remember. The memories disturbed him. He was not a man of passion but one of cool reason. He had been rather alarmed at the passionate self that had emerged during that particular encounter. He looked forward to returning to Mobley and then Bristol. After that, he hoped, he would never see her again. The memories would fade.

He made his bow and would have hastened away, but Mrs. Cross called to him.

"Mr. Downes," she cried. "Oh, Mr. Downes, might we impose upon you for a few minutes, I wonder? My niece is unwell."

He could see when he looked more closely at Lady Stapleton that she was leaning rather heavily on her aunt's arm and that her face and even her lips were ashen pale and her eyes half closed—and that until her aunt spoke his name, she had been quite unaware of his presence.

Her eyes jolted open and her glance locked with his.

THE POVISES HAD already left for the Continent with a group of friends and acquaintances. They intended to wander south at a leisurely pace and spend Christmas in Italy. Helena might have gone with them. Indeed, they had urged her to do so, and so had Mr. Crutchley, who had had designs on her for a number of years past, though she had never given him any encouragement. It was sure to be a gay party. She would have enjoyed herself immensely if she had gone along. She would have avoided this dreariest of dreary winters in England— and it was still only November. She could have stayed away until spring or even longer. Perhaps she could even have persuaded her aunt to go with her if she had set her mind to it.

But she had not gone.

She did not know why. She was certainly not enjoying London. There were almost daily entertainments, and she attended most of them for her aunt's sake. The company, though sparse, was congenial. She was treated with respect and even with warmth wherever she went— even on that evening when she had worn her bronze satin and Lady Francis Kneller had quite frankly and quite sincerely commended her bravery. Being in one comfortable home was certainly preferable to moving from one inn to another. And coach travel day after day could be tedious and even downright uncomfortable. She should be happy. Or since happiness was not a possible state for her, contented. She should be contented.

She felt lethargic and even ill. Her aunt had a bad cold soon after returning to town, but Helena did not catch it from her. It would have been better if she had, she thought. She would have suffered for a few days and then recovered. As it was, she felt constantly unwell without any specific symptoms that she might treat. Even getting out of bed in the mornings—her favorite time of day—had become a chore. Sometimes she lay late in bed, awake and bored and uncomfortable, but lacking the energy to get up, only to feel faintly nauseated and unable to eat any breakfast when she did make the effort.

She knew why she felt that way, of course. She was living through an obsession—and it was no new thing. If it had been, perhaps she would have been better able to deal with it. But it was not new. She had been obsessed once before and just the memory of it—long suppressed but never quite hidden below consciousness—could have her poised with her head hanging over the close stool, fighting to keep the last meal down.

Now she was obsessed again. Not in any way she could explain clearly to herself. Although she saw him almost daily, she never again felt the urge to seduce him—though the knowledge that it would not be an easy thing to do a second time was almost a temptation in itself. She just could not keep her eyes off him when he was in a room with her. Though that was not strictly accurate. She rarely looked directly at him. She would scorn to do so. He would surely notice. Other people would. She kept her eyes off him. But every other part of her being was drawn to him as if to a powerful magnet.

She was not even sure that it was just a sexual awareness. She imagined sometimes being in bed with him again, doing with him the things they had done on that one night they had spent together. But though the thoughts were undeniably arousing, she always knew that it was not that she wanted. Not just that anyway. She did not know what she wanted.

She wanted to forget him. That was what she wanted. She hated him. Those words they had spoken while waltzing would not fade from her mind.

Are we nothing, then? Nothing at all to each other?

We are nothing. We cannot be. Because there was that night.

There was a deep pit of emptiness in her stomach every time she heard the echo of those words of his—and she heard it almost constantly.

She should go away. She should have gone with the Povises. She had stayed for her aunt's sake, she had told herself. But when had she ever considered anyone's feelings except her own? When had she ever had a selfless motive for anything she had ever done—or not done? She should go away. She should go to Scotland for Christmas—horrid thought. But *he* would be going away for Christmas. He would be going to his father's estate near Bristol. She had heard Lady Francis Kneller talking about it. The Grainger girl would doubtless be going there, too. They would be betrothed—and married by the spring. Perhaps then she would know some peace.

Peace! What a ridiculous hope. Her last chance for any kind of peace had disappeared over a year ago with the marriage of another man.

She decided to accompany her aunt to the library one morning, despite the fact that she felt not only nauseous but even dizzy at breakfast, and even though her aunt urged her to go back to bed for an hour. She would feel better for a little fresh air, she replied.

She did not feel better. She sat with a newspaper while her aunt chose a book, but she did not read even the headlines. She was too busy imagining the humiliation should she vomit in such a public place. She mastered the urge as she had done on every previous occasion, even in the privacy of her own rooms.

But a wave of dizziness took her as they reached the door on their way out. It was so strong that her aunt noticed and became alarmed. She took Helena's arm and Helena unashamedly leaned on her for support. She drew a few deep breaths of the cold outside air, her eyes half closed. And then her aunt spoke.

"Mr. Downes," she called, her voice breathless with distress. "Oh, Mr. Downes, might we impose upon you for a few minutes, I wonder? My niece is unwell."

Helena's eyes snapped open. There he was, tall and broad and immaculately groomed and frowning at her as if he were quite out of humor. He of all people! There was suddenly another wave of nausea to be fought.

7

SHE PUSHED AWAY FROM HER AUNT'S SIDE AND stood upright. "I am quite well, I thank you," she said. "Good morning, Mr. Downes."

The effect of her proud posture and brisk words was quite marred by the fact that she swayed on the spot and would perhaps have fallen if Mrs. Cross had not grasped her arm and Edgar had not lunged forward to grab her by the waist.

"I am *quite well*," she said testily. "You may unhand me, sir."

"You are not well, Helena," her aunt insisted mildly. "Mr. Downes, *may* we impose upon you to call us a hackney cab?"

"No!" Lady Stapleton said as Edgar looked back over his shoulder toward the road. "Not a hackney cab. Not a carriage of any sort. I shall walk home. The fresh air will feel good. Thank you for your concern, Mr. Downes, but we need not detain you. My aunt's arm will be quite sufficient for my needs."

She was attempting her characteristic mocking smile, but it looked ghastly in combination with parchment white face and lips. The foolish woman was obviously trying to defy an early winter chill.

"I shall summon a hackney cab, ma'am," he said and turned away from her in order to hail one.

"I shall vomit if I have to set foot inside a carriage," she said from behind him. "There. Is that what you wanted, Mr. Downes? To hear me admit something so very ungenteel?"

"My dear Helena," her aunt said, "Mr. Downes is just being—"

"Mr. Downes is just being his usual overbearing self," Lady Stapleton said. "If you must offer your assistance, sir, give me your arm and escort me home. I can lean more heavily on yours than I could on Letty's."

"Helena, my dear." Mrs. Cross sounded shocked. "Mr. Downes probably has business elsewhere."

"Then he can be late," her niece retorted, taking Edgar's offered arm and leaning much of her weight on it. "Oh, I do wish I had gone to Italy with the Povises. How tiresome to be in England when it is so cold and sunless and cheerless."

"I have no business that cannot be delayed, ma'am," Edgar told Mrs. Cross. "I shall escort you home, Lady Stapleton, and then go to fetch a physician if you will tell me which. I suppose you have not consulted him lately." It was a statement rather than a question.

"How kind of you, sir," Mrs. Cross said.

"I do not consult a physician every time I am subjected to an overheated library and half faint from the stuffiness," Lady Stapleton said. "I shall be quite myself in a moment."

But she was very far from being herself even five minutes later. She continued to lean heavily on his arm and walked rather slowly along the street. She did not speak again, even to contradict Mrs. Cross, who proceeded to tell Edgar that her niece had not been in the best of health for some little while. By the time they came in sight of her house, her eyes were half closed and her footsteps lagged more than ever.

"Perhaps, ma'am," Edgar suggested to Mrs. Cross,

"you could go ahead to knock on the door and have it open by the time Lady Stapleton arrives there." And without warning to his flagging companion, he stopped, released her arm, and scooped her up into his arms.

She spoke then while her one arm came about his neck and her head dropped to his shoulder. "Damn you, Edgar," she said, reminding him of how she had sworn at him on a previous occasion. "Damn you. I suppose you were waiting outside that library for the express purpose of humiliating me. How I hate you." But she did not struggle to be set down.

"Your effusive expressions of gratitude can wait until you are feeling more the thing," he said.

The flat-nosed pugilist was in the hall and looked to be bracing himself to take his mistress in his own arms. Edgar swept by him with hardly a glance and carried his burden upstairs. She was certainly no light weight. He was thankful when he saw Mrs. Cross outside Lady Stapleton's bedchamber, holding open the door. Had she been ascending the stairs behind them, he might have forgotten that he was not supposed to know where the lady's bedchamber was.

He set her down on the bed and stood back while her aunt removed her bonnet and a maid, who had rushed in behind them, drew off her half boots. She was still terribly pale.

"Who is your physician?" he asked.

"I have none." She opened her eyes and looked up at him. Some of her hair had come loose with the bonnet. The richness of its chestnut waves only served to make her face look more colorless. "I have no need of physicians, Mr. Downes. I need a warm drink and a rest. I daresay I shall see you at Lady Carew's musical evening tonight."

"Oh, I think not, Helena," Mrs. Cross said. "I will send a note around. The marchioness will understand."

"You need a physician," Edgar said.

"And you may go to the devil, sir," she said sharply. "Might I expect to be granted the privacy of my own room? It is not seemly for you to be standing there looking at me here, is it?" The old mockery was back in both her face and her voice. It was the very room and the very bed, of course . . .

"When you are feeling better, Helena," Mrs. Cross said with gentle gravity, "you will wish to apologize to Mr. Downes. He has been extraordinarily kind to us this morning, and there is no impropriety with both Marie and me here, too. We will leave you to Marie's care now. Sir, will you come to the drawing room for tea or coffee—or something stronger, perhaps?"

"Thank you, ma'am," he said, turning toward the door, "but I really do have business elsewhere. I shall call tomorrow morning, if I may, to ask how Lady Stapleton does."

Lady Stapleton, he saw when he glanced back at the bed before leaving the room, was lying with her eyes closed and a contemptuous smile curling her lip.

"I am worried about her," Mrs. Cross said after he had closed the door. "She is not herself. She has always had so much restless energy. Now she seems merely restless."

"Would *you* like me to summon a physician, ma'am?" he asked.

"Against Helena's wishes?" she said, raising her eyebrows and laughing. "You do not know my niece, Mr. Downes. She was unpardonably rude to you this morning. I do apologize for her. I am sure she will do so for herself when she feels better and remembers a few of the things she said to you."

Edgar doubted it. "I understand that Lady Stapleton prides herself on her independence, ma'am," he said.

"She was embarrassed to have to accept my assistance this morning. No apology is necessary."

They were in the hall already and the manservant, looking his usual surly self, was waiting to open the door onto the street.

"You are gracious, sir," Mrs. Cross said.

He wished she would see a physician, Edgar thought as he strode along the street in an effort not to be quite impossibly late for a meeting he had arranged with a business associate. She was not the type of woman to be always having the vapors and relying upon men to support her to the nearest sofa. She had hated having to accept his help this morning. She had even damned him—and called him by his first name. Her indisposition was very real, and it had been going on for some time if her aunt was to be believed.

He was worried about her.

And then he frowned and caught the thought. *Worried* about her? About Lady Stapleton, who meant nothing to him? How had they expressed it between them during that evening when they had been waltzing? They were not adversaries or friends or lovers. They were nothing. They could be nothing, because there had been that night.

But there had been that night. He had known her body with thorough intimacy. He had known exhilarating and blazing passion with her.

Yes, he supposed she was *something*. Not anything that could be put into words, but something. Because there had been that night.

And so he was worried about her.

SHE HAD ALLOWED Marie to undress her and tuck her into bed. She had allowed her aunt back into her room to draw the curtains across the window and to send for a hot drink of weak tea—the thought of chocolate or coffee was just too nauseating. She had allowed them both to fuss—though she hated people fussing over her.

And now she had been left alone to sleep. She felt as far from sleep as she had ever felt. She lay staring up at the large silk rosette that formed the peak of the canopy over her bed. She could not believe how foolish she was. She was stunned by her own naivete.

Although her husband had been fifty-four when she married him and sixty-one when he died, he had been a vigorous man. He had had her almost nightly for the first year and with frequency after that, almost to the end. She had never conceived. She had come to believe that the fault was in herself. Although Christian had had only the one son, she had been told that his first wife had had an appalling number of stillbirths and miscarriages.

The possibility of conception had not occurred to her when she had lain with Edgar Downes—either before or during or after. Not even when she had begun to feel persistently unwell.

She was careless about her own cycle. Her monthly flow, that great nuisance to which all women were subjected, almost always took her by surprise. She had no idea if she was strictly regular or not. She was one of the fortunate women who were not troubled by either pain or discomfort or a heavy flow.

And so for a number of weeks she had allowed symptoms so obvious that they were like a hard fist jabbing at her chin to pass her by unnoticed. Even now, when she set her mind to it, she could not remember when her last flow had been. She was almost sure there had been none for a while—none since that night, anyway. She was almost sure enough to say that she was quite certain. Oh, yes, of course she was certain. And that had been well over a month ago.

She had been feeling lethargic and nauseated—especially in the mornings. Her breasts had been feeling tender to the touch.

As she stared upward, strong suspicion turned unwillingly to certainty—and to a mindless, clawing terror. She closed her eyes as the canopy began to swing about her—and then opened them again. Dizziness was only worsened when one closed one's eyes. She drew deep breaths, held them, and released them slowly through her mouth.

At the age of six-and-thirty she was with child.

She was pregnant.

She was going to swell up to a grotesque enormity just like a young bride. And then there was going to be a baby. A child. A person. For her to nurture.

No.

No, she could not do it. She could not face the embarrassment. Or the shame. Though she did not care the snap of two fingers for the shame. But the embarrassment! She was six-and-thirty. She had been a widow for ten years. If the *ton* suspected that she occasionally took lovers—and her carelessness of strict propriety had made that almost inevitable—then they would guess, too, that she was worldly-wise and knowledgeable enough to take care of herself. It was unpardonably gauche to allow oneself to be impregnated, especially when one did not have a live husband upon whose paternity to foist the love child.

She would be the laughingstock.

She did not care about that. Why should she care what people thought about her? She had not cared for a long time.

Her terror had little to do with either shame or embarrassment. It had everything to do with the fact that there was going to be a *baby*. A child who was half hers and would come from her body. A child she would be expected to nurse and to love and to teach.

She had involved someone else, drawn someone else into her own darkness. A child. An innocent.

Her mind reached frantically about. If she searched carefully for a good home, if she gave the baby up at birth, if she was careful never to see it again, never to let it know who or what its mother was, would the child have a chance?

But she could not think clearly. She had only just realized the truth, though it had been staring her in the face for some time. He had stopped a short distance from the house and taken her totally by surprise by picking her up and carrying her the rest of the way. She had felt the strength of his arms and the sturdiness of his body—and she had known in a blinding flash the nature of her obsession with him. Her body had been speaking for a few weeks but her mind had not been listening. She had this man's child growing inside her.

And so she had damned him and would have used worse language on him if she had had the energy.

Where would she go? She closed her eyes and found to her relief that the dizziness had gone. Scotland? Her cousins were respectable people. They would not appreciate the notion of entertaining a pregnant woman whose husband had died ten years ago. Italy? She could find the Povises and their party. If she told the story well enough, they would be amused by it. They were worldly enough to accept that such things happened.

She could not tell this story amusingly. There was a *child* involved. An innocent.

Where, then? Somewhere else in Europe? Somewhere here in England?

She could not think straight. She needed to sleep. She was mortally tired. If she could but sleep, she could clear her head and then think and plan rationally. If she could but sleep . . .

But she kept seeing Edgar Downes standing beside her bed, looking even more massive and forbidding than usual in his caped greatcoat, his booted feet set apart on her carpet, his face frowning down at her as he suggested fetching a physician.

And more alarmingly, she kept seeing him above her on the bed, his weight pressing her down, his hot seed gushing deep inside her. She kept feeling herself being impregnated.

She hated him. She did not blame him for anything. It had been all her fault. She had seduced him and had taken no precautions to avoid the consequences. But she hated him anyway.

He of all people must never know the truth. She would never be able to live with that humiliation. He would probably proceed to take charge, to send her somewhere where she could bear the child in comfort and secrecy. He would probably find a home for it. He would probably support it until it was adult and he could find it suitable employment. He would see her as just a weak woman who could not possibly manage alone.

He must never find out. He was not going to organize the life of *her* child. He was not going to take her child away from her or lift from her shoulders the responsibility of caring for it. It was her child. It was inside her body. Now. And not *it*. He. Or she. A real person.

She was biting her upper lip. After a while she tasted blood. She did not sleep.

LADY STAPLETON AND Mrs. Cross were not at the Carews' musical evening. Mrs. Cross had sent a note making their excuses, the marchioness explained when someone noted their absence. Lady Stapleton was indisposed.

It was only surprising that most of them remained healthy in such dreary weather, someone remarked.

Fanny Grainger had mentioned seeing Lady Stapleton at the library looking quite ill, Lady Grainger reported.

She had been looking not quite herself for a few weeks, the Countess of Thornhill said. Poor lady. Some winter chills were very hard to shake.

But look at the gowns she wore, Mrs. Turner remarked—or rather did not wear, her tone implied. It was no wonder she took chills.

No one picked up that particular conversational cue.

"I must pay her a call," Cora Kneller announced in the carriage on the way home. "I wonder if she has seen a physician. At least she is fortunate to have Mrs. Cross to tend to her. Mrs. Cross is a very amiable and sensible lady. I like her excessively."

"I shall come with you, Cora," her brother said.

"Oh good." She looked only pleased and not even mildly suspicious, as Lord Francis did. "I will not need your escort then, Francis. You may take the children to the park."

"They will probably take me, my love," he said. "But I shall allow myself to be dragged along."

And so Edgar made his promised morning call in company with his sister. He hoped that Lady Stapleton would have kept to her bed so that they might make their inquiries of Mrs. Cross and spend just a short while in conversation with her. But when they were shown up to the drawing room, it was to find both ladies there.

Lady Stapleton was looking more herself. There was little color in her cheeks, but she was looking composed and was dressed with her usual elegance. She even favored Edgar with her usual mocking smile as she greeted him. He and Cora were invited to have a seat and Mrs. Cross rang for tea.

"I was quite disturbed to hear last evening that you were indisposed," Cora said. "I can see for myself this morning that you are still not quite the thing. I do hope you have consulted a physician."

Lady Stapleton smiled at Edgar. "I have not," she said in her velvet voice. "I do not believe in physicians. But thank you for your concern, Lady Francis. And for yours, sir."

Edgar said nothing. He merely inclined his head.

"Letty tells me that I owe you an apology," she said. "She tells me I was rude to you yesterday. I cannot remember saying anything I did not mean, but perhaps I was feeling ill enough to say something to offend. I do beg your pardon."

"Yesterday?" Cora said with bright curiosity. "Did you see Lady Stapleton yesterday, Edgar, and said nothing last evening when we were discussing her absence? How provoking of you!"

"Ah, but doubtless Mr. Downes was too modest to admit to his own gallantry," Lady Stapleton said, her eyes mocking him. "I leaned heavily on his arm all the way home from the library, and he actually carried me the last few yards and all the way upstairs to my bedchamber. My aunt was with us, I hasten to add. Your brother has amazing strength, Lady Francis. I weigh a ton."

"Oh, Edgar." Cora looked at him curiously. "How thoughtful of you. And you did not say a word about it. I am not surprised that you wished to come to pay your respects today. But *you* are quite well, ma'am?" She turned her attention to Mrs. Cross.

The two of them proceeded to discuss Lady Stapleton's health almost as if the lady herself was not present. Mrs. Cross was worried because her niece had been under the weather for a week or more—yes, definitely more—but refused to seek a cure. She was ill enough each morning to be quite unable to eat any breakfast and her energy seemed to flag several times each day. She had come near to fainting on more than one occasion. And such behavior was quite unlike her.

Lady Stapleton kept her gaze on Edgar while they spoke, a look of mocking amusement in her eyes.

"I know just what it is like to be unable to eat breakfast," Cora said. "I sympathize with you, Lady Stapleton. It happened to me during the early months when I was expecting all four of my children. And yet breakfast has always been my favorite meal."

Lady Stapleton raised both eyebrows, but continued to look at Edgar. "Goodness me," she said. "We will be embarrassing Mr. Downes. I do believe he is blushing."

He was not blushing, but he was feeling remarkably uncomfortable. Only Cora would speak so indelicately in mixed company.

"Oh, Edgar will not mind," Cora said. "Will you, Edgar? But of course in my case, Lady Stapleton, it was a natural effect of my condition and passed off within a month or two. So did the dreadful tiredness. I do hate being tired during the day. But in your case such symptoms are unnatural and should be confided to a physician. It is unmannerly of me to press you on the issue, however, when I am not a relative or even a particularly close acquaintance. I am a concerned acquaintance, though."

"Thank you," Lady Stapleton said. "You are kind."

The conversation moved on to a more general discussion of health and by natural progressions through the weather and Christmas and some of the more attractive shops on Oxford Street.

Edgar did not participate. His discomfort had turned to something more extreme, though he was trying to tell himself not to be so foolish. She was his age, she had once told him. As far as he knew, she had never had children, though she had been married for a number of years and had admitted to numerous lovers since her widowhood. Was it possible for a woman to have a child at the age of six-and-thirty? Foolish question. Of course it was possible. He knew women who had borne children at an even more advanced age. But a first child? Was it possible? After years of barrenness or else years of careful guarding against such a thing?

It surely was not possible. How she would laugh at him if she knew the suspicions that were rushing their course through his brain. Just because Cora had compared the early months of her pregnancies with Lady Stapleton's illness. What an absurdity for him to take the extra step of making the direct comparison.

But then Cora did not know—and in her innocence would not even suspect—that the lady had had a lover just over a month ago. Neither would her aunt suspect it.

"And what are your plans for Christmas, Mr. Downes?" Mrs. Cross asked him suddenly.

He stared at her blankly for a moment. "I will be going down to Mobley Abbey, ma'am, to spend the holiday with my father," he said.

"There will be quite a house party there," Cora said. "Francis and I and the children will be going, of course, and several of our friends. I am looking forward to it excessively."

"And Mr. Downes's future bride will be there, Letty," Lady Stapleton said, looking at Edgar as he spoke. "Did you not know that he has come to town for the express purpose of choosing a bride from the *ton*? He is to take her to Mobley Abbey to present her to his father for approval. A Christmas bride. Is that not romantic?" She made it sound anything but.

This time Edgar really did flush.

"Now you are the one to have embarrassed Mr. Downes, Helena," Mrs. Cross said reproachfully. "But there is nothing to be embarrassed about, sir. I wish you joy of your quest. Any young lady would be fortunate indeed to be your choice."

"Thank you, ma'am," he said and noticed with some relief that Cora was getting to her feet to take her leave. He stood up and the other two ladies did likewise. He made his bow to them and then waited while Cora thought of something else she must tell Mrs. Cross before they left. He looked closely at Lady Stapleton, who smiled back at him.

Are you with child? he wanted to blurt out. But it was a ridiculous notion. Bizarre. She was a thirty-six-year-old widow. With whom he happened to have had sexual relations—twice—just over a month before. And now she was suffering from morning sickness and unusual tiredness and fainting spells when she tried to push on with her usual daily activities. And she was unwilling to see a physician.

He felt dizzy himself for a moment.

He could not imagine a worse disaster. It could not possibly be. But what other explanation could there be? Morning sickness. Tiredness. Even he was aware of those two symptoms as very characteristic of pregnancy in its early stages.

He followed his sister downstairs with some longing for the fresh air beyond the front door—even if it was chilly, damp, windblown air. He had to think. He had to convince himself of his own foolishness. But was it more foolish to think that it might be or to imagine that it could not possibly be?

Was she pregnant?

By him?

8

HELENA HAD DECIDED TO STAY IN TOWN OVER
Christmas. After a few days of suppressed terror
and near panic, she calmed down sufficiently to decide
that she had to plan carefully, but that there was no
immediate hurry. She was a little over one month
pregnant. Soon the nausea and the tiredness would pass
off. Her condition would not be evident for a few
months yet. She need not dash off somewhere in a blind
panic. There was time to think and to plan.

Soon most of her acquaintances would disperse to
their various country estates for the holiday. Some
would remain and others would arrive, but the people
she most wanted to be rid of would be gone. Edgar
Downes would be gone and so would that bold, curiously appealing sister of his and her family. They were
taking a number of other people with them to Mobley
Abbey—the Carews, the Bridgwaters, the Thornhills,
the Greenwalds. And very probably the Graingers, too.

She felt sorry for Fanny Grainger, though it was not
normally in her nature to feel sorry for people. Perhaps
she pitied the girl because she was reminded of herself at
that age, or a little younger. So unhappy and fatalistic.
So very obedient. Like a lamb to the slaughter, to use the
old cliché. Fanny would be quite suffocated by Edgar
Downes.

She forced herself to attend most of the social functions to which she was invited—and she was invited everywhere—while she was careful to curtail her morning activities and to keep most of her afternoons free so that she might rest. She succeeded in feeling and looking a little better than she had with the result that her aunt, though not quite satisfied, stopped pressing her to consult a physician.

Sooner or later, Helena thought, she was going to have to see a doctor. How embarrassing that was going to be. But she would think of it when the time came—after Christmas. By then she would have decided where to go and exactly what to do with the child. Perhaps she would keep it, she thought sometimes, and live somewhere on the Continent with it, thumbing her nose at public opinion. Probably she would give it up to a carefully chosen family and disappear from its life. She was not worthy of being a mother.

She took care to think of the child as *it*. Terror could return in a hurry when she began to think of its personhood and to wonder about its gender and appearance. Would it be a boy who would look like *him*? She would shake off the speculations. She could not imagine a real live child, born of her own body, in helpless need of her arms and her breasts and her love.

She was incapable of love. She knew nothing of nurturing.

Oh, yes, she rather thought she would give up the child. *It*.

She saw Edgar Downes frequently. They became very skilled at avoiding each other, at sitting far from each other at dinner and supper tables, at joining different conversational or card-playing groups, at sitting on opposite sides of a room during concerts. They never ignored each other—that might have been as noticeable to a society hungry for something to gossip about as if they had been constantly in each other's pocket. When they did come face-to-face, they smiled politely and he asked about her health and she assured him that she was quite well, thank you.

They watched each other. Not with their eyes—a strange notion. They were *aware* of each other. She was sure it worked both ways. She felt that he watched her, though whenever she glanced at him to confirm the feeling, she was almost always wrong. When he asked about her health, she sensed that the question was not a mere courtesy. For days after he had carried her to her bed and then called on her with his sister, she had half expected him to return with a physician. It was just the sort of thing she would expect him to do—take charge, impose his will upon someone who had no wish to be beholden to him in any way, do what he thought was best regardless of her feelings.

And she was always aware of him. She could not rid herself of the obsession and in the end stopped trying. Soon he would be gone and she would not have daily reminders of him. Within eight months his child would be gone—from her womb and from her life. She would have her own life, her own particular hell, back again.

She thought of him constantly—not sexual thoughts. They would have been understandable and not particularly disturbing. She kept thinking of him escorting her home, his arm solid and steady beneath her own, his pace reduced to fit hers. She kept thinking of him lifting her into his arms and carrying her into the house and up two flights of stairs as if she weighed no more than a feather. She kept thinking of his near-silence when he had called with Lady Francis, of that frowning, intent look with which he had regarded her, as if he were genuinely worried about her health. She kept imagining herself leaning into his strength, abandoning all the burdens of her life to him, letting him deal with them for her. She kept thinking of herself sleeping in his arms. Just sleeping—nothing else. Total relaxation and oblivion. Safety. Peace.

She hated the feeling. She hated the weakness of her thoughts. And so she hated him even as she was obsessed by him.

By the middle of December she was impatient for his departure. He had come to choose a bride. He had chosen her long ago. Let him take her to his father, then, and begin a grand Christmas celebration. She could not understand why he delayed. She resented the delay. She wanted to be free of him.

She wanted desperately to be free. And she laughed contemptuously to herself whenever she caught herself in the thought. Had she forgotten that there would never be freedom, either in this life or the next? Had hope somehow been reborn in her even as she knew that despair was the only end of any hope? She had dulled her sensibilities to reality before that dreadful evening when desperate need had tempted her to seduce Edgar Downes. Perhaps, she sometimes thought, she would have fought the temptation harder if she had had even an inkling of the fact that he would not be easily forgotten. That he would impregnate her.

She waited with mingled patience and impatience for him to be gone.

EDGAR HAD ALWAYS thought of himself as a decisive man, both by nature and training. He had never been a procrastinator—until now.

He delayed in making his intentions clear to Miss Grainger and her parents. And he delayed in speaking with Lady Stapleton and putting his suspicions into words. As a result, with only two weeks to go until

Christmas, he suddenly found himself in a dreadful coil indeed.

He was at a dance at Mrs. Parmeter's—she and her husband were newly arrived in London to take in the Christmas parties. He had just finished dancing a set of country dances with the Duchess of Bridgwater and had joined a group that included Sir Webster. The conversation, inevitably he supposed considering the date, centered about Christmas and everyone's plans for the holiday.

"Your father is to entertain quite a large house party at Mobley Abbey, I hear, Mr. Downes," Mrs. Parmeter said, smiling at him with marked condescension. As a new arrival she was not as accustomed as most of her other guests to finding herself entertaining a mere merchant.

"Yes, indeed, ma'am," he said. "He is delighted that there will be such a large number, children included. He is passionately fond of children."

Sir Webster was coughing against the back of his hand and shifting his weight from foot to foot. "I must commend you on the number of guests with whom you have filled your drawing room, ma'am," he said.

"Yes." Mrs. Parmeter smiled graciously and vaguely. "And Sir Webster was telling us that he and his lady and *Miss Grainger* are to be among the guests, Mr. Downes," she said, placing particular emphasis on the one name. She raised her eyebrows archly. "Is there to be an interesting announcement during Christmas, sir?"

"Oh, I say." Sir Webster sounded suitably mortified. "I was merely saying, ma'am—"

"I am certainly hoping that Sir Webster and Lady Grainger and their daughter will be among my father's guests," Edgar said, aghast at what he was being forced into—as a businessman he had perfected the art of avoiding being maneuvered into anything he had not pondered and decided for himself. At least he had the sense to leave the woman's final question alone.

"I am sure you are, sir," Mrs. Parmeter said. "You know, I suppose, that Lady Grainger's father is Baron Suffield?"

"Yes, indeed, ma'am," Edgar said.

She turned her conversation on other members of the group and soon enough Edgar found himself with Sir Webster, a little apart from the rest of them.

"I say—" that gentleman began. "Mrs. Parmeter totally misunderstood me, you know. I was merely saying—" But he could not seem to remember what it was he had been merely saying.

Perhaps, Edgar thought, it was as well to have his hand forced. He had only two weeks left in which to keep his promise. There was no one more suitable—or more available—than Miss Grainger. There was that young man of hers, of course—he should have found a way of dealing with that problem by now. And there was that other problem, too—but no. She appeared to have recovered from her indisposition whatever it had been, though she still seemed paler than he remembered her to have looked. He could not do better than Miss Grainger—not in the time allowed, at least. And perhaps he had carried the courtship rather too far to back off now without humiliating the girl and her family. Certainly the father seemed to expect a declaration.

"But my father would be delighted to entertain you and your wife and daughter at Mobley, sir," Edgar said, releasing the man from his well-deserved embarrassment. "And my sister and I would be delighted, too, if you would join us and other of our friends there for Christmas. If you have no other plans, that is. I realize that this is rather short notice."

"No," Sir Webster said quickly, "we have no other plans, sir. We were thinking of staying in town to enjoy the festivities. That was our plan when we came here. We were undecided whether to stay, too, for the Season. Fanny would enjoy it and it is time to bring her out, I suppose. It is difficult to part with a daughter, Mr. Downes. Very difficult. One wants all that is the best for her. We will accept your gracious invitation, sir. Thank you. And we will decide later about the Season."

There would be no Season if he came up to scratch, Edgar understood. And probably no Season if he did not, either. The Graingers were said to be too poor to afford such an expense. But he was not going to pick up the cue this time. He merely smiled and bowed and informed Sir Webster that Cora would write to their father tomorrow.

His father would read eagerly between the lines of that particular letter, he thought. Or perhaps not between the lines either. Cora would surely inform him that Miss Grainger was the one, that he might prepare to meet his future daughter-in-law within the fortnight.

Edgar felt half robbed of breath. But it was a deed that must be done. It was time to stop dragging his feet. Young Jack Sperling could not be helped. This was the real world. And the girl's age could not be helped. Young ladies were married to older men all the time. He would be kind to her and generous to her. He would treat her with affection. So would his father and Cora. She would be taken to the bosom of their family with enthusiasm, he did not doubt. She would learn to settle to a marriage that could be no worse than thousands of marriages that were contracted every year. And he would settle, too. He would enjoy having children of his own. Like his father, he was fond of children.

Children of his own. There—that thought again. That nagging suspicion. His eyes found out Lady Stapleton. She was at the other side of the room—without ever looking at each other for any length of time, they always seemed to maneuver matters so—talking and laughing with Mr. Parmeter and the Earl of Thornhill. She was wearing the scarlet gown she had worn that first night— the one with all the tiny buttons down the back. It must have taken him all of five minutes. . . .

She looked healthy enough and cheerful enough. She looked pale. She did not look as if she felt nauseated. But this was the evening rather than the morning. Besides, Cora had said that the feeling passed after a couple of months. It was two months since . . . Well, it was two months. She did not look larger. But it was only two months.

It could not possibly be. Beautiful and alluring as she looked, it was a mature beauty and a mature allure. But she was only six-and-thirty. She was still in her fertile years. She had never had a child before—at least he did not believe so. Why would she conceive now? But why not?

Such conflicting thoughts had teemed in his head for the past two weeks. They had woven themselves into his dreams—when he had been able to sleep. They had kept him awake.

He caught her eye across the room, something that rarely happened. But instead of looking away from each other, both continued to look as if daring the other to be the first to lose courage. She raised one mocking eyebrow.

He despised indecisiveness. If there was one single factor that could keep a man from success in the business world, he had always found, it was just that—being indecisive, allowing misplaced caution and unformed worries to hold one back from action that one knew must be taken. He knew he must talk with her. And time was running out. He should already have left for Mobley. He must do so within the next few days.

He must talk to Lady Stapleton first. He did not want

to—he would do almost anything to get out of doing so if he could. But he could not. Not if he was to know any peace of mind over Christmas. He walked across the center of the drawing room, empty now between sets, and she smiled that smile of hers to see him come. She did not turn away or even look away from him.

"Ma'am?" He bowed to her. "May I have the honor of dancing the next set with you?"

"But of course, Mr. Downes," she said. That low velvet voice of hers always jolted him, no matter how often he heard it. "It is a waltz, and I know you perform the steps well." She set her hand in his. It was quite cold.

"And how do you do, ma'am?" he asked her when they had taken their positions on the floor and waited for the music to begin.

"Very well, thank you, Mr. Downes." Her perfume brought back memories.

There was no dodging around it, he decided as the pianist began playing and he set his hand at the back of her waist and took her other in his own. And so he simply asked the question.

"Are you with child?" His voice was so low that he was not sure the sound of it would carry to her ears.

Clearly it did. She mastered her surprise almost instantly and smiled with brutal contempt. "You must think yourself one devil of a fine lover, Mr. Downes," she said. "Is it the factor by which you measure your success? Have you peopled Bristol with bastard children?"

But not quite instantly enough. For the merest fraction of a second—had he not been looking for it he would certainly have missed it—there had been something other than contempt in her eyes. There had been fright, panic.

"No," he said. "But I believe I have got you with child." Now that the words were out, now that he had seen that fleeting reaction, he felt curiously calm. Almost cold.

"Do you?" she said. "And do you realize how absurd your assumption is, sir? Do you know how old I am?"

"You told me once," he said. "I do not believe you are past your childbearing years. Are you?"

"You are impertinent, sir," she said. "You dare ask such a question of a lady, of a virtual stranger?"

"A stranger whom I bedded two months ago," he said. "One who is to bear my child seven months from now, if I am not much mistaken."

She smiled at him—a bright social smile, as much for the benefit of the other dancers and watchers as for his, he guessed. "You, Mr. Downes," she said, "may go to hell."

"But I notice," he said, "that you have not said no, it is not true. I notice such things, ma'am. I have been and still am a lawyer. Is it that you are afraid to lie? Let me hear it. Yes or no. Are you with child?"

"But I am not on the witness stand, Mr. Downes," she said. "I do not have to answer your questions. And I scorn to react to your charge that I am afraid to answer. I will not answer. I choose not to."

"Have you seen a physician?" he asked her.

She looked into his eyes and smiled. "You are a divine waltzer, Mr. Downes," she said. "I believe it is because you are so large. One instinctively trusts your lead."

"Do you still suffer from morning sickness?" he asked.

"Of course," she said, "it is not just your size, is it? One cannot imagine enjoying a waltz with an ox. You have a superior sense of rhythm." Her smile turned wicked.

"I shall find out for myself tomorrow," he said. "You once invited me to escort you to one of the galleries. I accept. Tomorrow morning will be the time. We have arranged it this evening. You may tell Mrs. Cross that if you will. If you will not, I will tell her when I come for you that I have come to discuss your pregnancy."

"Damn you, Mr. Downes," she said sharply. "You have the manners of an ox even if not the dancing skills of one."

"Tomorrow morning," he said. "And if you have any idea of bringing your aunt with you, be warned that we will have our frank talk anyway. I assume she does not know?"

"Damn you to hell," she said.

"Since we are dancing for pleasure," he said, "we might as well concentrate on our enjoyment in silence for the rest of the set. I believe we have nothing further to say to each other until tomorrow."

"How your underlings must hate you," she said. "I am not your underling, Mr. Downes. I will not be overborne by you. And I will not be blackmailed by you."

"Will you not?" he said. "You will tell Mrs. Cross the truth, then, and have that servant of yours refuse me admittance tomorrow morning? I believe I might enjoy pitting my strength against his."

"Damn you," she said again. "Damn you. Damn you."

Neither of them spoke after that. When the music drew to an end, he escorted her to her aunt, stayed to exchange civilities with that lady for a few minutes, and then took himself off to the other side of the room.

He felt rather as if he had been tossed into the air by that ox she had spoken of and then trodden into the ground by it after landing. It was true, then. He could no longer lull himself with the conviction that his suspicions were absurd. She had not admitted the truth, but the very absence of such an admission was confirmation enough.

She was with child. By him. He felt as dizzy, as disoriented, as if the idea had only now been planted in his brain.

What the devil were they going to do?

And why the devil did he need to pose that question to himself?

SHE DAMNED HIM to hell and back throughout a sleepless night. She broke a favorite trinket dish when she picked it up from her dressing table and hurled it against the door. She considered calling his bluff and telling her aunt the truth, though she had hoped to go away somewhere alone so that no one need know, and then instructing Hobbes to deny him entry.

But he would come tomorrow morning even if she told her aunt and even if Hobbes tried to prevent him. She had great faith in Hobbes's strength and determination, but she had a nasty feeling that neither would prevail against Edgar Downes. He would come and drag the truth from her and proceed to take charge of the situation no matter what she did.

She would not dance to his tune. Oh, she would not. She did not doubt that he would plan everything down to the smallest detail. She did not doubt that he would find her a safe and comfortable nest in which to hide during the remainder of her confinement and that he would find the child a respectable home afterward. He would do it all with professional efficiency and confidentiality. No one would ever suspect the truth. No one would ever know that the two of them had been more to each other than casual social acquaintances. And he would pay for everything. She did not doubt that either. Every bill would be sent to him.

She would not allow it to happen. She would shout the truth from the rooftops before she would allow him to protect her reputation and her safety. She would keep her child and take it with her wherever she went rather than allow him neatly to hide its very existence.

And yet, she thought, mocking herself, she did not even have the courage to tell her aunt. She would go out with him tomorrow morning, two acquaintances visiting a gallery together, a perfectly respectable thing to do, and she would allow herself to be browbeaten.

Never!

She would fight Edgar Downes to the death if necessary. The melodramatic thought had her lip curling in scorn again.

She mentioned to her aunt at the breakfast table that Mr. Downes would be calling later to escort her to the Royal Academy. He had mentioned wanting to go there while they had danced the evening before and she had commented that it was one of her favorite places. And so he had asked to escort her there this morning.

"I have promised to show him all the best paintings," she said.

Mrs. Cross looked closely at her. "Are you feeling well enough, Helena?" she asked. "I have become so accustomed to your staying at home in the mornings that I have arranged to go out myself."

"Splendid," Helena said. "You are going shopping?"

"With a few other ladies," Mrs. Cross said. "Will you mind?"

"I hardly need a chaperone at my age, Letty," Helena said. "I believe Mr. Downes is a trustworthy escort."

"Absolutely," her aunt agreed. "He is an exceedingly pleasant man. I was quite sharp with Mrs. Parmeter last evening when she remarked on his background as if she expected all of us to begin to tear him apart. Mr. Downes is more the gentleman than many born to the rank, I told her. I believe he has a soft spot for you, Helena. It is a shame that as his father's only son he feels duty bound to marry a young lady so that he may set up his nursery and get an heir for that estate near Bristol. The Grainger girl will not suit him, though she is pretty and has a sweet enough nature. She has not had the time or opportunity to develop enough character."

"And I have?" Helena smiled. "You think he would be better off with me, Letty? Poor Mr. Downes."

"You would lead him a merry dance, I daresay," Mrs. Cross said. "But I believe he would be equal to the task. However, he must choose a young lady."

"How lowering," Helena said with a laugh. "But I would not be young again for a million pounds, Letty. I shudder to remember the girl I was."

She would gain one advantage over Mr. Edgar Downes this morning at least, she thought while she began to talk about other things with her aunt. She would confront him on home ground. Her aunt was going out for the morning. That would mean that she and Mr. Downes need not leave the house. She would not have to be smilingly polite lest other people in the streets or at the gallery take note. She could shout and scream and throw things to her heart's content. She could use whatever language suited her mood.

Only one thing she seemed incapable of doing—at least she had been last night. She could not seem to lie to Edgar Downes. She could get rid of him in a moment if only she could do that. But she scorned to lie. She would withhold the truth if she could, but she would not lie.

She went upstairs after breakfast to change her dress and have her hair restyled. She wanted to look and feel her very best before it came time to cope with her visitor.

She waited for an hour in the drawing room before he came. She had instructed Hobbes to show him up when he arrived.

9

*E*DGAR WAS RATHER SURPRISED TO BE ADMITTED TO her house without question. The manservant, his face quite impassive, led the way upstairs, knocked on the drawing room door, opened it, and announced him.

She was there alone, standing by the fireplace, looking remarkably handsome in a dark green morning gown of simple, classic design. Her chin was lifted proudly. She was unsmiling, the customary mocking expression absent from her face. She was not ready for the outdoors.

"Thank you, Hobbes," she said. "Good morning, Mr. Downes."

Her face was pale. There were shadows beneath her eyes. Perhaps, he thought, she had slept as little as he. The thought that this proud, elegant woman was pregnant with his child was still dizzying. It still threatened to rob him of breath.

"I suppose it was too much to expect," he said, "that you would not somehow twist the situation to impose some sort of command over it. We are not to view portraits and landscapes?"

"Not today or any other day, Mr. Downes," she said. "Not together at least. My aunt is from home. I would have had Hobbes deny you admittance but you would have made a scene. You are so ungenteel. If you have something to say that is more sensible than what you were saying last evening, please say it and then leave. I have other plans."

He could not help but admire her coolness even while he was irritated by it. Most women in her situation would be distraught and clinging and demanding to know his intentions.

"Thank you for offering," he said, walking farther into the room after removing his greatcoat—the servant had not offered to take it downstairs—and tossing it onto a chair. "I believe I will sit down. But do have a seat yourself, ma'am. I am gentleman enough to know that I may not sit until you do."

"You are impertinent, Mr. Downes," she said.

"But then I am also, of course," he said, gesturing toward the chair closest to her, "quite bourgeois, ma'am."

She sat and so did he. She was furious, he saw, though she would, of course, scorn to glare. She sat with her back ramrod straight and her jaw set in a hard line.

"You are with child," he said.

She said nothing.

"It is a reality that will not go away," he said. It had taken the whole of a sleepless night finally to admit that to himself. "It must be dealt with."

"Nothing in my life will be dealt with by you, Mr. Downes," she said. "I deal with my own problems, thank you very much. I believe this visit is at an end."

"I believe, ma'am," he said, "it is *our* problem."

"No!" Her nostrils flared and both her hands curled into fists in her lap. "You will not treat this as a piece of business, Mr. Downes, to be dealt with coldly and efficiently and then forgotten about. I will not have a quiet hideaway found for me or a discreet midwife. I will not have a decent, respectable home found for the child so that I may return to my usual life with no one the wiser. You may be expert at dominating your subordinates with that confident, commanding air of yours. You will not dominate me."

Good Lord!

He leaned back in his chair, set his elbows on the arms, and steepled his fingers beneath his chin. He stared at her for a long time before speaking.

"You realize, I suppose," he said at last, "what you have admitted to me." If there had been one thread of hope left in him, it was gone. On the whole, he was glad of it. He liked to have issues crystal clear in his mind.

There was a flush of color to her cheeks. But her expression did not change. She did not speak.

"You have misunderstood my character," he said. "There will be no hideaway, no decent home for the child away from his mother, no resumption of your old way of life, no sweeping of anything under the carpet. We will marry, of course."

Her head snapped back rather as if he had punched her on the chin. Her eyes widened and her eyebrows shot up. And then she laughed.

"Marry!" she said. "We will marry? You jest, sir, of course."

"I do not jest," he said. "Of course."

"Mr. Downes." All the old mockery was back in her face. No, it was more than mockery—it was open contempt. "Do you seriously imagine that *I* would marry *you*? You are presumptuous, sir. I bid you a good morning." She was on her feet.

"Sit down," he told her quietly and sat where he was, engaging in a silent battle of wills with her. He never lost such battles. This time, after a full minute of tension, he tacitly agreed to accept a compromise when she turned and crossed the room to the window. She stood with her back to him, looking out. He remained seated.

"I thank you for your gracious offer, Mr. Downes," she said, "but my answer is no. There. You have done the decent thing and I have been civil. We are even. Please leave now."

"We will marry by special license before going down to Mobley Abbey for Christmas," he said.

She laughed again. "Your Christmas bride," she said. "You are determined to have her one way or another, then? But have you not already invited Miss Grainger in that capacity? Do you have ambitions to set up a harem, Mr. Downes?"

He dared not think of that invitation to the Graingers. Not yet. Experience had taught him that only one sticky problem could be dealt with at a time. He was dealing with this one now.

"Better still," he said, "we could take the license with us and marry there. It would please my father."

"Your father would be quite ecstatic," she said, "to find that you had brought home a bride as old as yourself. He wants grandchildren, I do not doubt."

"And that is exactly what he will have, ma'am," he said.

He could see from the hunching of her shoulders that she had only just realized her mistake. Although she must have known for a lot longer than he, although she was carrying the child in her own womb, he supposed that the truth must seem as unreal to her as it did to him.

"It will be easier if you accept reality," he said. "If we both do. We had our pleasure of each other two months ago without a thought to the possible consequences. But there have been consequences. They are in the form of an innocent child who does not deserve the stigma of bastardy. We have created him or her. It is our duty to give him parents who are married to each other and to nurture him to the best of our ability. We have become rather unimportant as individuals, Lady Stapleton. There is someone else to whose whole life this issue is quite central—and yet that person is at the mercy of what is happening in this room this morning."

"Damn you," she said.

"Which would you prefer?" he asked her briskly. "To marry here or at Mobley? The choice is yours."

"How clever you are, Mr. Downes." She turned to look at him. "Giving the illusion of freedom of choice when you have me tied hand and foot and gagged, too. I will make no choice. I have not even said I will marry you. In my world, you know—it may be different with people of your class—a woman has to say that she does or that she will before her marriage can be declared valid. So I do still have some freedom, you see."

He got to his feet and walked toward her. But she held up both hands as he drew close.

"No," she said. "That is far enough. You are too tall and too large, Mr. Downes. I hate large men."

"Because you are afraid you will not have total mastery over them?" he said.

"For exactly that reason." Her voice was sharp. "I made a mistake two months ago. I rarely make mistakes. I chose the wrong man. You are too—too *big*. You suffocate me. Go away. I have been remarkably civil to you this morning. I can become ferociously uncivil when aroused. Go away." Her breathing was ragged. She was agitated.

"I am not going to hurt you," he told her. "I am not going to touch you against your will." He clasped his hands behind his back.

She laughed. "Are those the sentiments of an ardent bridegroom, Mr. Downes?" she said. "Do you speak only in the present tense or do your words have a more universal meaning? You would never touch me against my will? You would be facing an arid, celibate life, sir, unless you would take your ease with mistresses."

"I have a strong belief in marital fidelity," he said.

"How bourgeois!" She laughed again.

"Yes."

"Mr. Downes." Her arms dropped to her sides. Both the agitation and the contempt were gone from her face and she looked at him more earnestly than she had ever done before. Her face was pale again. "I cannot marry you. I cannot be a wife. I cannot be a mother."

He searched her eyes but they gave nothing away. They never did. This woman hid very effectively behind her many masks, he realized suddenly. He did not know her at all, even though he had had thorough sexual knowledge of her body.

"Why not?" he asked.

"Because." She smiled the old smile. "Because, Mr. Downes. Because."

"And yet," he said, "you are to be a <u>mother</u> whether you wish it or not. The deed is done and cannot be undone."

She closed her eyes and looked as if she were about to sway on her feet. But she mastered herself and opened her eyes again. "I will deal with it," she said. "I cannot keep the child. I cannot marry you. I would destroy both of you. Believe me, Mr. Downes. I speak the truth."

He frowned, trying to read her eyes again. But there were no depths to them. They were quite unreadable. "Who hurt you?" he asked her. He remembered asking her the question before.

She laughed. "No one," she said. "Absolutely no one, sir."

"I am going to be your husband," he said. "I would hope to be your companion and even your friend as well. There may be many years of life ahead for us."

"You are not going to be talked out of this, are you?" she said. "You are not going to take no for an answer. Are you?"

He shook his head.

"Well, then." Her head went back and both her eyes and her lips mocked him. "Behold your Christmas bride, Mr. Downes. It is a Christmas and a bride that you will come to regret, but we all choose our own personal hells with our eyes wide open, I have found. And it will happen at Mobley. I would see the ecstasy in your father's eyes as we tie the eternal knot." There was harsh bitterness in her voice.

He inclined his head to her. "I do not believe I could ever regret doing the right thing, ma'am," he said. "And before you can tell me how bourgeois a sentiment that is, let me forestall you. I believe we bourgeoisie have a firmer, less cynical commitment to decency and honor than some of the gentry and aristocracy. Though I daresay that like all generalizations there are almost as many exceptions as there are adherents to the rule."

"I will not allow you to dominate me," she said.

"I would not wish to dominate a wife," he told her.

"Or to touch me."

"As you wish," he said.

"I will make you burn for me, Edgar," she said. "But will not let you touch me."

"Perhaps," he said.

Her lip curled. "I cannot make you quarrel, can I?" she said. "I would love to have a flaming row with you, Mr. Downes. It is your power over me, perhaps, that you will not allow it."

"Perhaps," he agreed.

"Do you realize how frustrating it is," she asked him, "to quarrel with someone who will not quarrel back?"

"Probably as frustrating," he said, "as it is going to be to burn for you when you refuse to burn for me."

She smiled slowly at him. "I believe," she said, "that if I did not resent and hate you so much, Mr. Downes, I might almost like you."

He did not hate her or particularly resent her. He did

not like the situation in which he found himself, but in all fairness he could not foist the blame entirely on her. It took two to create a child, and neither of them had been reluctant to engage in the activity that had left her pregnant. He did not like her. She was bitter and sharp-tongued and did nothing to hide her contempt for his origins. But there was something about her that excited him. There was her sexual allure, of course. He had no doubt that his frustrations would be very real indeed if she meant what she said. But it was not just a sexual thing. There was something challenging, stimulating about her. She would not be easy to manage, but he was not sure he wanted to manage her. She would never be a comfortable companion, but then comfort in companionship could become tedious. Life with her would never be tedious.

"Have I silenced you at last?" she asked. "Are you wounded? Are you struggling not to humiliate yourself by confessing that you *love* me?"

"I do not love you," he said quietly. "But you are to be my wife and to bear my child. I will try to respect and like you, ma'am. I will try to feel an affection for you. It will not be impossible, perhaps. We are to share a child. I will certainly love our child, as will you. We will have that to bring us together."

"Why, Mr. Downes," she said, "I do believe there is a streak of the romantic in you after all."

The door opened behind them.

"Oh," Mrs. Cross said, startled. "Mr. Downes is here with you. I am so sorry, Helena. I assumed you were alone. I wondered why you were back so soon."

"You need not leave, Aunt," Lady Stapleton said, moving past Edgar to take Mrs. Cross by the arm. She was smiling when she turned back to him. "You must make your curtsy to Mr. Downes, who is now my affianced husband. We are to marry at Mobley Abbey before Christmas."

Mrs. Cross's face was the picture of astonishment. She almost gaped at Edgar. He bowed to her.

"I have offered for Lady Stapleton's hand, ma'am," he told her, "and she has done me the great honor of accepting me."

"Oh, come now, Mr. Downes." Lady Stapleton sounded amused. "This is my aunt you are talking to. The truth is, Letty, that I am two months with child. Edgar and I became too—*ardent* one night before your return from the country and having learned of the consequences of that night, he has rushed here to make amends. He is going to make an honest woman of me. Wish us joy."

Mrs. Cross appeared speechless for a few moments. "I do," she said finally. "Oh, I do indeed. Pardon me, Helena, Mr. Downes, but I do not know quite what to say. I do wish you joy."

"Of course you do," Lady Stapleton said. "You commented just this morning, did you not, that Mr. Downes had a soft spot for me." Her eyes mocked him even as her aunt flushed and looked mortified. "It appears you were right."

"Ma'am." Edgar addressed himself to Mrs. Cross, ignoring the bitter levity of his betrothed's tone. "We will be marrying by special license at Mobley Abbey, as Lady Stapleton mentioned. My father and my sister will be in attendance, as well as a number of our friends. I would be honored if you would be there, too, and would remain to spend Christmas with us. My father would be honored."

"How kind of you, sir." The lady was recovering some of her composure. "How very kind. I would, of course, like to be at Helena's wedding. And I have no other plans for the holiday."

Edgar looked at Lady Stapleton. "There will perhaps be time to invite other members of your family or other particular friends if you wish," he said. "Is there anyone?"

"No," she said. "This is no grand wedding celebration we are planning, Edgar. This is a marriage of necessity."

"Your stepson is at Brookhurst only thirty miles from Mobley, is he not?" he said. "Perhaps—"

Her face became a mask of some strong emotion— horror, terror, revulsion, he could not tell which.

"No!" she said icily. "I said no, Mr. Downes. No! I will have my aunt with me. She will be family enough. She is the only relative I wish to acknowledge. But, yes, you must come, Letty. I will not be able to do this without you. I do not wish to do it at all, but Mr. Downes has been his usual obnoxious, domineering self. I shall lead him a merry dance, as you said I would if I ever married him, but he has been warned and has remained obdurate. On his own head be it, then. But you must certainly come to Mobley with me."

"Have you offered Mr. Downes a cup of tea, Helena?" her aunt asked, looking about her at the empty tables.

"No, I have not," her niece said. "I have been trying to get rid of him since he set foot inside the door. He will not leave."

"Helena!" her aunt said, looking mortified again. "Mr. Downes, do let me send for some tea or coffee."

"Thank you, ma'am." He smiled. "But I have other business to attend to. I shall see you both in my sister's drawing room this evening? I shall have the announcement made there and put in tomorrow morning's papers. Good day to you, Mrs. Cross. And to you, Lady Stapleton." He bowed to each of them as he retrieved his greatcoat.

"I must remember," Lady Stapleton said, "to start

offering you tea whenever I set eyes on you, Edgar. It seems the only sure way to be rid of you."

He smiled at her as he let himself out of the room, feeling unexpectedly amused. For a mere moment there seemed to be an answering gleam in her own eyes.

His betrothed. Soon to be his wife. The mother of his child. He shook his head as he descended the stairs in an effort to clear it of that dizziness again.

EDGAR WAS GLAD to get out again during the afternoon. He had arrived home to find both Cora and Francis there, having just returned from their usual morning outing with their children.

"Edgar," Cora had said, smiling brightly, "have you concluded all your business? Are you going to be ready to leave for Mobley tomorrow after tonight's farewell party? We met Lady Grainger and Miss Grainger in the park, did we not, Francis? They are extremely gratified to have been invited to Mobley. I have written to Papa to tell him—"

Cora's monologues could sometimes continue for a considerable length of time. Edgar had cut her off.

"Lady Stapleton and Mrs. Cross will be coming, too," he had told her and Francis. Francis's eyebrows had gone up.

"Are they?" Cora had said. "Oh. How splendid. We will be a merry house party. Papa will—"

"I will be marrying Lady Stapleton at Mobley before Christmas," Edgar had announced.

For once Cora had been speechless—and inelegantly open-mouthed. Lord Francis's eyebrows had remained elevated.

There had been no point in mincing matters. It was rather too late for that. "She is two months with child," he had said. "With my child, that is. We will be marrying."

Francis had shaken his hand and congratulated him and said all that was proper. Cora had been first speechless and then garrulous. By the time Edgar escaped the house, she had talked herself into believing that she, that he, that Francis, that everyone concerned and unconcerned must be blissfully happy with the betrothal. Lady Stapleton would be *just* the bride for Edgar, Cora had declared. Lady Stapleton would not allow herself to be swept along by the power of his character, and he would be the happier for it. Cora had never been so pleased by anything in her life, and Papa would be deliriously happy. Francis was called upon to corroborate these chuckle-headed notions.

"I believe it might well turn into a good match, my love," he had said less effusively than she, but with apparent sincerity. "I cannot imagine Edgar being satisfied with anything less. And the lady certainly has character—and beauty."

But of course Cora had issued the reminder Edgar had not needed before he made his escape.

"Oh, Edgar!" Her eyes had grown as wide as saucers and her hand had flown to her mouth and collided with it with a painful-sounding slap. "Whatever are you going to do about Fanny Grainger? You have all but *offered* for her. And she is coming to *Mobley*."

Edgar had no idea what he was going to do about Fanny Grainger, apart from the fact that he was not going to marry her. He had not offered for her, but he had come uncomfortably close. And last evening he had even taken the all-but-final step of inviting her and her parents to spend Christmas at Mobley. Everyone of course took for granted that he had invited her there for only one reason.

He liked the girl, even though he had not wished to

marry her. The last thing he wanted to do was to leave her publicly humiliated. But it seemed that that was what he was fated to do. Unless . . .

It was purely by chance—entirely, amazingly coincidental—that as he was walking along Oxford Street he caught a glimpse of the young man she had met on almost the exact same spot a few weeks ago when Edgar had come upon them. Jack Sperling was hurrying along, his head down, clearly intent on getting where he was going in as little time as possible. One could understand why. The wind cut down the street rather like a knife.

Edgar stepped to one side to impede his progress. Sperling looked up, startled. "I do beg your pardon," he said before frowning and looking distinctly unfriendly. "Oh, you," he added.

"Good afternoon." Edgar touched the brim of his beaver hat and did what it was not in his nature to do— he acted on the spur of the moment. "Mr. Sperling, is it not?"

"I am in a hurry," the young man said ungraciously.

"I wonder if I could persuade you not to be?" Edgar said.

Unfriendliness turned to open hostility. "Oh, you need not fear that your territory is going to be poached upon," he said. "She has sent me a letter this morning and has explained that it will be the last. *She* will not see me again, and *I* will not see her. We both have some sense of honor. Sir," he added, making the word sound like an insult.

"I really must persuade you not to be in a hurry," Edgar said. "I need to talk to you."

"I have nothing to say to you," Jack Sperling said. "Except this. If you once mistreat her and if I ever hear of it, then you had better learn to watch your back." His voice shook.

"It is dashed cold out here," Edgar said, shivering.

"That coffee shop is bound to be a great deal warmer. I believe they serve good coffee. Let us go and have some."

"You may drop dead, sir," the young man said.

"I do hope not," Edgar said. "Let me say this. I am going to be married within the next week or so—but not to Miss Grainger. However, she is to be a guest at my father's home and I feel a certain sense of responsibility for her happiness, since I seem to have been at least partly responsible for her unhappiness. Perhaps you and I could discuss the matter in civil fashion together?"

Jack Sperling stared at him for a few moments, deep suspicion in his face. Then he turned abruptly and strode in the direction of the coffee shop.

They emerged half an hour later and went their separate ways after bidding each other a civil good afternoon. His father was going to have far more than he bargained for this Christmas, Edgar thought, having added yet one more guest to the list.

10

THE MARRIAGE OF LADY STAPLETON AND EDGAR Downes was solemnized in the small church at the village of Mobley, two miles from the abbey, six days before Christmas. There was a respectable number of guests in attendance, all the invited house guests having already arrived for the holiday, with the exception of the Graingers and Jack Sperling. A few of Edgar's closer colleagues and some of the elder Mr. Downes's old friends had been invited to come out from Bristol.

Edgar's first intention, which was to marry quickly and quietly in London, had been set aside—partly by Lady Stapleton's choice. There was no point in undue stealth. The truth would soon be known whether they tried to stifle it or not. And neither one of them made any attempt to stifle it. She had announced the truth to her aunt; he had confessed it to his sister and brother-in-law. She had talked about it quite freely and unblushingly during the party at which the announcement of their betrothal was made—just as if there were nothing shameful in such an admission and nothing ungenteel about such a public topic of conversation.

But then Lady Stapleton had always been known for her outspoken ways—and for treading very close to the edge of respectability without ever stepping quite beyond.

Lady Stapleton and Mrs. Cross had shared a carriage to Mobley Abbey with Cora and her youngest child, Annabelle. Lord Francis had ridden with Edgar, one or other of the former's three sons as often as not up before them. The Duke and Duchess of Bridgwater with their infant son, the Earl and Countess of Thornhill, the Marquess and Marchioness of Carew, the Earl and Countess of Greenwald, all with three children apiece, had left London in a vast cavalcade of carriages a day later.

Before any of them had arrived, wedding preparations had been in full flight at Mobley—Cora had written again to her father. And the elder Mr. Downes had greeted his future daughter-in-law with hearty good humor, regardless of either her age or her condition.

For a few days there was no chance to think about Christmas. The wedding superseded it in importance and excitement value. Edgar had brought home a Christmas bride.

HELENA ARMED HERSELF with scorn—for herself and her own weakness in agreeing to this marriage, for Edgar's foolish sense of honor, for the whole hypocrisy of the joyful nuptials for which everyone seemed to be preparing.

She had prepared herself to find his father coarse and vulgar. She found instead a man who was loud and hearty and who bore an almost uncanny physical resemblance to his son—but who was not vulgar. He lacked Edgar's refinement of speech and manner—he had, of course, had his son educated in the best schools—but he was no less genteel than many gentlemen of her acquaintance. She had prepared herself to find Mobley Abbey a garish and distasteful display of wealth. A great deal of wealth had quite obviously been expended on its restoration so that its ecclesiastical origins were breathtakingly apparent; at the same time it was a cozy and comfortable private home. Every last detail gave evidence of impeccable taste.

It was disappointing, perhaps, to have little outside of herself on which to turn her scorn. But then she had never deceived herself about the main object of her bitterness and hatred. She had always been fair about that at least.

At first she decided to wear her bronze silk for her wedding. But she had an unaccustomed attack of conscience just the day before. None of these people—not even Edgar—had deserved such a show of vulgarity. She had an ensemble she had bought for a winter fête in Vienna and had worn only once—she had never found a suitable occasion on which to wear it again. She wore it for her wedding—a simple, expertly designed white wool dress with round neck, straight, long sleeves, and straight skirt slightly flaring from its high waistline; a white pelisse and bonnet, both trimmed with white fur; and a white muff and half boots.

At least there was an element of irony in the simple, elegant, eminently respectable attire, she thought, surveying herself in the mirror before leaving for the church. It was a wonderfully virginal outfit.

She did not want to marry. Not Edgar. Anyone but him. But there was no choice, of course. She would not allow the twinge of panic she felt to grow into anything larger. She smiled mockingly at her image. She was a bride—again. She wondered if she would make as much a disaster of this marriage as she had of the first. Undoubtedly she would. But he had been warned. He could never say he had not been.

She had asked the Marquees of Carew if he would be so good as to give her away, though she imagined that that foolish formality might have been dispensed with if she had talked to the vicar. The idea of a thirty-six-year-old widow having to be given away to a new husband was rather absurd. She had asked Lord Carew because he was a mild-mannered, kindly gentleman. Sometimes he reminded her of—no! He did not. He walked with a limp and had even been thoughtful enough to ask her if it would embarrass her. She had assured him it would not. It rather fascinated her to observe that the marchioness, who was many times more beautiful than he was handsome, nevertheless seemed to worship the ground he trod on. But Helena had never denied the existence of romantic and marital love—only of it as a possibility in her own life.

Her bridegroom was dressed very elegantly and fashionably in a dark blue, form-fitting tailed coat, buff pantaloons, white linen, and highly polished Hessians. She looked at him dispassionately as she walked toward him along the aisle of the small old church, oblivious to the guests, who turned their heads to watch her approach, and oblivious to either the marquess's limp or the steadying hand he had laid over her own on his arm. Edgar Downes looked solid and handsome and very much in command of his own life. He looked magnificent.

She experienced a growingly familiar feeling as she stood beside him and the marquess gave her hand into his. The feeling of being small and frail and helpless—and safe and secure. All illusions. His eyes, she saw when she looked up, were steady on hers. She did not want to gaze back, but having once looked, she had no choice. She would not lower her eyes and play the part of the demure bride. She half smiled at him, hiding her fear behind her customary mask.

Fear? Yes, she admitted, turning the mockery inward, too. Fear.

She listened to him promise her the moon and the stars in a firm voice that must have carried to the back pew of the church. She heard herself, almost as if she listened to someone else, promise him her soul. She watched the shiny gold ring, bright symbol of ownership, come to rest on her finger. She heard the vicar declaring that they were man and wife. She lifted her face to her new husband, feeling a wave of the nausea that had been disappearing over the past week.

He looked into her eyes and then at her lips, which she had drawn into a smile again. And then he took her completely by surprise. He clasped both her hands in his, bowed over them, and raised them one at a time to his lips.

She could have howled with fury. Tears sprang to her eyes and she bit hard on her upper lip. With her eyes and her lips she might have mocked his kiss on the mouth. She might have reminded him silently of his promise never to touch her without her permission. She might have put him subtly in the wrong. His kiss on her hands was startling in the illusion it gave of reverence and tenderness. She had to fight a painful ache in her throat to keep the humiliating tears from spilling over. But he must have seen them swimming in her eyes—he looked into them as soon as he raised his head. How she hated him.

He was her husband. And already he was establishing mastery.

BEFORE SUSPECTING HER pregnancy, he had not once thought of marrying her. He had been horrified by his suspicions and even more so by their confirmation. He had felt that he was being forced into something very much against his will. He had not wanted to marry her.

And yet once it had become fact, once he had persuaded her to accept him, once he had acquired the special license, once the wedding preparations had been set in motion, he had felt a curious elation, a strange sense of—rightness. He found it hard to believe that the obvious had been staring him in the face ever since his arrival in London and he had not opened up his eyes and seen.

She was the very woman for him.

She was a woman of character and experience, someone he would find an interesting and a stimulating companion. He knew that he had a strong tendency to dominate other people, to take charge, to insist on doing things the way he knew they must be done. It was a tendency that worked to his advantage in his professional life. It was a tendency that might well be disastrous in his marriage. He would make a timid mouse out of a young, inexperienced girl—Miss Grainger, for example—within a month of wedding her. He did not want a timid mouse. He wanted a companion.

Even one who had sworn that she would never allow him to touch her. Even one who had promised to lead him a merry dance. Even one who rarely looked at him without that mockery in her eyes and on her lips.

He had always intended to make a marriage with whomever he ended up wedding. He intended to make a marriage with Helena Stapleton. A real marriage. The challenge of overcoming such hostility was strangely exhilarating. And he would overcome it.

The woman herself was exciting, of course. She was extremely beautiful, the sort of woman who was probably lovelier now in her maturity than she had been as a young girl. Or perhaps it was just that he was a mature man who saw more beauty in a woman of his own age than in someone who was little more than a child.

By the time his wedding day arrived, Edgar had admitted to himself that he was in love with his bride. He would not go as far as believing that he loved her. He was not even sure he liked her. He did not know her well enough to know if the unpleasant side of her nature she delighted in showing to him was the product of a basically unpleasant disposition or if it was merely the outer symptom of a troubled, wounded soul. He rather suspected the latter, though she denied having ever been deeply hurt. He faced the challenge of getting to know her. He might well not like her when he did. And even if he did, he might never grow to love her as he had always dreamed of loving a wife.

But he was certainly *in* love with her. It was a secret which he intended to guard very carefully indeed, for a lifetime if necessary. The woman did not need any more weapons than she already possessed.

His wedding was like a dream to him. And as with many dreams, he determinedly imprinted every detail on his memory so that he would be able to relive it in the future. There was his father, hearty and proud—and afraid for the son whom he loved with unabashed tenderness. There was Cora, armed with half a dozen of Francis's large handkerchiefs because she always cried at weddings, she had explained, but was sure to cry *oceans* at her only brother's. And there was Francis beside her, looking faintly amused and also solicitous of the wife he adored. There were all the other guests, an illustrious gathering for the wedding of a man who could not even claim the title of gentleman for himself.

And then there was his bride—and once she appeared, nothing and no one else mattered until they were out on the church steps some time later. She usually wore vivid colors and dramatically daring styles and looked vibrantly beautiful. This morning, all in pure white from head to toe, she looked almost ethereal. It was an incongruous word to use of her of all people. Her beauty robbed him of breath and of coherent thought. He felt, he thought in some alarm as she came closer to the altar rail, almost like weeping. He did not do so.

He spoke his commitment to her and to their marriage

in the guise of the words of the nuptial service. He ignored the slight tone of mockery with which she made her promises to him. She would live those promises and mean them eventually. She was going to be a challenge, but he had never yet failed in any of the challenges he had set himself. And success had never been as important to him as it was with this one.

She was his wife. He heard the vicar announce the fact and felt the shock of the reality of the words. She was his wife. It was the moment at which he was invited to kiss her, though the vicar did not say so in words. He felt the expectation in the gathered guests. She lifted her face to his—and he saw the mockery there and remembered the promise he had made her. This was ritual, of course, and hardly subject to that promise. But he would give her no weapon wittingly.

He kissed the backs of her hands instead of her lips and for that public moment made no secret of his feelings for his new wife. He felt a moment of exultation when he raised his head and saw the brightness of tears in her eyes. But he did not doubt she would make him pay for that moment of weakness.

Oh, he did not doubt it. He counted on it!

He led his bride from the dark unreality of the church interior into the reality of a cold, bright December outdoors.

"You look remarkably beautiful this morning, Helena," he told her in the brief moment of privacy before their guests came spilling out after them.

"Oh, and so do you, Edgar," she said carelessly. "Remarkably beautiful."

Touché!

HELENA WAS FEELING irritable by the time she was finally alone in her own bedchamber for the night. The combination of a wedding and an imminent Christmas was enough, it seemed, to transport everyone to great heights of delirious joy. What she had done by coming here with Edgar and marrying him was land herself in the middle of glorious domesticity.

It was the last thing she wanted.

Domesticity terrified her more than anything else in life.

The elder Mr. Downes—her father-in-law, who had actually invited her today to call him *Papa*—seemed endlessly genial. The noise and activity by which he had been surrounded all day—by which they had *all* been surrounded—had been appalling to say the least. The adults had been in high spirits. There was no word to describe in what the children had been—and there had been hordes of children, none of whom had been confined to the nursery. Helena had understood—she hoped fervently that she had misunderstood—that they would not be this side of Christmas.

She had found it impossible to sort them all out, to work out which children belonged to which adults, which names belonged to which children. The smallest infant belonged to the Bridgwaters, and she *thought* she knew which four belonged to Cora and Francis. Gracious heaven, they were her niece and nephews. But the others were unidentified and unidentifiable. And yet her father-in-law knew them all by name and they all knew him by name. He was Grandpapa to every last one of them—except to the one who could not yet talk and even he had bounced on the grandparental knee, gurgling and chuckling with glee.

She would go mad if every day between now and Christmas was like today, Helena thought. Unalloyed exuberance and merriment. Families. Happy couples— were there no *un*happy couples in this family or among their friends? Except for Edgar and herself, of course.

And children. Children made her decidedly nervous. She did not like being around them. She did not like them being around her. And yet she was to have one of her own.

She was poking at the fire, trying to coax the coals into a position in which they would burn for a long time, when the door opened abruptly behind her and Edgar walked in, wearing a dressing gown. She stood up and glared, the poker clutched in one hand.

"And what do you think you are doing here?" she asked him, preparing for battle, almost glad that there was to be someone on whom to vent her irritation. It might be their wedding night, but there were going to be no exceptions to the rule. If he wanted to know how loudly and how embarrassingly she could squawk, let him take one step farther into the room.

He took it. And then another.

"Going to bed here," he said. "Sleeping here. It is my room, Helena. Ours. I slept elsewhere until tonight for form's sake."

"Oh, no, it is not ours," she said. "It is yours or it is mine. If it is yours, I shall go somewhere else. You will not break your promise as easily as that, Edgar."

"I have no intention of breaking my promise." His voice and his whole demeanor were maddeningly cool. "The bed is wide enough to accommodate both of us without touching, and I have enough control over my instincts and emotions to keep my hands off you. We will both sleep here. In my family—in my world, I believe—husbands and wives sleep in the same bed. All night, every night."

"And you have not the courage to fight family tradition," she said, throwing into her voice all the contempt she could muster.

"I have not the inclination," he said, removing his dressing gown and tossing it over the back of a chair.

She was relieved to see that he wore a decent nightshirt beneath. "You are quite safe from me, Helena. And you need to sleep. I would guess that you have not been doing enough of it lately."

"I am looking haggard, I suppose," she said testily.

"Pale and interesting." He smiled. "Come to bed. Even with that fire, the room is chilly."

There was no point in arguing with Edgar when he was cool and reasonable, she was finding. And he was always cool and reasonable. But one day she was going to goad him into a loud, undignified brawl, and then he would find that he had met his match.

She lay on her back, staring up at the canopy, her eyes gradually accustoming themselves to the darkness. He lay on his side facing away from her. He said nothing. He made no move to break his promise. She fumed. How could he expect her to *sleep*?

Was he sleeping? She listened for the sound of his breathing. She would surely hear it if he slept. Yet he was apparently relaxed. He was probably in the process, she thought, of having a good night's rest just as if he slept alone or with a bundle of rags beside him. How could he *sleep*? How could he humiliate her so?

"Damn you, Edgar," she said. One of these times she would think of something original to say, but at the moment she was not in the business of originality.

He turned over to face her and propped himself on one elbow. He rested the side of his head on his hand. "My only hope," he said, "is that you will not be standing beside St. Peter when I appear at the pearly gates."

"I am not in the mood for silly jokes," she said. "This is ridiculous. I am nothing better than a puppet, forced to move whenever you jerk on a string. I do not like the feeling."

"If you feel strings connecting you and me," he said,

"they are of your own devising, Helena. I will not touch you—even with a string."

"Damn your damnable control," she told him. "I will have none of it. Make love to me. It is what we both wish to do. Let us do it, then." She surged onto her side and put herself against him. She was immediately engulfed by heat and hard muscles and masculinity—and a soaring desire. She rubbed her breasts against his chest and reached for his mouth with her own.

He kissed her back softly and without passion. She drew back her head, breathing hard.

"It is for mutual comfort, Helena," he said quietly, "and for the procreation of children. Sometimes it is for love. It is not for anger or punishment. We will not punish each other with angry passion. You need to sleep." He slipped an arm beneath her head and drew her more snugly against him. "Relax and let yourself sleep, then."

She thought she would want to die of humiliation if it had not been for one thing. He was fully aroused. She could feel the hardness of his erection against her abdomen. It was not that she had failed to make him want her, then. It was just that he wanted a submissive wife, who would give him comfort rather than passion. Never! She had only passion to give.

"Go to sleep," he murmured against her ear.

"I thought you were ruthless, Edgar," she said into his shoulder. "I expected an overbearing tyrant. I expected that you would take advantage of the smallest opportunity to get past that promise and master me. I should have known the truth when you would not quarrel with me. You think to master me in this way, do you not?"

"Go to sleep, Helena," he said, his voice sounding weary. "We are not engaged in battle but in a marriage. Go to sleep." He kissed her temple.

She closed her eyes and was quiet for a while. If he knew her as she really was, he would not wish to share a bed with her, she thought. Once he got to know her, he would leave her alone fast enough. She would be alone again. She was alone now. But he was seducing her senses with this holding and cuddling and these murmured words. He was giving her the illusion of comfort.

"Comfort," she said. "It is for comfort, you say. Do you think I do not need comfort, Edgar? Do you think it? Do you? Do you think I am made of iron?"

He sighed and dipped his head to take her mouth. His was open this time and warm and responsive. "No," he said. "I do not think that."

"Make love to me, then," she said. "Let us do it for comfort, Edgar." She was being abject. She was almost crying and her voice revealed the fact. But she would think of that later. She would despise herself—and hate him—later. At this moment she was desperate for comfort and she would not remember that there was no comfort. That there could not be any. Ever.

He lifted her nightgown and his nightshirt before turning her onto her back, coming on top of her with the whole of his weight, and pushing her legs wide apart with his knees. She would have expected to hate being immobilized by his weight. But it was deliriously arousing. There was no foreplay. She would have expected to wish for it, to need it. But she wanted only to be penetrated, to be stretched, to be filled, to be ridden hard and deep.

He was a man of such control, her husband. He was hot and damp with need. He was rigid with desire. But he worked her slowly, withdrawing almost completely before thrusting firmly and deeply inward again. If there had been foreplay, she would have been in a frenzy of passion by the time he entered her, clamping about him with inner muscles to draw him to climax and to reach desperately for her own fleeting moment of happiness.

But there had been no foreplay. Incredibly, she felt herself gradually relaxing, lying still and open beneath him, taking exquisite enjoyment from the rhythmic strokes with which he loved her. She had no idea how many minutes passed—but it seemed like a long, long time—before she heard herself moaning and realized that enjoyment had turned to a pleasurable ache and that he was going to take her over the edge to peace and happiness without any active participation on her part. For a moment she considered fighting such passivity, but the ache, the certainty that he was going to take her through it and past it to the other side was too seductive to be denied.

She sighed and shivered beneath him as he made it happen and then with dreamy lethargy observed while he completed his own journey toward comfort. It was a moment of happiness blissfully extended into several moments—a gift she accepted with quiet gratitude. The moments would pass, but for now they were hers to hold in her body and her soul. They were like the peace that was supposed to come with Christmas. And for these moments—they would pass—she loved him utterly. She adored him.

He moved off her and drew her against him again. They were both warm and sweaty. She breathed in the smell of him.

"Comforted?" he asked softly.

"Mmm," she said.

"Sleep now, then," he told her.

"Mmm." Had she been just a little wider awake, perhaps she would have fought him since the suggestion had been issued as a command. But she slid into instant obedience.

11

$\mathcal{A}$LTHOUGH IT WAS THE WEEK BEFORE CHRISTMAS and life could not be said to be following any normal pattern, nevertheless Helena began to have some inkling of how her life had changed. Permanently changed.

No longer would she travel almost constantly. The realization did not upset her enormously. Traveling could be far more uncomfortable and tedious than those who only longed to do it could ever realize. More disturbing was the understanding of why she had traveled and why she had never arrived at any ultimate destination. She had traveled for escape. It was true that she had derived great pleasure from her experiences, but never as much as she had hoped for. She knew finally, as she supposed she had known all along, that she could never in this life—and perhaps beyond this life, too—leave behind the thing she most wished to escape. She could never escape from herself. Wherever she went, she took herself with her. Yes, she had known it before. She had known that she lived in her own particular hell.

She would live at Mobley Abbey much of the time from now on. Edgar explained to her that his ties with his father had always been close ones and would undoubtedly remain so. For the rest of the time she would live in Bristol, in a home she had not yet seen. It was a large home, Edgar had told her. From the sketchy descriptions he had given of it in answer to her questions, she guessed that it was also an elegant home.

She was Mrs. Downes. Her title had never meant a great deal to her. She would have shed it if she could after her first husband's death. It was a reminder of a part of her life she would forget if she could. But there had been a certain dash to being Lady Stapleton, wealthy, independent widow. She had carefully cultivated that image of herself. There was something very solidly respectable about being Mrs. Edgar Downes.

She was part of a family. Not just some cousins in Scotland and an aunt whom she treated as much as a friend as a relative, but a real family, who prided themselves on their familial closeness.

Cora had hugged her hard immediately after the wedding and cried over her and insisted that they be on a first-name basis now that they were sisters. And so must her husband and Helena, she had commanded. They really had been given no choice in the matter. Lord Francis had laughed and Helena had thought how attractive laugh lines in the corners of a man's eyes could be.

"Shall we bow to tyranny?" he had asked her, bowing over her hand. "I say we should. I must be plain Francis to you from this moment on, if you please."

What choice had Helena had but to reply graciously in kind?

Her father-in-law, that genial older version of Edgar—genial, yes, but Helena had the strange feeling that she would not wish to be the person to cross his will in any matter of importance—was all that was paternal. One would almost have sworn that he was delighted by his son's choice of a bride. He rose from the table when she entered the breakfast parlor the morning after her wedding, mortifyingly late, and reached out both hands for hers. He had kept a chair empty beside him.

"Good morning, Daughter," he said, taking both her hands in his, wringing them painfully hard, and drawing her close enough to plant a hearty kiss on her cheek.

Again, what choice did she have? She could not reply to such a greeting with a mere curt good morning. She could not call him Mr. Downes.

"Good morning, Papa," she said and took the chair beside him. The combination of calling him that and of realizing that this was the morning after her wedding night and the eyes of all the family and house guests and of Edgar himself, seated farther down the table, were on her caused her to disgrace herself utterly. She blushed. Everyone in the room knew why she and Edgar had married—and yet on the morning after her wedding night she *blushed*. How terribly gauche!

She felt trapped. Trapped into something she could not escape simply by packing her bags and planning her itinerary to wherever her fancy led her. This was to be her life, perhaps forever. And last night she had given up the one illusion of freedom and power she had still possessed. She had lacked his control, and so she had given up the greater good for—for what? Not for passion. There had been surprisingly little of that. Not even for pleasure. There had been pleasure—quite intense pleasure, in fact—but it was not for that she had begged. She had begged for comfort. And he had comforted her.

The memory frightened her. It suggested that she had needed him. Worse, it suggested that he could satisfy her need. She had been so satisfied that she had slept the night through without once waking, even when he had left the bed. But she needed no one! She refused to need anyone. Least of all Edgar. She would be swallowed up whole by him. And then, because she did not enjoy the sensation of being swallowed whole, she would find ways to fight back, to fight free. And she would destroy him. He did not deserve the misery of a shrewish wife.

She conversed brightly at the breakfast table, telling her father-in-law and her aunt, who sat at his other side, about Christmases she had spent in Vienna and Paris and Rome. Soon her audience consisted of most of the people at the table.

"And this year," Mr. Downes said, patting her hand on the table, "you will enjoy a good old-fashioned English Christmas, Daughter. There is nothing to compare to it, I daresay, though I have never been to those other places to judge for myself. I have never had a hankering for foreign parts."

"There will be the greenery to gather for the house decorations," Cora said, "and the decorating itself. And the children's party on Christmas Day and the adult ball in the evening. There will be baskets to deliver and skating parties down at the lake—the ice will be firm enough in a day or two if the weather stays cold. There will be—oh, so much. I am so *glad* that Christmas is here this year. And Helena, *you* shall help with all the plans since you are more senior in this family now than I am. You are Edgar's wife." She looked quite unabashed at having been supplanted in the role of hostess.

"It would not surprise me if there were even snow for Christmas," Mrs. Cross said, looking toward the window and drawing general attention that way. The outdoor world did indeed look gray and chilly.

"Of course there will be snow, ma'am," Mr. Downes said. "I have decreed that this is to be a perfect Christmas."

"The children will be ecstatic," the Earl of Thornhill said.

"The children of *all* ages," his wife said with a smile. "No one is more exuberant on a sleigh than Gabriel."

"And no one makes more angelic snow angels than Jane," the Earl of Greenwald said.

"I may have to challenge you on that issue," the Marquess of Carew said with a grin, "and put forward the claims of my own wife. Samantha's snow angels come with haloes."

"I notice," Cora said, "that you are conspicuously silent, Francis."

"It is against my religion, my love," he said, "to fight duels at Christmastime. Now any other time . . ." He raised his eyebrows and winked at her.

"I believe, Corey," Edgar said, "there are in the hierarchy of heavenly beings warrior angels as well as cherubic ones."

Francis laughed. So did everyone else at the table, Cora loudest of all.

"What an abomination brothers are," she said. "You are welcome to him, Helena. Perhaps you can teach him some manners."

Helena smiled and met Edgar's eyes along the table—he looked despicably handsome and at ease—but she could not join in the lively banter. It was too—cozy. Too alluring. Too tempting. It continued without her participation.

Edgar must be put in his place this morning, she decided, before he could get any ideas about last night's having begun an era of domestic bliss. And so at the end of the meal, when he waited at the door to escort her from the room, she ignored his offered arm.

"Oh, you need not worry about me, Edgar," she said carelessly. "I have things to do. You may amuse yourself to your heart's content with the other gentlemen or with whatever it is you do when you are at Mobley."

"You will need boots and a warm cloak and bonnet," he told her. "Everyone has been so caught up in the events surrounding our wedding during the past few days that my father is feeling that he has been derelict in his duties as host. He is taking everyone on an exploratory walk about the park. Most of his guests, like you, are here for the first time, you see."

"Oh," she said. And so once again she had no choice. She had not been asked if she would like to trek about the park on a gray, cold day, in company with a number of other couples. She was half of a couple now and it was assumed that she would do what Edgar decided they should do. Besides, he was the heir to all this. Of course she must go. It would be ill-mannered to refuse. And she was finding it very hard here at Mobley to be bad mannered.

"Take my arm," he said. "I will come up with you."

Staying aloof would have to be a mental thing, then, she decided. And perhaps something of a physical thing, too. Tonight she would reestablish the rules. He would learn that though she had allowed him to touch her once, she had not issued a general invitation to conjugal relations at his pleasure.

"You are feeling well enough to walk?" he asked her as they entered their bedchamber.

It was the excuse she might have thought of for herself downstairs. It was the easy solution. But she would not use her condition as an excuse for anything. She would not hide behind female frailty.

"I am quite well, thank you," she said, slipping her arm from his and making her way to her dressing room. "Why would I not be? I am expecting a baby, Edgar. Thousands of women are doing it every day."

"But only one of them is my wife," he said. "And only one of them is expecting *my* baby."

She did not even try to interpret the tone of his voice. If he was trying to establish ownership, he might save his breath. He had done that quite effectively yesterday. She belonged to him body and soul. But she would not curl into the safety and comfort that fact offered her.

"I hope, Edgar," she called from inside her dressing

room, making sure that there would be no mistaking the tone of her voice at least, "you are not going to start fussing over me. How tiresome that would be."

The bedchamber was empty when she came back into it. He had gone into his own dressing room. She was not sure whether he had heard her or not.

The walk was going to be far worse of an ordeal than she had anticipated, she saw immediately on their return downstairs. The hall was teeming with not only adult humans but also hordes of infant humans, too. Every child had spilled from the nursery in order to enjoy the walk. The noise was well above comfort level. Helena grimaced and would have returned to her room if she decently could.

She, it soon became apparent, was to be favored by the personal escort of her father-in-law. He took her arm and directed Edgar to escort her aunt.

And so by association she became the focal point of all the frolicking children as they walked. Mr. Downes had four grandchildren of his own among the group and clearly he was one of their favorite humans. But there were ten other children—Helena finally counted them all—who had fully adopted him during the few days of their acquaintance with him. And so every discovery along their route, from a misshapen, cracked chestnut to a gray, bedraggled bird feather was excuse enough to dash up to "Grandpapa" so that he might scrutinize the treasure and exclaim on its uniqueness. And Helena was called upon to exclaim enthusiastically about everything, too.

The Bridgwater baby was too heavy for his mama and papa to carry by turns, Mr. Downes decided after they had walked through a landscaped grotto and about the base of a grassy hill, which the older children had to run over, whooshing down the far side with extended arms and loud shrieks like a flock of demented birds. And so he enticed the babe into his own arms and made it bounce and laugh as he tickled it and talked nonsense to it. And then he decided that he would pass along the privilege and the pleasure to his new daughter-in-law.

Helena found herself carrying the rosy-cheeked little boy, who gazed at her in the hope that this new play-mate would prove as entertaining as the last. The inno-cence of babyhood shone out at her from his eyes and the total trust of a child who had not yet learned the treachery of the world or of those he most loved.

She was terrified. And fascinated. And very close to tears. She smiled and kissed him and made a play out of stealing the apples from his cheeks. He chuckled and bounced and invited a repetition of the game. He was soft and warm and surprisingly light. He had tiny white baby teeth.

Helena drew in a deep breath. She had a surprising memory of wanting children of her own during the early years of her first marriage, of her disappointment each month when she had discovered that she had not con-ceived. She had been so relieved later and ever since to be childless that she had forgotten that once upon a time she had craved the experience of motherhood. There was a child in her womb—now. This time next year, if all went well, she could be holding her own baby like this, though hers would be somewhat younger.

A surge of yearning hit her low in her womb, almost like a pain. And then an equivalent dose of panic made her want to drop the Bridgwater child and run as far and as fast as she could go. She was being seduced by domesticity.

"Let me take him from you, ma'am." The Duke of Bridgwater was a coldly handsome man, whom she would have considered austere if she had not occasion-ally glimpsed the warmth of his relations with his wife and son. "He entertains the erroneous belief that the arms of adults were made to be bounced in. Come along, rascal."

The child was perfectly happy to be back with his papa. He proceeded to bounce and gurgle.

"Ah, the memories, Daughter," Mr. Downes said. "Having my children small was the happiest time of my life. I would have had more if my dear Mrs. Downes had not died giving birth to Cora. After that, I did not have the heart to remarry and have children with another wife."

If Christian had lived, Helena thought, he would be older than her father-in-law was now. He would have been seventy-one. It was a fascinating thought. "Children like you," she said.

"It is because I like them," he said with a chuckle. "There is no child so naughty that I do not like him. And now I have grandchildren. I see Cora's children as often as I can. I will see yours more frequently. I will lure you from Bristol on every slight pretext. Be warned."

"I believe it will always be a pleasure to be at Mobley, sir," she said.

He looked at her with raised eyebrows.

"Papa," she added.

"I believe," he said as he turned onto a different path, leading the group downhill in the direction of what appeared to be extensive woods, "you will do very well for my son. He has waited perhaps overlong to choose a bride. His character has become set over the years and has grown in strength, in proportion to his successes in life. I was successful, Daughter, as witness Mobley Abbey, which I purchased rather than inherited. My son is many more times successful than I. It will take a strong woman to give him the sort of marriage he needs."

"You think I am a strong woman?" Helena asked.

"You were a widow for many years," he said, "when you have the beauty and the rank and wealth to have made an advantageous match at any time. You have traveled and been independent. Edgar reported to me that he had the devil's own time persuading you to marry him, despite the fact that you are with child. Yes, I believe you are a strong woman."

How looks could deceive, she thought.

A lake had come into view through the trees. A lake that was iced over.

"This will be the scene of some of our Christmas frolics," her father-in-law said. "There will be skating, I do believe. And the greenery will be gathered among these trees. We will make a great ritual of that, Daughter. Christmas is important in this family. Love and giving and peace and the birth of a child. It is a good time to have a houseful of children and other guests."

"Yes," she said.

"And a good time to have a new marriage," he said. "There are worse things to be than a Christmas bride."

The children were whooping and heading either for the lake or for the nearest climbable trees.

IT SEEMED THAT he was fated to have a very prickly wife, Edgar thought the morning after his wedding. He had had hopes after their wedding night that, if they could not exactly expect to find themselves embarking on a happily-ever-after, at least they would be able to enjoy a new rapport, a starting ground for the growth of understanding and affection. But as soon as she entered the breakfast parlor he had known that she had retreated once more behind her mask. She had looked beautiful and proud and aloof—and slightly mocking. He had known that she had no intention of allowing last night to soften their relations. Her rebuff as they left the breakfast room had not taken him at all by surprise.

He watched with interest as they walked outside and

he made conversation with Mrs. Cross. He watched both his father and his wife. His father, he knew, though he had said nothing to his son, was deeply disturbed by his marriage and the manner in which it had been brought about. Yet he talked jovially with Helena and involved her with the children who kept running up to him for attention and approval.

Helena disliked children, a fact that Edgar had come to realize with cold dread. And yet he learned during the course of the walk that it was not strictly the truth. When his father first deposited the Duke of Bridgwater's young son in her arms, she looked alarmed as if she did not know quite what to do with him. What she proceeded to do was amuse the child—and herself. Edgar watched, fascinated, as all the aloof mask came away and left simply a lovely woman playing with a child. The mask came back on as soon as Bridgwater took the baby away from her.

And then they were at the lake and everyone dispersed on various courses—the children to find the likeliest playgrounds, the adults to supervise and keep them from breaking something essential, like a neck. Cora was testing the ice with a stout stick, his father with the toe of his boot. Francis was bellowing at his youngest son to get off the ice—*now*! One group of children proceeded to play hide-and-seek among the tree trunks. The more adventurous took to the branches. Helena stood alone, looking as if she would sneak off back home if she could. Mrs. Cross had first bent to listen to something Thornhill's daughter was saying to her and had then allowed herself to be led away.

Edgar was about to close the distance between himself and his wife, though she looked quite unapproachable. Why could she not simply relax like everyone else and enjoy the outing? Was she so determined *not* to enjoy it? He felt a certain annoyance. But then Cora's youngest son, who had escaped both the ice and his father's wrath, tugged on his greatcoat and demanded that Uncle Edgar do up a button that had come undone at his neck. Edgar removed his gloves, went down on his haunches, and wrestled with the stubborn buttonhole.

When he stood up again, he could not immediately see Helena. But then he did. She was helping one of the Earl of Greenwald's young sons climb a tree. Edgar had noticed the lad standing forlornly watching some larger, bolder children, but lacking the courage to climb himself. Helena had gone to help him. She did so for all of ten minutes, patiently helping him find his footing on the bark and then slide out along one of the lower branches, encouraging him, congratulating him, laughing at his pleasure, catching him when he jumped, coaxing him when he lost his courage, starting all over again when he scampered back to the starting point.

She was that woman unmasked again—the one who forgot to be the dignified, cynical Lady Stapleton, the one who had forgotten her surroundings, the one who clearly loved children with a patient, compassionate warmth.

Edgar stood with his shoulder against a tree, watching, fascinated.

And then the child jumped with a bold lunge and bowled her right off her feet in his descent so that they both went down on the ground, the child squealing first with fright and then with delight when he realized he was not hurt, Helena laughing with sheer amusement.

She turned her head and caught herself being watched.

She lifted the child to his feet, dusted him off with one hand, directed him to his father, and sent him scampering away. She dusted herself off, her face like marble, and turned to walk away into the trees, in a direction no one else had taken. She did not look at Edgar or anyone else.

He sighed and stood where he was for a moment. Should he go after her? Or should he leave her alone to sulk? But sulk about what? That he had watched her? There was nothing secret in what she had been doing. She had been amongst the crowd, playing with one of the children. But her awareness that he was watching her had made her self-conscious or angry for some reason. It was impossible to know what was wrong.

He knew his wife as little today, Edgar thought, as he had known her that first evening, when he had looked up from his conversation with the Graingers and had seen her standing in the doorway, dressed in scarlet. She was a mystery to him—a prickly mystery. Sometimes he wondered if the mystery was worth probing.

But she was his wife.

And he was in love with her, even if he did not love or even particularly like her.

He pushed his shoulder away from the tree and went after her.

12

S HE HAD NOT WANDERED FAR. BUT SHE WAS HALF hidden behind the tree trunk against which she leaned. She was staring straight ahead and did not shift her gaze when Edgar came in sight. But he cut into it when he went to stand before her. He set one hand against the trunk beside her head and waited for her eyes to focus on his.

"Tired?" he asked.

"No."

"It has been a long walk for you," he said, "with the added strain of having to converse with a new father-in-law."

"Would you make a wilting violet of me, Edgar?" she asked, one corner of her mouth tilting upward. "It cannot be done. You should have married one of the young virgins."

"You are good with children," he said.

"Nonsense!" Her answer was surprisingly sharp. "I dislike them intensely."

"Greenwald's little boy had been abandoned by the older tree climbers," he said. "He would have been left in his loneliness if you had not noticed. You made him happy."

"Oh, how easy it is to make a child happy," she said impatiently, "and how tedious for the adult."

"You looked happy," he said.

"Edgar." She looked fully into his eyes. "You would possess me body and soul, would you not? It is in your nature to want total control over what is in your power. You possess my body and I suppose I will continue to allow you to do so, though I did resolve this morning to remind you of your promise and to force you on your honor to keep it. But there is that damnable detail of a shared bed, and I never could resist an available man. You will *not* possess my soul. You may prod and probe as much as you will, but you will not succeed. Be thankful that I will not allow you to do so."

He was hurt. Partly by her careless dismissal of him as merely an available man—but then such carelessness was characteristic of her. Mainly he was hurt to know that she was quite determined to keep him out of her life. He might possess her body but nothing else. More than ever she seemed like a stranger to him—a stranger who was not easy to like, but one he craved to know and longed to love.

"Is the reality of your soul so ugly, then?" he asked.

She smiled at him and lifted her gloved hands to rest on his chest. "You have no idea how appealing you look in this greatcoat with all its capes," she said, "and with that frown on your face. You look as if you could hold the world on your shoulders, Edgar, and solve all its problems while you did so."

"Perhaps," he said, "I could help solve your problems if you would share them with me, Helena."

She laughed. "Very well, then," she said. "Help me solve this one. How do I persuade a massive, masterly, frowning man to kiss me?"

He searched her eyes, frustrated and irritated.

She pulled a face and then favored him with her most mocking smile. "You like only more difficult problems,

Edgar?" she asked him. "Or is it that you have no wish to kiss me? How dreadfully lowering."

He kissed her—hard and open-mouthed. Her hands came to his shoulders, her body came against his, and for a few moments hot passion flared between them. Then he set his hands at her waist, moved her back against the tree, and set some space between them. Irritation had turned to anger.

"I do not like to be played with like a toy, Helena," he said, "to be used for your pleasure at your pleasure, to be seduced as a convenient way of changing the subject. I do not like to be mocked."

"You are very foolish, Edgar," she said. "You have just handed me a marvelous weapon. Do you not like to be *mocked*, my dear? I am an expert at mockery. I cannot be expected to resist the challenge you have just set to me."

"Do you hate me so much then?" he asked her.

She smiled. "I lust after you, Edgar," she said. "Even with your child in my womb, I still lust after you. Is it not enough?"

"What have I done to make you hate me?" he asked. "Must I take sole blame for your condition?"

"What have you done?" She raised her eyebrows. "You have married me, Edgar. You have made me respectable and safe and secure and rich. You *are* very wealthy, are you not? Wealthier than your father even before you inherit what is his? You have made me part of an eminently respectable family. You have brought me to this—to Mobley Abbey at Christmastime and surrounded me with respectable families and children. *Children* wherever I turn. It is to be what your father calls a good old-fashioned Christmas. I do not doubt it, if today is any indication—yet today Christmas has not even started. And if all this is not bad enough, you have tried to take my soul into yourself. You have suffocated me. I cannot breathe. This is what you have done to me."

"My God." His hand was back on the tree trunk beside her head. He had moved closer to her though he did not touch her. "My God, Helena, who was he? What did he do to you? Who was it who hurt you so badly?"

"You are a fool, Edgar," she said coldly. "No one has hurt me. No one ever has. It is I who have done all the hurting. It is in my nature. I am an evil creation. You do not want to know me. Be content with my body. It is yours. You do not want to know *me.*"

He did not believe her. Oh, yes, she hurt people. He did not doubt that he was not the first man she had used and scorned. But he did not believe it was in her very nature to behave thus. There would not be the bitterness in her smile and behind her eyes if she were simply amoral. Nor that something more than bitterness that he sometimes almost glimpsed, almost grasped. What was that other something? Despair? Something or someone had started it all. Probably someone. Some man. She had been very badly hurt at some time in her past. So badly that she had been unable to function as her real self ever since.

But how was he to find out, to help her when she had shut herself off so entirely from help?

There was a glimmering of hope, perhaps. The things that suffocated her must also frighten her—her marriage to him, his family, his father's guests and their children, Christmas. Why would she fear such benevolent things? Because they threatened her bitterness, her masks? The masks had come off briefly already this morning—first with the Bridgwater baby and then with the Greenwald child. And perhaps even last night when she had allowed herself to be comforted.

"You were right about one thing," she said. "I *am* tired. Take me home, Edgar. Fuss over your pregnant wife."

He took her arm in his and led her back to the others so that he could signal to his father that he was taking Helena back to the house. His father smiled and nodded and then bent down to give his attention to Jonathan, the Thornhills' youngest son. Greenwald's little boy briefly danced up to Helena and told her that he was going skating as soon as the ice was thick enough.

"I am going to skate like the wind," he told her.

"Oh, goodness," she said, touching a hand lightly to his woolly cap. "That *is* fast. Perhaps all we will see is a streak of light and it will be Stephen skating by."

He chuckled happily and danced away.

Her voice had been warm and tender. She might believe that she disliked children, but in reality she loved them altogether too well.

They walked in silence through the woods and up the slope to the wider path. She leaned on him rather heavily. He should not, he thought, have allowed her to make such a lengthy walk when only a week or so ago she had still been suffering from nausea and fatigue.

"Tell me about your first marriage," he said.

She laughed. "You will find nothing there," she said. "It lasted for seven years. He was older than your father. He treated me well. He adored me. That is not surprising, is it? I am reputed to have some beauty even now, but I was a pretty girl, Edgar. I turned heads wherever I went. I was his prize, his pet."

"You were never—with child?" he asked.

"No." She laughed again. "Never once, though not for lack of trying on his part. You can imagine my astonishment when you impregnated me, Edgar. Seven years of marriage and a million lovers since then had convinced me that I was safely barren."

Did she realize, he wondered, how her open and careless mention of those lovers cut into him? But he had no cause for complaint. He had never been deceived about her promiscuous past, of which he had been a part. She had never even tried to keep it a secret.

"His poor first wife suffered annual stillbirths and miscarriages for years and years," she said. "Was not I fortunate to be barren?"

"There was only one survivor?" he asked.

"Only Gerald, yes," she said. "Though why he survived when none of the others did was a mystery—or so Christian always said. He was neither tall nor robust nor handsome; he was shy and timid; he was not overly intelligent. He excelled at nothing he was supposed to excel at. He had only one talent—a girlish talent, according to his father. He played the pianoforte. I believe Christian would have been just as happy if none of his offspring had survived."

Her first husband did not sound to have been a pleasant man. Edgar could not imagine his own father being impatient with either him or Cora if they had been less than he had dreamed of their being. His father, for all his firm character and formidable abilities in his career, gave unconditional love to those nearest and dearest to him—and to their spouses, too. Had Sir Christian Stapleton treated Helena, as he appeared to have treated his only son, with such contempt that she had forever after treated herself that way? Could that account for her bitterness? Her despair?

"Your child will have his father's love," he told her. "Or hers. I do not care what its gender is or its looks or abilities or nature or talents or lack thereof. I do not care even if there are real handicaps. The child will be mine and will be deeply loved."

If he had thought to soften her, he was much mistaken.

"You think that now, Edgar," she said contemptuously. "But if it is a son and he has not your splendid physique or can look at two numbers and find himself unable to add them together or sneaks away to play the pianoforte when you are trying to train him to take over your business, then you will compare him to yourself and to his grandfather and you will find him wanting. And he will know himself despised and become a weak, fragile creature. But he may not come to me for comfort. I shall not give it. I shall turn my back on him. I will not have this pregnancy romanticized. I will not think in hazy terms of a cuddly baby and doting motherhood and strong, protective fatherhood. The stable at Bethlehem must have been drafty and uncomfortable and smelly and downright humiliating. How dare we make beatific images of it! It was nasty. That was the whole point. It was meant to be nasty just as the other end of that baby's life was. *This* is what I am prepared to do for you, that stable was meant to tell us. But instead of accepting reality and coping with it, we soften and sentimentalize everything. What did you *do* to inspire this impassioned and ridiculous monologue?"

"I dared to think of my child with love," he said, "though she or he is still in your womb."

"Oh, Edgar," she said wearily, "I did not realize you were such a decent man. One's first impression of you is of a large, masterful, ruthless man. Our first encounter merely confirmed me in that belief. I wish you were not so decent. I am terrified of decency."

"And I, ma'am," he admitted, "am totally baffled by you. You would have me believe that you are anything but decent. And yet you will help a lonely child climb a tree and touch his head with tenderness. And you will passionately defend a woman and child whose courage and suffering have been softened to nothing by the sweet sentiments that surround the Christmas story. And you keep me at arm's length so that I will not be drawn into your own unhappiness. That *is* the reason, is it not?"

She set the side of her head against his shoulder and sighed. "The walk out did not seem nearly this long," she said. "I am very weary, Edgar. Weary of being prodded and poked and invaded by your questions. Have done now. Come upstairs with me when we reach the house. Lie down with me. Hold me as you did last night. You did, did you not? All night? Your arm must have gone to sleep. Hold me again, then. And draw me farther into this terror of a marriage. Perhaps I will sleep and when I awake will have more energy with which to fight you. I will fight, you know. I hate you, you see."

Surprisingly he smiled and then actually chuckled aloud. She had spoken the words almost with tenderness.

Oh, yes, he would draw her farther into the terror—of their marriage, of her new family, of her proximity to children, of Christmas. She was right about one thing. He could be a ruthless man when his mind was set upon something. His mind was set upon something now. More than his mind—his heart was set upon it. He wanted a marriage with this woman.

A real marriage.

He had spotted her weakness now—she had handed him the knowledge on a platter. He was an expert—a ruthless expert—at finding out weaknesses and probing and worrying them until he had gained just what he wanted. He would have to say that Helena, Mrs. Edgar Downes, did not stand one chance in a million.

Except that she was quite irritatingly stubborn. A worthy opponent. He could not stand an opponent who cowered into submission at the first indication of the formidable nature of his foe. There was no challenge in such a fight. Helena was not such an opponent. She could still tell him she hated him, even while conceding a physical need for his arms to hold her.

"Shall I carry you the rest of the way?" he asked her, feeling her weariness.

"If you try it, Edgar," she said, "I shall bar the door of

your bedchamber against you from this day forward and screech out most unladylike answers to anything you care to call through it. I shall shame you in front of your father and your sister and all these other nauseatingly respectable people. I am not a sack of potatoes to be lugged about merely because I have the despicable misfortune to be in a delicate condition and to be your property."

"A simple no, thank you would have sufficed," he said.

"I wish you were not so large," she said. "I wish you were small and puny. I *hate* your largeness."

"I believe," he said as they stepped inside the house, "I have understood your message. Come. I'll take you up and hold you while you sleep."

"Oh, go away," she said, dropping his arm, "and play billiards or drink port or do whatever it is you do to make another million pounds before Christmas. I have no need of you or of sleep either. I shall write some letters."

"After you have rested," he said firmly, taking her arm and drawing it through his again. "And if it is a real quarrel you are hankering for, Helena, I am almost in the mood to oblige you." He led her toward the stairs.

"Damn you," she said. "I am not. I am too weary."

He chuckled again.

JACK SPERLING ARRIVED at Mobley Abbey early in the afternoon, the Graingers just before teatime.

Jack was shown into the library on his arrival, and Edgar joined him there with his father.

"Sperling," he said, inclining his head to the young man, who bowed to him. "I am pleased to see that you had a safe journey. This is the young gentleman I spoke of, Father."

"Mr. Sperling." The elder Mr. Downes frowned and looked him over from head to toe. "You are a very young gentleman."

"I am two-and-twenty, sir," the young man said, flushing.

"And I daresay that like most young gentlemen you like to spend money as fast as you can get your hands on it," Mr. Downes said. "Or faster."

The flush deepened. Jack squared his shoulders. "I have worked for my living for the past year, sir," he said. "Everything I earn, everything I can spare from feeding myself and setting a roof over my head is used to pay off debts that I did not incur."

"Yes, yes," Mr. Downes said, his frown suggestive of irritation. "You are foolish enough to beggar yourself for the sake of an extravagant father, I daresay. For the sake of that ridiculous notion of a gentleman's honor."

The young man's nostrils flared. "Sir," he said, "with all due respect I will not hear my father insulted. And a gentleman's honor is his most precious possession."

Mr. Downes waved a dismissive hand. "If you work for my son and me, young man," he said, "you may grow rich. But if you intend to spend your hard-earned pounds on paying a father's debts, you are not the man for us. You will need more expensive and more fashionable clothes than those you are wearing and more than a decent roof over your head. You will need a wife who can do you credit in the business world. I believe you have a lady in mind. You will need to think of yourself, not of creditors to whom you owe nothing if you but forget about a gentleman's honor. The opportunity is there. My son has already offered it and I am prepared to agree with him. But only if you are prepared to make yourself into a single-minded businessman. Are you?"

Jack had turned pale. He could work for these two powerful men, who knew how to be successful, how to grow rich. As a gentleman with a gentleman's education and experience as his father's steward and more lately as a London clerk, he could be trained by them, groomed by them for rapid promotion until he was in a position to make his own independent fortune. It was the chance of a lifetime, a dream situation. He would be able to offer for Fanny Grainger. All he had to do was swallow a few principles and say yes.

Edgar watched his face. This was not an approach he would have taken himself. His father had grown up in a harsher world.

"No, sir." Jack Sperling's face was parchment white. The words were almost whispered. But they were quite unmistakable. "No, thank you, sir. I shall return to town by stage. I thank you for your time. And for yours, sir." His eyes turned on Edgar.

"Why not?" Mr. Downes barked. "Because you are a *gentleman*, I suppose. Foolish puppy."

"Yes, sir," Jack said, very much on his dignity. "Because I am a gentleman and proud of it. I would rather starve as a gentleman, sir, than live as a rich man as a— As a—" He bowed abruptly. "Good day to you."

"Sit down, Mr. Sperling," Mr. Downes said, indicating a chair behind the young man. "My son judged you rightly, it seems. I might have known as much. We have business to discuss. Men who go into trade for the sole purpose of getting rich, even if it means turning their backs upon all their responsibilities and obligations and even if it means riding roughshod over the persons and livelihoods and feelings of everyone else—such men often do prosper. But they are not men I care to know or do business with. You are not such a man, it seems."

Jack looked from him to Edgar.

"It was a test," Edgar said, shrugging. "You have passed it."

"I would have appreciated your trust, sir," the young man said stiffly, "without the test. I am a gentleman."

"And I am not, Mr. Sperling," Mr. Downes said. "I am a businessman. Sit down. You are a fortunate young man. You know, I suppose, what gave my son the idea of taking you on as a bright prospect for our business."

"Mr. Downes was obliged to marry Lady Stapleton," Jack Sperling said, "and wished to reduce the humiliation to Miss Grainger, who expected his offer. Yes, I understand, sir."

"It is in our interest to make you an acceptable groom for the lady," Mr. Downes said, "who will be arriving here with her mama and papa before the day is out, I daresay." Jack Sperling flushed again. "But make no mistake, young man. There is no question of your being paid off. We demand work of our employees."

"I would not accept a single farthing that I had not earned, sir," Jack said. "Or accept a bride who had been bought for me."

"And about your father's property," Mr. Downes said. "Your *late* father?"

The young man inclined his head. "He died more than a year ago," he said.

"And the property?" Mr. Downes was drumming the fingers of one hand on the arm of his chair. "It has been sold?"

"Not yet," Jack said. "It is in a state of some dilapidation."

"I am willing to buy it," Mr. Downes said. "As an investment. As a business venture. When the time is right I will sell it again for a profit—or my son will if it is after my time. To you, Mr. Sperling. When you can afford to buy it. It will not come cheaply."

Edgar noted the whiteness of the young man's knuckles as his hands gripped the chair arms. "I would not expect it to, sir," he said. "Thank you, sir."

"We are good to our employees, Mr. Sperling," Mr. Downes said. "We also expect a great deal of them."

"Yes, sir."

"For the next week, we will expect you to enjoy Christmas at Mobley and to court that young lady with great care. Her father does not know you are to be here unless you have informed the lady and she has informed him. He will not take kindly to a suitor who is to be a clerk in my son's business until he has earned his first promotion—not when he expected my son himself."

"No, sir."

"He will perhaps be reconciled when he understands that you are a favored employee," Mr. Downes continued. "One who is expected to rise rapidly in the business world and eventually rival us in wealth and influence. Being a gentleman himself, he will doubtless be even further reconciled when he knows that our business is to invest in buying and improving your father's property with a view to preparing it as your country residence when you achieve stature in the company."

The young man's eyes closed tightly. "Yes, sir."

Mr. Downes looked at his son. "I believe we have said everything that needs to be said." He raised his eyebrows. "Have we forgotten anything?"

Edgar smiled. "I believe not," he said. "Except to thank Mr. Sperling for his willingness to help me out of a tight spot."

"You will go to Bristol when my son returns there after Christmas, then," Mr. Downes said. "He will put you to work. For a trial period, it is to be understood. Pull the bell rope, will you please, Edgar? My butler will show you to your room, Mr. Sperling, and explain to you how to find the drawing room. We will be pleased to see you there for tea at four o'clock."

"Thank you, sir." Jack got to his feet and bowed. He

inclined his head to Edgar. He followed the butler from the room.

"I have never regretted my retirement," Mr. Downes said after the door had closed behind them. He chuckled. "But it feels damned good to come out of it once in a while. I believe you judged his character well, Edgar. I thought for one moment that he was going to challenge me to a duel."

"You were formidable." Edgar laughed, too. "Poor young man. One almost forgot that he is the one doing me a favor."

"One cannot afford to have weak employees merely as a favor, Edgar," his father said. "That young man will do very nicely indeed if I am any judge of character. You do not regret the young lady?"

"I am married to Helena," Edgar said rather stiffly.

"The answer you would give, of course," his father said. "Damn it, Edgar, we did not go around bedding respectable women before marrying them in my day. I am disappointed in you. But you have done the right thing and one can only hope all will turn out for the best. She is a handsome woman and a woman of character. Though one wonders what she was about, allowing herself to be bedded and her a lady."

"That is her concern, Father," Edgar said firmly, "and mine."

"The right answer again." Mr. Downes rose to his feet. "I have promised to show Mrs. Cross the conservatory. A very ladylike person, Edgar. She reminds me of your mother, or the way your mother would have been." He sighed. "Sometimes I let a few days go by without thinking about her. I must be getting old."

"You must be forgiving yourself at last," Edgar said quietly.

"Hmm." His father led the way from the room.

13

The Graingers arrived at Mobley Abbey in time to join the family and the other guests in the drawing room for tea. Helena had at first been rather surprised to find that they still planned to come for Christmas, even after learning of Edgar's betrothal and imminent marriage to her. But it was not so very surprising after she had had time to think about it a little more.

The Graingers were not wealthy. It was very close to Christmas. If they admitted to their disappointment and returned to their own home, they would be compelled to go to the expense of celebrating the holiday there with all their expectations at an end. General opinion had it that Sir Webster would not be able to afford to take his daughter back to town for a Season. She would sink into spinsterhood and he would have the expense of her keep for the rest of his life.

They had lost the very wealthy Edgar Downes as a matrimonial prospect, but spending Christmas at Mobley Abbey would at least give them the chance of continuing in the company of several of the *ton*'s elite, of enjoying the hospitality of wealthy hosts, and of keeping their hopes alive for a little longer. In such a social setting, who knew what might turn up?

And so it was not so surprising after all that they had come, Helena thought, greeting them as they appeared in the drawing room. They were gracious in their congratulations to her. Miss Grainger was quite warm in hers.

"Mrs. Downes," she said. "I am very pleased for you. I am sure you will be happy. I like Mr. Downes," she added and blushed.

Helena guessed that the girl was sincere. She would have married Edgar without a murmur of protest, but she would have been overwhelmed by him.

"Thank you," she said and saw the girl almost at the same moment suddenly stare off to her right as if her eyes would pop from their sockets. She visibly paled.

"Oh," she murmured almost inaudibly.

Edgar had come up and was greeting the Graingers. Helena linked her arm through Fanny's. "Come and meet my father-in-law," she said. He was speaking with Helena's aunt and the young man who had arrived earlier. Helena had been introduced to him but had not had a chance to converse with him.

"Papa," she said, "this is Miss Grainger, just lately arrived from London with her mama and papa."

Fanny curtsied and focused the whole of her attention on Mr. Downes. It seemed to Helena that she was close to fainting.

"Ah," Mr. Downes said heartily. "As pretty as a picture. Welcome to my home, Miss Grainger. And—Sir Webster and Lady Grainger?" Edgar had brought them across the room. "Welcome. You met Mrs. Cross in London, I daresay. Allow me to present Mr. Sperling, a young gentleman my son recently discovered in London as a particularly bright prospect for our business. We need gentlemen of education and breeding and enterprise to fill the more challenging positions and to rise to heights of responsibility and authority and wealth. I daresay that in five or ten years Mr. Sperling may make me look like a pauper." He rubbed his hands together and laughed merrily.

Mr. Sperling bowed. Fanny curtsied deeply without once looking at him. Sir Webster cleared his throat.

"We are acquainted with Mr. Sperling," he said. "We are—or were—neighbors. How d'ye do, Sperling?" He had pokered up quite noticeably.

"Acquainted? Neighbors?" Mr. Downes was all astonishment. "Well now. Who says that coincidences never happen these days? Amazing, is it not, Edgar?"

"Astonishing," Edgar agreed. "You and Lady Grainger—and Miss Grainger, too—will be able to help us make Mr. Sperling feel more at home over Christmas, then, sir."

"Yes, certainly. My dear Mrs. Cross," Mr. Downes was saying, beaming with hearty good humor, "please do pour the tea, if you would be so good."

Helena caught him alone after he had escorted her aunt to the tea tray. The Carews, she noticed, those kindest of kind people, were taking a clearly uncomfortable Mr. Sperling and Fanny Grainger under their wing while Edgar had taken the Graingers to join Cora and Francis.

"Sit here, Daughter," Mr. Downes said, indicating a large wing chair beside the fire. "We have to be careful to look after you properly. It was thoughtless of me to take you so far from the house this morning."

"Nonsense," she said briskly. "What are you up to, Papa?"

"Up to?" He looked at her in astonishment. "I am protecting my daughter-in-law and my future grandchild. Both are important to me."

"Thank you." She smiled. "Who is Mr. Sperling? No." She held up a staying hand. "Not the story about Edgar's having discovered a prodigy quite by chance. The real story."

His eyes were shrewd and searching. "Edgar has not told you?" he asked.

"Let me guess." She perched on the edge of the chair he had indicated and looked up at him. "It does not take a great deal of ingenuity, you know. Mr. Sperling is a young and rather good-looking gentleman. He is a neighbor of the Graingers. Fanny Grainger, when she set eyes on him a few minutes ago, came very near to fainting—a little excessive for purely neighborly sentiment. His own face, when we came closer, turned parchment pale. Can he by any chance be the ineligible suitor? The man she is not allowed to marry?"

"I suppose," her father-in-law conceded, "since we have just established that coincidences do happen, it might be possible, Daughter."

"And Edgar, feeling guilty that the necessity of marrying me forced him to let down the Graingers, whose hopes he had raised," Helena said, "devised this scheme of making Mr. Sperling more eligible and bringing the lovers together. And you are aiding and abetting him, Papa. A more unlikely pair of matchmakers it would be difficult to find."

"But make no mistake," Mr. Downes said. "Business interests always come first with Edgar, as with me. He would not have brought that young man to Mobley or offered him the sort of employment that will involve a great deal of trust on his part if he had not been convinced that Mr. Sperling was the man for the job. There is no sentiment in this, Daughter, but only business."

"Poppycock!" she said, startling him again. "Perhaps the two of you believe the myth that has grown up around you that you are ruthless, hard-nosed, heartless businessmen to whom the making of money is the be-all and end-all of existence. Like most myths, it has hardly a grain of truth to it. You are soft to the core of your foolish hearts. You, sir, are an impostor."

His eyes twinkled at her. "It is Christmas, Daughter," he said. "Even men like my son and me dream of happy endings at Christmas, especially those involving love and romance. Leave us to our dreams."

Edgar, Helena noticed, was laughing with the rest of his group and setting an arm loosely about Cora's shoulders in an unconscious gesture of brotherly affection. He looked relaxed and carefree. But dreams—they were the one thing she must never cultivate. When one dreamed, one began to hope. One began to have images of happiness and of peace. Peace on earth and goodwill to all men. How she hated Christmas.

Her father-in-law patted her shoulder even as her aunt brought them their tea. "Let me dream, Daughter," he said. And she knew somehow that he was no longer talking about Fanny Grainger and Mr. Sperling.

THE NEXT DAY saw the return of some of the wedding guests who had come out from Bristol for that occasion and now came to Mobley Abbey to spend Christmas. Some of Edgar's personal friends were among them and some of his father's. Almost without exception, they had sons and daughters of marriageable age.

He had invited them, Mr. Downes explained to his son, when it had become obvious to him that his home was to be filled with aristocratic guests. He had welcomed the connections—he had wanted both his son and his daughter to marry into their class, after all—but he would not turn his back on his own. He was a man who aimed always to expand the horizons of his life, not one who allowed the old horizons to fade behind him as he aggressively pursued the new.

"But more than that, Edgar," he explained, "I realized the great gap there would be between the older, married guests and the children, with only Miss Grainger between. This was when it appeared that you would be celebrating your betrothal to her over Christmas. It seemed important that she have company of her own age. Under the changed circumstances, it seems even more important. And I like young people. They liven up a man's old age."

"The old man being you, I suppose," Edgar said with a grin. "You have more energy than any two of the rest of us put together, Papa."

His father chuckled.

But Edgar was pleased with the addition of more young people and of his own friends. He was more relaxed. He was able to see Fanny Grainger and Jack Sperling relax more.

The house guests had all arrived safely—and only just in time. The following night, the night before the planned excursion to gather greenery for decorating the house, brought a huge fall of snow, one that blanketed the ground and cut them off at least for a day or two from anywhere that could not be reached by foot.

"Look," Edgar said, leaning against the window sill of his bedchamber just after he had got out of bed. He turned his head to glance at Helena, who was still lying there, awake. "Come and look."

"It is too cold," she complained.

"Nonsense," he said, "the fire has already been lit." But he went to fetch her a warm dressing gown and set it about her as she got out of bed, grumbling. "Come and look."

He kept an arm about her shoulders as she looked out at the snow and the lowering clouds which threatened more. Indeed more was already sifting down in soft, dancing flakes. She said nothing, but he saw wonder in her eyes for a moment—the eternal wonder that children from one to ninety always feel at the first fall of snow.

"Snow for Christmas," she said at last, her voice cool. "How very timely. Everyone will be delighted."

"My first snowball will be targeted for the back of your neck," he said. "I will treat you to that delicious feeling of snow melting in slow trickles down your back."

"How childish you are, Edgar," she said. "But why the back of the neck? My first one will splatter right in your face."

"Is this a declaration of war?" he asked.

"It is merely the natural reaction to a threat," she said. "Will the gathering of greenery have to be canceled? That snow must be several inches deep."

"Canceled?" he said. "Quite the contrary. What could be better designed to arouse the spirit of Christmas than the gathering of greenery in the snow? There will be so many distractions that the task will take at least twice as long as usual. But distractions can be enormous fun."

"Yes," she said with a sigh.

It struck him suddenly that he was happy. He was at Mobley Abbey with his family and friends, and Christmas was just a few days away. There was enough snow outside that it could not possibly all melt before Christmas. And he was standing in the window of his almost warm bedchamber with his arm about his pregnant wife. It was strange how happiness could creep up on a man and reveal itself in such unspectacular details.

He dipped his head and kissed her. She did not resist. They had made love each night of their marriage and though there had been little passion in the encounters, there had been the warmth of enjoyment—for both of them. He turned her against him, opened her mouth with his own, and reached his tongue inside. One of her arms came about his neck and her fingers twined themselves in his hair.

He would enjoy making love with her in the morning,

he thought, with the snow outside and all the excitement of that fact and the Christmas preparations awaiting them. There could surely be no better way to start a day. It felt good to be a married man.

She drew back her head. "Don't, Edgar," she said.

He released her immediately. How foolish to have forgotten that it was Helena with all her prickliness to whom he was married. "I beg your pardon," he said. "I thought I had been given permission to have conjugal relations with you."

"Don't be deceived by snow and Christmas," she said. "Don't imagine tenderness where there is none, Edgar—either in yourself or in me. We married because I seduced you and we enjoyed a night of lust and conceived a child. It can be a workable marriage. I like your father and your sister and your friends. And I am reconciled to living in one place—even Bristol, heaven help me—and doing all the domestic things like running your home and being your hostess. I am even resigned to being a mother and will search out the best nurse for the child. But we must not begin to imagine that there is tenderness. There is none."

If he had fully believed her, he would have been chilled to the bone. As it was, he felt as if someone had thrown a pail of snow through the window and doused him with it.

"There must at least be an attempt at affection," he said.

"I cannot feel affection," she said. "Don't try to tempt me into it, Edgar. You are a handsome man and I am strongly attracted to you. I will not try to deny that what we do together on that bed is intensely pleasurable to me. But it is a thing of the body, not of the emotions. I respect you as a man. I do believe sometimes I even like you. Do the same for me if you must. But do not waste emotion on me."

"You are my *wife*," he said.

"I hurt badly what I am fond of," she said. "I hurt badly and forever. I do not *want* to be fond of you, Edgar. And I am not trying to be cruel. You are a decent man—I do wish you were not, but you are. Don't make me fond of you."

Did she realize what she was saying? She was *fond* of him and desperately fighting the feeling. But what had she done? He had been very deaf, he realized. She had insisted every time he had asked that no one had ever hurt her, that she had done the hurting. He had not listened. Someone must have hurt her, he had thought, and he had asked his questions accordingly. He had asked the wrong questions. Whom had she hurt? *I hurt badly and forever.* The words might have sounded theatrical coming from anyone else. But Helena meant them. And he had felt the bitterness in her, the despair, the refusal to be drawn free of her masks, the refusal to love or be loved.

"Very well, then," he said and smiled at her. "We will enjoy a relationship of respect and perhaps even liking and of unbridled lust. It sounds good to me, especially the last part."

He drew one of her rare amused smiles from her. "Damn you," she said without any conviction at all.

"We had better dress and go downstairs," he said, "before all the snow melts."

"I would hate that snowball to miss its destiny and never collide with your face," she said.

THEY WERE BACK down by the lake, spread along one of its banks, searching for holly and mistletoe and well-shaped evergreen boughs of the right size. The lake itself was like a vast flat empty field of snow on which some of the children—and three or four of the young people, too—had made long slides while whooping with delight. The snow would have to be swept off before anyone could skate, though the ice had been pronounced by the head gardener to be thick enough to bear any human weight. But the skating would have to wait until tomorrow, they had all been told. Today was strictly for the gathering of greenery and the decorating of the house.

Of course it had turned out not to be strictly for any such thing, just as Edgar had predicted. There had been a great deal of horseplay and noise ever since the first one of them had set foot outside the house. A vicious snowball fight had been waged and won and lost before any of them had succeeded in getting even twenty yards from the house. Edgar's first snowball had been safely deflected by Helena's shoulder—she had seen it coming. Her own had landed squarely in the middle of his laughing face.

"If you think to win any war against me, Edgar," she had told him while he shook his head like a wet dog and wiped his face with his snowy gloves, "let that be a warning to you."

"You win," he had said, smiling ruefully and setting a hand at the back of her neck. When he had picked up a palmful of snow she did not know. But every drop of it, she would swear, had found its way down inside her cloak and dress.

Samantha, Marchioness of Carew, and Jane, Countess of Greenwald, had shown all the little girls and some of the older ones, too, how to make snow angels and soon there was a heavenly host of them spread out on what was usually a lawn.

By slow degrees they had all made their way to the lake and the woods and been divided into work parties. Both her father-in-law and her husband had tried to persuade Helena to return to the house instead of going all the way. She wished they had not. She might have gone back if she had been left to herself. But once challenged, she had had no choice but to go. Not that she felt too weak or fatigued. She just did not want any more merriment.

In the event she soon became involved in it. It really was irresistible. There were children to be helped and children to be played with and young people and people of her own generation to be laughed with. She had forgotten how warm and wonderful family life could be. She had forgotten how exhilarating a good old-fashioned English Christmas could be. She had forgotten how sheerly pleasurable it was to relax and interact with other people of all ages, talking and teasing and laughing.

It was so easy to be seduced by Christmas. The thought was conscious in her mind more than once, but she could not seem to fight against it. Stephen, the little Greenwald boy, appeared to have adopted her as a favored aunt and had persuaded a few of the other children of similar age to do likewise. When she should have been directing them in the carrying of a largish pile of holly to the central cache close to the lake, she found herself instead dancing in a ring with the children, chanting "Ring around the rosy" and actually tossing herself into the snow with them when everyone's favorite line had been chanted—"We all fall down." And laughing as merrily as any of them as she staggered back to her feet and dusted herself off.

She had known it would happen. She had fought weakly against it and allowed Christmas and the snow to win—for now. Perhaps even in the afterlife, she thought, there were brief vacations from hell. Perhaps only so that it would appear even worse afterward. She tried not to watch Edgar climbing trees for mistletoe, lifting nephews and a niece and other children on his broad shoulders by turns so that they could reach the desired holly branches—why did the best ones always seem to be above the reach of an outstretched arm? Why were the best of all things just beyond one's grasp?

A surprise awaited everyone when the greenery was finally gathered and piled neatly in one place ready to be hauled back to the house. A group of warmly clad gardeners and house servants had built a large bonfire and were busy warming chocolate and roasting chestnuts over it.

They all suddenly realized how cold they were and how tired and thirsty—and hungry. There was a great deal of foot stamping and glove slapping and talking and laughing. And someone—Helena thought it was probably one of the Bristol guests—started singing, a bold gamble when he might have ended up singing an embarrassed solo. But of course he did not. Soon they were all singing one carol after another and being very merry and very sentimental and only marginally musical. Helena shivered and found a log on which to sit, her gloved hands warming about her chocolate cup.

"I suppose," Edgar said, seating himself beside her, "I will have my head bitten off when I ask if you are overtired?"

"Yes," she said, "I suppose you will."

He had been offering affection this morning. It was something Edgar would do, of course. A perfectionist in all things, he would not be satisfied with a forced marriage to a woman whose behavior in London must have disgusted as well as excited him. He would try to create a marriage of affection out of what they had. And she had rebuffed him.

Would it be possible? she wondered and was frightened by the question which expressed itself quite verbally in her mind. The answer was very clear to her. Of course it would be possible. One could not respect a man and like him and admire him and find him attractive and enjoy intimacies with him without there being the possibility of affection for him. Indeed, if she let down all her inner guard, she might even admit to herself . . . No!

Dared she allow the element of affection to creep into their relationship? Perhaps after all there was an end to punishment and self-loathing. Perhaps Edgar was strong enough . . . Certainly he was stronger than . . . No!

Her cup was empty and had lost its comforting warmth. She set it down on the ground at her feet. When Edgar took her hand in his, she curled her fingers about it. He was singing with everyone else. He had a good tenor voice. She had not heard him sing before. He was her husband. Their lives were linked together for all time. It was his child she carried. They were to be parents together—perhaps more than once. That was a new thought. Perhaps they would have more than one child. There would be other occasions like this down the years.

Did she dare to let go and simply enjoy? When someone else, because of her, would suffer for the rest of a lifetime?

She turned her head to look at her husband. Decent, strong, honorable Edgar. Who deserved far better. But who would never have it unless she dared give more in her marriage than she had been prepared to give. And who might forever be sorry if she did.

He looked back at her and stopped singing. He smiled and lowered his head to kiss her briefly on the lips. A small token of—affection. Was he going to pay her warning no heed, then?

"Such a bleak look, Helena," he said. "Yet you have been looking so happy."

"Let us not start this again," she said.

But his next words had her jumping to her feet in terror and panic.

"Tell me about your stepson," he said. "Tell me about Sir Gerald Stapleton."

She turned and stumbled off in the direction of the house. She tried to shake off his arm when he caught up to her and took her in his grasp.

"I was right, then," he said. "I picked on the right person. Steady, Helena. You cannot run all the way home. We will walk. You cannot run from yourself either. Have you not realized that yet? And you will not run from me. But we will take it slowly—both the walk and the other. Slow your steps."

A chaplain praying over a condemned man must speak in just that quiet, soothing voice, she thought.

"Damn you, Edgar!" she cried. "Damn you, damn you, damn you!"

"Calm yourself," he said. "Walk slowly. There is no hurry."

"I hate you," she said. "Oh, how I hate you. You are loathsome and I hate you. Damn you," she added for good measure.

14

$\mathcal{I}$NCREDIBLY, NOTHING MORE WAS SAID ON THE SUBject of Helena's stepson. They walked home in silence and Edgar took her straight to their bedchamber, where she slumped wearily onto the bed, taking the time only to remove her boots and outdoor garments before she did so. He went to stand at the window until he looked over his shoulder and noticed that she had not covered herself, though the room was rather chilly. He wrapped the top quilt carefully about her to the chin. She was already asleep.

She slept deeply for two hours while Edgar first watched her, then returned to his place at the window, and finally went downstairs when he saw that everyone else was coming back to the house, loaded with greenery. He helped to carry armfuls inside while their original bearers stamped snow-packed boots on the steps and slapped at snowy clothing. He took the Bridgwater baby from the duke's arms and had unwound him from his many layers of warm clothing before a few of the nurses came hurrying downstairs to whisk him and most of the other children back up to the nursery with them. They were to be tidied and warmed and fed and put down for an obligatory rest before the excitement was to resume with the decoration of the house.

Edgar told several people who asked that his wife had merely felt herself tiring and was now having a sleep.

"I warned her that it would be too much for her," Mr. Downes said. "You should have taken a firmer hand with her yourself, Edgar. You must not allow her to risk her health."

"I believe Helena is not one to take orders meekly, Papa," Edgar said.

"Oh, dear, no," Mrs. Cross agreed. "There was never anyone more stubborn than Helena, Mr. Downes. But she was exceedingly happy this morning. She still has a way with children, just as she always used to have. Children warm quickly to her, perhaps because she warms quickly to them. Yes, thank you, sir. You are most kind." Mr. Downes was taking her cloak and bonnet from her and looking around in vain for a footman who might be standing about doing nothing.

"Let me take you to the drawing room, ma'am," Edgar said, offering his arm, "where there will be a warm fire and probably some warm drinks too before nuncheon."

"Thank you," she said. "I must admit to feeling chilly. But I do not know when I have enjoyed myself as much as I have this morning, Mr. Downes. You cannot know what it means to me to be part of such a happy family Christmas."

"You always will be from now on, ma'am," he said, "if my wife and I have anything to say in the matter. Did you ever visit Helena during her first marriage?"

"Oh, yes, indeed," she said, "two or three times. She had a gift for happiness in those days. I suppose the marriage was not entirely to her liking—Sir Christian Stapleton was so much older than she, you know. But she made the best of it. She had that vibrancy and those smiles." She smiled herself. "Perhaps they will come back now. I am confident they will. This is a far better match for her."

"Thank you," he said. "I hope you are right. Did you know Sir Christian's son?"

"Poor boy," she said. "He was very lonely and timid and not much loved by his father, I believe. But Helena was good to him. She set herself to mothering him and shielding him from his father's impatience—she could always wheedle him with her sunny ways. They both worshiped her. But you do not want to be hearing this, Mr. Downes. That was a long time ago. I am very glad Helena has a chance at last to have a child of her own— and a husband of her own age. I was shocked at first and was perhaps not as kind to you as I ought to have been. I do apologize for that. You are a fine young man, I believe."

"You were all that was gracious, ma'am," he said. "Take this chair while I fetch you a drink. You should be warm again in a moment."

By the time Helena woke up nuncheon was over— Edgar had a tray sent up to her—and the drawing room, the dining room, the ballroom, and the hall were being cleared, ready for the decorating. The older children had already come downstairs and the younger ones were being brought just as she came down herself. There was much to do and many people to do it. It was certainly not the time for a serious talk.

Edgar had been appointed to direct most of the men and some of the bigger children in the decoration of the ballroom. It involved much climbing of ladders and leaning out precariously into space. Cora shrieked when she saw her eldest son, ten rungs up one of the ladders, intent on handing his father a hammer. She showed every intention of climbing up herself to rescue him, though she was terrified of heights, and was banished to the drawing room.

Stephanie, Duchess of Bridgwater, and Fanny Grainger, self-proclaimed experts in the making of kissing boughs, were constructing the main one for the drawing room with the help of some of the other ladies. Helena, self-proclaimed nonexpert, was making another with the help of far too many children for any degree of efficiency. She had thrown herself into the task, Edgar noticed, with bright-faced enthusiasm. Of course the sleep had done her good, she had assured his father and a few other people who had thought to ask. All her energy was restored and redoubled. She smiled dazzlingly. She ignored her husband as if he did not exist.

She could not continue to do so indefinitely, of course. Finally all was done and they were summoned to the drawing room for hot punch—hot lemonade for the children—and for the first annual ceremony of the raising of the kissing bough, Mr. Downes announced when they were all assembled. Adults chuckled and children squealed with laughter.

It was finally in place at the very center of the room below the chandelier. They all gazed at it admiringly. The Marquess of Carew began a round of applause and Fanny blushed while the duchess laughed.

"It would seem appropriate to me," Mr. Downes said, "for the bough to be put to the test by the new bride and groom. We have to be sure that it works."

There was renewed applause. There were renewed shrieks from the children. The Earl of Thornhill whistled.

"Pucker up, Edgar, old chap," Lord Francis said.

Well, Edgar thought, stepping forward and reaching for his wife's hand, he had not kissed her at their wedding. He supposed he owed everyone this.

"Now, let me see." He played to the audience, setting his hands on Helena's shoulders and looking upward with a frown of concentration. "Ah, yes, there. Dead center. That should work." He grinned at her. She gazed back, the afternoon's bright gaiety still in her face. "Happy Christmas, Mrs. Downes."

They lingered over the kiss, entirely for the benefit of their cheering audience. It was not exactly his idea of an erotic experience, Edgar thought, to indulge in public kissing. But he was surprised by the tide of warmth that flooded over him. Not physical warmth—or at least not *sexual* warmth. Just the warmth of love, he and his wife literally surrounded by family and friends at Christmas.

He smiled down at her when they were finished. "It works exceedingly well," he said. "But we do not expect anyone to believe it merely because we have said so. Do we, my love? You are all welcome to try for yourselves."

Rosamond, young daughter of the Carews, pulled the marquess out beneath the bough, and he bent over her, smiling, and kissed her to the accompaniment of much laughter. No one, it seemed, was prepared to take Edgar at his word or that of anyone who came after him and confirmed his opinion. Hardly anyone went unkissed, and those who did—those children of middle years who were both too old and too young to kiss and pulled gargoyle faces at the very thought—did so entirely from choice.

Jack Sperling and Fanny Grainger were almost the last. Edgar had watched them grow progressively more self-conscious and uncomfortable until finally Jack got up his courage, strode toward her, and led her onto the recently vacated space beneath the bough with all the firm determination any self-respecting man of business could possibly want in an employee. Their lips clung together with very obvious yearning—for perhaps the duration of one whole second. And then she scurried away, scarlet to the tips of her ears, her eyes avoiding those of her suitor—and those of her barely smiling parents.

The elder Mr. Downes was last.

"Well, Mrs. Cross," he said heartily, "I am not sure I believe all these young folk. There is something sorry seeming about that bough, pretty as it is and loaded down with mistletoe as it is. I believe you and I should see what all the fuss is about."

Mrs. Cross did not argue or even blush, Edgar was interested to note. She stepped quietly under the bough and lifted her face. "I believe we should, sir," she said.

It felt strange watching his father kissing a woman, even if it was just a public Christmas kiss beneath mistletoe. One tended not to think of one's own father in such terms. It was not the sort of smacking kiss his father often bestowed on Cora and his grandchildren. Brief and decorous though it was, it was definitely the sort of kiss a man exchanges with a woman.

"Well, what do you say, ma'am?" His father was frowning ferociously and acting to the audience of shrieking, bouncing children, who had lost some interest in the proceeding until Grandpapa had decided to take a turn.

"I think I would have to say it really is a kissing bough, sir," Mrs. Cross said calmly and seriously. "I would have to say it works very nicely indeed."

"My sentiments entirely," he said. "Now I am not so sure about the monstrous concoction of ribbons and bows that is hanging in the hall. The children's creation with the help of my daughter-in-law, I believe. *That* is no kissing bough." He still had his hands on Mrs. Cross's waist, Edgar noticed, while grimacing from the noise of children screeching in indignation.

"*What?*" his father said, looking about him in some amazement. "It *is?*"

The children responded like a Greek chorus.

And so nothing would do but Mr. Downes had to tuck Mrs. Cross's arm beneath his and lead them all in an unruly procession down the stairs to the hall, where Helena's grotesque and ragged creation hung in all its tasteless glory. He kissed Mrs. Cross again, with a resounding smack of the lips this time, and pronounced the children's kissing bough even more effective than the one in the drawing room.

The children burst into mass hysteria.

It had been a thoroughly enjoyable afternoon for all. But parents were only human, after all. The children were gradually herded in the direction of the nursery, where it fell to the lot of their poor nurses to calm their high spirits. Something resembling quiet descended on the house. The conservatory would be the quietest place of all, Edgar thought. He would take his wife there. They could not suspend indefinitely the talk that this morning's revelation had made inevitable.

He had to find out about Gerald Stapleton.

But Cora had other ideas. She reached Helena's side before he did. "The children's party on Christmas Day needs to be planned, Helena," she said, "as well as the ball in the evening. Papa has had all the invitations sent out, of course, and the cook has all the food plans well in hand. But there is much else to be organized. Shall we spend an hour on it now?"

"Of course," Helena said. "Just you and I, Cora?"

"Stephanie was a governess before she was a duchess," Cora said. "Did you know that? She is wonderful with children."

"Then we will ask her if she wishes to help us plan games," Helena said.

They went away to some destination unknown, taking the duchess with them as well as the wife and daughter of one of Edgar's Bristol friends. After they returned, it was time to change for dinner. And dinner, with so many guests, and with so many Christmas decorations to be exclaimed over and so many Christmas plans to be divulged and discussed, lasted a great long while. So did coffee in the drawing room afterward, with several of the young people entertaining the company informally with pianoforte recitals and singing.

But it could not be postponed until bedtime, Edgar decided. And certainly not until tomorrow. He had started this. He had thought methodically through all he knew of Helena, and all she had told him, and not told him, and had concluded that her first husband was not the key figure in her present unhappiness and bitterness. It was far more likely to have been the son. Her reaction to his question this morning had left him in no doubt whatsoever. She had been so shocked and so distressed that she had not even tried to deceive him with impassivity.

They must talk. She must tell him everything. Both for her own sake and for the sake of their marriage. Perhaps forcing her to confront her past in his hearing was entirely the wrong thing to do. The bitterness that was always at the back of her eyes and just behind her smiles might burst through and destroy the fragile control she had imposed on her own life. The baring of her soul, which she had repeatedly told him she would never do, might well destroy their marriage almost before it had begun. She might loathe him with a very real intensity for the rest of their lives.

But their marriage stood no real chance if she kept her secrets. They might live together as man and wife in some amity and harmony for many years. But they would be amicable strangers who just happened to share a name, a home, a bed, and a child or two. He wanted more than that. He could not be satisfied with so little. He was willing to risk—he *had* to risk—the little they had in the hope that he would get everything in return and with the very real risk that he would lose everything.

But then his life was constantly lived on a series of

carefully calculated risks. Of course, as an experienced and successful businessman, he never risked all or even nearly all on one venture. No single failure had ever ruined him, just as no single success had ever made him. This time it was different. This time he risked everything—everything he had, everything he was.

He had realized in the course of the day that he was not only in love with her. He loved her.

He might well be headed toward self-destruction. But he had no choice.

She was conversing with a group of his friends. She was being her most vibrant, fascinating self, and they were all charmed by her, he could see. He touched her on the arm, smiled, and joined in the conversation for a few minutes before addressing himself just to her.

"It is a wonderfully clear night," he said. "The sky will look lovely from the conservatory. Come and see it there with me?"

She smiled and he caught a brief glimpse of desperation behind her eyes.

"That is the most blatantly contrived invitation a man ever offered his new bride, Edgar," one of his friends said. "We have all done it in our time. 'Come and see the stars, my love.'"

The laughter that greeted his words was entirely good-natured.

"Take no notice, Edgar," one of the wives told him. "Horace is merely envious because he did not think of it first."

"I will come and see the stars," Helena said in her lowest, most velvet voice, leaving with their friends the impression that she expected not to see a single one of them.

Which was, in a sense, true.

* * *

HE STOOD AT one of the wide windows of the conservatory, his hands clasped at his back, his feet slightly apart. He was looking outward, upward at the stars. He looked comfortable, relaxed. She knew it was a false impression.

She liked the conservatory, though she had not had the chance to spend much time here. There were numerous plants and the warmth of a summer garden. Yet the outdoors was fully visible through the many windows. The contrast with the snowy outdoors this evening was quite marked. The sky was indeed clear.

"The stars are bright," she said. "But you must not expect to see the Bethlehem star yet, Edgar. It is two nights too early."

"Yes," he said.

She had not approached the windows herself. She had seated herself on a wrought-iron seat beneath a giant palm. She felt curiously calm, resigned. She supposed that from the moment she had set eyes on Edgar Downes and had felt that overpowering need to do more than merely flirt with him this moment had become inevitable. She had become a firm believer in fate. Why had she returned to London at very much an off-season for polite society? Why had he chosen such an inopportune time to go to London to choose a bride?

It was because they had been fated to meet. Because *this* had been fated.

"He was fourteen when I married his father," she said. "He was just a child. When you are nineteen, Edgar, a fourteen-year-old seems like a child. He was small and thin and timid and unappealing. He did not have much promise." Because she had been unhappy herself and a little bewildered, she had felt instant sympathy for the boy, more than if he had been handsome and robust and confident.

"But you liked him," Edgar said.

"He had had a sad life," she said. "His mother abandoned him when he was eight years old to go and live with her two sisters. He had adored her and had felt adored in return. Christian tried to soften the blow by telling him that she was dead. But when she really did die five years later, Gerald suddenly found himself thrust into mourning for her and knew that she had loved him so little. Or so it seemed. One cannot really know the truth about that woman, I suppose. Everything about him irritated Christian. Poor Gerald! He could do nothing right."

"And so you became a new mother to him?" he asked.

"More like an elder sister perhaps," she said. "I talked to him and listened to him. I helped him with his lessons, especially with arithmetic, which made no sense at all to him. When Christian was from home I listened to him play the pianoforte and sometimes sang to his accompaniment. He had real talent, Edgar, but he was ashamed of it because his father saw it as unmanly. I helped him get over his terrible conviction that he was unlovable and worthless and stupid. He was none of the three. He was sweet. It is a weak word to use of a boy, but it is the right word to use of Gerald. There was such sweetness in him." He had filled such a void in her life.

"I suppose," Edgar said, breaking the silence she had been unaware of, "he fell in love with you."

"No," she said. "He grew up. At eighteen he was pleasing to look at and very sweet natured. He was—he was youthful."

Edgar had braced his arms wide on the windowsill and hung his head. "You seduced him," he said. He was breathing heavily. "Your husband's son."

She set her head back against the palm and closed her eyes. "I loved him," she said. "As a *person* I loved him. He was sweet and trusting and far more intelligent and talented than he realized. And he was vulnerable. His sense of his own worth was so very fragile. I knew it and feared for him. And I—I wanted him. I was horrified. I hated myself—*hated* myself. You could not know how much. No one could hate me as I hated myself. I tried to fight but I was very weak. I was sitting one day on a bridge, one of the most picturesque spots in the park at Brookhurst, and he was coming toward me looking bright and eager about something—I can no longer remember what. I took his hands and—Well. I frightened him and he ran away. Of all the shame I have felt since, I do not believe I have ever known any of greater intensity than I felt after he had gone. And yet it happened twice more before he persuaded Christian to send him away to university."

She had thought of killing herself, she remembered. She had even wondered how she might best do it. She had not had enough courage even for that.

"Now tell me that you are glad I have told you, Edgar," she said after a while. "Tell me you are proud to have such a wife."

There was another lengthy silence. "You were young," he said, "and found yourself in an arranged marriage with a much older man. There were only five years between you and your stepson. You were lonely."

"Is it for me you try to make excuses, Edgar?" she asked. "Or for yourself? Are you trying to convince yourself that you have not made such a disastrous marriage after all? There are no excuses. What I did was unforgivable."

"Did you beg his pardon later?" he asked. "Did he refuse to grant it?"

"I saw him only once after he left for university," she said. "It was at his father's funeral three years later. We did not speak. There are certain things for which one cannot ask for pardon, Edgar, because there is no pardon."

He turned to look at her at last. "You have been too hard on yourself," he said. "It was an ugly thing, what you did, but nothing is beyond pardon. And it was a long time ago. You have changed."

"I seduced you a little over two months ago," she said.

"I am your equal in age and experience, Helena," he said, "as I suppose all your lovers have been. You have had to convince yourself that you are promiscuous, have you not? You have had to punish yourself, to convince yourself that you are evil. It is time you put the past behind you."

"The past is always with me, Edgar," she said. "The past had consequences. I destroyed him."

"That is doubtless an exaggeration," he said. "He would not dally with his father's wife and went away. Good for him. He showed some strength of character. Perhaps in some way the experience was even the making of him. You have been too hard on yourself."

"It is what I hoped would happen," she said. "I went to Scotland after Christian's death and waited and waited for word that Gerald was somehow settled in life. Then I went traveling and waited again. I finally heard news of him last year in the late summer. Doubtless you would have, too, Edgar, if you moved in *ton*nish circles. Doubtless Cora and Francis heard. He married."

"Well, then." He had come to stand in front of her. He was frowning down at her. "He has married. He has found peace and contentment. He has doubtless forgotten what has so obsessed you."

"Fool!" she said. "I finally confirmed him in what all the experiences of his life had pointed to—that he was unlovable and worthless. He married a whore, Edgar."

"A whore?" he said. "Those are strong words."

"From a woman who has admitted to having had many lovers?" she said. "Perhaps. But she worked in a brothel. Half the male population of London paid for her services, I daresay. I suppose that is where Gerald met her. He took her and made her his mistress and then married her. Is that the action of a man with any sense of self-worth?"

"I do not know," he said. "I do not know the two people or the circumstances."

She laughed without any humor whatsoever. "I do know Gerald," she said. "It is just what he would do and just the sort of thing that for years I dreaded to hear. He thought himself worthy of nothing better in a wife than a whore."

"How old was he last year?" Edgar asked. "Twenty-nine? Thirty?"

"No," she said, "you will not use that argument with me, Edgar. I will not allow you to talk me out of my belief in my own responsibility for what has become of him. I will not let you forgive me. You do not have the power. No one does."

He went down on his haunches and reached out his hands to her.

"Touch me now," she said, "and I will never forgive you. A hug will not solve it, Edgar. I am not the one who needs the hug. And you cannot comfort me. There is no comfort. There is no forgiveness. And do not pretend you do not feel disgust—for what I did, for what I trapped you into, for the fact that I am bearing your child."

He drew breath and sighed audibly. "How long ago did this happen, Helena?" he asked. "Ten years? Twelve?"

"Thirteen," she said.

"Thirteen." He gazed at her. "You have lived in a self-made hell for thirteen years. My dear, it will not do. It just will not do."

"I am tired." She got to her feet, careful not to touch him. "I am going to bed. I am sorry you have to share it with me, Edgar. If you wish to make other arrangements—"

He grabbed her then and drew her against him and she felt the full force of his strength. Although she fought him, she could not free herself. After a few moments she did not even try. She sagged against him, soaking up his warmth and his strength, breathing in the smell of him. Feeling the lure of a nonexistent peace.

"Hate me if you will," he said, "but I will touch you and hold you. When we go to bed I will make love to you. You are my wife. And if you are so unworthy to be forgiven and to be loved, Helena, why is it that I can forgive you? Why is it that I love you?"

She breathed in slowly and deeply. "I am so tired, Edgar," she said. So tired. Always tired. Not just from her pregnancy, surely. She was soul-weary. "Please. I am so tired." Was that abject voice hers?

"We will go to bed, then," he said. "But I want you to see something first." He led her to the window, one arm firmly about her waist. "You see?" He pointed upward to one star that was brighter than all the others. "It is there, Helena. Not only on the night of Christmas Eve. Always if we just look for it. There is always hope."

"Dreamer," she said, her voice shaky. "Sentimentalist. Edgar, you are supposed to be a man of reason and cold good sense."

"I am also a man who loves," he said. "I always have, from childhood on. And I am what you are stuck with. For life, I am afraid. I'll never let you forget that star is always there."

There was such a mingling of despair and hope in her that her chest felt tight and her throat sore. She buried her face against his shoulder and said nothing. After a few minutes of silence he took her up to bed.

15

*E*DGAR WAS UP BEFORE DAWN THE NEXT MORNING, a little earlier than usual. The fire had not yet been made up. He shivered as he stretched his arms above his head and looked out through the window. As last night's clear sky had suggested, there had been no more snow.

He was tired. Nevertheless he was glad to be up. He had slept only in fits and starts through the night, and he had felt Helena's sleeplessness, though they had not spoken and had lain turned away from each other for most of the night after he had made love to her.

Her story had been ugly enough. What she had done had been truly shameful. She had been a married woman, however little say she had had in the choice of her husband. She had known and understood the boy's vulnerability—and he had been her husband's son. She had been old enough to know better, and of course she *had* known better. The attraction, the desire had been understandable—the son had been far closer to her own age than the father. That she had given in to temptation was blameworthy. She had been morally weak.

Her conscience had not been correspondingly weak. She had punished herself ever since. She had refused either to ask forgiveness or to forgive herself simply because she thought her sin unforgivable. She had never allowed herself to be happy or to love—or be loved. He guessed that her extensive travels had been her way of trying to escape from herself. It might be said that true repentance should have made her celibate. But Edgar believed he had been right in what he had said to her the night before. She had punished herself with promiscuity, with the conviction that she was truly depraved.

Their marriage stood not one chance in a million of bringing either of them contentment. Unless . . .

It would be an enormous risk. He had known that all through the night. She was quite convinced that she had destroyed her stepson, that her betrayal had been the final straw in an unhappy life of abuse. And she had been quite certain of her facts when describing the man's marriage. He had married a prostitute taken from a London brothel.

It seemed very probable that she was right. And if she was, there would never be any peace for her. He might argue until kingdom come that Sir Gerald Stapleton had been abused by both his father and mother, far more important people in his life than she had ever been, and that he had not used his individual freedom when he was old enough to fight back against his image of himself as a victim. Helena would forever blame herself.

And so he must do today the only thing he could do. It was the only hope left, however slim it might be. He must remember what he had told his wife last night about the star. It was always there, the Christmas star perhaps, constant symbol of hope. There must always be hope. The only thing left when there was no hope was despair. Helena had lived too long with despair.

Her stillness and quietness did not deceive him. She was awake, as she had been most of the night. He crossed to the bed and set a hand on her shoulder.

"I am going to Bristol," he said. "There is some business that must be taken care of before the holiday. I will stay at the house tonight and return tomorrow."

He expected questions. What business could possibly have arisen so suddenly two days before Christmas when there had not even been any post yesterday?

"Yes," she said. "All right."

He squeezed her shoulder. "Get some rest," he said.

"Yes."

The dusk of dawn had still not given place to the full light of day when Edgar led his horse from the stables, set it to a cautious pace to allow it to become accustomed to the snowy roads, and set his course for Brookhurst, thirty miles away.

IT WAS AN enormous relief to have Edgar gone for the day. It would have been difficult to face him in the morning after the night before. Helena was annoyed with herself for giving in to his constant needling and pestering. She should never have told him the truth. She had done so as a self-indulgence. It had felt surprisingly cathartic sitting there in the quiet, darkened conservatory, reliving those memories for someone else's ears. She almost envied papists their confessionals.

But it had not just been self-indulgence. She had owed him the truth. He was her husband. And therein lay the true problem. She was unaccustomed to thinking sympathetically about another person, caring about his feelings. It was something she had not done in years. And something she ought not to do now. What good could ever come of her sympathy, of her compassion?

She cared about him. He was a decent man, and he had been good to her. But she must not care *for* him or allow herself to be comforted *by* his care. She remembered what he had said the night before—*why is it that I love you?* She shook her head to rid her mind of the sound of his voice saying those words.

She was glad he had gone. There was no business in

Bristol, of course. His friends had looked surprised and his father astonished when she had given that as an explanation for his absence. He had gone there so that he could be away from her for a day, so that he could think and plan. There would be a greater distance between them by the time he returned, once he had had the chance to digest fully what she had told him. And a greater distance on her part, too—she must return to the aloofness, the air of mockery that had become second nature to her for a number of years but that had been deserting her since their marriage. She was glad she had not told him the one, final truth.

She was glad he had gone.

She spent a busy day. She walked into the village during the morning with Cora and Jane, Countess of Greenwald, to purchase some prizes for the children's games at the Christmas party. The children, the young people, and most of the men had gone out to the hill to ride the sleds down its snowy slopes. After nuncheon she was banished to her room by her father-in-law for a rest and was surprised to find that she slept soundly for a whole hour. And then she went outside when it became obvious that the duke and duchess, who were going to build a snowman for their little boy, had acquired a sizable train of other small children determined to go along to see and to help.

"You are remarkably good with children, Mrs. Downes," the Duke of Bridgwater told her when three snowmen of varying sizes and artistic merit were standing in a row. "So is Stephanie. I might have stayed inside the house and toasted my toes at the fire."

It was surprising in a way that he had not done so. Helena had been acquainted with him for several years and had always known him as an austere, correct, rather toplofty aristocrat. He still gave that impression when one did not see him in company with his wife or his son.

Their company was obviously preferable to toasted toes this afternoon, despite his words.

For a moment Helena felt a pang of emptiness. She favored the duke with her mocking smile. "It must be incipient maternity that is causing me to behave so much out of character, your grace," she said. "I have never before been accused of anything as shudderingly awful as being good with children."

"I do beg your pardon, ma'am," he said with a gleam in his eye. "I experienced much the same horror less than a month ago when my butler observed me to be galloping—*galloping*, ma'am—along an upper corridor of my home with my son on my shoulders. Why I confess to this next detail I do not know—I was *whinnying*." He grimaced.

Helena laughed.

The evening was spent in the drawing room. Family and guests passed the time with music and cards and conversation and a vigorous game of charades, suggested by the young son and daughter of one of Mr. Downes's friends and participated in with great enthusiasm by all the young people and a few of the older ones, too.

A definite romance was developing between Fanny Grainger and Mr. Sperling, Helena noticed. They were being very careful and very discreet and were watched almost every moment by Sir Webster and Lady Grainger, who dared not appear too disapproving, but who were far from being enthusiastic. But matters had been helped along by her father-in-law's apparently careless remark at tea that Edgar's business was to buy and renovate Mr. Sperling's country estate as a future home for the young man when he should have risen high enough in the company's ranks to need it as a sign of status.

Edgar either felt very guilty about Miss Grainger, Helena concluded, or he had a great soft heart, inherited with far tougher attributes from his father. She strongly favored the soft heart theory.

It felt good to be alone again, Helena thought, to be free of him for one day at least. She wondered if he had got safely to Bristol. She wondered if he had dressed warmly enough for the journey or if he had caught a chill. She wondered what he was doing this evening. Was he sitting at home, brooding? Or enjoying his solitude? Was he out visiting friends or otherwise amusing himself? She wondered if he kept mistresses. She supposed he must have over the years. He was six-and-thirty after all and had never before been married. Besides, he was an experienced and skilled lover. But she could not somehow imagine the very respectable, very bourgeois Edgar Downes keeping a mistress now that he had a wife. Not that she would mind. But she had a sudden image of Edgar doing with another woman what he did with her in their bed upstairs and felt decidedly irritable—and even murderous.

She did not care what he was doing tonight in Bristol. She was just happy to be able to converse and laugh and even join in the charades without feeling his eyes on her.

Was he thinking about her?

She hoped he was not wasting time and energy doing any such thing, since she was certainly not thinking about him.

SIR GERALD STAPLETON's butler would see if he was at home, he told Edgar with a stiff bow when the latter presented himself and his card at the main doors of Brookhurst late in the afternoon. He showed Edgar into a salon leading off the hall.

At least, Edgar thought, the long journey had not been quite in vain. Stapleton might refuse to see him, but clearly he had not gone away for Christmas. The butler would have known very well then that he was not at home. He stood at the window. There was as much snow here as at Mobley. It was an elegant house. The park was large and attractive, even with its snow cover.

He turned when the door opened again. The man who stepped inside did not surprise him, except perhaps in one detail. He was not particularly tall or broad or handsome. He was well dressed though with no extravagance of taste. There was something quite ordinary and unremarkable about his appearance. Except for his pleasant, open countenance—that was the surprise. Though a man might look that way merely out of politeness when he had a visitor, of course.

"Mr. Downes?" he said, looking at the card in his hand.

Edgar inclined his head. "From Bristol, as you see on the card," he said. "My father owns Mobley Abbey thirty miles from here."

"Ah, yes," Sir Gerald Stapleton said. "That is why the name seemed familiar to me. The snow must make for slow travel. You are on your way to Mobley for Christmas? I am glad you found Brookhurst on your way and decided to break your journey here. I will send for refreshments."

"I came from Mobley Abbey today," Edgar said, "specifically to see and to speak with you. I am recently married. My wife was Lady Stapleton, your father's widow."

Sir Gerald's expression became instantly more guarded. "I see," he said. "My felicitations to you."

"Thank you," Edgar said. It was very difficult to know how to proceed. "And to my wife?" he asked.

Sir Gerald looked down at the card and placed it absently into a pocket. He was clearly considering his reply. "I mean you no offense, sir," he said at last. "I have no kind feelings for Mrs. Downes."

Ah. It was not simply a case then of something Helena had blown quite out of proportion with reality. Sir Gerald Stapleton had neither forgotten nor forgiven.

"Then you mean me offense," Edgar said quietly.

Sir Gerald half smiled. "I would offer you the hospitality of my home," he said, "but we would both be more comfortable, I believe, if you stayed at the village inn. It is a posting inn and quite respectable. I thank you for informing me."

"She believes she destroyed you," Edgar said.

Sir Gerald pursed his lips for a moment. "She did not do that," he said. "You may inform her so, if you wish."

"She believes she betrayed your trust at a time in your life when you were particularly vulnerable," Edgar said. "She believes you have never recovered from her selfish cruelty. And so she has never forgiven herself or stopped punishing herself."

"Helena?" Sir Gerald said, walking toward the fireplace and staring down at the fire burning there. "She was so much in command of herself. So confident. So without conscience. I remember her at my father's funeral, cold and proud—and newly wealthy. I beg your pardon, sir. I speak of your wife and do not expect you to remain quiet while you hear her maligned. You may assure her that she has had no lasting effect on my life. You may even say, if you will, that I wish her well in her new marriage. That is all I have to say on the subject. If we can find some other topic of mutual interest, I will order hot refreshment to warm you before you return to the cold. I would like to hear about Mobley Abbey. I hear that it has been restored to some of its earlier splendor."

There was no avoiding it. "My wife believes that your marriage was an outcome of your lasting unhappiness," Edgar said, wondering if he was going to find himself fighting a duel before the day was out—or at dawn the next day.

"My marriage." Sir Gerald's face had lost all traces of good humor. "Have a care what you say about my marriage, sir. It is not open for discussion. I believe it would be best for both of us if we bade each other a civil good afternoon while we still may."

"Sir Gerald," Edgar said, "I love my wife."

Sir Gerald closed his eyes and drew breath audibly. "You can love such a woman," he said, "and yet you believe that I cannot? You believe that I must have married out of contempt for my wife and contempt for myself?"

"It is what my wife believes," Edgar said.

Sir Gerald stood with his back to the fire for a long while in silence. Finally he strode toward the door and Edgar prepared to see him leave and to know that he must return to Mobley with nothing more comforting for Helena than an assurance from her stepson that she had no permanent effect on his life. But Sir Gerald stood in the doorway, calling instructions to his butler.

"Ask Lady Stapleton if she would be so good as to step down here," he said.

He returned to his position before the fire without looking at Edgar or exchanging another word with him. A few minutes passed before the door opened again.

She was a complete surprise. She was small, slender, dark-haired, decently dressed, and very pretty in an entirely wholesome way. She had a bright, intelligent face. She glanced at Edgar and then looked at her husband in inquiry.

"Priss?" Sir Gerald held out one arm to her, his expression softened to what was unmistakably a deep affection. "Come here, my love. This is Mr. Edgar Downes of Bristol. He has recently married Helena. My wife, Lady Stapleton, sir."

She looked first into her husband's face with obvious concern and deep fondness as she moved toward him until he could circle her waist with his arm and draw her protectively to his side. Then she turned to Edgar. Her eyes were calm and candid. "Mr. Downes," she said, "I wish you happy."

"You sent Peter back to the nursery?" Sir Gerald asked her.

"Yes." She smiled at him and then turned back to Edgar. "Has my husband offered you refreshments, Mr. Downes? It is a chilly day."

She spoke with refined accents and with a graciousness that appeared to come naturally to her.

"Priss." Sir Gerald took one of her hands in both of his. "Mr. Downes says that Helena has never forgotten what happened and has never forgiven herself."

"I told you she probably had not, Gerald," she said.

"She believes she destroyed me," he said.

She tipped her head to one side and looked at him with such tenderness that Edgar found himself almost holding his breath. "She was very nearly right," she said.

Sir Gerald closed his eyes briefly. "She considers our marriage as evidence that she succeeded," he said.

"It is understandable that she should think that," she said gently.

"She wants my forgiveness." He looked up. "I suppose that *is* why you came, Mr. Downes? I cannot give it. But you may describe my wife to her, if you wish, and tell her that Lady Stapleton is the woman I honor above all other women and love more than my own life. Will it suffice? If it will not, I have nothing more to offer, I am afraid."

Edgar found himself locking eyes with Lady Stapleton and feeling shock at the sympathy that passed between them.

"If Mrs. Downes has not forgotten the pain of that

time in her life, sir," she said, "neither has my husband. It is a wound very easily rubbed raw. I have tried to convince Gerald that in reality there are very few people who are monsters without conscience. I have told him that Helena has probably always regretted what happened. She is very unhappy?"

"Very, ma'am," he said.

"And you are fond of her." It was a statement, not a question. Her intelligent eyes searched his face.

"Yes, ma'am."

"Gerald." She turned to him and looked earnestly at him. "Here is your chance for final peace. If you forgive her, you may finally forget."

Edgar tried to picture her performing her tricks at a London brothel. It was impossible.

"You are soft-hearted and sweet-natured, Priss," her husband said. "I cannot forgive her. You know I cannot."

"And yet," she said softly, flushing, "you forgave me."

"There was nothing to forgive," he said hotly. "Good God, Priss, there was *nothing to forgive.*"

"Only because you knew me from the inside," she said. "Only because you knew of my suffering and my yearning to rise above my suffering. There are few deeds in this life beyond forgiveness, Gerald. For our own sakes we must forgive as much as for the sake of the person we forgive. I find it hard to forgive Helena. She made you so desperately unsure of yourself. But without her, dear, I would never have met you. I would still be where you found me. And so I can forgive her. She is unhappy and has been for all these years, I daresay."

Sir Gerald stood with bowed head and closed eyes. "You are too good, my love," he said after a while.

"Suffering teaches one compassion, Gerald," she said. "You know that. You can feel compassion for everyone except Helena, I believe. Mr. Downes, there is a bigger and warmer fire burning in the drawing room. Will you come up there? You still have had no refreshments. And it is dusk outside already. Will you stay here for tonight? You cannot possibly drive all the way home, and inns are dreary places at which to put up. Stay with us?"

Edgar looked at Sir Gerald, who had raised his head.

"Please accept our hospitality," he said. "Ride back to Mobley Abbey tomorrow and inform Mrs. Downes that she has my full and free forgiveness." His voice was stiff, his face set and pale. But the words were spoken quite firmly.

"Thank you," Edgar said. "I will stay."

Lady Stapleton smiled. "Come upstairs, then," she said. "I hope you like children, Mr. Downes. Our son Peter was very cross to be taken back to the nursery so early. I will have him brought back down if I may. He is a little over a year old and terrorizes his mama and papa." She crossed the room and linked her arm through Edgar's.

"I like children," he said. "My wife and I are expecting one of our own next summer."

"Oh?" she said. "Oh, splendid. And Gerald and I, too, Mr. Downes."

THE DRAWING ROOM was cozy and looked lived-in. Its surfaces were strewn with books and needlework, but not with breakables. The reason was evident as soon as Peter Stapleton arrived in the room. He toddled about, exploring everything with energetic curiosity, before climbing onto his father's lap and playing with his watch chain and fob.

The room was decorated for Christmas. A warm fire burned in the hearth. Sir Gerald sat in his chair by the fire, looking at ease with his child on his lap. Lady Stapleton bent her head over her embroidery after pouring the tea and handing around the cups and a plate of cakes.

It was a warm family circle, into which Edgar had been drawn by the courtesy of his hostess, who soon had him talking about his life in Bristol and about Mobley Abbey.

But it was Christmas and there was no sign of other guests and no sign that they were preparing to go elsewhere for the holiday. They were to spend it alone? He asked the question.

"Yes." Lady Stapleton smiled. "The Earl of Severn, Gerald's friend, invited us to Severn Park, but his mother and all his family are to be there and we would not intrude on a family party."

Sir Gerald's eyes watched his wife gravely.

"We are happy here together," he said.

They were not. Contented, perhaps. They were a couple who very clearly shared an unusually deep love for each other. But perhaps circumstances had deepened it. Lady Stapleton had been a whore. She would now be a pariah in society.

"I wish," Edgar said, taking himself as much by surprise as he took them, "you would return to Mobley Abbey with me tomorrow and spend Christmas there."

They both looked at him, quite startled. "To Mobley?" Lady Stapleton said.

"Impossible!" her husband said at the same moment.

"I would like you and my wife to meet each other again," Edgar said to Sir Gerald. "To see each other as people again. To recapture, perhaps, some of the sympathy and friendship you once shared. Christmas would seem the ideal time."

"You push too hard, sir," Sir Gerald said stiffly.

"There is a large house party there," Edgar said, turning to Lady Stapleton. "My father and I have friends and their families there, all members of the merchant class. My sister—she is Lady Francis Kneller—has several of her friends there with their families. They are aristocrats and include the Duke and Duchess of Bridgwater and the Marquess and Marchioness of Carew. It would be pleasant to add three more people to our number."

She was a woman of dignity and courage, he saw. She did not look away from him as she spoke. "I believe you are fully aware, sir," she said, "of what I once was and always will be in the eyes of respectable society. I am not ashamed of my past, Mr. Downes, because it was a means of survival and I survived, but I am well aware of the restrictions it imposes upon the rest of my life. I have accepted them. So has Gerald. I thank you for your invitation, but we must decline."

"I believe," he said, not at all sure he was right, "that you might well find your fears ill-founded, ma'am. I went into polite society myself a few months ago when I was in London. I am what is contemptuously called a cit, yet I was treated with unfailing courtesy wherever I went. I know our situations are not comparable, but I know too that my father and my sister will receive with courtesy and warmth anyone I introduce to them as my friend. Lord Francis Kneller and his friends are people of true gentility. And my wife needs absolution," he added.

"Mr. Downes." She had tears in her large, intelligent eyes. "It is impossible, sir."

"I will not take my wife into a situation that might pain her," Sir Gerald said. "I will not have her treated with contempt or worse by people who are by far her inferior."

Edgar's eyes focused on the little boy, who had wriggled off his father's lap and was into his mother's silk threads, undetected.

"There are children of all ages at Mobley," he said. "I counted fourteen, but there may well be three or four

more than that. Children have an annoying tendency
not to stand and be counted. Your child would have
other children to play with for Christmas, ma'am."

She bit her lower lip and he saw her eyes before she
turned them on her husband. They were filled with
yearning. Her child was her weakness, then. And she
expected another. How she must fear for their future,
isolated from other children of their class.

"Gerald—" she said.

"Priss." There were both pain and tenderness in Sir
Gerald's voice.

If he had calculated wrongly, Edgar thought, he had
several people headed in the direction of disaster. He felt
a moment's panic. But it was the sort of exhilarated
panic with which he was familiar in his business life. It
was a calculated risk he took. Forgiveness was not
enough. Helena needed to know that she had not permanently blighted the life of her stepson. Contented as
the Stapletons clearly were together, they were equally
clearly not living entirely happy lives. And those lives
would grow progressively less happy as the years went
on and their children began to grow up.

"Please come," he said. "I will promise you the happiest Christmas you have ever known."

Lady Stapleton smiled at him, her moment of weakness
already being pushed aside in favor of her usual serenity.
"You can do no such thing, Mr. Downes," she said. "We
would not put such responsibility on your shoulders. It
is just as likely to be the most uncomfortable Christmas
of our lives. But I think we should go. Gerald, I think we
should."

"Priss." He frowned. "I could not bear it. . . ."

"And I cannot bear to hide here for the rest of my
life," she said. "I cannot bear to keep you hiding here.
And Peter adores other children. You can see that at
church each week. Besides, I want to meet Helena. I

want you to see her again. I want—oh, Gerald, I want freedom even if it must come at the expense of some contentment. I want freedom—for both of us and for Peter and the new baby."

"Then we will go," he said. "Mr. Downes, I hope you know what you are doing. But that is unfair. As my wife says, you cannot be held fully responsible for what we decide to do. Let us bring everything into the open, then. I will see Helena, and Priss will be taken into society. And Peter will be given other children with whom to play. We will leave in the morning? Christmas Eve? You are quite sure, Priss?"

"Quite sure, dear." She smiled at him with a calm she could not possibly be feeling.

But then Edgar, too, sat outwardly calm while inwardly he quaked at the enormity of what he had just set in motion.

Sir Gerald and his wife pounced simultaneously in the direction of their son, who was absorbed in making an impossible tangle of bright threads.

16

CHRISTMAS EVE. IT HAD BEEN A RELATIVELY QUIET day for Helena. Although several of the adults had made visits to the village for last-minute purchases, and the young people had gone outside for a walk and come back again with enough snow on their persons to suggest that they had also engaged in a snowball fight, and several individual couples had taken their children outside for various forms of exercise—despite these things, there had been a general air of laziness and waiting about the day. Everyone conserved energy for Christmas itself, which would start in the evening.

Dinner was to be an hour earlier than usual. The carolers would come during the evening, and Mr. Downes and all his guests would greet them in the hall and ply them with hot wassail and mince pies after they had sung their carols. Then there would be church in the village, which it seemed everyone except the younger children was planning to attend. And afterward a gathering in the drawing room to provide warm beverages after the chilly walk and to usher in the new day.

Christmas Day itself, of course, would be frantically busy, what with the usual feasting and gift-giving with which the day was always associated and the children's party in the afternoon and the ball in the evening.

Her father-in-law had not insisted today that Helena

rest after nuncheon, though he did ask her if she felt quite well. He and everyone else, of course, wondered why Edgar had gone to Bristol just two days before Christmas and why he was still not back on the afternoon of Christmas Eve. She could feel the worry and strain behind Mr. Downes's smile and Cora's. She decided of her own accord an hour before tea to retire to her room for a rest.

She did not sleep. She was not really tired. That first phase of pregnancy was over, she realized. She had come for escape more than rest. There was such an air of eager anticipation in the house and of domestic contentment. One would have thought that in such a sizable house party there would be some quarreling and bickering, some jealousies or simple dislikes. There were virtually none, apart from a few minor squabbles among the children.

It was just too good to be true. It was cloying.

She felt lonely. As she had always felt—almost all her life. It seemed to her that she had always been on the outside looking in. Yet when she had tried to get in, to be a participant in a warm love relationship, she had done a terrible thing, trying to add a dimension to that love that just did not belong to it. And so she had destroyed everything—everything! If she had only remained patient and true to Christian, she realized now—and it would not have been very difficult, as he had always been good to her—she might have mourned his death for a year and still been young enough to find someone else with whom to be happy.

But then she would never have met Edgar, or if she had, she would have been married to someone else. Would that have made a difference? If she had been married this autumn and had met him in the Greenwald's drawing room, would she have recognized him in that single long glance across the room as that one person who could make her life complete? As the one love of her life?

She lay on her bed, gazing upward, swallowing several times in an attempt to rid herself of the gurgle in her throat.

Would she? Would she have fallen as headlong, as irrevocably in love with him no matter what the circumstances of her life? Had they been made for each other? It was a ridiculous question to ask herself. She did not believe in such sentimental rot. Made for each other!

But had they been?

She wished they had not met at all.

If they had not met, she would be in Italy now. She would be celebrating the sort of Christmas she was accustomed to. There would be no warm domestic bliss within a mile of her. She would not have been happy, of course. She could never be happy. But she would have been on familiar ground, in familiar company. She would have been in control of her life and her destiny. She would have kept her heart safely cocooned in ice.

Would he come home today? she wondered. Would he come for Christmas at all? But surely he would. He would come for his father's sake. Surely he would.

What if he did not? What if he never came?

She had never been so awash in self-pity, she thought. She hated feeling so abject. She hated him. Yes, she did. She hated him.

And then the door of her bedchamber opened and she turned her head to look. He stood in the open doorway for a few moments, looking back at her, before stepping inside and closing the door behind him.

She closed her eyes.

ALL DAY EDGAR had been almost sick with worry. He was taking an enormous risk with several people's lives.

If things went awry, he might have made life immeasurably worse for both Sir Gerald and Lady Stapleton as well as for Helena. He might have destroyed his marriage. He might have exposed his father to censure for behavior unbecoming a man with pretensions to gentility.

But events had been set in motion and all he could do now was try to direct them and control them as best he could.

The Stapletons had not changed their minds overnight. And so they set off early for Mobley Abbey on Christmas Eve on roads that were still covered with snow and still had to be traveled with care. Sir Gerald, Edgar noticed, was very tense. His wife was calm and outwardly serene. Each of them, Edgar had learned during his short acquaintance with them, felt a deep and protective love for the other. Without a doubt they had found comfort and peace and harmony together. Equally without a doubt, they were two wounded people whose wounds had filmed over quite nicely during a little more than a year of marriage—their marriage, he guessed, must have coincided almost exactly with the birth of their son. But were the wounds healed? If they were not, this journey to Mobley might rip them open again and make them harder than ever to heal.

They arrived at Mobley Abbey in the middle of the afternoon, having made good time. Edgar, who had ridden, set down the steps of the carriage himself, though it was Sir Gerald who handed his wife and sleeping child out onto the terrace. The child's nurse came hurrying from the accompanying carriage and took the baby, and Edgar directed a footman to escort them to the nursery and summon the housekeeper. He took Sir Gerald and Lady Stapleton to the library, which he was thankful to find empty, ordered refreshments brought for them, and excused himself.

He went first to the drawing room. Helena was not there. His father was, together with a number of his guests.

"Edgar!" Cora came hurrying toward him and took his arm. "You wretch! How dare you absent yourself for almost two full days so close to Christmas? Helena has been quite disconsolate and I have scarce removed my eyes from the sky for fear lest another snowstorm prevent your coming back. It is to be hoped that you went to Bristol to purchase a suitably extravagant Christmas present for your wife. Some *almost* priceless jewel, perhaps?"

"Edgar," his father said, rising from the sofa on which he had been sitting and conversing with Mrs. Cross, "it is good to see you home before dark. Whatever did take you to Bristol?"

"I did not go to Bristol," Edgar said. "I told Helena I was going there because I wished to keep my real destination a secret. We are all surrounded by family and friends while Helena has only one aunt here." He bowed in Mrs. Cross's direction. "I went to see her stepson, Sir Gerald Stapleton, at Brookhurst and persuade him to come back with me to spend Christmas."

"Splendid!" Mr. Downes rubbed his hands together. "The more the merrier. My daughter-in-law's stepson, you say, Edgar?"

"What a very kind thought Mr. Downes," Mrs. Cross said.

"Sir Gerald Stapleton?" Cora's voice had risen almost to a squeak. "And he has come, Edgar? *Alone?*"

Cora had always been as transparent as newly polished crystal. The questions she had asked only very thinly veiled the one she had not asked. Edgar looked steadily at her and at his brother-in-law beyond her.

"It is Christmas," he said. "I have brought Lady Stapleton, too, of course, and their son. If you will excuse me, Papa. I must find Helena and take her to meet them in the library. Do you know where she is?"

"She is upstairs resting," Mr. Downes said. "This will do her the world of good, Edgar. She has been somewhat low in spirits, I fancy. But then your absence would account for that." The statement seemed more like a question. But Edgar did not stay to pursue it. He left the room and, almost sick with apprehension, went up to his bedchamber.

She was lying on the bed, though she was not asleep. Their eyes met and held for a few moments and he knew with dreadful clarity that the future of her life and his, the future of their marriage, rested upon the events of the next hour. He stepped inside the room and shut the door. She closed her eyes, calmly shutting him out. She looked quite unmoved by the sight of him. Perhaps she had not missed him at all. Perhaps she had hoped he would not return for Christmas.

He sat down on the edge of the bed and touched the backs of his fingers to her cheek. She still did not open her eyes. He leaned down and kissed her softly on the lips. He felt a strong urge to avoid the moment, to keep the Stapletons waiting indefinitely in the library.

"Your father will be happy you have returned, Edgar," she said without opening her eyes. "So will Cora. Go and have tea with them. As you will observe, I am trying to rest."

"I have brought other guests," he said. "They are in the library. I want you to meet them."

She opened her eyes then. "More friends?" she said. "How pleasant for you. I will meet them later."

She was in one of her prickly moods. It did not bode well.

"Now," he said. "I wish you to meet them now."

"Oh, well, Edgar," she said, "when you play lord and master, you know, you are quite irresistible. If you would care to stop looming so menacingly over me, I will get up and jump to your command."

Very prickly. He went to stand at the window while she got up and straightened her dress and made sure at the mirror that her hair was tidy.

"I am ready," she said. "Give me your arm and lead me to the library. I shall be the gracious hostess, Edgar, never fear. You need not glower so."

He had not been glowering. He was merely terrified. Was he going about this the right way? Should he warn her? But if he did that, the chances were good that she would flatly refuse to accompany him to the library. And then what would he do?

He nodded to a footman when they reached the hall, and the man opened the library doors. Edgar drew a slow, deep breath.

"SIR GERALD AND Lady Stapleton." Cora whirled around and looked at her husband, her eyes wide with dismay.

"My new daughter's stepson," Mr. Downes said, beaming at Mrs. Cross and resuming his seat beside her. "And his wife and son. More family. When was there ever such a happy Christmas, ma'am?"

"I am sure I have never known a happier, sir," Mrs. Cross said placidly.

"Tell me what you know of Sir Gerald Stapleton," Mr. Downes directed her. "I daresay Edgar will bring them to tea soon."

"Yes, my love," Lord Francis said, going to Cora's side.

"Oh, dear," Cora said. "Whatever can Edgar have been thinking of? Perhaps he does not even know." She looked suddenly belligerent and glared beyond her husband to the group of their friends, who were regarding her in silence. She lifted her chin. "Well, *I* will be civil to her. She is Helena's relative by marriage, even if it is only a *step* relationship. And she is Edgar's and Papa's guest. No one need expect me to be uncivil."

"I would be vastly disappointed in you if you were, Cora," her husband said mildly.

"And why would anyone even think of treating a lady, the wife of a baronet, a fellow guest in this home, with incivility?" the Earl of Thornhill asked, eyebrows raised.

"You do not remember who she is, Gabriel?" his wife asked. "Though I do hope you will repeat your words, even when you do."

"The lady did something indiscreet, Jennifer?" he asked, though it was obvious to all his listeners that he knew the answer very well and had done so from the start. "Everyone has done something indiscreet. I remember a time when you and I were seen kissing by a whole ballroomful of dancers—while you were betrothed to another man."

"Oh, bravo, Gabe," Lord Francis said as the countess blushed rosily. "The rest of us have been tactfully forgetting that incident ever since. Though something very similar happened to Cora and me. Not that we were kissing. We were laughing and holding each other up. But it looked for all the world as if we were engaged in a deep embrace—and it caused a delicious scandal."

"The *ton* is so foolish," Cora said.

"Sir Gerald and Lady Stapleton are guests in this home," the Duke of Bridgwater said. "As are Stephanie and I, Cora. I shall not peruse them through my quizzing glass or along the length of my nose. You may set your mind at ease."

"Of course," the duchess said, "Alistair does both those things to perfection, but he reserves them for pretentious people. I can remember a time when I was reduced to near-destitution, Cora. I can remember the fear. I was fortunate. Alistair came along to rescue me."

"There are all too many ladies who are not so fortunate," the Marquess of Carew said gently. "The instinct to survive is a strong one. I honor those who, reduced to desperation, contrive a way of surviving that does not involve robbery or murder or harm to anyone else except the person herself. Lady Stapleton is, I believe, a lady who has survived."

"Oh, Hartley," his wife said, patting his hand, "you would find goodness in a murderer about to be hanged, I do declare."

"I would certainly try, love," he said, smiling at her.

"I know the Countess of Severn," Jane, Countess of Greenwald, said. "She and the earl have befriended the Stapletons. They would not have done so if Lady Stapleton was impossibly vulgar, would they?"

"There, my love," Lord Francis said, setting an arm about Cora's waist. "You might have had more faith in your friends and in me."

"Yes," she said. "Thank you. Now I wonder how poor Helena will be feeling about all this. Edgar and his surprises! One is reminded of the saying about bulls charging at gates."

"I believe both Edgar and Helena may be trusted," Lord Francis said. "I do believe those two, by hook or by crook, are going to end up quite devoted to each other."

"I hope you are right," Cora said with a loud sigh.

"What was that, Francis?" Mr. Downes called across the room. "Edgar and my daughter-in-law? Of course they are devoted to each other. He went off to bring her this secret present and she has been moping at his absence. I have great hopes. Not even hopes. Certainties. What say you, ma'am?" He turned to Mrs. Cross.

"I will say this, sir," she said. "If any man can tame

my niece, Mr. Edgar Downes is that man. And if any man deserves Helena's devotion, he is Mr. Edgar Downes."

"Precisely, ma'am." He patted her hand. "Precisely. Now where is that son of mine with our new guests? It is almost teatime."

HELENA LOOKED FIRST at the woman, who was standing to one side of the fireplace. A very genteel-looking young lady, she thought, slim and pretty, with intelligent eyes. She smiled and turned her eyes on the man. Pleasant looking, not very comfortable. Decidedly uncomfortable, in fact.

And then she recognized him.

Panic was like a hard ball inside her, fast swelling to explosion. She turned blindly, intent on getting out of the room as fast as she could. She found herself clawing at a very broad, very solid chest.

"Helena." His voice was impossibly steady. "Calm yourself."

She looked up wildly, recognized him, and was past that first moment and on to the next nightmare one. "I'll never forgive you for this," she whispered fiercely. "Let me past. I'll never forgive you."

"We have guests, my dear." His voice—and his face—was as hard as flint. "Turn and greet them."

Fury welled up in wake of the panic. She gazed into his face, her nostrils flaring, and then turned. "And *you*, Gerald," she said, looking directly at him. "What do *you* want here?"

"Hello, Helena," he said.

He looked as quiet, as gentle, as peaceful as he had always appeared. She could not believe that she had looked at him for a whole second without recognizing him. He had scarcely changed. Probably not at all. That outward appearance had always hidden his sense of rejection, insecurity, self-doubt.

"I have the honor of presenting my wife to you," he said. "Priscilla, Lady Stapleton. Helena, Mrs. Edgar Downes, my dear."

Helena's eyes stayed on him. "I have nothing to say to you, Gerald," she said, "and you can have nothing to say to me. I have no right to ask you to leave. You are my husband's guest. Excuse me, please."

She turned to find herself confronted by that same broad, solid chest.

"How foolish you are, Edgar," she said bitterly. "You think it is enough to bring us together in the same room? You think we will kiss and make up and proceed to live happily ever after? We certainly will not *kiss*. You foolish, interfering man. Let me past."

"Helena," he said, his voice arctic, "someone has been presented to you and you have not acknowledged the introduction. Is that the behavior of a lady?"

She gazed at him in utter incredulity. He dared instruct her on ladylike behavior? And to reprove her in the hearing of other people? She turned and looked at the woman. And walked toward her.

"Lady Stapleton. Priscilla," she said quietly, bitter mockery in her face, "I do beg your pardon. How pleased I am to make your acquaintance."

"I understand," the woman said, looking quite calmly into Helena's eyes. Her voice was as refined as her appearance. "I had as little wish for your acquaintance when it was first suggested to me, Helena, as you have for mine. I have had little enough reason to think kindly of you."

How dared she!

"Then I must think it remarkably kind of you to have overcome your scruples," Helena said sharply.

"I have done so for Gerald's sake," Lady Stapleton

said. "And for the sake of Mr. Downes, who is a true gentleman, and who cares for you."

The woman spoke with *dignity*. There was neither arrogance nor subservience in her and certainly no vulgarity—only dignity.

"I could live quite happily without his care," Helena said.

"Helena." It was Gerald this time. She turned to look at him and saw the boy she had loved so dearly grown into a man. "I never wanted to see you again. I never wanted to hear your name. I certainly never wanted to forgive you. Your husband is a persuasive man."

She closed her eyes. She could not imagine a worse nightmare than this if she had the devising of it. "I cannot blame you, Gerald," she said, feeling all the fight draining out of her. "I would have begged your pardon, perhaps, before your father died, at his funeral, during any of the years since, if I had felt the offense pardonable. But I did not feel it was. And so I have not begged pardon and will not do so now. I will take the offense to the grave with me. I have done enough permanent damage to your life without seeking shallow comfort for myself."

"I must correct you in one misapprehension," he said, his voice shaking and breathless. "I can see that you misapprehend. Forgive me, Priss? I met my wife under circumstances I am sure you are aware of, Helena. She had been forced into those circumstances, but even in the midst of them she remained cheerful and modest and kind and dignified. She has always been far my superior. If anyone is to be pitied in this marriage, it is she."

"Gerald—" Lady Stapleton began, but he held up a staying hand.

"She is not to be pitied," he said. "Neither am I. Priss is the love of my heart and I am by now confident in the conviction that I am the love of hers. I am not in the habit of airing such very private feelings in public, but I have seen from your manner and have heard from your husband that you have bitterly blamed yourself for what happened between us and have steadfastly refused to forgive yourself or allow yourself any sort of happiness. I thought I was still bitter. I thought I would never forgive you. But I have found during the past day that those are outmoded, petty feelings. You were young and unhappy—heaven knows *I* was never happy with my father either. And while youth and unhappiness do not excuse bad behavior, they do explain it. To hold a grudge for thirteen years and even beyond is in itself unpardonable. If it is my forgiveness you want, then, Helena, you have it—freely and sincerely given."

No. It could not possibly be as easy as that. The burden of years could not be lifted with a single short speech spoken in that gentle, well-remembered voice.

"No," she said stiffly. "It is not what I want, Gerald. It is not in your power."

"You will send him away still burdened, then?" Priscilla asked. "It is hard to offer forgiveness and be rejected. It makes one feel strangely guilty."

"It is Christmas." Edgar stepped forward. He had been a silent spectator of the proceedings until now. Helena deeply resented him. "We are all going to spend it here at Mobley Abbey. Together. And it is teatime. Time to go up to the drawing room. I wish to introduce you to my father and our other guests, Stapleton, Lady Stapleton."

They had not been introduced? *Lady Stapleton* had not yet been introduced to the Duke and Duchess of Bridgwater, the Marquess and Marchioness of Carew, the Earl and Countess of Thornhill, and everyone else? She would be *cut*. And she must know it. She must have known it before she came. Why had she come, then? For Gerald's sake? Did she love him so much? Would she risk such humiliation for his sake? So that he, too, might find a measure of peace? But Gerald had done nothing to regret. Except that she had refused to accept his forgiveness.

"Take my arm, Priss." Gerald's voice was tense with protective fear.

"No." Helena stepped forward and took the woman's arm herself. Gerald's wife was smaller than she, daintier. "We will go up together, Priscilla. I will present you to my father-in-law and my sister-in-law and my aunt. And to all our friends."

"Thank you, Helena," Priscilla said quietly. If she was afraid, she did not show it.

"I must show everyone what a delightful gift my husband has brought me on Christmas Eve," Helena said. "He has brought my stepson and his wife to spend Christmas with me."

"And our son," Priscilla said. "Peter. Thank you, Helena. Gerald has told me what a warm and charming woman you were. I can see that he was right. And you will see in the next day or two what a secure, contented man he is and you will forgive yourself and allow him to forgive you. I have seen enough suffering in my time to know all about the masks behind which it hides itself. It is time we all stopped suffering."

And this just before they stepped inside the drawing room to what was probably one of the worst ordeals of Priscilla's life?

"I can certainly admire courage," Helena said. "I will take you to my father-in-law first. You will like him and he will certainly like you."

"Thank you." Priscilla smiled. But her face was very pale for all that.

17

EDGAR GAZED UPWARD THROUGH THE WINDOW OF his bedchamber. By some miracle the sky was clear again. But then it was Christmas. One somehow believed in miracles at Christmas.

"Come here," he said without turning. He knew she was still sitting on the side of the bed brushing her hair, though her maid had already brushed it smooth and shining.

"I suppose," she said, "the Christmas star is shining as it was when we walked home from church a couple of hours ago. I suppose you want me to gaze on it with you and believe in the whole myth of Christmas."

"Yes," he said.

"Edgar." He heard her sigh. "You are such a romantic, such a sentimentalist. I would not have thought it of you."

"Come." He turned and stretched out one arm to her. She shrugged her shoulders and came. "There." He pointed upward unnecessarily. "Wait a moment." He left her side in order to blow out the candles and then joined her at the window again and set one arm about her waist. "There. Now there is nothing to compete with it. Tell me if you can that you do not believe in Christmas, even down to the last detail of that sordid stable."

She nestled her head on his shoulder and sighed. "I should be in Italy now," she said, "cocooned by cynicism. Why did I go to London this autumn, Edgar? Why did you? Why did we both go to the Greenwalds' drawing room that evening? Why did we look at each other and not look away again? Why did I conceive the very first time I lay with you when I have never done so before?"

"Perhaps we have our answer in Christmas," he said.

"Miracles?" The old mockery was back in her voice.

"Or something that was meant to be," he said. "I used not to believe in such things. I used to believe that I, like everyone else, was master of my own fate. But as one gets older, one can look back and realize that there has been a pattern to one's life—a pattern one did not devise or control."

"A series of coincidences?" she said.

"Yes," he said. "Something like that."

"The pattern of each of our lives merged during the autumn, then?" she said. "Poor Edgar. You have not deserved me. You are such a very decent man. I could have killed you this afternoon. Literally."

"Yes," he said, "I know."

She turned her head on his shoulder and closed her eyes. "She is very courageous," she said. "I could never do what she did today. She did it for him, Edgar. For Gerald."

"Yes," he said, "and for their son and their unborn child. And for herself. For them. You were wonderful. I was very proud of you."

She had taken Priscilla Stapleton about in the drawing room at teatime, introducing her to everyone as her stepson's wife, her own manner confident, charming, even regal. She had scarcely left the woman's side for the rest of the day. They had walked to and from church with Sir Gerald and his wife and shared a pew with them.

"But I did nothing," she said. "Everyone greeted her with courtesy and even warmth. It was as if they did not know, though I have no doubt whatsoever that they all did. She—Edgar, there is nothing vulgar in her at all."

"She is a lady," he said.

"Gerald is happy with her." Her eyes, he saw, had clenched more tightly shut. "He *is* happy. Is he, Edgar? Is he?" She looked up at him then, searching his eyes.

"I believe," he said, "the pattern of his life merged with the pattern of hers in a most unlikely place, Helena. Of course they are happy. I will not say they are in love, though I am sure they are. They *love* deeply. Yes, he is happy."

"And whole and at peace," she said. "I did not destroy him permanently."

"No, love," he said. "Not permanently."

She shivered.

"Cold?" he asked.

"But I might have," she said, "if he had not met Priscilla."

"And if she had not met him," he said. "They were both in the process of surviving, Helena. We do not know how well they would have done if they had not met each other. Perhaps they were both strong people who would have found their peace somehow alone. We do not know. Neither do they. I do believe, though, that they could not be so happy together if they merely used each other as emotional props. But they did meet, and so they are as we see them today."

She withdrew from him and rested her palms on the windowsill as she looked out. "I will not use you as an emotional prop either, Edgar," she said. "It would be easy to do. You organize and fix things, do you not? It comes naturally to you. You have seen that my life is all in pieces and you have sought to mend it, to put the pieces back together again, to make all right for me. You took a terrible risk today and won—as you almost always do, I suspect. It would be easy to lean into you as I was just doing, to allow you to manage my life. You can do it so much better than I, it seems. But it is my life. I must live it myself."

He felt chilled. But he had said it himself of her stepson and his wife—they could not be happy together if they depended too much upon each other. And he had spoken the truth. He could not be happy as the totally dominant partner in a marriage—even though by his nature he would always try to dominate, thinking he was merely protecting and cherishing his wife.

"Then you will do so," he said, "without my further interference. I am not sorry for what I did yesterday and today. I would do it again given the choice—because you are my wife and because I love you. But you must proceed from here, Helena—or not proceed. The choice is yours. I am going to bed. It is late and I am cold."

But she turned from the window to look at him, the old mocking smile on her lips—though he had the feeling that it was turned inward on herself rather than outward on him.

"I was not quarreling with you, Edgar," she said. "You do not need to pout like a boy. I want to make love. But not as we have done it since our marriage. I have allowed you your will because it has been so very enjoyable to do so. You are a superlative lover, unadventurous as are your methods."

He raised his eyebrows. Unadventurous?

"I want to be on top," she said. "I want to lead the way. I want you to lie still as I usually do and let me set the pace and choose the key moments. I want to make love to you."

He had never done it like that. It sounded vaguely wrong, vaguely sinful. He felt his breath quicken and his groin tighten. She was still smiling at him—and though she was dressed in a pale dressing gown with her hair in long waves down her back, she looked again in the faint light of the moon and stars like the scarlet lady of the Greenwalds' drawing room.

"Then what are we waiting for?" he asked.

He stripped off his nightshirt and lay on his back on the bed. He was thankful that a fire still burned in the grate, though the air felt chill enough—for the space of perhaps one minute. She kneeled, naked, beside him and began to make love to him with delicate, skilled hands and warm seeking mouth. The minx—of course she was skilled. He did not wish to discover where she had acquired those skills—though he really did not care. He had acquired his own with other women, but they no longer mattered. Just as the other men would no longer matter to her. He would see to it that they did not.

It was difficult to keep his hands resting on the bed, to submit to the sweet torture of a lovemaking that proceeded altogether too slowly for his comfort. It was hard to be passive, to allow himself to be led and controlled, to give up all his own initiative.

She came astride him when he thought the pain must surely soon get beyond him, positioned herself carefully, her knees wide, and slid firmly down onto him. His hands came to her hips with some urgency, but he remembered in time and gentled them, letting them rest idly there.

"Ah," she said, "you feel so good. So deep. You have not done this before, have you?"

"No."

"I will show you how good it feels to be mastered," she said, leaning over him and kissing him open-mouthed. "It does feel good, Edgar, provided it is only play. And this is play—intimate, wonderful play, which we all need in our lives. I do not wish to master you outside of this play—or you to master me. Only here. Now."

He gritted his teeth when she began to move, riding him with a leisurely rocking of her hips while she braced her hands on his shoulders and tipped back her head, her eyes closed. Fortunately the contracting of inner muscles told him that she was at an advanced stage of arousal herself. It was not long before she spoke again.

"Yes," she whispered fiercely. "Yes. Now, Edgar. *Now!*"

His hands tightened on her hips and he drove into her over and over again until they reached climax together.

"Ah, my love," she said in that throaty, velvet voice that most belonged here, in their bed. "Ah, my love." Her head was still tipped back, her eyes still closed.

He would perhaps not have heard the words if they had not sounded so strange and so new to his ears. He doubted that she heard them herself.

She did not lift herself away. She lowered herself onto him and straightened her legs so that they lay on either side of his. She snuggled her head into the hollow between his shoulder and neck and sighed.

"Do I weigh a ton?" she asked as he contrived somehow to pull the covers up over them.

"Only half," he told her.

"You are no gentleman, sir," she said. "You were supposed to reply that I feel like a mere feather."

"Two feathers," he said.

"Good night, Edgar. I did enjoy that."

"Good night, love." He kissed the side of her face. "And I enjoyed being mastered."

She laughed that throaty laugh of hers and was almost instantly asleep.

They were still coupled.

It was going to be an interesting marriage, he thought. It would never be a comfortable one. It might never be a

particularly happy one. But strangely, he felt more inclined to favor an interesting marriage over a comfortable one. And as for happiness—well, at this particular
moment he felt thoroughly happy. And life was made up
of moments. It was a shame that this one must be cut
short by sleep, but there would be other moments—
tomorrow or the next day or the next.

He slept.

CHRISTMAS DAY WAS one of those magical days that
Helena had studiously avoided for ten years. It was
everything that she had always most dreaded—a day
lived on emotion rather than on any sane rationality.
And the emotions, of course, were gaiety and love and
happiness. The Downes family, she concluded—her
father-in-law, her husband, her sister-in-law—used love
and generosity and kindness and openness as the guid-
ing principles of their own family lives, and they passed
on those feelings to everyone around them. It seemed
almost impossible that anyone *not* have a perfectly
happy Christmas in their home.

And it seemed that everyone did.

The morning was spent in gift-giving within each family group. For Helena there was a great deal more to do
than that. There were the servants to entertain for an
hour while Mr. Downes gave them generous gifts, and
there were baskets to be delivered to some of the poorer
families in their country cottages and in the village. Cora
and Francis delivered half of them, while Helena and
Edgar delivered the others.

It felt so very good—Helena was beginning to accept
the feeling, to open herself to it—to be a part of a family.
To recognize love around her, to accept that much of it
was directed her way—not for anything she had ever
done or not done, but simply because she was a member

of the family. To realize that she was beginning to love again, cautiously, fearfully, but without resistance.

She had decided to enjoy Christmas—this good old-fashioned English Christmas of her father-in-law's description. Tomorrow she would think things through, decide if she could allow her life to take a new course. But today she would not think. Today she would feel.

The young people had contrived to find time during the morning to walk out to the lake to skate. They were arriving back, rosy cheeked, high spirited, as Helena and Edgar were returning from their errands. Fanny Grainger and Jack Sperling were together, something they had been careful to avoid during the past few days.

Fanny smiled her sweet, shy smile. Jack inclined his head to them and spoke to Edgar.

"Might I have a word with you, sir?" he asked.

"Certainly," Edgar said, indicating the library. "Is it too private for my wife's ears?"

"No." Jack smiled at Helena and she adjusted her opinion of his looks. He was more than just mildly good looking. He was almost handsome. He offered his arm to Fanny and led her toward the library.

"Well." Edgar looked from one to the other of them when they were all inside the room. "The hot cider I asked for should be here soon. What shall we toast?"

"Nothing and everything." Jack laughed, but Helena noticed that his arm had crept about Fanny's waist and she was looking up at him with bright, eager eyes.

"It sounds like a reasonably good toast to me." Edgar smiled at Helena and indicated two chairs close to the fire. "Do sit down, Miss Grainger, and warm yourself. Now, of what does this nothing and this everything consist?"

"I have been granted permission by Sir Webster Grainger," Jack said, "to court Miss Grainger. There is to be no formal betrothal until I can prove that I am able to support her in the manner of life to which she is accustomed and no marriage until I am in a fair way to offering her a home worthy of a baronet's daughter. That may be years in the future. But F—Miss Grainger is young and I am but two-and-twenty. Waiting seems heaven when just a few weeks ago we thought even that an impossibility."

Helena hugged Fanny. She was not in the habit of hugging people—had not been for a long while. But she was genuinely happy for the girl and her young man. And she was happy for Edgar, who must have felt guilty about the expectations he had raised in the Graingers.

"Well." Edgar was smiling. "The long wait can perhaps be eased a little. Since you have become a close friend of my family, Miss Grainger, and you are to be a favored employee, Sperling—provided you prove yourself worthy of such a position, of course—I daresay the two of you might meet here or at my home in Bristol with fair frequency."

Fanny bit her lip, her eyes shining with tears.

"I thank you, sir," Jack Sperling said. "For everything. We both do, don't we, Fan?"

She nodded and turned her eyes on Helena. There was such happiness in them that Helena was dazzled. The girl had a long wait for her marriage—perhaps years. But happiness lay in hope. Perhaps in hope more than in any other single factor. The moment might be happy, but unless one could feel confident in the hope that there would be other such moments the happiness was worth little.

"I will be new to Bristol," Helena said. "And though I will have Edgar and have already met here some of his friends, I will still feel lonely for a while. Perhaps we can arrange for you to stay with me for a month or two in the spring, Fanny. I believe you have an aunt in Bristol? I would be pleased to make her acquaintance."

Two of the tears spilled over onto Fanny's cheeks. "Thank you," she murmured.

The hot cider had arrived. They were all still chilled from the outdoors. They toasted one another's happiness and Christmas itself and sipped on the welcome warmth of their drinks.

EDGAR DID NOT plan to attend the children's party in the ballroom during the afternoon. They could be dizzyingly noisy and active, even the fourteen who were house guests—fifteen now that the young and very exuberant Peter Stapleton had been added to their number. With several neighborhood children added, the resulting noise was deafening. He intended only to poke his head inside the door to make sure that the ballroom was not being taken to pieces a bit at a time.

In the event he stayed. Cora's four descended upon him just as if he had a giant child magnet pinned to his chest. Then Cora herself called to him and asked if he would head one of the four race teams with Gabriel, Hartley, and Francis. Then he spotted Priscilla Stapleton and his wife playing a game in a circle with the younger children. And finally he noticed that the person seated at the pianoforte ready to play the music for the game was Sir Gerald Stapleton.

It was his wife who kept him lingering in the ballroom even after he had served his sentence as race-team leader. Children always seemed the key to breaking through all her masks to the warm, vibrant, fun-loving woman she so obviously was. Perhaps she did not know it yet and perhaps she would resist it even when she did—but she was going to be a perfectly wonderful mother. Her resistance was understandable, of course. She had convinced herself that her stepson was a child when she had tried to corrupt him. And so she feared her effect on children.

But her effect was quite benevolent. The Greenwalds' Stephen adored her—she came third in his affections, behind only his mama and papa.

Edgar had decided to enjoy Christmas, to relax and let go of all his worries. He had decided not to try to control events or people any longer—not in his personal life, anyway. He had married Helena and he loved her. He had discovered her darkest secrets and had made an effort to give her the chance to put right what had happened in the past. She had not entirely spurned his efforts—she had been remarkably kind to Priscilla and to the child. She had been civil to Gerald. But she had not reacted quite as Edgar had hoped she would.

He could do no more. Or rather, he *would* do no more. The rest was up to her. If she chose to live in the hell of her own making she had inhabited for thirteen years, then so be it. He must allow it. He must allow her the freedom she craved and the freedom he knew was necessary in any relationship in which he engaged.

He was going to enjoy Christmas. It was certainly not difficult to do. Apart from the basic joyfulness of the day and its activities, there had been the happy—or potentially happy—outcome of his scheme to bring Fanny Grainger and Jack Sperling together. And there was more. His father had made several appearances at the children's party and had been mobbed each time. On his final appearance, just as the party was coming to an end, he invited Edgar and Helena, Cora and Francis to his private sitting room.

"After all," he said as they made their way there, "a man is entitled to snatch a half hour of Christmas Day to spend just with his very nearest and dearest."

But there was someone else in the sitting room when they arrived there. Edgar suppressed a smile. They would have to have been blind and foolish during the past week not to have guessed that some such thing was in the works.

Mrs. Cross smiled at them, but she looked a little less placid than her usual self. She looked very slightly anxious.

Mr. Downes cleared his throat after tea had been poured and they had all made bright, self-conscious conversation for a few minutes. "Edgar, Cora," he began, "you are my children and of course will inherit my fortune after my time. Edgar will inherit Mobley, but I have seen to it that Cora will receive almost as much since it seems unfair to me that my daughter should be treated with less favor than my son. You are wealthy in your own right, Edgar, as you are in yours, Francis. It would seem to me, therefore, that perhaps neither of my children would be too upset to find that they will receive a little less than they have always expected."

"Papa," Cora said, "I have never *seen* you so embarrassed. Why do you not simply say what you brought us here to say?"

"My love," Francis said, "you cannot know how difficult it is for a man to say such a thing. You ladies have no idea."

Helena was smiling at her aunt, who was attempting to remove a particularly stubborn—and invisible—speck of lint from her skirt.

"Neither Cora nor I covet your property or your wealth, Papa," Edgar said. "We love *you*. We would rather have you with us forever. Certainly while we do have you, we want nothing more than your happiness. Do we, Corey?"

"How foolish," she said, "that I am even called upon to answer that. Papa! Could you ever have doubted it?"

"No." Their father actually look sheepish. "I loved your mother dearly. I want all here present to know that and not to doubt it for a moment."

There was a chorus of protests.

"Your children never have, Joseph," Mrs. Cross said, looking up at last. "Of course, they never have. Neither have I. You loved Mrs. Downes just as I loved Mr. Cross."

Mr. Downes cleared his throat again. "This may come as a great surprise—" he began, but he was halted by another cry—of hilarity this time. He frowned. "Mrs. Letitia Cross has done me the great honor of accepting my hand in marriage," he said with an admirable attempt at dignity.

There was a great clamor then, just as if they really had all been taken by surprise. Cora was crying and demanding a handkerchief of Francis, who was busy shaking his father-in-law's hand. Helena was hugging her aunt tightly and shedding a tear or two of her own. Edgar waited his turn, wondering that it had never happened before. His father, with a huge heart and a universe of love to give, had mourned his wife for almost thirty years and lavished all his love on his children. But they were both wed now and paternal love was not enough to satisfy a man's heart for a leftover lifetime.

Mrs. Cross was a fortunate lady. But then, Edgar thought, his father was probably a fortunate man, too.

His father turned to him, damp-eyed—and frowning ferociously. Edgar caught him in a bear hug.

$\mathscr{H}$ELENA HAD WORN HER SCARLET GOWN TO THE Christmas ball. It was perhaps a little daring for an entertainment in a country home, especially when she was a matron of six-and-thirty. More especially when she was fast losing her waistline. But it was not indecent—and the soft folds of the high-waisted skirt hid the slight bulge of her pregnancy—and it suited her mood. She felt brightly festive.

And desperately unwilling for the day to be over. It almost was. It was already late in the evening, after supper.

Tomorrow Christmas would linger, but in all essentials it would be over. Just as it always was. The great myth lifted one's spirits only to dash them afterward even lower than they had been before. She had feared it this year and sworn to resist it, but she had given in to it. Christmas!

But having given in, she would take from the celebrations all she could. And give, too. That was an essential part of it, the giving. And it was that she had shunned as much as the taking—more. She was terrified of giving. Once upon a time she believed she had had a generous spirit. Despite the disappointment of a lost love at the age of nineteen, she had put a great deal into her marriage with Christian. She might have settled into unhappiness and bitterness and revulsion, but she had not done so. She had set out to make him happy and had succeeded, God help her. But she had focused the largest measure of her generosity and the sympathy of her loving heart on Gerald. She had tried to help him overcome the setbacks of his mother's desertion and his father's dislike. She had tried to help him gain confidence in himself, to realize that he was a boy worthy of respect and love.

And then she had destroyed him.

But not forever. She had perhaps overestimated her own importance. She had harmed him. She had made him suffer, perhaps for a long time. But he had recovered. And she dared to believe that he was now happy. He was still gentle, quiet Gerald, but he was at peace with himself. She did not know all the circumstances surrounding his strange marriage, but there was no doubt of the fact that he and Priscilla were devoted to each other and suited each other perfectly. And their son, little Peter, was a darling. Today there was an extra glow of happiness about all three of them. Peter must have been starved for the company of other children. He had steadfastly made up for lost time. Priscilla had been accepted at Mobley just as if she had never been anything but a lady. Helena guessed that her happiness was as much for Gerald's sake as her own. He would no longer feel that he must absent himself from society for her sake. And Gerald's happiness doubtless had a similar unselfish cause. His wife need no longer hide away from the company of her peers.

Helena watched them dance a cotillion as she danced with her father-in-law. Though they were not the only ones she watched. There were Edgar and her aunt—dear Letty. She was quietly contented. She would have a home of her own again at last and a husband who was clearly very fond indeed of her—as she was of him. And never again would she find herself in the position of being dependent upon relatives.

If she had not married Edgar, Helena thought, her aunt would not have met Mr. Downes and would never have found this new happiness. Neither would he. If she had not married Edgar, Fanny Grainger would not now be dancing with Jack Sperling and looking as glowingly happy as if she expected her nuptials within the month. She would instead be dancing with Edgar and wearing forced smiles. If Helena had not married Edgar, Gerald and Priscilla would be at Brookhurst, alone with their son, trying to convince themselves that they were utterly happy.

Really, when she thought about it, very cautiously, so that she would not jump to the wrong conclusions, nothing very disastrous had happened lately for which she could blame herself. Except that she had forced Edgar into marrying her—though he was the one who had done the actual forcing. He did not seem wildly unhappy. He claimed to love her. He had said so several times. She had refused to hear, refused to react.

She had been afraid to believe it. She had been afraid it was true.

It was as if a door had been held wide for her for several days now, a door beyond which were bright sunlight and birdsong and the perfumes of a thousand flowers. All she had to do was step outside and the door would close forever on the darkness from which she had emerged. But she had been afraid to take that single step. If she did, perhaps she would find storm clouds blocking out the sunlight and silencing the singing and stifling the perfumes. Perhaps she would spoil it all.

But she had not spoiled anything yet this Christmas. Perhaps she should dare. Perhaps she could take that step. If all turned to disaster, then she could only find herself back where she expected to be anyway. What was there to lose?

It seemed suddenly that there was a great deal to lose. The cotillion had ended and her father-in-law was kissing her hand and Edgar was smiling and bending his head to hear something Letty was saying to him. Cora was laughing loudly over something with one of Edgar's friends, and Francis was smiling in some amusement at the sound. The Duke of Bridgwater was joining Gerald and Priscilla—and addressing himself to Priscilla. He must be asking her for the next set. The smell of the pine boughs and the holly with which the ballroom was festooned outdid the smells of the various perfumes worn by the guests. There was a very strong feeling of Christmas.

Oh, yes, there was a great deal to lose. But the sunlight and the birdsong and the flowers beckoned. Edgar was coming toward her. The next set was to be a waltz. She longed to dance it with him. But not this one, she decided suddenly. Not yet. Later she would waltz with him if there was another before the ball ended. She turned and hurried away without looking at him, so that he would think she had not seen him.

"The next is to be a waltz," she said unnecessarily as she joined the duke and Gerald and Priscilla.

"Yes, indeed," his grace said. "Lady Stapleton has agreed to dance it with me."

It seemed strange to hear another woman called that, to realize that the name was no longer hers. She was not sorry, Helena thought. *Mrs. Downes* sounded a great deal more prosaic than *Lady Stapleton*, but the name seemed somehow to give her a new identity, a new chance.

"Splendid," she said. "Then you must dance it with me, Gerald. It would never do for you to be a wallflower."

He looked at her in some surprise, but she linked her arm through his and smiled dazzlingly at him. They had not avoided each other since that first meeting in the library the day before, but they had not sought each other out either.

"It would be my pleasure, Helena," he said.

And so they waltzed together, smiling and silent for a few minutes.

"I am glad we came," he said stiffly after a while. "Mr. Downes and your husband have been extraordinarily kind to Priss and to me. So has everyone else. And Peter is ecstatic."

"I am glad," she said. She was aware that she wore her mocking smile. It was something to which she clung almost in terror. But it was something that must go. She stopped smiling. "I really am glad, Gerald. She is charming and delightful. You have made a wonderful match."

"Yes," he said. "And I might say the same of you, Helena. He is a man of character."

"Yes." She smiled at him and this time it was a real smile. He smiled back.

"Gerald." She was alarmed to find her vision blurring. She blinked her eyes firmly. "Gerald, I am so very sorry. I have never been able to say it because I thought my sin unforgivable. I thought its effects permanent and irreversible. I was wrong. I was, was I not? It is not a meaningless indulgence to say I am sorry?"

"It never was," he said. "It never is, Helena. There is nothing beyond forgiveness—even when the effects are irreversible. We all do terrible things. All of us. For a long time before our marriage I treated Priss as if the label of her profession was the sum total of her character. If that is not an apparently unforgivable sin, I do not know what is. I had to lose her before I realized what a precious jewel had been within my grasp. You do not have a monopoly on dastardly deeds."

"If I had asked forgiveness at your father's funeral," she asked him, "would you have forgiven me, Gerald?" Had she been responsible, too, for all the wasted years?

He did not answer for a while. He took her into an intricate twirl about one corner of the dance floor. "I do not know," he said at last. "Perhaps not. I felt terribly betrayed, the more so because I had loved you more than I had loved anyone else in my life since my mother. But in time I believe it would have helped to know that at least you had a conscience, that you regretted what had happened. Until a few days ago I assumed that you felt no guilt at all—though Priss has always maintained that you must. Priss has the gift of putting herself into other people's souls and understanding what must be going on deep within them even when the outer person shows no sign of it. And she did not even know you."

"I am hoping," she said, "that I can have the honor of a close friendship with my stepdaughter-in-law. If you can say again what you said yesterday, Gerald, and mean it. Can you forgive me? Will you?"

He smiled at her, all the warm affection and trust she had used to see in his face there again. "Priss was right," he said. "She so often is. The one flaw to my peace of mind has been my enduring resentment of you. I have accepted my father for what he was and am no longer hurt by the memory of his dislike. I like the person I am, even though I am not the person he would have had me be. And I have the memory of my mother back. She did not desert me, Helena. She was banished—by my father—and forbidden to see me or communicate with me in any way. I visited my aunts and found out the truth from them."

"Oh, Gerald—" Helena said, feeling all the old pain for his brokenness.

"Sometime," he said, "perhaps I could tell you the whole story. It brought pain. It also brought ultimate peace. She loved me. And you loved me. I have thought about it during the past few days and have realized that it is true. You were very good to me—and not for ulterior motives as I have thought since. You did not plot. You were merely—young and lonely. But even if all my worst fears had been correct, Helena—about my mother, about you—they would not be an excuse for the failed, miserable life to which you thought you had doomed me. I am an individual with a mind and a will of my own. We all have to live life with the cards that have been dealt us. We all—most of us—have the chance to make of life what we will. You would not have been responsible for my failed life—I would have been."

"You are generous," she said.

"No." He shook his head. "Just reaching the age of maturity, I hope. Have you really denied yourself happiness for thirteen years, Helena?"

"I did not deserve it," she said.

"You deserve it now." He twirled her again. "And happiness is yours for the taking, is it not? I believe he is fond of you, Helena. I do not wish to divulge any secrets, but you must know anyway. He told Priss and me when he came to Brookhurst that he loves you. We have both seen since coming here that it is true. He is the man for you, you know. He is strong and assertive and yet sensitive and loving. It is quite a combination. You must be happy to be having a child. I remember how you used to share your disappointments with me when you were first married—because you felt you could not talk to my father on such a topic, you said. How you longed for a child! And how good you were with the children you encountered—myself included."

"I have been afraid of being a mother," she told him.

"Do not be." Their roles had been reversed, she realized suddenly. He was the comforter, the reassurer, the one to convince her that she was capable of love and worthy of love. "All the little children here adore you, Helena, including Peter, who is shy of almost all adults except Priss and me. He fought with the rest of the children this afternoon to be the one to hold your hand in their circle games. You will be a wonderful mother."

"I am so old," she said, pulling a face.

"God—or nature if you will—does not make mistakes," he said. "If you are able to be a mother at your age, then you are not too old to be a mother. Enjoy it. Parenthood is wonderful, Helena. Exhausting and terrifying and wonderful. Like life."

"Gerald," she said. But there was nothing more to say. Some feelings were quite beyond words. And hers at this particular moment ran far too deep even for tears. "Oh, Gerald."

He smiled.

"YOU WANT TO DO *what*?"

Edgar bent his head closer to his wife's, though he had heard her perfectly clearly. The ball was over, the guests who were not staying at the house had all left, the house guests had begun to drift away to bed, the servants had been instructed to leave the clearing away until morning. And he was eager to get to bed. Helena had glowed all evening—especially after the waltz which he had wanted, but which she had danced with her stepson. She looked more beautiful even than usual. Edgar was feeling decidedly amorous.

"I want to go skating," she told him again.

"Skating," he said. "At one o'clock in the morning. After a dizzyingly busy day. With a mile to walk to the lake and a mile back. In arctically cold weather. When you are pregnant. Are you mad?"

"Edgar," she said, "don't be tiresome. It is so bourgeois

to feel that one must go to bed merely because it is late and one has had a busy day and it is cold outside."

"Bourgeois," he said. "I would substitute the word *sane*."

But she whirled about and with a single clap of the hands and a raising of arms she had everyone's attention.

"It is Christmas," she said, "and a beautiful night. The ball is over but the night is not. And Christmas is not. Edgar and I are going skating. Who else wants to come?"

Everyone looked as stunned as Edgar had felt when she first mentioned such madness. But within moments he could see the attraction of the idea take hold just as it was doing with him. The young people were almost instantly enthusiastic, and then a few of the older couples looked at each other doubtfully, sheepishly, inquiringly.

"That is one of the best ideas I have heard today, Daughter," Mr. Downes said, rubbing his hands together. "Letitia, my dear, how do you fancy the thought of a walk to the lake?"

"I fancy it very well, Joseph," Mrs. Cross replied placidly. "But I hope not just a walk. I have not skated in years. I have an inclination to do so again."

And that was that. They were going, a large party of them, with only a few older couples wise enough to resist the prevailing madness. At one o'clock in the morning they were going skating!

"You see, Edgar?" his wife said. "Everyone is not as tiresome and as staid as you."

"Or as bourgeois," he said. "I should not allow you to skate, Helena, or to exert yourself any more today. You are with child. Can you even skate?"

"Darling," she said, "I have spent winters in Vienna. What do you think I did for entertainment? Of course, I skate. Do you want me to teach you?"

Darling?

"I shall escort you upstairs," he said, offering his arm. "You will change into something *warm*. We will walk to the lake at a sedate pace and you will skate *for a short while* with my support. You are not to put your health at greater risk than that. Do you understand me, Helena? I must be mad, too, to give in to such a whim."

"I said I would lead you a merry dance, Edgar," she said, smiling brightly at him. "The word *merry* was the key one." She slipped her arm through his. "I will not risk the safety of your heir, never fear. He—or she—is more important to me than almost anything else in my life. But I am not yet willing to let go of Christmas. Perhaps I never will. I will carry Christmas about with me every day for the rest of my life, a sprig of holly behind one ear, mistletoe behind the other."

She was in a strange mood. He was not sure what to make of it. The only thing he could do for the time being was go along with it. And there *was* something strangely alluring about the prospect of going skating on a lake one mile distant at something after one o'clock of a December morning.

"The holly would be decidedly uncomfortable," he said.

"You are such a realist, darling," she said. "But you could kiss me beneath the other ear whenever you wished without fear that I might protest."

He chuckled. *Darling* again? Yes, life with Helena really was going to be interesting. Not that there was just the future tense involved. It *was* interesting.

SHE HAD MARRIED a tyrant, Helena thought cheerfully—she had told him so, too. The surface of the ice was, of course, marred by an overall powdering of snow which had blown across it since it had last been skated upon. And in a few places there were thicker finger drifts. It took several of the men ten minutes to sweep it clean again while everyone else cheered them on and kept as warm as it was possible to keep at almost two o'clock on a winter's night.

Edgar had flatly refused to allow Helena to wield one of the brooms. He had even threatened, in the hearing of his father and everyone else present, to sling her over his shoulder and carry her back to the house if she cared to continue arguing with him. She had smiled sweetly and called him a tyrant—in the hearing of his father and everyone else.

And then, as if that were not bad enough, he had taken her arm firmly through his when they took to the ice, and skated with her about the perimeter of the cleared ice just as if they were a sedate middle-aged couple. That they were precisely that made no difference at all to her accusation of tyranny.

"I suppose," he said when she protested, "that you wish to execute some dizzying twirls and death-defying leaps for our edification."

"Well, I did wish to *skate,* Edgar," she told him.

"You may do so next year," he told her, "when the babe is warm in his cot at home and safe from his mother's recklessness."

"Or hers," she said.

"Or hers."

"Edgar," she asked him, "is it horridly vulgar to be increasing at my age?"

"Horridly," he said.

"I am going to be embarrassingly large within the next few months," she said. "I have already misplaced my waist somewhere."

"I had noticed," he said.

"And doubtless think I look like a pudding," she said.

"Actually," he said, "I think you look rather beautiful and will look more so the larger you grow."

"I do not normally look beautiful, then?" she asked.

"Helena." He drew her to a stop, and four couples immediately zoomed past them. "If you are trying to quarrel with me again, desist. One of these days I shall oblige you. I promise. It is inevitable that we have a few corkers of quarrels down the years. But not today. Not tonight."

"Hmm." She sighed. "Damn you, Edgar. How tiresome you are."

"Guilty," he said. "And bourgeois and tyrannical. And in love with you."

This time she heard and paid attention. This time she dared to consider that perhaps it was true. And that perhaps it was time to respond in kind. But she could not say it just like that. It was something that had to be approached with tortuous care, something to be crept up on and leapt on unawares so that the words would come out almost of their own volition. Besides, she was terrified. Her legs felt like jelly and she was breathless. It was not the walk or the skating that had done it. She was not that unfit.

"If we are not to skate even at a snail's pace, Edgar," she said, "perhaps we should retire from the ice altogether."

"I'll take you home," he said. "You must be tired."

"I do not want to go home," she said, looking up to see that the stars were no longer visible. Clouds had moved over. "We are going to have fresh snow. Tomorrow we will probably be housebound. Let us find a tree behind which we can be somewhat private. I want to kiss you. Quite wickedly."

He laughed. "Why waste a lascivious kiss against a tree," he asked, "when we would be only *somewhat* private? Why not go back home where we can make use of a perfectly comfortable and entirely private bed—and do more than just kiss?"

"Because I want to be kissed *now*," she said, wrestling her arm free of his grip and taking him by the hand. She began to skate across the center of the ice's surface in the direction of the bank. "And because I may lose my courage during the walk back to the house."

"Courage?" he said.

But she would say no more. They narrowly missed colliding with Letty and her father-in-law. They removed their skates on the bank. They almost chose a tree that was already occupied—by Fanny Grainger and Jack Sperling. They finally found one with a lovely broad trunk against which she could lean. She set her arms about him and lifted her face to his.

"You are quite mad," he told her.

"Are you glad?" she whispered, her lips brushing his. "Tell me you are glad."

"I am glad," he said.

"Edgar," she said, "he has forgiven me."

"Yes, love," he said, "I know."

"I have loved during this Christmas season and have been loved," she said, "and I have brought disaster on no one."

"No," he said, and she could see the flash of his teeth in the near darkness as he smiled. "Not unless everyone comes down with a chill tomorrow."

"What a horrid threat," she said. "It is just what I might expect of you."

He kissed her—hard and long. And then more softly and long, his tongue stroking into her mouth and creating a definite heat to combat the chill of the night.

"You have brought happiness to a large number of people," he said at last. "You are genuinely loved. Especially by me. I do not want to burden you with the knowledge, Helena, and you need never worry about feeling less strongly yourself, but I love you more than I thought it possible to love any woman. I do not regret what happened. I do not regret marrying you. I do not care if you lead me a merry dance, though I hope it will always be as merry as this particular one. I only care that you are mine, that I am the man honored to be your husband for as long as we both live. There. I will not say it again. You must not be distressed."

"Damn you, Edgar," she said. "If you maintain a stoic silence on the subject for even one week I shall lead you the *un*merriest dance you could ever imagine."

He kissed her softly again.

"Edgar." She kept her eyes closed when the kiss ended. "I have lied to you."

He sighed and set his forehead against hers for a moment. "I thought we came here to kiss wickedly," he said.

"Apart from Christian," she said, "I have never been with any man but you."

"What?" His voice was puzzled. She did not open her eyes to see his expression.

"But I could not *tell* you that," she said. "You would have thought you were *special* to me. You would have thought me—*vulnerable*."

"Helena," he said softly.

"You were," she said. "I was. You are. I am. Damn you, Edgar," she said crossly, "I thought it was *men* who were supposed to find this difficult to say."

"Say what?" She could see when she dared to peep that he was smiling again—grinning actually. He knew very well what she could not say and the knowledge was making him cocky.

"I-love-you." She said it fast, her eyes closed. There. It had not been so difficult to say after all. And then she heard a loud, inelegant sob and realized with some horror that it had come from her.

"I love you," she wailed as his arms came about her

like iron bands and she collided full length with his massive body. "I love you. Damn you, Edgar. I love you."

"Yes, love," he said soothingly against one of her ears. "Yes, love."

"I love you."

"Yes, love."

"What a tedious conversation."

"Yes, love."

She was snickering and snorting against his shoulder then, and he was chuckling enough to shake as he held her.

"Well, I do," she accused him.

"I know."

"And you have nothing better to say than that?"

"Nothing *better*," he said, putting a little distance between them from the waist up. "Except a tentative, tiresome, bourgeois suggestion that perhaps it is time to retire to our bed."

"Tiresome and bourgeois suddenly sound like very desirable things," she said.

They smiled slowly at each other and could seem to find nothing better or more satisfying to do for the space of a whole minute or so.

"What are we waiting for?" she asked eventually.

"For you to lead the way," he said. "You will start damning me or otherwise insulting me if I decide to play lord and master."

"Oh, Edgar," she said, taking his arm. "Let us go *together*, shall we? To the house and to bed? Let us make love together—to each other. Whose silly idea was it to come out here anyway?"

"I would not touch that question with a thirty-foot pole," he said.

"Wise man, darling." She nestled her head against his shoulder as they walked.

Epilogue

CORA HAD COME HURTLING DOWN TO THE DRAWING room of the Bristol house, in her usual undignified manner. But she had said only that all was well and that Edgar must go up immediately. When Francis had raised his eyebrows in expectation of more information and Mr. Downes had openly asked for it, she had smiled dazzlingly and asked her brother if he was about to faint.

He had stridden from the room without further ado and taken the stairs to the bedchamber two at a time— even though there *was* a strange buzzing in his head and the air in his nostrils felt cold.

All is well, Cora had said.

His father's new wife came bustling toward him when he opened the bedchamber door, the doctor at her heels, bag in hand. Letty beamed at him and stood on her toes to kiss his cheek; the doctor bowed and made his exit with her.

Edgar was left alone. Though not quite alone. Helena was lying on the bed, pale and silent, her eyes closed. Beyond her was a small bundle that had him swallowing convulsively. It was moving and making soft fussing noises. But it was not his main concern. She looked too still and too pale for all to be well—and she had labored for all of fourteen hours. He took a few fearful steps toward the bed. Was it possible that she was . . .

"Damn you, Edgar," she said without opening her eyes. Her voice sounded strangely normal. "If I had known—though I might have guessed, of course—that you would beget such large children, I would not in a million years have seduced you."

He could feel no amusement. Only relief—and guilt. It had been unbearably hard to pace downstairs, his father and Francis in tow, for fourteen hours. What must it have been like . . .

"You had a hard time," he told her just as if she did not know it for herself. "I am so sorry, Helena. I wish I could have suffered the pain for you."

She opened her eyes and looked up at him. "He well nigh tore me apart," she told him.

He winced even as one of her words caught him like a blow low in his stomach. *"He?"* He swallowed again. "We have a son, Helena?" Not that the gender mattered. He had rather hoped for a daughter. What he really meant was—*we have a child, Helena?* Fruit of his body and hers? Product of their love? Their very own baby? The miracle of it all left him feeling paralyzed.

"Are you pleased that I have done my duty like a good wife?" she asked him. "I have presented you with an heir for the Downes fortune."

"To hell with the Downes fortune," he said, forgetting himself in the emotion of the moment. "We have a child, my love. A baby."

She smiled fleetingly. He could see that she was desperate with weariness.

"Meet your son," she said, and she turned to draw back the blanket from the moving bundle. A red, wrinkled, ugly little face, its eyes gazing vacantly about it, was revealed to his view—for a moment. Then he lost sight of it.

"Foolish Edgar," his wife said. "How bourgeois to weep at sight of your newborn child. You are supposed to look closely for a moment to assure yourself that he has the requisite number of eyes, noses, and mouths, all in the appropriate places, and then you are supposed to return to your brandy and your dogs and your hunting."

"Am I?" She was lifting the bundle and then holding it up to him. He did not dare. He would drop it. How could human life be so small? "But I am bourgeois, Helena, and so I will cry at the sight of my son." He took the bundle gingerly into his own arms. It was warm and soft and alive.

"Is he not the most beautiful child ever born?" Her voice had lost its mocking tone.

"Yes." He lifted the bundle and set his lips lightly to the soft, warm cheek of his son. "At *least* the most beautiful. Thank you, my love." He reached over her to set the child back on the bed before he could drop it in his clumsiness. He smiled at her. "You must rest now."

"Oh, damn you," she said, lifting one hand to dash across her cheeks. "Now you have started me weeping. It is because I am tired after all that damnable *work*. I would not do it otherwise."

But she grabbed for him as he would have straightened up and moved away. She wrapped her arms tightly about his neck and hid her face against his neckcloth. "Edgar," she said fiercely, "we have a *child*. At the age of seven-and-thirty!"

"Yes." He kissed the top of her head. "And Priscilla and Gerald have a new daughter. A letter came just this morning. All is well, my love."

She said nothing, but she sighed aloud against him and relaxed. She had forgiven herself for the past, he knew, and had set up a close relationship with her former stepson and his wife. But a part of her would always yearn to know that they were eternally happy, that what she had done no longer had any negative effect on their lives.

"All is well," he whispered again.

And all *was* well, he thought as he kissed her, got up from the bed, and crossed quietly to the door. Their marriage, begun under such inauspicious circumstances, was bringing them more joy than they could possibly have expected; his father and Letty were contentedly married; Gerald and Priscilla were being accepted by society; the business was prospering; and he was a father.

He was a father!

"I love you, Edgar Downes," she said as his hand closed about the knob of the door. Her eyes were closed again, he saw. But there was a smile on her pale face. "And if I had everything to do over, I would seduce you again. I swear I would."

He grinned at her even though she did not open her eyes. "It *was* a night to remember," he said, "in more ways than one. But it can be repeated and will be. Not now. Not soon. But it will happen—with me as seducer. I owe it to you—and to myself. You have been given fair warning."

He could hear her chuckling softly as he let himself out of the room and shut the door behind him before going back downstairs to rejoice with his family.

He and Helena were parents. They had a child.

He took the stairs down two at a time.

Christmas Beau

1

*I*T FELT STRANGE TO BE DRESSING UP TO GO OUT again. And strange to be wearing a blue gown. She had gone straight from black to colors when her year of mourning had ended the week before, with no intermediate stages of gray or lavender.

Not only strange. It felt somehow wrong to be dressing to go out to enjoy herself with the children in bed in the nursery. Especially since she had during the past week denied them what might have brought them great pleasure. She had refused to go to Scotland with her parents in order to spend Christmas with her sister. The journey would be too tedious for the children, she had decided, especially Kate, who was scarcely three years old.

A whole month before that she had refused an invitation to spend Christmas with Andrew's family at Ammanlea, although there was the country estate for the children to run free on and several other children for them to play with. She had refused because she had always felt almost as if her identity was swallowed up by their large numbers. And because she did not particularly want any reminders of Andrew.

The thought brought further guilt. He had been her husband, after all, and father of her two children.

It seemed that they would be spending Christmas

alone together in London, the three of them, with Amy. It was a bleak prospect, though preferable to either of the two alternatives.

Blue. Judith Easton ran her hands lightly over the soft silk of her new evening gown and looked down at the flounces at the hem and the blue silk slippers beneath. Her favorite color. How very delightful it was to look down and not see unrelieved black. Even after a week the novelty of being out of mourning had not worn off.

Her fair hair had been looped down over her ears and dressed in ringlets at the back of her head. It was an elegant style, she thought, though perhaps she should be donning a turban as more in keeping with her age and widowed status.

She was twenty-six years old. Did she look it? she wondered, glancing in the mirror. She did not feel that old. Being back in London again and living in her parents' home while they were in Scotland, the years seemed to roll away. It did not seem as if almost eight years had passed since her come-out Season. Though there were two children in the nursery to prove that it was indeed so.

She turned from the mirror and picked up her cloak and fan. She did not want to think of her come-out Season. The memories made her shudder with shame and embarrassment. The only consolation had always been that she had escaped from a dreaded marriage. But then, the one that had replaced it had quickly brought disillusion and heartache.

She tiptoed into the nursery, but Rupert was sitting up in bed frowning over a book, and even Kate was still awake, her cheeks flushed, her dark eyes wide.

"Mama," she asked, her lower lip wobbling, "don't be gone long."

"By the time you wake in the morning," Judith said, bending over the child to kiss her, "I shall have been home a long time. Nurse will be close by. You have nothing to fear. And Aunt Amy will be in the house."

"Mr. Freeman will not still be here tomorrow, Mama, will he?" Rupert asked with a frown, looking at her over the top of his book.

"He is being obliging enough to escort me to Lady Clancy's this evening," Judith said, crossing to her son's bed and kissing the top of his head. "That is all."

"Good," Rupert said, ducking his head down behind his book again.

Claude Freeman was a former acquaintance of Andrew's, who had come to pay his respects to her when she came to London two months before and had called at regular intervals ever since. He was a large man with a pompous manner. Unfortunately, his overhearty efforts to befriend her children had met with no success.

"I must go," Judith said, straightening up and smiling at both children. "Mr. Freeman will be waiting downstairs for me. Sleep well."

"Mama," Kate said, "you look pretty."

Judith smiled and blew a kiss.

She still felt guilty as she went down the stairs. She and Andrew had lived in the country for all of their married life. The only social occasions she had known for several years had been the dinners and assemblies there, and they had not been numerous. Though it would be more accurate to say that *she* had lived in the country all that time. Andrew had frequently spent weeks and even months alone in town.

Claude was in the hallway, looking large and imposing in his evening cloak and silk hat. He looked even larger in comparison with Amy, who was tiny and birdlike. A battle with smallpox as a child had left her pale and undergrown, her complexion marred by a few pockmarks. She had been made for marriage and motherhood, Judith had always thought, but both had eluded her thanks to the cruelty of fate. She was Andrew's elder sister. Judith had invited her to live with them after his death since no one else in the family appeared to want her. Amy had accepted with unexpected eagerness.

"Judith," Amy said as Claude took her cloak from her hands and wrapped it about her shoulders, "how lovely you look again. Black is really not your color."

Nor was it Amy's. She did not need black to sap her of the last vestiges of color. Even her hair was a faded blond. Amy must be thirty-six years old, Judith thought. Time marched on.

"My sentiments exactly, Mrs. Easton," Claude said, standing back and making her an elegant bow. "I shall be the envy of the *ton* this evening."

Judith smiled. There was a definite excitement about going out again to a *ton* event, even if it was only a soirée and not a full ball. She had had a few invitations during the past month. She had chosen her first appearance with care.

Yes, there was a lifting of the spirits. There was no denying it. But there was also an apprehension that was making her stomach churn rather uncomfortably. She supposed that such a feeling was natural for someone returning to society after nearly eight years away. But there was more to it than that.

Would the old scandal be remembered? she wondered. Would she be snubbed? She did not really believe it would be quite as bad as that. Surely she would not have had any invitations at all if she were still considered to be in disgrace. And Claude would not be so eager to escort her if she was to be ostracized.

But there would doubtless be some who would remember that she had been formally betrothed for all of two months during the Season seven and a half years ago and that she had broken off that betrothal abruptly and without any public announcement—or any private explanation to her betrothed—in order to run off to the country to marry Andrew.

She had acted very badly. Even at the time, she had known that. But she had been so young, so terrified, so bewildered. She had found herself quite unable to face the consequences of her change of heart—no, there had been no change of heart since there had been no love or even affection involved in that betrothal. But however it was, she had been unable to do things properly. She had fled with her sister and her maid, leaving her parents to find the note she had left behind and to smooth things over as well as they were able before following along after her.

She smiled determinedly at Claude and took his arm. That was all eight years in the past, a girl's gaucherie. She was a different person now, with a different name. And she was about to begin her life without Andrew.

She was free. There was exhilaration in the thought.

"You are quite sure you will not come, too?" she asked Amy. It was a foolish question to ask when she was ready to step out the door, but it was not the first time she had asked.

"I have never attended a *ton* event, Judith," Amy said. "I would positively die and not know where to hide myself. You run along and have a lovely time. I shall stay here in case the children need me. And I shall imagine all the conquests you are making."

Judith laughed. "Good night, then," she said. "But one of these times I shall drag you out with me, Amy."

Her sister-in-law smiled, and looked wistful only as the door closed behind Judith and Mr. Freeman. How she sometimes wished . . . But she was far too old for such wishes. And she must count her blessings. At last she had a home where she felt wanted and useful. And she was in London, where she had always wanted to be.

Amy turned and climbed the stairs to her sitting room.

Judith's exhilaration continued. Lord and Lady Clancy received her graciously, and Claude took her about their drawing room on his arm until they stopped at a group where she found the conversation particularly interesting. Soon Claude had wandered off, and she felt as thoroughly comfortable as if she had never been away.

For perhaps the span of ten minutes, anyway.

At the end of that time, the lady standing next to Judith stood back with a smile to admit a new member to the group.

"Ah," she said, "so you did come after all, my lord. Do join us. You know everyone, of course. Except perhaps Mrs. Easton? The Marquess of Denbigh, ma'am."

Was it possible for one's stomach to perform a complete somersault? Judith wondered if her thoughts were capable of such coherence. Certainly it was possible for one's knees to be almost too weak to support one's person.

He had not changed, unless it was possible for him to look even harsher and more morose than he had looked eight years before. He was very tall, a good six inches taller than Andrew had been. He looked thin at first glance, but there was a breadth of chest and of shoulders that suggested fitness and strength. That had not changed with the years either, one glance told her.

His face was still narrow, angular, harsh, his lips thin, his eyes a steely gray, the eyelids drooped over them so that they might have looked sleepy had they not looked hawkish instead. His dark hair had the suggestion of gray at the temples. That was new. But he was only—what? Thirty-four? Thirty-five years old?

The sight of him and his proximity could still fill her with a quite unreasonable terror and revulsion. Unreasonable because he had never treated her harshly or with anything less than a perfectly correct courtesy. But then, there had never been any suggestion of warmth either.

She had always wanted to run a million miles whenever he came into a room. She wanted to run now. She wanted to run somewhere where there would be air to draw into her lungs.

"Mrs. Easton," he said in that unexpectedly soft voice she had forgotten until now. And he bowed stiffly to her.

"My lord." She curtsied.

"But of course they know each other," a gentleman in the group said with a booming laugh. "I do believe they were betrothed once upon a time. Is that not so, Max?"

"Yes," the Marquess of Denbigh said, those steely eyes boring through her, not the faintest hint of a smile on his face—but then she had never ever seen him smile. "A long time ago."

"I THINK NOT, Nora," the Marquess of Denbigh had said three evenings before the night of the soirée. He had called to pay his respects to the Clancys between acts at the theater.

"We scarcely see you in town, Max," Lady Clancy protested. "It must be two years at the very least since you were here last. And yet even when you are here, you refuse to go about. It is most provoking. I am considering disowning you as my cousin."

"Second cousin," he corrected, putting his quizzing glass to his eye and gazing lazily about the theater at all the boxes. "And I am here tonight, so I can hardly be accused of being a total recluse."

"But alone in your box," she said. "It is inhuman, Max. One word and you might have come with us. Are you sure you cannot be persuaded to come to my soirée? It would be a great coup for me. Word that you are in town has caused a considerable stir, you know. If you are intending to remain for the Season, you will be having a whole host of mamas sharpening their matchmaking skills again."

"They would be well advised to spend their energies on projects more likely to bring them success," he said, still perusing the other boxes through his glass.

"One wonders why you have come to town at all," she said rather crossly, "if not to mingle with society."

"I have to call on Weston among others," he said. "I have fears that after two years I may no longer be fashionable, Nora."

She made a sound that was perilously close to a snort. "What utter nonsense," she said. "You would look elegant dressed in a sack, Max. It is that presence you have. Are you looking for someone in particular?"

He dropped his quizzing glass unhurriedly and clasped his hands behind his back. "No," he said. "I was only marveling at how few faces I know."

"They would begin to look far more familiar if you would just do more with your invitations than drop them in a wastebasket," she said. "That is what you do with them, I presume?"

"Ah, not quite," he said. "But I do believe that is what my secretary does with them."

"It is most irritating," she said. "December is not a month when society abounds in London, Max. But it seems that there is no reasoning with you. There never was. And there—you have made me thoroughly cross when I am normally of quite sanguine disposition. You had better return to your box and be alone with yourself as you seem to wish to be. The next act must be due to begin."

Lord Clancy had turned from his conversation with a lady guest who shared his box. He laughed. "Nora has been quite determined to be the first and only hostess to lure you out this side of Christmas, Max," he said. "She has forgotten that since this morning there has been good reason for you not to come."

"Quite right. I had forgotten," Lady Clancy said, "though it all happened such a long time ago that I daresay it makes no difference to anyone now. Mrs. Easton sent an acceptance of her invitation this morning. Judith Easton, Max. Lord Blakeford's daughter."

"Yes," the marquess said, looking down into the pit of the theater, his hands still at his back, "I know who Mrs. Easton is."

"I thought she would have gone to Scotland with Blakeford and his wife," Lord Clancy said. "They have gone for Christmas, apparently. But she has stayed here. Nora sent her an invitation to her soirée. It is an unfortunate coincidence that she should be in town at the same time as you, Max. She has not been here for more years than you, I believe. In fact, I do not recall seeing her here since she ran off with Easton."

"That is all old news," Lady Clancy said briskly. "You had better take yourself off, Max. I am planning not to talk to you for a whole month if you will not come to my soirée—not that I am likely to see you in that time to display my displeasure to you, of course."

The Marquess of Denbigh sighed. "If it is so important to you, Nora," he said, "then I shall look in for half an hour or so. Will that satisfy you?"

She smiled and opened her fan. "It is amazing what a little coercion can accomplish," she said. "Yes, I am satisfied. Now, will you take a seat here, or are you planning to insist on returning to your own box?"

"I shall return to my own," he said, bowing to the occupants of the box.

But he did not return to his box. He left the theater and walked home, his carriage not having been directed to return for him until the end of the performance.

So she was coming out of hiding at last. She was going to be at Nora's. Well, then, he would see her there.

Eight years was a long time—or seven and a half to be more accurate. He supposed she would have changed. She had been eighteen then, fresh from the schoolroom, fresh from the country, shy, sweet, pretty—he never had been able to find the words to describe her as she had been then. Words made her sound uninteresting, no different from dozens of other young girls making their come-out. Judith Farrington had been different.

Or to him she had been different.

She would be twenty-six years old now. A woman. A widow. The mother of two young children. And her marriage could not have been a happy one—unless she had not known, of course. But how could a wife not know, even if she spent all of her married life in the country, that her husband lived a life of dissipation and debauchery?

She would be different now. She was bound to be.

He wanted to see the difference. He had waited for it a long time, especially since the death of her husband in a barroom brawl—that was what it had been, despite the official story that he had died in a skirmish with thieves.

He had waited. And come to London as soon as he knew that she was there. And waited again for her to begin to appear in public. And finally, it seemed, she was to appear at Nora's soirée.

He would be there, too. He had a score to settle with Judith Easton. Revenge to take. He had a great deal of leftover hatred to work out of his heart and his soul.

He had waited a long time for this.

His eyes found her immediately when he entered Lord Clancy's drawing room three evenings later. Indeed, he hardly needed the evidence of his eyes that she was there. There had always been something about her that appealed very strongly to a sixth sense in him.

"Come," Lady Clancy said, linking her arm through his and noting the direction of his gaze. "You do not need to be embarrassed by her presence, Max. I shall take you over to Lord Davenport's group. Caroline Reave is there, too. Conversation is never dull when she is part of it."

"Thank you, Nora," he said, resisting the pressure of her arm, "but I can find my own way about. I have not forgotten how to do it in two years away from town."

She shrugged and smiled. "I might have known that you would confront the situation head to head," she said. "Perhaps I should have warned Mrs. Easton as I warned you."

Ah, so she had not been warned, he thought as he strolled across the room toward the group of which she was a part.

Yes, she was different. She was slender still, but with a woman's figure, not a girl's. Her hair was more elegantly dressed, with ringlets only at the back, not clustered all over her head as they had used to be. She carried herself proudly. He had not yet seen her face.

And then Dorothy Hopkins saw him and stood aside to admit him to the group, and he was able to stand right beside her and turn and make his bow to her, since Dorothy seemed to have forgotten the old connection and mentioned her particularly by name.

"Mrs. Easton," he said.

It was impossible to know her reaction. She spoke to him and curtsied to him, but her expression was calm and unfathomable—as it had always been. He had not known at that time that she hid herself behind that calmness. Her flight with Easton had taken him totally by surprise, had shattered him utterly.

Yes, her face had changed, too. She had been pretty as

a girl, with all the freshness of youth and eagerness for an approaching womanhood. She was beautiful now, with some of the knowledge of life etching character into her face.

"A long time ago," he said in reply to a remark made by someone in the group.

He did not take his eyes off Judith Easton or particularly note the embarrassment of the other members of the group, who had just been reminded of their former connection. He hardly noticed that their embarrassment drew them a little away from the two of them, so that soon they were almost isolated.

She was not looking quite into his eyes, he saw, but at his chin, perhaps, or his neckcloth or his nose. But her chin was up, and there was that calmness about her. He had dreamed once of transforming that calmness into passion once they were married. He had not known that behind it she was totally indifferent to him, perhaps even hostile.

It had been an arranged match, of course, favored by his father and her parents. He had been a viscount at the time. He had not succeeded to his father's title until three years before. But she had shown no open reluctance to his proposal. He had attributed her quietness to shyness. He had dreamed of awakening her to womanhood. He had dreamed of putting an end to his own loneliness, his own inability to relate to women, except those of the wrong class. He had loved her quite totally and quite unreasonably from the first moment he set eyes on her.

They had been betrothed for two months before she abandoned him, without any warning whatsoever and no explanation. They were to have been married one month later.

"Eight years, I believe," he said to her.

It was seven years and seven months, to be exact. She

had been to the opera with him and two other couples. He had escorted her home, kissed her hand in the hallway of her father's house—he had never kissed more than her hand—and bidden her good night. That was the last he had seen of her until now.

"Yes," she said. "Almost."

"I must offer my belated condolences on your bereavement," he said.

"Thank you." She was twisting her glass around and around in her hands, the only sign that her calmness was something of a facade.

He made no attempt to continue the conversation. He wanted to see if there would be any other crack in her armor.

She continued to twist her glass, setting one palm against the base while she did so. She raised her eyes to his mouth, drew breath as if she would speak, but said nothing. She lifted her glass to her mouth to drink, though he did not believe her lips touched the liquid.

"Excuse me," she said finally. "Please excuse me."

It was only as his eyes followed her across the room that he realized that a great deal of attention was on them. She had probably realized it the whole time. That was good. He was not the least bit sorry. If she was embarrassed, good. It was a beginning.

He did not know quite when love had turned to hatred. Not for several months after her desertion, anyway. Disbelief had quickly turned to panic and a wild flight, first to the Lake District, and then to Scotland. Panic had turned to numbness, and numbness had finally given way to a deeply painful, almost debilitating heartbreak. For months he had dragged himself about on his walking tour, not wanting to get up in the mornings, not wanting to eat, not able to sleep, not wanting to live.

He had continued to get up in the mornings, he had

continued to eat, he had slept when exhaustion claimed him. And eventually he had persuaded himself to go on living. He had done it by bringing himself deliberately to hate her, to hate her heartlessness and her contempt for honor and decency.

And yet hatred could be as destructive as heartbreak. He had found himself after his return to London hungry for news of her, going out of his way to acquire it—not easily done when she never came to town. He had found himself viciously satisfied when it became evident that Easton was returning to his old ways. She had preferred Easton to him. Let her live with the consequences.

Finally he had had to take himself off to his estate in the country to begin a wholly new life for himself, to try to stop the bitterness and the hatred from consuming him and destroying his soul.

He had succeeded to a large extent. He had focused the love she had spurned on other persons. And yet always there was the hunger for news of her. The birth of her children. The death of her husband. Her return to London.

And overpowering all his resolves, all his common sense, the need to see her again, to avenge himself on her, to even the score. He had been horrified at himself when he had heard of her arrival in London and had realized the violence of his suppressed feelings. Despite the meaningfulness, the contentment of his new life, they had been there the whole time, the old feelings, and they had proved quite irresistible. They had driven him back to London to see her again.

The Marquess of Denbigh turned abruptly and left both the room and Lord Clancy's house.

2

THE WEATHER WAS BITTERLY COLD FOR DECEMBER. Although there had been only a few flurries of snow, there had been heavy frost several mornings and some icy fog. And it was said that the River Thames was frozen over, though Judith had not driven that way to see for herself.

One was tempted to huddle indoors in such weather, staying as close to the fire and as far from the doors as possible. But Judith had lived in the country for most of her life and loved the outdoors. Besides, she had two young and energetic children who needed to be taken beyond the confines of the house at least once a day. It had become their habit to take a walk in Hyde Park each afternoon. Amy usually accompanied them there.

"One stiffens up quite painfully and feels altogether out of sorts when one stays by the fire for two days in a row," Amy said. "So exercise it must be. Old age is creeping up on me, Judith, I swear. Although sometimes I declare it is galloping, not creeping at all. I had to pull a white hair from its root just this morning."

Amy was a favorite with Kate because she was always willing to listen gravely and attentively to the child's often incomprehensible prattling. She had always seemed to know what Kate was talking about, even in those earlier days when no one but Amy—and Judith, of course—had even believed that the child was talking English.

"I just wish," Judith said, her hands thrust deep inside a fur muff as they walked along one of the paths in the park two days after Lady Clancy's soirée, "that taking one's exercise was not so utterly uncomfortable sometimes. I would be convinced that I had dropped my nose somewhere along the way if I could not see it when I cross my eyes. It must be poppy red."

"To match your cheeks," Amy said. "You look quite as pretty as ever, Judith, have no fear."

"I just hope I will not have to appear at the Mumford ball tonight with ruddy cheeks and nose," Judith said. "Indeed, I wish I did not have to appear there at all. Or I wish you would come, too, Amy. Won't you?"

"Me?" Amy laughed. "Maurice once told me that I would be an embarrassment to gentlemen at a ball since I scarce reach above the waist of even the shortest of them. Henry agreed with him and so did Andrew. They made altogether too merry with the idea, but they were quite right. Besides, I am far too old to attend a ball in any function other than as a chaperone. And since you do not need a chaperone, Judith, I shall remain at home."

Judith felt her jaw tightening with anger. How could Amy have remained so cheerful all her life, considering the treatment she had always received from her family? They were ashamed of her, embarrassed by her. They had always liked to keep her at home, away from company, where she would not be seen.

Judith had tackled Andrew about it on one occasion, before she had learned that he did not have a heart at all. She had accused him and his brothers of cruelty for persuading Amy against attending a summer fair in a neighboring town.

"We have her best interests at heart," he had said.

"We don't want her hurt, Jude. She might as well stay with the family, where her appearance does not make any difference."

"Perhaps one day," she said now, "we can drive down to the river to see if it is true about the ice. Claude says that if it thickens any further there will be tents and booths set up right on the river and a frost fair. But I am sure he exaggerates."

"But how exciting it would be," Amy said. "Booths? To sell things, do you think, Judith? But of course they would if it is to be likened to a fair. Perhaps we can buy some Christmas gifts there. I have not bought any yet, and there are only three weeks to go."

Amy entered into the excitement of the prospect and pushed from her mind the mention of the ball. Balls were not for her. It was too late for her. There had been a time when she had dreamed of London and the Season and a come-out. It was true that her glass had always told her that she was small and plain, and of course she had those unfortunate pockmarks on her forehead and chin. But she had been a girl and she had dreamed.

Her father had never taken her to London. And finally it had dawned on her that he considered her unmarriageable. She had gradually accepted reality herself. She was an old maid and must remain so. She learned to take pleasure from other people's happiness and to love other people's children.

"Run along, by all means," she said when Kate tugged at her hand. "Aunt Amy is quite incapable of breaking into a run." She released her niece's hand and watched her race forward to join Rupert.

Judith watched the two children ahead of them. Rupert was a ship in full sail and was weaving and dipping about an imaginary ocean. Kate was hopping on first one leg and then the other.

It was hard to believe that Christmas was approaching.

There was no feel of it, no atmosphere to herald the season. Christmas had always been a well-celebrated occasion in her family, and for a moment she regretted having decided against the long journey to Scotland and her sister's family. It would have been good once they had arrived there.

And in Andrew's family, too, it was always a big occasion. It was traditional for the whole family to gather together at Ammanlea, and she had been expected to join them after her marriage and abandon her own family's traditions. She had always hated it. Almost the only activities had ever been card playing and heavy drinking.

Even last year. They had all been in deep mourning for Andrew and the nursery had been the only room in the house to be decorated. But the drinking and the card playing had gone on unabated despite the blackness and the gloom of all their clothing.

She had come almost to hate Christmas for seven years. "We must decorate the house," she said. "We must find a way of celebrating and making Christmas a joyous occasion for the children, Amy, even though there will be just the four of us and the servants." She looked at her sister-in-law with some concern. "Are you sure you do not want to go home, Amy? You have never been away at Christmas, have you?"

"I am sure." Amy smiled. "I will miss all the children. I must admit that. But there are some things I will not miss, Judith. It will be lovely to be quiet with you and Rupert and Kate. Yes, we will decorate the house and go to church and sing carols. Perhaps carolers will come to the house. Does that happen in London, I wonder? It would be very pleasant, would it not?"

Yes, it would be pleasant, Judith thought. Strangely, although the prospect of their very small gathering seemed somewhat bleak, she was looking forward to Christmas for the first time in many years.

Invitations continued to arrive at the house daily. She could if she wished, she knew, be very busy and very gay all over Christmas. And she was determined to go out, to meet society again, to enjoy herself, to feel young again, of some worth again. But not too much. She would not sacrifice her children's happiness at Christmas for her own. And she would not leave Amy at home night after night while she abandoned herself to a life of gaiety.

Besides, she was a little afraid to go out. In some ways she was dreading that evening's ball. Would he be there again? she wondered.

It was a question she tried not to ask herself. There was no way of knowing the answer until the evening came. And even if he were, she told herself, it would not matter. For that very awkward first meeting was over, and they had had nothing whatsoever to say to each other and would be at some pains to avoid each other forever after.

There was no reason for the sleeplessness and the vivid, bizarre dreams of the past two nights and the breathless feeling of something like terror whenever her thoughts touched on him.

It was all eight years in the past. They had grown up since then—though he, of course, had been her present age at the time it had happened. And they were civilized beings. There was no reason to wonder why he had made no effort to make conversation when they had been awkwardly stranded together at Lady Clancy's. It was merely that he was morose by nature, as he always had been. It was absurd to feel that she should have rushed into some explanation, some apology.

It had been a shock to realize that it had been the first time she had set eyes on him since that night of the opera when her flight with Andrew had already been planned for the following day. That night she had sat through the whole performance without once concentrating on it, anxious about the plans for the morrow, breathless with the knowledge that the viscount, seated slightly behind her in the box, had been watching her more than the performance with those hooded and steely eyes. And she remembered wondering if he suspected, if he would do something to foil her plans, something to force her into staying with him and marrying him after all.

"He is slowing down," Amy said, and Judith realized with a jolt that her sister-in-law had been commenting on the approach of a rider and expressing the hope that he would not gallop too close to the children.

And looking up, Judith felt that disconcerting somer-saulting of her stomach again. The rider, with a billow-ing black cloak, drew his equally black stallion to a halt, removed his beaver hat, and sketched them a bow.

"Mrs. Easton," the Marquess of Denbigh said. "Good afternoon to you."

She inclined her head. "Good afternoon, my lord," she said, expecting him to move on without further delay. She was surprised he had stopped at all.

He did not move on. He looked inquiringly at Amy.

"May I present my sister-in-law, Miss Easton, my lord?" she said. "The Marquess of Denbigh, Amy."

Amy smiled and curtsied as he made her a deeper bow than the one with which he had greeted Judith.

"I am pleased to make your acquaintance, my lord," Amy said.

"Likewise, ma'am," he said. "I did not know that your brother had any sisters."

"I have always lived in the country," Amy said. "But when Judith came to London and needed a companion, then I gladly agreed to accompany her. I have always wanted to see London."

"I hope you are having your wish granted, ma'am,"

he said. "You have visited the Tower and Westminster Abbey and St. Paul's? And the museum?"

"Westminster Abbey, yes," Amy said. "But we still have a great deal of exploring to do, don't we, Judith? We are going to drive down to the river tomorrow, or perhaps the day after since Judith is to attend a ball this evening and is likely to be late home. Have you heard that it is frozen over, my lord?"

"Indeed, yes," he said. "There is likely to be a fair in progress before the end of the week, or so I have heard."

"So it is not idle rumor," Amy said, smiling in satisfaction. "What do you think of that, Judith?"

Judith was not given a chance to express her opinion. The children had come running up, Kate to grasp her cloak and half hide behind the safety of its folds, Rupert to admire the marquess's horse.

"Will he kick if I pat his side, sir?" he asked. "He is a prime goer."

A prime goer! The phrase came straight from Maurice's vocabulary. It sounded strange coming from the mouth of a six-year-old child.

"Stand back, if you please, Rupert," she said firmly.

"He is a prime goer," the marquess agreed. "And I am afraid he is likely to kick, or at least to sidle restlessly away if you reach out to him in that timid manner and then snatch your hand away. You will convey your nervousness to him."

Rupert stepped back, snubbed.

"However, you may ride on his back, if you wish," the marquess said, "and show him that you are not at all afraid of him despite his great size."

Judith reached out a hand as Rupert's eyes grew as wide as saucers.

"Really, sir?" he asked. "Up in front of you?"

The marquess looked down at the boy without smiling

so that Judith felt herself inhaling and reaching down a hand to cover Kate's head protectively.

"I don't believe a big boy like you need ride in front of anyone," Lord Denbigh said. And he swung down from the saddle, dwarfing them all in the progress. He looked rather like a rider from hell, Judith thought, with his black cloak swinging down over the tops of his boots, and his immense height.

"I can ride in the saddle?" Rupert gazed worshipfully up at the marquess. "Uncle Maurice says I am a half pint and must not ride anything larger than a pony until I am ten or eleven."

"Perhaps Uncle Maurice was thinking of your riding alone," the marquess said. "It would indeed not be advisable at your age to ride a spirited horse on your own. I shall assist you, sir."

And he stooped down, lifted the boy into the saddle, kept one arm at the back of the saddle to catch him if he should begin to slide off, and handed the boy the reins with the other.

"Just a short distance," he said, "if your mama has no objection."

Judith said nothing.

"Oh, how splendid," Amy said. "How kind of you, my lord. I am sure you have made a friend for life."

They did not go far, merely along the path for a short distance and back again. Judith stood very still and watched tensely. Her son's auburn curls—he was very like Andrew—glowed in marked contrast to the blackness of the man who walked at the side of the horse. She was terrified for some unaccountable reason. It was not for her son's safety. The horse was walking at a quite sedate pace, and the man's arm was ready to save the child from any fall.

She did not know what terrified her.

"There," the marquess said, lifting Rupert down to

the ground again, "you will be a famous horseman when you grow up."

"Will I? Did you see, Mama?" Rupert screeched, his face alight with excitement and triumph. "I was riding him all alone."

"Yes." Judith smiled at him. "You were very clever, Rupert."

"Do you think so?" he asked. "Will I be able to have a horse this summer, Mama, instead of a stupid pony? I will be almost seven by then. Will you tell Uncle Maurice?"

She cupped his face briefly with her hands and looked up to thank the marquess. And then she froze in horror as she saw him looking down at a tiny auburn-haired little figure who was tugging at his cloak.

"Me, too," Kate was saying.

"No," Judith said sharply. And then, more calmly, "We have taken enough of his lordship's time, Kate. We must thank him and allow him to be on his way."

"Pegasus does not have a saddle for a lady," the marquess said. "But if you ask your mama and she says yes, I will take you up before me for a short distance."

"Please, Mama." Large brown eyes—also Andrew's—looked pleadingly up at her.

But was Kate not terrified of the man? Judith thought in wonder and panic. How could she bear the thought of being taken up before him on the great horse and led away from her mother and her aunt and brother? Kate was not normally the boldest of children.

"Very well," she said. She fixed her eyes on his chin. "If it is no great inconvenience to you, my lord."

He swung back up into the saddle again and reached down for the child, whom Judith lifted toward him. His hands touched her own briefly and she felt that she must surely suffocate. She stepped back as he settled Kate on the horse's back before him, and her daughter stared down at her with eyes that seemed as large as her face.

"How very kind of him," Amy said quietly as they rode away along the path. "There are not many gentlemen who would have such patience with children, Judith—including these children's own uncles."

"Yes," Judith said. "It is kind of him. And also unutterably embarrassing."

He took his leave of them and rode away as soon as he had returned with Kate and handed her down into Judith's waiting arms.

"What a very unfortunate meeting," she said when he had ridden out of earshot and the children's excitement had died down enough that they rushed ahead along the path again.

"Unfortunate?" Amy said. "Oh, no, Judith. You must not feel embarrassed. He was under no compulsion to be so kind to the children. But where did you make his acquaintance? At Lady Clancy's?"

"Yes," Judith said. "And before, Amy. He was—and I suppose still is—the Viscount Evendon."

"Evendon?" Amy was quiet for a moment. "The man to whom you were betrothed, Judith? Really? It is very good of him to be so civil, then." She stared back along the path at the disappearing figure of the marquess.

"Yes," Judith said.

And it was good of him. He had been remarkably civil to take such notice of her children. Why, then, did she feel frightened, almost as if he had attempted to kidnap them? Why did she not feel at all that an olive branch had been extended?

Was it just her guilt? Or was it something else?

IT HAD BEEN impossible to discover if she intended to go to the Mumford ball short of asking the question of

Mumford himself. And even he probably would not know since he had expressed a certain distaste for all the elaborate preparations Lady Mumford was making and a determination to stay within the safe walls of White's until he could stay there no longer.

The Marquess of Denbigh did not ask Mumford. He merely spent his days at White's and kept his ears open. It was amazing what gossip passed within the walls of the club. The story of his coming face-to-face with Judith Easton at Nora's had become common knowledge, of course. Some men avoided the topic in his presence, assuming that he would be embarrassed by a reminder of the way he had been jilted eight years before.

Fortunately, some gentlemen considered that he needed consoling.

"I hear you ran into Mrs. Easton at Clancy's," Bertie Levin said. "Unfortunate that, old chap."

The marquess shrugged. "Ancient history has no particular interest for me," he said.

"Too bad that you had to return at just the time when she is here," Bertie said. "Easton never brought her, you know."

"Is that so?" The marquess polished his quizzing glass.

"She might have interfered with his other pleasures," Bertie said with a chuckle.

"Yes," the marquess said. "They were well known."

"Though why he would want to get into the muslin company when he had such a looker for a wife eludes my understanding," Bertie said. "She is well rid of him, if you were to ask me."

"To be uncharitable," the marquess said, "I would have to say that perhaps the world is well rid of him."

"She don't go about much, by all accounts," Bertie said. "It was unfortunate that you ran into her at

Clancy's. Especially since you don't go about much yourself." He laughed heartily.

"Yes," Lord Denbigh said.

"She is a model mother, according to Freeman," Bertie said. "Cannot be pried from her children and all that. Walks them in the park every afternoon despite the weather. That would certainly not suit Freeman." He chuckled again. "At least you can be warned about that, Denbigh, and avoid the place."

"Yes," the marquess said, dropping his quizzing glass on its black ribbon. "Though ancient history, as I said before, does not excite me."

"Well," Bertie said, getting to his feet, "I never could understand why she dropped you for Easton, Denbigh. Most females would kill for a chance at you. Maybe money and titles and all that did not interest the chit. And Easton was a handsome devil, one must admit. I have to fetch my mother from my aunt's. She will shoot me with a dueling pistol if I am late."

The marquess inclined his head and watched Bertie leave the room. Then he consulted his watch. Scarcely past luncheon time. At what time during the afternoons? he wondered. Early or late? He supposed that the only way he would find out was to ride to the park himself both early and late. He got to his feet.

He was fortunate enough not to have to ride there for longer than an hour. Obviously, early afternoon was the time for their walk. Four of them. Judith Easton herself, the two children, who both resembled Easton to a remarkable degree, and the little bird of a woman who was introduced to him as Easton's sister.

He rode away after giving each of the children a brief ride, well satisfied with the encounter. He knew now for certain that she was indeed planning to attend the Mumford ball. And he knew something else, too, something about her children and something about her sister-in-law.

And something about her, too. Clearly, her children were everything in the world to her.

Perhaps he could make something of those facts. The desire for revenge had burned in him with increased fervor since he had seen her again at Nora's.

Since the park was empty at that time of the day and of the year, he increased his horse's speed to a canter. Fortunately, he would not have to sit around any longer, wondering how he was to come upon her again. He would see her again that evening.

He could scarcely wait for the hours to pass.

THE MUMFORD BALL was not what might be called a great squeeze—not of the kind, anyway, that Judith had known in her come-out Season. But then, as Lady Mumford explained to her almost apologetically before the dancing began, it was the wrong time of year for grand *ton* events. Even those people who spent the winter in town were beginning to take themselves off for Christmas parties in the country.

Judith did not lament the lack of crowds. There were quite enough guests present to make it a pleasant occasion. Claude led her into the opening quadrille, and Lord Clancy was waiting to dance with her the set of country dances that followed.

And he was not there, she thought with some relief as the second set began. The Marquess of Denbigh was not there. Perhaps it was as well that Amy had mentioned her own plans in his hearing that afternoon, though she had been alarmed at the time. If he had intended to come, surely he would have changed his mind after that.

But her early pleasure in the evening dissipated

halfway through the second set while she was laughing at something Lord Clancy said as he twirled her down the set.

He was standing alone in the doorway of the ball-room, dressed in black evening clothes and immaculately white linen and lace. He was the only gentleman clad in black. He looked more than ever like a hawk or some other bird of prey.

He would be as intent on ignoring her, she told herself as another gentleman twirled her back down the set, as she would be on ignoring him. She was not going to let him spoil her evening. She looked very deliberately across the ballroom at him just to prove her theory to herself.

He was staring back, his eyes hooded and intent.

She whisked her eyes away from him and made some remark to Lord Clancy and smiled broadly at him. And she kept her attention on the dance for all of five more minutes without giving in to the urge to look back to the doorway.

He would have moved away from there, she persuaded herself at last. He would have found a group of people with whom to converse. She turned her head to look.

He stood in exactly the same place. And he was still looking steadily at her.

By the time the set came to an end almost ten minutes later, Judith felt quite unnerved. She could not walk without feeling that her movements were jerky. She could not smile without feeling as if she were behaving artificially. She could not laugh without hearing the trill of her own voice. And she could not talk without losing the trend of her own words or listen without suddenly realizing that she was not hearing a word.

And each time she turned her head, sometimes deliberately, sometimes under the pretense of looking elsewhere close by, he was standing in the same place. Lady Mumford joined him there, but still he looked quite steadily at her, Judith found.

She had not realized that the ballroom was quite so hot and stuffy.

3

She was wearing an apricot-colored gown of simple but elegant design. It was neither too low nor too high at the bosom, and it was fashionably high-waisted, falling in soft folds to the scalloped hemline. She wore white lace gloves and white slippers. Her hair was dressed as it had been at the soirée.

She looked beautiful, as she had looked in the park that afternoon with reddened cheeks and nose and hair somewhat windblown beneath her bonnet.

The Marquess of Denbigh stood in the doorway of Lord Mumford's ballroom looking at her. If she had been grief-stricken at the death of her husband, then she had recovered her spirits in the year since. She was laughing quite merrily.

He watched her until he knew she was aware of his presence. And then he continued to watch her, knowing that his gaze would disconcert her. He knew that even when she was not darting glances at him she was aware of his steady scrutiny. And he knew that when she looked at people or objects close to him, smiling in apparent enjoyment of the evening, she was really seeing him out of the corner of her eye. He knew that when she looked full at him it was in the hope that his attention had been taken by someone or something else.

He watched her even when he knew that other people

must be noticing the focus of his attention and even when Lady Mumford came to speak with him to apologize for the fact that she and Mumford had not been at the door to greet him. He knew he was late, he explained to her. He did not expect them to stand at the door all evening merely in order to greet latecomers.

Finally, after he had stood in the doorway for well over half an hour, a set ended and Judith Easton joined a group of guests and deliberately turned her back on him. It was a very straight back. If she was uncomfortable— and he knew very well that she was—then she was going to do nothing outwardly to show it.

She had always had that control over her emotions even as a girl. Unfortunately, at that time he had mistaken control for sweetness and shyness.

He strolled toward her. Nothing in her posture suggested that she knew he had moved from his position in the doorway. But as he approached another lady said something to her and she turned her head sharply just as he came up to her. He nodded a greeting to the whole group and turned to her.

"Mrs. Easton," he said, "will you do me the honor of waltzing with me?"

She inhaled visibly as she lifted her eyes to him.

"Oh, I say," said a florid-faced gentleman with whom the marquess was not acquainted, "I was just about to ask you myself, ma'am."

"Thank you," she said, ignoring the florid-faced gentleman, seeming in fact not even to have heard him. She stepped away from the group. He felt himself also inhaling slowly when the music started and he touched her for the first time in almost eight years. Her waist was still small and supple beneath the folds of her gown— even after two children. Her hand was still slim and soft. She wore the same perfume. He could not identify it, but he knew instantly that he had not smelled it since he had last been close to her. Long eyelashes, darker than her hair, still fanned her cheeks.

He had never waltzed with her before. The waltz had come into fashion since their betrothal. But she danced it as well and as daintily as she had used to dance the quadrille or the minuet.

She looked up to his chin. "I want to thank you for letting my children ride your horse this afternoon, my lord," she said. "You gave them a great deal of pleasure."

"I am fond of children," he said, and watched her raise her eyes briefly to his.

Perhaps she did not believe him. Probably she did not. And of course he had not been motivated chiefly by his love for children that afternoon, though he had liked the boy's enthusiasm and the girl's quiet trust.

What had he done wrong? he wondered as he had wondered hundreds—thousands—of times years before. Why had she preferred Easton to him? He had had the rank and the wealth and the prospects. It was true that Easton had been good-looking and charming with the ladies. But the man had also had a reputation as something of a rake.

Probably that had been it, he had concluded long ago. Perhaps it had been the eternal attraction of the rake. He on the other hand had always behaved toward her with perfect decorum and restraint. Perhaps she would have liked him better if he had displayed his feelings on occasion. But he had thought a display of feelings inappropriate before their wedding night. A night that had never come. Besides, he had never been easy with women of his own class.

"You are planning to make London your home?" he asked.

"For a while," she said.

"You are joining your husband's family for Christmas?" he asked.

She hesitated. "No," she said. "We are going to be quiet here alone for a change. My parents went to Millicent's in Scotland, but I decided that my daughter is too young for the lengthy journey. We are not going to stay with Andrew's family this year."

"Ah," he said. "London can be sparsely populated and a little lonely at Christmas."

"I have two young children and a sister-in-law," she said. "We will not be lonely."

That was the end of their conversation. He had found out what he wanted to know, and he had no wish to entertain her. He watched her as they waltzed, not taking his eyes from her face, totally unconcerned by the attention he must be drawing from the other guests—or by the embarrassment he must be causing her.

She remained calm, though he could feel a certain tightening of muscles beneath his hand at her waist.

Had she ever regretted jilting him? he wondered. Once the stars had faded from her eyes and she had realized—as she surely must have done—what kind of man she had married, had she remained in love with him, loyal to the feelings that had sent her running guiltily to his arms?

Or did she sometimes regret the man she had wronged? He supposed the answer depended upon whether she had been hostile to him or merely indifferent. Perhaps she had been hostile. Having grown up in a womanless home, he had never learned that easy charm with women that seemed to come so easily to other men. Perhaps she had actively disliked him. Perhaps she had never for one moment regretted her decision. His jaw tightened and his lips thinned.

Toward the end of the waltz he thought that she would open the conversation again. She drew breath and looked up resolutely into his eyes. But whatever words she planned to say were not spoken after all. She let out the breath through her mouth and continued to look into his eyes as he gazed steadily back. And finally her own wavered and fell.

He felt almost like laughing. But it was far too early to gloat. His revenge had scarcely begun yet.

"Thank you, my lord," she said, smiling at his chin when he returned her to her group at the end of the set. "That was pleasant."

"The pleasure was mine, ma'am," he said, bowing to her as she lifted her hand from his arm.

And he sought out Lady Mumford, complimented her on the success of her ball, bade her good night, and left the house.

JUDITH AWOKE THE following morning when a little figure climbed onto her bed carefully so as not to wake her, and burrowed beneath the bedclothes beside her.

"Mm," she said, reaching out a hand and ruffling auburn curls, "am I being an old sleepyhead?"

"Yes," Kate said. "Aunt Amy is painting with Rupert and Nurse is busy, and I escaped."

Judith chuckled. "Did you?" she said. "Have I slept the whole morning away?"

"Did you have fun, Mama?" the child asked.

Judith laughed again and swung her legs over the side of the bed. She sat up and stretched. Goodness, someone had been in and built up the fire without her even knowing.

"I had lots of fun," she said. "I danced all night until I thought I must have blisters on every toe." She turned and tucked the blankets under Kate's chin. "Are you going to have a sleep?" she asked. "Shh."

Kate chuckled and kicked the blankets away. She

bounded to her feet and scrambled off the bed. "We are going to the river tomorrow," she said. "Aunt Amy said so. We can walk on it, Mama. It is all over ice." And she was gone from the room.

Judith smiled and noted that the water in the pitcher on the washstand was warm. She must have been very deeply asleep. She supposed it was not surprising. She had still been awake when daylight broke and had quite resigned herself to a completely sleepless night. But as so often happens on such occasions, she had fallen asleep with the coming of day.

She had had fun indeed, she thought, her hand pausing as it poured water into the china basin. Fun! She could not recall a worse disaster of an evening.

Except that that was a ridiculous assessment. Claude had been attentive without being annoyingly so. She had mingled with ease and renewed some old acquaintances and made some new. She had danced every set except the one she had sat out with Colonel Hyde. It had been a wonderful evening. She had always loved dancing more than any other social activity.

And yet when she had come home and lain down, humming to herself, determined to remember only the gaiety and the successes, it had been he she had seen as soon as she closed her eyes. The Marquess of Denbigh, standing motionless and dark in the doorway of the ballroom for what had seemed hours and for what had probably been close to one—staring at her with that harsh angular face and those hooded gray eyes.

Why? Was he so outraged at her return to town and his domain? Was he trying to make her so uncomfortable that she would leave for the country without further delay? He had been trying to make her uncomfortable, she was convinced. She could not subscribe to Mrs. Summerberry's assessment.

"Mrs. Easton," that lady had said, tapping her on the

arm with her fan after he had left the ballroom not to return, "I do believe the marquess is still wearing the willow for you. Is there a chance that romance will blossom after all?"

Unfortunately, there had been other listeners, all of whom had turned interested eyes on Judith.

"Wearing the willow?" she had said with a laugh. "He never did. It was an arranged match, you know, and a mistake from the start. His feelings were no more engaged than mine. I believe he was just being civil dancing with me this evening, showing everyone that the past is in the past. And romance? I have experienced it once in my life and am now long past the age of such silliness."

But he was not being civil. She had lied when she said that. She knew that he was being anything but civil. Apart from those few words they had exchanged at the very start, he had made no attempt whatsoever to make conversation, and she had been feeling too tense to do so. And yet he had not taken his eyes off her. She had known it though for most of the time she had not had the courage to look up into his eyes.

Had he been gazing at her because he was wearing the willow for her, as Mrs. Summerberry had put it? No. She knew the answer was no. There had been a deliberate intent to embarrass her, to discompose her.

He had almost succeeded. She had almost cracked at the end and had looked up at him, determined to confront him, to demand an explanation of his behavior. But she had looked into his eyes, those keen gray eyes over which his eyelids drooped incongruously, giving an impression of sleepiness to an expression that was far from sleepy, and she had lost her nerve.

She had suddenly been even more intensely aware than she had been since the start of the waltz of his physical presence, of his great height and that impression of strength in his lean body that she was sure was no illusion, of some force—some quite unnameable force—that terrified her now even more than it had used to do.

For whereas eight years before she had considered him cold and unfeeling and had been afraid of being trapped in a marriage with a man she feared, now she could sense a very real animosity in him and felt like a weak victim being stalked by a bird of prey.

It was a foolish idea, a ridiculous idea. And yet, she thought as she rubbed a cloth hard over her face and neck, it had haunted her through what had remained of the night after she had arrived home. It had kept her from sleep.

At luncheon, which she and Amy took with the children, Judith announced that they would walk to St. James's Park that afternoon for a change.

"And the river tomorrow," she said. "We will see if it is safe to walk upon."

JUDITH WAS FEELING pleased with herself when they arrived back from their walk in St. James's. She could not be at all sure, of course, that the Marquess of Denbigh had ridden in Hyde Park that day, but if he had—and she had a strange feeling that he had—then he would have been foiled. He would have taken a lone and chilly ride for nothing.

She hoped that he had ridden there. Perhaps he would have realized by now that she could not so easily be made his victim.

And it was strange, she thought, repairing the damage made to her hair by her bonnet before going downstairs to the drawing room for tea, how she was assuming that the meeting in the park the afternoon before had been no accident. But how could it not have been? How could he have known?

The thought made her shiver. It was time for tea.

"We must buy some holly and ivy and other green-ery," Amy was saying to the children, who were also in the drawing room for tea, as had been their custom since arriving in town. "And how dreadful to be talking about buying when they have always been there for the gather-ing in the country. But never mind. And we will need some bows and bells and other decorations."

"We are going to buy them?" Rupert asked.

Amy frowned. "We must make as many as possible," she said. "It will be far more fun. There are boxes and boxes of decorations at Ammanlea. Here we must begin with nothing. But it will be fun, I promise you children. Perhaps we can even make a Nativity scene somehow." She smiled brightly.

"Perhaps after we have been down to the river tomor-row," Judith said, "we can go shopping and buy some length of ribbon to start making the bows and stream-ers. Shall we, Kate?"

The child's eyes grew round with wonder.

"I still think Christmas is going to be dull with no one else to play with," Rupert said dubiously.

Judith smiled determinedly. "We will play with one another," she said. "And there will be so many good things to eat and only the four of us to eat them that we will all burst and never be able to play again."

"We must sing carols while we make the decorations," Amy said. "I wonder if we could go carol singing about the square, Judith. Do you think the people here would think we had quite lost our senses? I will miss going caroling more than anything else."

Amy had a sweet voice and was always the most val-ued member of the carolers who traveled about the neighborhood at Ammanlea every Christmas. She would be missed that year.

"Perhaps," Judith said, but was interrupted by the

appearance of her father's butler, who had come into the room to announce the arrival of a gentleman below asking if he might call upon Mrs. Easton and Miss Easton.

"Upon me, too?" Amy said, brightening.

"The Marquess of Denbigh, ma'am," the butler said, inclining his head stiffly.

"We are from home," Judith said.

"Oh, famous," Rupert said, jumping to his feet. "Perhaps he has come to give me another ride, Mama."

"Riding," Kate said, clapping her hands.

"Oh, how very civil of him," Amy said. "Do show him up." But she flushed and looked at her sister-in-law. "I am sorry. Judith?"

Judith felt rather as if someone had punched her in the ribs. "He is calling on both of us?" she asked. "Then please show him up, Mr. Barta."

"Famous," Rupert said. "I think he is top of the trees, Mama."

Another of Maurice's phrases.

Kate moved from her chair to sit on the stool at Judith's feet. Judith stood.

"Good afternoon, my lord," she said, clasping her hands before her when he entered the room.

Amy swept him a deep curtsy and beamed at him. "How very civil of you to call, my lord," she said. "It is quite as cold outside today as it was yesterday, is it not?"

"It is indeed, ma'am," he said. "But I am afraid I played coward today and called out my carriage."

"Good afternoon, my lord," Rupert said.

Kate half hid behind Judith's skirt.

"Ah, the children are here, too," the marquess said. "And good day to you, sir, and to the young lady who believes that she is invisible although I can clearly see two large eyes and some auburn curls."

Kate chuckled and hid completely behind Judith.

"Won't you be seated, my lord?" Judith said coolly.

"The tea tray arrived a mere few minutes before you. I have not even poured yet."

"Then my timing is perfect," he said, seating himself as Amy resumed her place. "I came to assure myself that you have recovered from the exertions of last night's ball, ma'am."

"Yes, I thank you," Judith said. "It was a very pleasant evening."

He looked penetratingly at her while she looked coolly back. She scorned to lower her eyes in her own drawing room.

"And to assure myself that you took no chill from your walk in the park yesterday, ma'am," he said, turning his attention to Amy.

"Oh, no," Amy said. "We walk every day, you know. And it is my opinion that it is fresh air and exercise that keeps a person healthy and free of chills. Huddling by a fire all day and every day is a quite unhealthy practice."

"My feelings exactly, ma'am," he said. "But sometimes it is very hard to resist the temptation to keep oneself warm and cozy."

"It is a hard winter we are having so far," Amy said. "My only hope is that the snow will not come to prevent travel before Christmas. There will be many disappointed families, I am afraid, if their members cannot journey to be together."

"Yes, indeed," he said. "I have some guests coming to my home in Sussex for the holiday. I do not have any close family, but even so I will be hoping that both my guests and I will be able to travel. Loneliness is always hardest at Christmas for some reason."

"Yes," Amy said. "I remember . . ."

And to Judith's amazement they were off on a comfortable and lengthy coze, the two of them, ignoring her just as if she did not exist. And his manner with Amy was easy and pleasant, though of course he came no-where near smiling.

She was angry. And even more so when Rupert, his cake eaten, got to his feet and went to stand patiently beside the marquess's chair, waiting to be noticed. She tried to frown him back to his own place, but he did not look her way.

"And how are you today, sir?" the marquess asked eventually, he and Amy having finally come to a full agreement about the undesirability of being alone at Christmas.

"My grandpapa keeps the largest stable in Lincoln-shire," Rupert said gravely. "And the largest kennels, too. My papa would have taught me to ride but he died before I was old enough. Uncle Maurice was too busy last summer, but he will teach me when he has time. I am going to be a bruising rider."

The marquess set a hand on the boy's shoulder while Judith unconsciously held her breath. "I have no doubt of it," he said. "You sat Pegasus quite fearlessly yester-day."

Rupert almost visibly swelled with pride.

"I was not afraid either," an indignant little voice said from the stool at Judith's feet.

He looked across the room, his eyes touching on Judith for the first time for many minutes before drop-ping to Kate.

"I don't believe," he said, "I have ever seen a lady sit a horse with such quiet dignity."

Judith could not see Kate's reaction to his words. The child said nothing, but Amy was beaming down at her.

Everyone was having a perfectly amicable good time, she thought, controlling her anger and sipping on her tea. And if she had been furious the evening before at the way he had gazed so fixedly at her for an hour or longer, now she was indignant at the way he had so effectively ignored her almost from the moment of his entrance into her father's drawing room—*her* drawing room in her father's absence.

And what was his game? She could not believe this was the purely social call that it appeared to be.

No sooner had she had the thought than she discovered the answer—or doubtless a part of the answer, anyway.

"The ice is very firm on the Thames," he told Amy and the children. "Booths and tents are being moved out there constantly so that the river between the Blackfriar's Bridge and London Bridge is almost like a new busy thoroughfare. By tomorrow the fair will be in full swing, I am sure."

"Oh, famous!" Rupert yelled. "We are going there tomorrow."

"Yes," the marquess said. "I remember Miss Easton's saying so yesterday. And the thought occurred to me, sir, that you would have your hands very full indeed escorting three ladies to what will be a busy and perhaps rough celebration without some assistance from another gentleman. I have come to put my carriage and my person at everyone's disposal for tomorrow afternoon."

Judith felt herself turn cold despite the fact that the fire was roaring cheerfully in the fireplace.

"Famous!" Rupert said.

"How very civil of you indeed, my lord," Amy said. "And you are quite right, of course. It would not be at all the thing for Judith and me to go there with the children and no gentleman to escort us. I daresay there will be people of all classes there and some rogues and pickpockets, too. We are very obliged to you, I am sure. Are we not, Judith?"

Judith found herself finally being regarded steadily from those eyes, which were coming to unnerve her more than she cared to admit.

"Yes," she said. "You are very kind, my lord."

His eyes remained on her until they dropped to Kate, who had suddenly appeared, standing before his knees.

"We are going to buy ribbons," she told him. "For Christmas bows. Mama said."

"Are you?" he said. "Perhaps we will find some at the fair tomorrow. Yards and yards of ribbon and all colors of the rainbow, especially red and green for Christmas."

Kate returned solemnly to her stool.

The marquess stood up. "That is settled, then," he said. "I shall call for you ladies and gentleman after luncheon?"

"Thank you," Judith said, also rising to her feet.

"We will look forward to it immensely," Amy said. "It is very civil of you to think of us and our safety, my lord."

Everyone spoke at once after the marquess had left. The children were excited by the renewed certainty that they would indeed be going to the river the following day and by the fact that a gentleman was to take them there. Amy was quite ecstatic.

"I must confess," she said, "that I had not really considered the dangers of our going there alone, Judith. But now we do not have to worry at all, for I am sure that his lordship would only have to level a look at any impertinent fellow for him to melt into the ice. I shall feel quite perfectly safe with him and I shall feel that you and the children will be safe, too."

"I cannot like it," Judith said. "He is a stranger to us and has no obligation at all to put his time so much at our disposal."

Amy beamed at her. "I do not know what happened all those years ago," she said, "and I certainly cannot say I am sorry that you chose Andrew, Judith. I would not have known you else, and the children would not exist. But I can see that his lordship is going out of his way to win your favor again. And he is such a splendid and such a very civil gentleman."

"Upstairs, children," Judith said briskly, turning to pull the bell rope to have the tea tray removed. "Nurse will be waiting for you. Amy, you have mistaken his motives quite. He has no interest in me, you know. Why, he did not even speak with me at tea. It is quite as likely that his interest is in you. You must be very close to him in age, after all."

Amy laughed as the children left the room. "What a thoroughly nonsensical idea," she said. "It was perfectly obvious that he had nothing but a purely friendly interest in me, Judith. And I would have to say that age is the only thing the Marquess of Denbigh and I have in common. No, it is you with whom he is trying to fix his interest, mark my words."

"Amy." Judith covered her mouth with her hands. "Don't say so. Please don't say so. He makes my flesh creep."

Her sister-in-law looked at her in amazement. "Oh, no, Judith," she said. "Surely not. He is such a splendid man. But how insensitive I am being. It has been only a little longer than a year since Andrew passed away, has it not? Of course it is a little early for you to think of any other gentleman in that way. But never fear. The marquess is perfectly amiable and civil. He will not press unwelcome attentions on you, I am sure."

Amy had given up hope of matrimonial contentment for herself, but she loved to see those she cared for happy. And she cared for Judith more than for either of her other two sisters-in-law. Judith had not had a good marriage, Amy knew, but she had always remained true to it. She had made Andrew a good wife, and she was a good mother—and a good sister-in-law, too. Amy could imagine no greater happiness than seeing Judith well wed. Though of course, she thought a little sadly, when

Judith remarried, then she would have to return to Ammanlea.

Judith used the excuse of the removal of the tray to leave the room herself in order to return to her own room.

He was stalking his prey. She could feel it. And he was clever enough to get to her through her unsuspecting sister-in-law and children.

Because after eight years he wanted her back? Because he wanted to fix his interest with her, as Amy seemed to think?

No, not that. There was a certain expression in his eyes when he looked at her. He was not stalking her out of any soft sentiments, of that she was sure. But why, then? Punishment? Had she so wounded his pride and sense of consequence that she must be punished even eight years after the fact?

It must be that, she thought. She had made him feel and look foolish all those years ago. Now she must be punished.

She wondered with some fear and some anger what constituted punishment as far as the Marquess of Denbigh was concerned. Only what she had suffered so far, but at greater length? Embarrassment? Discomfort? Enforced hours in his company?

Or was there something else?

She shivered and despised herself for feeling fear.

4

He liked her children. He supposed that it might have been easier if he had not done so, and he had not particularly expected to do so since they were hers—and Easton's. But then in many ways it was not surprising. He had something of a weakness for children.

He liked the sister-in-law, too. She was unfortunately plain, with several pockmarks marring her complexion, and she was unusually small. He guessed that she was about his own age, well past the age of marriage for a woman. But there was an amiability about her and a kindness that he sensed. It was a pity that such women were so often denied the fulfillment of husbands and families.

Her friendliness, of course, and that of the children—even the little one could not maintain her shyness when there was something important to be said—could only make his task easier. It would all depend, he supposed, on the amount of power Judith Easton held over them and how well she liked to use that power even against their wishes. Her behavior of the afternoon before had suggested that making them happy was important to her. She had put up no fight against the proposed outing.

The Marquess of Denbigh rode out to the river and across the Blackfriar's Bridge during the morning. The icy fog that had gripped the city earlier was lifting and there was a magical, almost fairytale quality to the view below him on the river. Booths and tents were lined up in close and orderly formation on either side with a wide avenue of roughened ice between. Hawkers were loudly advertising their wares. Shoppers, sightseers, and the curious were wandering from stall to stall. There was a tantalizing aroma of cooking food wafting up to him.

It would do, he thought. He was fortunate that the rare occurrence of the Thames freezing over had happened at such an opportune time. He turned his horse's head for home again.

By the afternoon the fog had lifted right away and the sun was even trying, though not quite succeeding, to break through the high cloud cover. There was no significant wind. It was still cold, but pleasant for an outing. And the Eastons liked daily outings.

They were all ready to leave when he arrived, and came downstairs to the hallway without delay. The boy was openly excited. The little girl clung to her mother's cloak and smiled shyly at him from behind one of its folds until he looked at her. Then she disappeared altogether.

He bowed to them and bade them a good afternoon.

"The air is crisp," he said. "But you are all dressed warmly, I see. And there are warm foods and drinks down on the river, I have heard, and even a fire where meat is being roasted. I could smell it this morning."

"A fire on the ice?" Amy asked in amazement. "Will it not all melt?"

"Apparently not, ma'am," he said. "The ice is very thick indeed."

"Amazing!" she said.

He handed them into his carriage, lifting the little girl and setting her on her mother's knee. The boy scrambled in without assistance. Judith Easton had not said a word beyond the initial greeting and sat quietly and calmly smoothing her daughter's cloak over her knees.

"From my observations this morning," the marquess said, seating himself opposite Judith, his knees almost touching hers, and addressing his words to Amy, "it is quite a festive scene. The sort of excitement such an occasion engenders can also serve to make one quite unaware of the cold."

"To be quite honest," Amy said, "I would prefer extreme cold to extreme heat if I had to make a choice. Very hot summer days can quite sap one of energy."

The two of them carried on an amicable conversation during the journey while Kate stared wide-eyed from one to the other of them and Rupert sat with his face pressed to the window, watching what passed outside.

"Oh," he said eventually, stabbing a finger against the pane, "there, Mama. There, sir, do you see? Look, Aunt Amy."

And then they were all leaning toward the one window, gazing down from the bridge at London's newest street.

"May we get down?" Rupert demanded. "Oh, just wait until Uncle Maurice hears about this."

"We may," the marquess said. He looked across at Judith for the first time. The moss green of her bonnet and velvet cloak became her well, he thought. "Shall I instruct my coachman to return in two hours' time, ma'am?"

"As you wish," she said.

Two hours should be long enough for a start, he thought. He must not be impatient.

But the time passed quickly. There were vendors of everything one might want to buy from lace to boots, from books to smelling salts. And hawkers to persuade a person that he needed an item he had never felt a need of before. There were the tempting aromas of roasted

lamb and pork pies and tarts and chestnuts and the less
tempting one of cheap ale. And there were fortune-
tellers and portrait painters and card playing booths and
skittle alleys. There was everything one could possibly
imagine for the entertainment of all.

Amy was enjoying herself. She was in London and at
the very heart of its life and activity. And she was not
alone but with her sister-in-law and nephew and niece.
And they had the escort of a handsome gentleman. She
felt more light-hearted than she had felt for years.

"I am going to have my fortune told," she announced
recklessly when they came to the fortune-teller's booth.

Judith smiled at her.

"There can be nothing but good ahead for you,
ma'am," the marquess said gallantly.

Amy stepped inside the dark tent and gazed about,
fascinated. Oh, she had always loved fairs, though more
often than not after her early girlhood she had been refused permission to go.

She sat down before the gaudy, veiled figure of the
fortune-teller with her crystal ball and waited expectantly, feeling like a hopeful girl again and smiling inwardly at the thought.

But she was feeling disappointed a minute later—the
fortune-teller must have mistaken her age, she thought—
but only a little disappointed. She was in the land of
make-believe and she refused to allow reality to intrude
too chillingly.

Romance, the fortune-teller had predicted. With a
gentleman she had not met yet but would meet soon.
And children—lots of them. That was the detail that
was most disappointing, since it was so obviously the
most impossible.

But no matter. She would dream of her gentleman in
the coming days and laugh herself out of melancholy

when he failed to put in an appearance in her life. There was a whole fair waiting to be enjoyed outside the tent.

"Thank you," she said formally, getting to her feet.

"How very foolish," she said, laughing and blushing when she rejoined the others. "I am to find love and romance soon, it seems, with a gentleman I have never before set my eyes on, and am to live happily ever after. I wonder if she ever says anything different to any lady who is unmarried. One would, after all, feel that one had wasted one's money if one were told that there were only misery and loneliness ahead." She said nothing about the many children.

"Perhaps we should put the matter to the test," the marquess said. "Mrs. Easton must have her fortune told, too."

"I have no wish to waste money on such nonsense," Judith said.

"Then I shall waste it for you," he said. "Come, we must find what delights life has in store for you."

"Yes, Mama," Rupert said, jumping up and down on the spot. "Go on."

"Go, Mama," Kate said.

She looked rather as if she were going to her own execution, the marquess thought, but she went. He in the meanwhile swung Rupert up onto his shoulders when the boy complained that he could not see for the crowds.

"You were quite right, Amy," Judith said when she came out of the tent. "My own fortune was remarkably similar to yours. As if I am looking for love and romance at this stage of my life!" Her tone was scornful.

"And what is he to look like?" Amy asked.

"Oh, tall, dark, and handsome, of course," Judith said, flushing. "What else?"

"Well, there our fortunes differ," Amy said. "Now it is your turn, my lord."

"It would be interesting, would it not?" he said. "I

wonder how many tall, dark, and handsome ladies there are in England?"

Amy laughed.

"Down you go, then, my lad," the marquess said, setting Rupert down on the ice again. "I shall take you up again when I come out."

"I see much darkness in your life," the fortune-teller told him a few moments later. "And a great deal of light, too. A great deal of light. But the darkness threatens it."

Lord Denbigh had never been to a fortune-teller before. He supposed that there were a few fortunes to be told and that each listener could be relied upon to twist the words to suit his own case. One merely had to be clever with vague generalities. He was amused.

"Ah," the fortune-teller said, "but Christmas may save you if you keep in mind that it is a time of peace and goodwill. I see a great battle raging in your soul between light and darkness. But the joy of Christmas will help the light to banish the darkness—if you do not fight too strongly against it."

Well. That was it? Nothing about romance and love and marriage and happily-ever-afters? That was to be reserved exclusively for the female customers? He rose and nodded to the fortune-teller. It would be a kindness to tell her, perhaps, that if all her women customers were to find the romance she promised them, then men should be alerted to their needs.

"Nothing," he said to the ladies when he went outside again. "There is to be no romance in my future, alas. Only the promise of a happy Christmas if I do not do something to spoil the occasion."

"Ah," Amy said. "How disappointing, my lord. But I am glad that you can expect a good Christmas."

He leaned down and swung Rupert up onto his shoulders again. Judith watched him, her lips tightening.

The marquess bought the children each a tart and all

of them a hot drink of chocolate. And when Kate spotted a stall that sold ribbons, he bought her long lengths of green and red over Judith's protests and Amy's exclamations on his kindness.

"It amazes me," Amy said when they paused to watch the portrait painter draw his likenesses, "how he can hold the charcoal and wield it so skillfully without freezing his fingers off. But the portraits are quite well done."

"Have your picture drawn with your good lady, guv'nor?" the artist's assistant asked, looking from the marquess to Judith. "And with the lovely children, too, if you want, guv. 'Alf a sovereign for all four of you."

"No, thank you," Judith said quickly.

Rupert shouted with glee from his perch on the marquess's shoulders. "He is not our father," he exclaimed to the assistant.

Kate was tugging at Judith's cloak.

"Mama," she said when Judith looked down, "may I have my pictures?"

"Your portrait done?" Judith said, smiling down at her and passing a hand beneath her chin. "You would have to sit very still and would get very cold."

"No longer than five minutes, mum," the assistant assured her briskly. "The child's likeness in five minutes, satisfaction guaranteed or your money back. Two and sixpence for the child, mum."

"A shilling," the marquess said. "One and sixpence if it is a good likeness."

"Done, guv," the assistant said. "And worth two shillings it will be if it's worth a penny. Let the little lady take a chair."

Kate smiled wonderingly up at the marquess and her mother and aunt and allowed Judith to seat her on the chair indicated. And she sat very still, her feet dangling a few inches above the ice, her hands clasped in her lap, only her eyes moving.

"How sweet she looks," Amy said. "Would you like to be next, Rupert?"

"Pooh," the boy said. "I don't want to sit for my picture." But he did squirm to be set down so that he could walk around to the side of the artist and watch the progress of the portrait.

Judith wandered to a book stall a few feet away after a couple of minutes. But she was not to be allowed to browse in peace. A man with one arm outstretched and draped from shoulder to wrist in necklaces of varying degrees of gaudiness accosted her and tried to interest her in his wares. Another man came up on her other side with a tray of bangles.

The marquess watched her laugh and shake her head, looking from one to the other. They moved in closer on either side of her, pressing their wares on her. Her reticule dangled from her right arm.

He walked toward her and set one hand lightly against the back of her neck. "You are not considering buying more baubles, are you, my love?" he asked, at the same time picking up her reticule and tucking it into the crook of her arm.

She looked around at him, her eyes wide and startled.

"These pearls for the lidy, guv?" the necklace seller asked. "Real pearls wiv a real diamond clasp? A bargain they are today, guv."

"I am sure they are," the marquess said. "Unfortunately the lady already has three different strings of pearls." He held up a staying hand. "And all the other jewels she could possibly wear in a lifetime."

The bangle seller had already faded away.

"You're missin' the bargain of a lifetime, guv," the hawker said, and he turned and made his way to a group of three ladies who had stopped nearby.

The marquess removed his hand from Judith's neck.

"That was one reason why you needed a male escort," he said.

"They were harmlessly trying to sell their wares," she said stiffly. "I did not need your interference, my lord."

"You would have been easy prey," he said. "They would not even have had to draw attention to themselves by racing off with your reticule. The bangle seller was lifting it so skillfully off your arm that you probably would not even have missed it until they had disappeared among the crowds."

She looked down at the reticule she now held against her side. "That is ridiculous," she said. "They were merely selling their wares."

"They were merely thieving," he said. "However, since no harm has been done, I suppose it does not matter if you do not believe me. But do be careful. This type of scene is a pickpocket's heaven."

"He was really about to steal my reticule?" she asked, frowning.

"As surely as the clasp on that pearl necklace was glass," he said.

She was looking directly into his eyes. He had never quite been able to put a name to the color of her eyes. They were not exactly green, not exactly gray. They were certainly not blue—not altogether so, anyway. But they were bright and beautiful eyes, the colored circle outlined by a dark line, almost as if it had been drawn in with a fine pen. He had once fancied it possible to drown in her eyes.

"Thank you," she said. She did not smile. He knew that it had taken her a great effort to acknowledge her gratitude. She turned abruptly to the portrait painter's booth.

The portrait was finished and Kate was holding it in her hands and gazing at it wide-eyed. Her aunt was exclaiming in delight over it while Rupert regarded it critically, head to one side.

"Look, Mama." Kate held out the portrait for her mother's inspection. Judith took it and the marquess looked at it over her shoulder. A little girl sat stiffly on a chair, her feet dangling in space, her hands in her lap. Two large dark eyes peeped from beneath the poke of a bonnet. It could have been any child anywhere.

"Oh, lovely," Judith said. "I will have to find a frame for it at home and hang it in my bedchamber. How clever of you to sit still all that time, Kate."

The marquess paid the assistant one shilling and sixpence. Kate was pulling on the tassel of one of his Hessian boots as he put his purse away in a safe inside pocket.

"Yes, ma'am?" he said, looking down at her.

She pointed upward and smiled at him. He stooped down closer to her.

"Ride up there," she said.

She weighed no more than a feather. He swung her up onto one shoulder and wrapped an arm firmly about her. She put one arm about his head beneath his beaver hat and spread her palm over his ear. And she sat very still and quiet.

It was his one regret. No, perhaps not the only one. But it was one regret of his life that he had not had children of his own. He had dreamed of it once, of course. When he was twenty-six years old he had been very eager to marry and begin his family. He had hoped that Judith would want several children. He had suffered too much loneliness himself from being an only child.

He should, he supposed, have shaken off his disappointment and his heartache more firmly and chosen again. He might still have found contentment with another woman and he might certainly have had his family. But it seemed too late now at the age of thirty-four to begin the process of finding a woman with whom he might be compatible. He had loved once, and the experience seemed to have sapped all his desire to search for love again.

Rupert was holding his free hand, he realized suddenly, and telling him in his piping voice how he would skate like the wind if he only had skates with him. Faster than the wind. He would skate so fast that no one would even see him.

Judith walked to his side, her eyes on her children, almost as if she believed that he would disappear with them if she relaxed her vigil for one moment. Amy walked at his other side, still gazing about her with bright interest.

"I'm cold," Kate announced suddenly.

They were strolling back toward the bridge where the carriage was to meet them, and the slight movement of air was against their faces.

"It is chilly," Amy agreed, "though you were quite right in what you said earlier, my lord. The excitement of the occasion makes one almost forget that it is a cold winter's day."

"We will warm ourselves at the roasting fire," the marquess said, leading the way there.

And indeed the heat from the flames was very welcome. While Rupert dashed forward, his hands outheld, Lord Denbigh lifted Kate down carefully from his shoulder, stooped down behind her and unbuttoned his greatcoat to wrap about her, and held her little hands up to the blaze.

"Better?" he asked.

She nodded. He took her hands and rubbed them firmly together and then held them to the blaze again. He looked up at Amy.

"It feels good, does it not?" he said.

"Wonderful," she agreed.

He looked up at Judith. "Warm again?" he asked.

"Yes, thank you," she said.

"Only those wot's buyin' meat is welcome to warm their 'ands, guv," the man who was tending the cooking said, and he stretched out a hand to catch the shilling that the marquess tossed to him.

"Is that better?" the marquess asked Kate after a couple of minutes, rubbing her hands together again.

She nodded once more to him, turned, and raised her arms to him. He wrapped his coat more firmly about her and lifted her.

"I think the carriage will be waiting by the time we have strolled back to the bridge," he said. "Has everyone seen enough?"

"Oh, yes, indeed," Amy said. "This has been very wonderful, my lord."

"This has been the best day of my life," Rupert said.

"May I take Kate, my lord?" Judith asked. "She must be getting heavy."

"As light as a feather," he said, glancing down and realizing that the child had fallen asleep against his chest.

He had a strange feeling, almost as if butterflies were fluttering through his stomach. She was warm and relaxed inside his coat. He could hear her deep breathing when he bent his head closer. No, it was more than butterflies. He felt almost like crying.

She might have been his, he thought, if only things had turned out differently. She might have had his dark hair or her mother's fair coloring. He swallowed and shook off the thought.

Judith Easton had seen to it that that had never happened.

He allowed his coachman to help the ladies into the carriage and climbed in carefully himself in order not to waken the child. He shifted her in his arms so that she lay on his lap, her head on his arm. Her mouth fell open as her head tipped back.

"Poor Kate," Amy said. "She has tired herself out. But she has had such a very happy afternoon, my lord. I am sure she will not stop talking about this for days."

Judith Easton, the marquess saw as he looked steadily across the carriage at her, had her eyes on her daughter. She was biting at her lower lip.

"But there is so much in London to delight children," he said. "And adults, too. You have not yet been to the Tower, Miss Easton?"

Judith's eyes lifted to his and held. He did not look away from her.

"No," Amy replied. "But we have been meaning to do so ever since we came to town, have we not, Judith? I am longing to see the Crown Jewels."

"The menagerie there is not as impressive as it used to be, I believe," he said. "But it is still worth a visit and is the delight of all children who see it."

"Yes!" Rupert said. "Is there a lion, sir?"

"There is," the marquess said. "And also an elephant."

"A lion!" Rupert said. "I wonder if it has ever eaten anyone."

"Oh, I don't believe so, dear," Amy said. "It must be in a safe cage."

Judith lifted her chin slightly. She knew very well what was coming, the marquess thought, his eyes still on hers. And she knew that she was powerless to avert it.

"There are all sorts of armor and torture instruments on display, too," he said, "including the block and ax with which people's heads used to be chopped off. Children inevitably enjoy seeing them even more than they enjoy the lion."

Rupert made a chopping motion at his own neck with the side of one hand.

"Perhaps you would allow me to escort you all there one afternoon, ma'am," he said. "It would be my pleasure."

He watched her mouth lift in a half smile, though there was no amusement in her eyes. She said nothing.

"Yes!" Rupert said. "May we, Mama?"

"How extraordinarily civil of you, my lord," Amy said, delight in her voice.

"Thank you," Judith said softly, that half smile still on her lips. "It would be our pleasure, my lord."

"Then it is settled," he said as his carriage jolted slightly to a halt outside their home. "Shall we say three afternoons from now?"

She inclined her head.

Five minutes later he drove away alone, having laid the child in her mother's arms inside the hallway of the house and declined an invitation to go upstairs for tea.

So Judith Easton was divining his game, was she? He wondered if she had even a glimmering of an understanding of the whole of it. And he wondered if she would be able to guard against it even if she did.

He would see to it that she did not. For the plan was now whole in his mind and he was quite confident of its success. The sister-in-law and the children were eating out of his hand already. And she cared for their happiness.

He would make it succeed. For now more than ever, having seen her again, having had some of the old wounds aggravated again, he wanted her to suffer. Almost exactly as he had suffered.

Almost exactly.

JUDITH CARRIED THE still-sleeping Kate upstairs to the nursery and laid her down carefully on her bed. She loosened the child's bonnet and slid it from her head, unlaced her boots and eased them off her feet.

Well, she thought, the Marquess of Denbigh was doing very nicely for himself. If punishment was his motive—and it must be that—then he was succeeding very well. Not only was he ruining the days and the evenings of her return to town and society, but he was insinuating himself very firmly into the approval and even the affections of her sister-in-law and her children.

Amy was already looking upon him as something of a hero. If she heard her sister-in-law talk one more time about his great civility and kindness, Judith thought, she would surely scream. And if Amy one more time suggested, as she had done after he came to tea and again a few minutes before when the door had closed behind him, that he had a *tendre* for her, Judith, and was trying to fix his interest with her, she would—scream. She most certainly would.

He had already won the children's confidence. It was hard to understand how he had done it. The man never smiled, and he had those harsh features and that stiff manner that had always half frightened her. And yet she could not push from her mind the images of Rupert riding on his shoulder and Kate huddled inside his greatcoat, her small hands in his large ones held out to the blaze of the fire. Or of Kate on his shoulder and Rupert's hand in his, her son's voice raised in excitement. Or of Kate asleep inside his coat and on his lap in the carriage.

Judith smoothed a hand over the soft auburn curls of her daughter and tiptoed from the nursery bedchamber.

She hated him. All the old revulsion and fear had been intensified into hatred. He was playing a game with her and for the time she seemed quite powerless to fight him.

She thought suddenly of his hand coming to rest against the back of her neck and the shudders and flames it had sent shooting downward through her breasts and her womb to her knees. And of his soft cultured voice calling her "my love." She fought breathlessness and fury.

Well, she thought, she could wait him out. If he thought that she would break, that she would lash out at him in fury—perhaps in public—and give him the satisfaction of knowing that his punishment was having its effect, then he would be disappointed. She could wait.

There were less than three weeks left before Christmas. He had said that he was going home to the country for the holiday. And it was unlikely that he would change his plans—he had mentioned the fact that he had invited guests. So she had perhaps two weeks at the most to endure. Probably less.

She could endure for that long. And when he returned to town after Christmas, he would find her gone. She would go back home to the country herself. Perhaps it would be cowardly to do so, but there would also be good reason for going. The children needed the greater freedom and stability of a country home in which to grow up, she told herself. It was all very well to have to come to London for her own sake when her mourning period ended. But she would not be selfish forever. The countryside was the place for children.

Yes, she would endure for another two weeks. And after that he would be powerless to interfere further with her life.

And she would never give him the satisfaction of knowing that he had ruined this brief return to town for her.

5

DURING THE NEXT WEEK SHE SAW HIM FOUR TIMES IN all. It was endurable, she told herself. Barely. Surely, soon he would remove to his country estate.

He was at Mrs. Colbourne's musical evening the day before he had agreed to take them to the Tower. She sat with Claude Freeman and a few other acquaintances, watching the pianist seated at the grand pianoforte in the center of the room, listening to his skilled renditions of Mozart and Beethoven, wishing that her fingers would obey her will as the pianist's did his.

And all the time she was aware of the Marquess of Denbigh at the edge of her vision to the right. He was staring at her, she thought, until her breathing became a strained and a conscious exercise and her concentration on the music disappeared almost entirely. And yet since he was on a different side of the room from her, it was just as likely that he was staring at the pianist. She could not bring herself to look at him.

She did dart a look finally, unable to bear the strain any longer. He was watching the pianist. And yet her look drew his and their eyes met for a moment before she withdrew hers.

Why was it, she wondered, that all the other guests within her line of vision seemed a blur of faces and color while he stood out in startling detail? He was not even wearing black tonight to make him noticeable. His coat was blue.

Was it that he was so much more handsome than any other gentleman present? Yet she had never thought of him as handsome. Quite the opposite, in fact. His face was thin and angular, his nose too prominent, his lips too thin, his eyes too penetrating, his eyelids too lazy.

No, he was not handsome. Distinguished looking perhaps? Yes, definitely distinguished looking in a cold, austere way. She thought suddenly of the fortune-teller's prediction about a tall, dark, handsome man, and shivered. And the woman had told her that she knew the man already, that her love for him would come upon her quite unexpectedly. There had been children in her future, too. Several of them. She had once dreamed of having a large family.

She focused her eyes and concentrated her mind on the pianist and his music.

The marquess came during the interval to pay his respects and to ask after the health of Amy and the children. He did not stay longer than a couple of minutes.

"You say that Denbigh escorted you and your family to the ice fair?" Claude said with a frown when the marquess had walked away. "I wish you had called upon me instead, Mrs. Easton. I would, of course, have advised against the visit. It is a vulgar show, or so I have heard. I would not have considered it desirable to have you rub shoulders with ruffians and thieves. And the children might have been in some danger. But then, I do not suppose Denbigh even so much as noticed your children."

She wished he had not, Judith thought, seeing again the image of Lord Denbigh with Kate on his shoulder and Rupert holding his hand.

"He was being civil," she said.

"I should watch his civility, if I were you," Claude said. "You have crossed his will once, ma'am, if you will forgive me for reminding you. I do not believe he would take kindly to its happening a second time."

Judith looked up at him indignantly.

"Pardon me," he said. "But people are saying, you know, that perhaps you are regretting your former decision."

"Are they?" she said, her voice tight with anger. "Are they, indeed?"

But she caught herself just in time and turned from him to resume her seat. She drew a few deep and steadying breaths. She closed her eyes briefly. She had been about to rip up at Claude in an appallingly public place, to tell him exactly what she thought of his impertinent and interfering words and of the *ton*'s foolish opinions.

And yet her anger was not really against Claude at all, or against the *ton*. It was against the Marquess of Denbigh, who had arranged all this, who was stalking her relentlessly, and who was intent on making her look a fool in the eyes of society. A rejected fool.

Well, let him keep on trying. She would never give him the satisfaction of showing anger or any other negative emotion in public. And let people say what they would. People would gossip no matter what. She had no control over that, only over her own behavior. And she supposed that a little gossip was no more than she deserved. She did deserve some punishment for her less than exemplary behavior almost eight years before.

She did not look at the marquess again that evening.

THEY VISITED THE Tower of London the next day and St. Paul's Cathedral two days after that. If she really had been setting her cap at the man, Judith thought, or even if she had liked him, she would have to say that both afternoons were a great success. Amy and the children certainly thought so.

Amy and Kate, hand in hand, watched the birds in the menagerie while Lord Denbigh and Rupert lingered over their perusal of the lion and the elephant and other animals. The marquess answered Rupert's questions about them, about where they were from, how they would have lived in those countries, what they would have eaten, how they would have hunted. He delighted the boy by giving all the gory details while Judith stood helplessly and disapprovingly beside them.

But her disapproval was foolish, she told herself. Boys enjoyed hearing of some of the crueler realities of life. And those realities existed no matter how sheltered she wished her children to be from them. Andrew, she knew, would have wanted his son to grow up a "real man," as he would have put it. And so would Maurice and Henry.

It was doubtless good for Rupert to be with a man occasionally, instead of always with her and Amy. If only the man were not the Marquess of Denbigh! Perhaps she should have gone to Andrew's family for Christmas after all, she thought fleetingly.

Amy exclaimed over the Crown Jewels, and Kate, in Judith's arms, gazed at them silent and wide-eyed.

"Pretty, Mama," was all she said, pointing at a crown. Judith looked at the armory and even at a few of the instruments of torture, which the marquess explained to Rupert and Amy. But she refused to look at the block and ax. She turned away with Kate while Rupert laughed and jeered.

"I should stay with you, Judith," Amy said. "All this is quite ghastly. But I must confess that it is also fascinating."

Somehow, as they were strolling away from the White Tower on their way back to the carriage, it happened that the children hurried ahead with Amy to gaze down into the moat and Judith was left walking beside the marquess.

"You have recovered?" he asked. "You looked for a few minutes as if you were about to faint."

"It is horrible," she said, "what human beings can do to other human beings."

"You do not believe, then," he said, "that criminals should be punished?"

"Of course," she said. "But torture? And execution by ax?"

"Many criminals have themselves used cruelty," he said. "Many have killed or betrayed their country. Do they not deserve to be treated accordingly? Do you not believe in execution, Mrs. Easton?"

"I don't know," she said. "I suppose I do. Anyone who kills deserves to die himself—I suppose. But what sort of an example do we set thieves and murderers when we return brutality for their brutality—in the name of law? It does not quite make sense."

"I would guess that you have never witnessed a hanging at Tyburn," he said. "Some people would not miss such an entertainment for all the world."

She shuddered and raised a gloved hand to her mouth.

And then her other hand was taken in a firm clasp and drawn through his arm.

"Your son loves animals," he said. "He was telling me all about his grandfather's dogs, particularly the one shaggy fellow which is allowed inside the house."

"Shaggy?" she said. "That is its name, you know. Sometimes it is difficult to know which end is which. There are a few dogs at home, too, but I would not allow any to be brought with us because London is not quite the place for pets, I believe. Besides, my father would not have taken kindly to having his home overrun by the animal kingdom."

"It is one advantage of living in the country," he said. "A great advantage for children. Animals were almost my only companions when I was growing up. Your children are fortunate that they have each other."

She looked up at him, startled. He had just given her almost the only human glimpse of himself she had ever had. He had no brothers and sisters. She had known that. She had never thought of what that might have meant to him. Son of the late Marquess of Denbigh, his mother dead since his infancy. An only child. Animals had been his only companions. Had he been lonely, then? But she did not want to start thinking of him as a person.

And she realized that she was strolling with him, her arm drawn firmly through his, conversing just as if they were friends or at least friendly acquaintances. She was relieved to see the moat ahead and Amy and the children standing on the bridge looking down into the water. She used the excuse of Kate's turning to wave a hand at her to withdraw her arm from the marquess's and hurry forward.

At least Kate had not fallen beneath his spell that afternoon, she thought a little spitefully as the child lifted her arms to be carried the rest of the distance to the carriage.

But even that triumph was to be short-lived. When they were seated in the carriage, Kate wriggled off Judith's lap and climbed onto the marquess's. He continued naming to Rupert all the towers in the outer walls and pointing them out through the windows as they drove away. But he opened the top two buttons of his greatcoat, drew out his quizzing glass on its black ribbon, and handed it to Kate.

She played with it quietly for a while before lifting it to her eye and peering through it at her brother. Rupert shrieked with laughter.

"Look at her eye!" he said, and Amy and Judith

laughed, too, as Kate gazed from one to the other, the glass held to one hugely magnified eye.

The children laughed and giggled for the rest of the journey. It was a merry homecoming.

AMY AS WELL as Judith was part of Claude Freeman's party at the theater on the evening of the following day. The marquess was there, too, and came to pay his respects between acts. Fortunately, Judith found, talking determinedly with Mrs. Fortescue, who was also one of their party, he directed his attentions and his conversation to Amy.

Amy was enchanted and as excited as any child being given a rare treat. She had never been to the theater before and had never seen so many splendidly dressed people all gathered in one place. Best of all, she thought, gazing about her, no one was staring at her. She was a very plain, very middle-aged-lady, she told herself. Not a monster. Sometimes her family members had protected her—or themselves—so closely that she had felt as if she must be some freak of nature.

"I cannot believe all the splendor of it," she told the Marquess of Denbigh. "The velvet and gold and the chandeliers. And the acting. I was never so well entertained in my life."

"It is your first visit to the theater?" he asked, his eyes looking kindly at her.

And she realized that her reactions must appear very naive to him. But she did not care. The marquess, for all his splendor and very handsome looks and impressive title, would not laugh at her. He was a kind gentleman and she liked him excessively. If only Judith . . .

But Judith was pointedly talking to someone else and for some reason did not like the marquess. Or else she felt embarrassed about what had happened all those years ago.

But Lord Denbigh had clearly forgiven her for that and was quite as clearly trying to fix his interest with her no matter how hard Judith tried to deny the fact.

She wished she had Judith's chance, Amy thought a little wistfully. Not with the marquess, of course. That would be ridiculous.

"The play is about to resume, ma'am," Lord Denbigh said, getting to his feet. "I shall take my leave of you and look forward to escorting you to St. Paul's tomorrow."

He took her hand and raised it to his lips. Amy felt ridiculously pleased. She felt even more pleased when he glanced toward Judith, although Judith was studiously looking the other way.

AT ST. PAUL'S the following day they wandered in some awe about the nave, dwarfed by the hugeness and majesty of the cathedral. Judith had never been there before. She had never been comfortable with heights, but the Whispering Gallery did not look too high up when one looked from below—the dome still soared above it—so she agreed to Rupert's persuasions and climbed the stone steps resolutely. Amy stayed down below with Kate.

But she felt the bottom fall out of her stomach when she stepped out onto the gallery, which circled the base of the dome. The nave of the cathedral looked very far down, the people there like ants. She did not even look long enough to distinguish Amy and Kate.

Rupert was running around the gallery, the marquess strolling after him. She stood against the wall, her palms resting against it at her back, willing her heart to stop thumping and her legs to regain their bones. She took a few tentative sideways steps. She looked nonchalantly about her but not down. It still seemed a very long way up to the top of the dome and the Thornhill frescoes painted there.

"It has nothing to do with cowardice, you know." She had not even noticed the Marquess of Denbigh coming back toward her. "It is an actual affliction that some people have. Your head can tell you that the gallery is broad and well railed, that there is no possible way you can fall. But still you can be paralyzed with terror. A friend who suffers in the same way has told me that it is not so much the fear of falling as the fear of jumping. Is that right?"

He was standing in front of her, perfectly at ease, filling her line of vision. He spoke quietly, as he usually did. For once in his presence she felt her heart quieting.

"Yes," she said. "It is a very annoying terror. One feels like the typical helpless woman."

"The friend I spoke of," he said, "is a man and weighs fifteen stone if he weighs an ounce and is as handy with his fives as any pugilist one would care to meet. Take my arm. Your son, you will see, is across from us, waving down to his sister and his aunt."

Judith felt her stomach somersault again.

"He is perfectly safe," he said, "and will be delighted if we join him there. Walk next to the wall and imagine that we are strolling in Hyde Park. Look at my arm, if you wish, or at my shoulder. You have a lively and curious son. You must look forward to nurturing his curiosity."

No, she thought firmly as she told him of her own plans to employ a tutor for a few years and the plans of her brothers-in-law to send him to school when he was older—Rupert would after all be head of the family after the passing of his grandfather—no, she would not grow to like him. She would not mistake his behavior either here and now or briefly at the Tower for kindness.

There was no kindness in the Marquess of Denbigh. Only a cold, calculating mind. Only the desire to punish her by winning the affection of her children and by inflicting his unwanted company on her and by making her look foolish and rejected in the eyes of society.

She must not even begin to doubt what she had so strongly sensed from the first moment of seeing him again.

"Your son will want to test the theory that a word whispered at one side of the gallery can be clearly heard at the other," he said just before they came up to Rupert. "But since you must whisper with your mouth to the wall and listen with your ear to it, that should pose no great problem for you."

Despite herself she found herself relaxing. His words were reassuring. Even more so was his tall strong body between her and the rail of the gallery.

He took them to Gunter's for tea and cakes before returning them home. He spoke of Christmas and his eagerness to return to his estate.

"There is nowhere quite like the country and a houseful of people for celebrating Christmas," he concluded, while Amy gazed wistfully at him and both children were unusually silent.

"There were always lots of cousins at Grandpapa's," Rupert said at last.

"But this year we will have each other," Judith said briskly, "and will be able to do just as we please all day long."

His words had been ill-considered, she thought. If his intention had been to make her feel guilt at having deprived her children and her sister-in-law of other company over the holiday, then he had succeeded. But it was one thing to hurt her, and quite another to depress the spirits of her family.

He had miscalculated. It was his purpose, surely, to

win over the others. She felt an almost spiteful satisfaction at his one slip.

And an even greater satisfaction at the realization that he must surely leave for the country within the following few days.

IT WAS SNOWING in a halfhearted way. Enough to whiten one's hat and shoulders and to blind one's vision as one rode. Enough to remind one of the coming season. But not enough to settle on the traveled thoroughfares and obstruct traffic.

Even so, the Marquess of Denbigh frowned up at the sky as he rode through the park. Perhaps he was foolish not to have gone into Essex before now. He had guests to prepare for, after all. And even if the weather should prevent the arrival of his guests, there were plenty of other people who needed his presence at Denbigh Park and would be disappointed if he did not arrive. All the children were to stay at the house for two nights—on Christmas Eve and Christmas Day—as they had the year before, and were looking forward to the treat almost as if he had offered them a month in Italy, according to both Mrs. Harrison's and Cornwell's letters.

It would not do to be stranded in town by snow.

But he had not wanted to jump his fences as far as Judith Easton was concerned. He had been proceeding with those plans as slowly as he dared. Too slowly perhaps. He was maybe seeing too much of her. And too much of her children and that good-natured sister-in-law of hers. He was becoming too fond of them.

One danger he had become particularly aware of in the past few days: He must not allow himself to like Judith Easton in any way. It was true—he had played on the fact—that she cared for the happiness of her family and hated to deny them pleasure. And it was true that she was a good mother, spending much of her days with her children instead of abandoning them to a nurse's care. He approved of the way she did not try to overprotect her children, especially the boy.

And there was something admirable about her courage. She had walked the whole circle of the Whispering Gallery at St. Paul's with him, even though he had known from the slight tremor in her voice that she had been terrified, and she had looked down at her son's direction and waved to her daughter and sister-in-law in the nave below. She had unconsciously gripped his arm a little tighter at that moment. She had spent ten whole minutes testing the acoustics of the Whispering Gallery to please her son.

But knowing someone was courageous was not the same thing as liking that person or growing soft in one's intentions for that person. He had always known that she was a woman well in command of her emotions. Or at least, he had known it since that morning after the opera when her white-faced father had called on him to bring his betrothal to an end.

No, courage, control over emotions did not necessarily make a person likable. And even the most vicious and degenerate of creatures were capable of showing mother love.

He rode in the direction of Lord Blakeford's home. The ladies would in all likelihood have returned from their afternoon's walk, if they had taken it in this weather. He hoped so, at least. This was the visit he had been building toward since his arrival in London. He drew some deep and steadying breaths. He hoped the children would be downstairs for tea. He would be far more confident of success if they were.

They were. In fact, the tea tray had not yet been brought in, and Lord Denbigh realized as he followed the butler into the drawing room that the ladies had only just risen from the floor, where a game of spillikins was in progress. Miss Easton was smoothing out the folds of her dress and laughing, rather flustered. Judith was busy sticking out her chin and clasping her hands calmly in front of her.

"Good afternoon, my lord," she said.

"How civil of you to call on us, my lord," Amy said. "Have you come to join us for tea?"

"I came to get myself out of the snow for a few minutes," he said, "and to assure myself that you are all well after our outing yesterday. But if I am being invited to tea, ma'am, I will most gratefully accept."

"Do you have Pegasus with you, sir?" Rupert asked.

"Yes, indeed," the marquess said, rubbing his hands together to warm them. "But he looked rather like a white-haired old man by the time we arrived here. He was quite covered with snow."

Kate chuckled. "Old man," she said.

Judith had no choice in the matter, as he had intended. Soon he was seated by the fire with Kate on his knee showing him some of the Christmas bows they had made already from the ribbons he had purchased at the river booth. Amy was telling him that they had forgone their walk that day in order to drive to Oxford Street to shop for their Christmas gifts.

"I bought Mama a—" Kate began.

"Sh," Amy said. "Secrets, love."

"—pair of scissors," Kate whispered in his ear, tickling it.

Judith was pouring tea from the tray, which had just arrived.

"She will be delighted with that," the marquess said, looking into the wide dark eyes gazing eagerly into his and resisting the urge to hug the child.

He let conversation flow of its own volition for a while. But matters were made easy for him. The children, and their aunt, too, had Christmas very much on their minds.

"I do believe we will be able to buy greenery at the markets, my lord, will we not?" Amy asked. "It would not seem like Christmas without greenery. And we have several of the bows with which to decorate it made already. I regret that we will not be able to gather our own this year."

"Yes," he said, "I would find it strange, too. There are masses of holly bushes at Denbigh Park. The soil must be very suited to them there. They are almost always laden with berries. And the pine trees are so thick that they do not miss the boughs cut from them. I have sometimes been accused of making my home look like an indoor forest at Christmas."

Amy sighed. "I was very happy to come here with Judith and the children," she said, "and I know I will not regret my first Christmas away from home. But if there is one thing I will miss more than any other it is the caroling. There is nothing that more joyfully conveys the spirit of Christmas, I always think, than going from house to house singing the old carols and seeing the smiles on everyone's faces and tasting the wassail and the cider and the fruitcake. I have suggested that the four of us go caroling here, but every time I do so Rupert looks scornful, Kate will only smile, and Judith looks embarrassed." She laughed.

"There was never a strong tradition of caroling in my neighborhood," he said, "until a lady new to the area began it two years ago. It has taken well, but most of her singers are children. She is always pleading for new adult voices to help lead the singing."

Amy sighed again.

"Last year," Rupert said, "Rodney had a whole boxful of tin soldiers and we set them up in the nursery and had a war that lasted for two whole days. You never saw such fun, sir. There were seven or eight of us playing all the time and sometimes the girls joined in, too. My side won because we had Bevin playing with us. He is twelve years old."

Kate had found the marquess's quizzing glass again and was quietly playing with it.

"My house is going to be overrun with boys and girls this year," Lord Denbigh said. "Twenty altogether—ten boys and ten girls. They were there last year, too, and I am quite confident in saying that it was the best Christmas Denbigh has ever known. Of course, my guests have to be warned. Some people do not consider such boisterous fun to their taste. But no one refused last year and no one has yet refused this year."

"Ten boys?" Rupert said wistfully.

"The youngest five and the oldest eleven," the marquess said. "I imagine it will be a very enjoyable Christmas for everyone who will be there, adults and children alike." He looked at Judith for the first time since he had sat down. She was looking at him tensely, her cup stranded halfway between her saucer and her mouth. *Yes, my lady,* he told her with his eyes. *Oh, yes indeed.* "Holly. Ivy. Pine boughs. Decorations. A Yule log. Good food and drink. Games. Dancing. Caroling and church going. Outdoor exercise. Skating. Perhaps sledding and snowballs if the snow decides to come in earnest."

"Skating," Rupert said, longing in his voice. "I can skate like the wind. Papa said so when we used to skate before he died."

Kate was patting the marquess's waistcoat with her free hand. He looked down at her.

"Yes, ma'am?" he said. "What may I do for you?"

"Can we come?"

"Kate!" Judith's cup clattered back into her saucer.

"Actually," he said, "my very reason for coming here

today was to invite you. Would you like to come?" He looked from Kate to Rupert.

Rupert jumped to his feet. "Mama, too?" he yelled.

"Aunt Amy, too?" Kate asked.

"All of you," he said. "I cannot quite imagine Christmas without you. Will you do me the honor of coming, ma'am?" He looked directly at Amy. "Despite the shortness of the notice?"

"Oh." Amy clasped her hands to her bosom and looked across at Judith.

"Ye-e-es!" Rupert cried.

Kate looked fixedly up into the marquess's face.

"Ma'am?" Lord Denbigh looked at Judith, whose face had lost all color. "Perhaps I should have asked you privately? It looks as if your family will be disappointed if you say no and you would, very unfairly, seem to be the villain. But it will please me more than I can say if you accept."

"Oh, Judith," Amy said, "it would be so wonderful."

"Lord Denbigh's housekeeper will not be expecting four extra guests," Judith said in a strangled voice.

"My housekeeper is always ready for guests," the marquess said. "She has learned from experience that they may descend upon her at any time and in any numbers."

"But it must be your decision," Amy said. "I told you when I came to live with you, Judith, that I would go wherever you wished to go and do whatever you wished to do. I meant it."

Judith turned her eyes from the marquess's to look first at her sister-in-law's resigned expression and then at her son's tensely excited one. And at Kate, who was looking at her with wide, solemn eyes.

"Please, Mama?" Rupert said.

"It is extremely kind of you to invite us, my lord," she said. "We accept."

There was great jubilation in the room while she held the marquess's eyes for longer than necessary. *Yes, my lady,* he told her silently. *Now do you begin to understand?*

When he rose to take his leave five minutes later, she rose, too, and accompanied him from the room and down the stairs.

"Why?" she asked him quietly as they descended the stairs side by side. "Have you not punished me enough?"

"Punished?" He looked at her, eyebrows raised.

"You know what I mean," she said. "Please do not pretend innocence. You have stalked me ever since that evening in Lady Clancy's drawing room. You have done all in your power to make me uncomfortable, to make me the topic of gossip and speculation. And you have used my children against me. Today more than ever. Yes, of course you should have spoken with me about this invitation first. But you knew very well what your answer would have been. When is this punishment to end?"

He stopped at the bottom of the stairs and turned to frown down at her. "Punishment?" he said. "Is that how you see my attentions, Judith? Is that how you always saw them? I have used your children, yes, and your sister-in-law. That is somewhat dishonorable, I will confess. But I will use all the means at my disposal. I have waited almost eight years for my second chance with you. I do not wish to squander it as I did the first."

He held her amazed eyes with his own as he took her nerveless hand from her side and raised it to his lips.

She was still standing at the foot of the stairs after he had donned his greatcoat and gathered up his hat and gloves. He looked at her once more before nodding to her father's butler to open the outer door for him.

And he stood for a moment on the steps outside, smiling grimly to himself.

6

THE MARQUESS OF DENBIGH LEFT TOWN TWO DAYS
later. Fortunately, the snow had done no more
than powder the fields and the hedgerows beside the
highways. And the weather remained too cold, some
said, for there to be danger of much snow.

His guests were not due to arrive until three days before Christmas, but there was much he wished to do
before then. He must make sure that invitations were
sent out for the ball on Christmas Day. His neighbors
would be expecting them, of course, since he had made
it a regular occurrence since his assumption of the title.
But still, the formalities must be observed.

And then he must make sure that all satisfactory arrangements had been made for the children. Ever since
bringing them to the village of Denbigh two years before, he had tried to make Christmas special for them—
having them to stay at the house for two nights,
providing a variety of activities for their entertainment,
filling them with good foods, encouraging them to contribute to the life of the neighborhood by forming a caroling party, making sure that they felt wanted and loved.

This year Cornwell and Mrs. Harrison had reported
that the children were preparing a Christmas pageant.
He would have to decide when would be the best time
for its performance. The evening of Christmas Eve

would seem to be the most suitable time, but that would interfere with the caroling and the church service.

Perhaps the afternoon? he thought. Or the evening before? Or Christmas Day?

He ran through his guest list in his mind. Sir William and Lady Tushingham would be there. They were a childless couple of late middle years, who boasted constantly and tediously about their numerous nephews and nieces but who seemed always to be excluded from invitations at Christmas. And Rockford, who was known—and avoided—at White's as a bore with his lengthy stories that were of no interest to anyone but himself, and who had as few family members as he had friends. Nora and Clement had agreed to come this year as their only daughter was spending the holiday with her husband's family. And his elderly aunts, Aunt Edith and Aunt Frieda, who had never refused an invitation to Denbigh Park since the death of his father, their brother, from whom they had been estranged.

And the Eastons, of course. He wondered how high in the instep Judith Easton was and how well it would please her when she discovered who all the children he had spoken of were. He wondered if she would approve of her son and daughter mingling with the riffraff of the London slums. He smiled grimly at the thought.

He had brought them to Denbigh a little more than two years before after sharing several bottles of port with his friend Spencer Cornwell one evening. Spence was impoverished, though of good family, and restless and disillusioned with life. He was a man with a social conscience and a longing to reform the world and the knowledge and experience to know that there was nothing one man could do to change anything. Cornwell had fast been becoming a cynic.

Except that somehow through the fog of liquor and gloom they had both agreed that one man could perhaps do something on a very small scale, something that would do nothing whatsoever to right all the world's wrongs, but something that might make a difference to one other life, or perhaps two lives or a dozen lives or twenty.

And so the idea for the project had been born. The Marquess of Denbigh had provided the capital and the moral support—and a good deal of time and love, too. He had been surprised by the latter. How could one love riffraff—and frequently foulmouthed and rebellious riffraff at that? But he did. Spence had gathered the children—abandoned orphans, thieving ruffians who had no other way by which to survive, gin addicts, one sweep's boy, one girl who had already been hired out twice by her father for prostitution. And Mrs. Harrison had been employed to care for the girls.

They lived in two separate houses in the village, the boys in one, the girls in the other, six of each at first, now ten, perhaps twenty with more houses and more staff in the coming year. Two years of heaven and hell all rolled into one, according to Spence's cheerful report. In that time they had lost only one child, who had disappeared without trace for a long time. Word had it eventually that he was back at his old haunts in London.

The marquess wondered how Judith would react to sharing a house with twenty slum children for Christmas. He should have warned her, he supposed, told her and her sister-in-law the full truth. Undoubtedly he should have. He always warned his other guests, gave them an opportunity to refuse his invitation if they so chose.

He watched the scenery grow more familiar beyond the carriage windows. It would be good to be home again. He had been happy there for three years, since the death of his father. Or almost happy, at least. And almost not lonely. He had good neighbors and a few good friends. And he had the children.

Watching the approach of home, the events of the past two weeks began to seem somewhat unreal. And he wondered if he had done the right thing, dashing up to London as soon as word reached him that she was there. And concocting and putting into action his plan of revenge—a plan to hurt as he had been hurt.

But of course it was not so much a question of right and wrong as one of compulsion. Should he have resisted the urge—need—to go? *Could* he have resisted?

The old hatred had lived dormant in him for so long that he had been almost unaware of its existence until he heard of the death of her husband. Perhaps it would have died completely away with time if Easton had lived. But he had not, and the hatred had surfaced again.

"When is this punishment to end?" she had asked him just two days before.

He rested his head back against the cushions of his carriage and closed his eyes. Not yet, my lady. Not quite yet.

But did he want her to suffer as he had suffered? He thought back to the pain, dulled by time but still bad enough to make his spirits plummet.

Yes, he did want it. She deserved it. She should be made to know what her selfish and careless rejection had done to another human heart. She deserved to suffer. He wanted to see her suffer.

He wanted to break her heart as she had broken his.

He opened his eyes. Except that his hatred, his plans for revenge, seemed unreal in this setting. He had found happiness here in the past few years—or near happiness, anyway. And he had found it from companionship and friendship and love—and from giving. He had found peace here if not happiness.

Would he be happy after he had completed his revenge on Judith Easton?

He closed his eyes again and saw her as she had been eight years before: shy, wide-eyed, an alluring girl, someone with whom he had tumbled headlong in love from the first moment of meeting. Someone whom he had been so anxious to please and impress that he had found it even more impossible than usual to relax and converse easily with her. Someone who had set his heart on fire and his dreams in flight.

And he remembered again that visit from her father putting an end to it all. Just the memory made the bottom fall out of his stomach again.

Yes, he would be happy. Or satisfied, at least. Justice would have been done.

KATE WAS ASLEEP on Amy's lap, a fistful of Amy's cloak clutched in one hand. Rupert should have been asleep but was not. He was fretful and had jumped to the window twenty times within the past hour demanding to know when they would be there.

Judith did not know when they would be there. She had never been either to Denbigh Park or to that part of the country before. All she knew was that it would be an enormous relief to be at the end of the journey but that she wished she could be anywhere on earth but where she was going.

Her anger had not abated since the afternoon during which she had been trapped into accepting this invitation. But she had been forced to keep it within herself. Amy was quite delighted by the prospect of spending Christmas in the country after all, part of a large group of people. And the children were wildly excited. Judith had voiced no objections, realizing how selfish she had been to have decided against spending the holiday with Andrew's family that year.

Amy of course was delighted not only by the invitation but also by what she considered the motive behind it.

"Can you truly say," she had asked after the marquess had left the house, "that you no longer believe he has a *tendre* for you, Judith? Do you still refuse to recognize that he is trying to fix his interest with you?"

"I do not know why he has asked us," Judith had said, "but certainly not for that reason, Amy."

Her sister-in-law had clucked her tongue.

But Judith had lain awake for a long time that night. He had said that he had waited eight years for a second chance with her. He had called her by her given name. He had kissed her hand, something he had done several times during their betrothal.

She could not believe him. She *would* not believe him. And yet her breath had caught in her throat at the sound of her name on his lips and she had felt the old churning of revulsion in her stomach when he had kissed her hand.

Except that it was not revulsion. She had been very young and inexperienced when they were betrothed. She had called it revulsion then—that breathless awareness, that urge to run and run in order to find air to breathe, that terror of something she had not understood.

She had called it revulsion now, too, for a couple of weeks, from mere force of habit. But it was not that. She had recognized it for what it was at the foot of the stairs when he had kissed her hand. And the realization of the truth terrified her far more than the revulsion ever had.

It was a raw sexual awareness of him that she felt. A sort of horrified attraction. A purely physical thing, for she did not like him at all—and that was a gross understatement. She disliked him and was convinced, despite his words and actions, that he disliked her, too. She distrusted him.

And yet she wanted him in a way she had never wanted any man, or expected to do. She wanted him in a way she had never wanted Andrew, even during those weeks when she had been falling in love with him and contemplating breaking a formally contracted betrothal. In a way she had never wanted him even after their marriage during that first year when she had been in love— the only good year.

And so if the Marquess of Denbigh was trying to punish her—and it had to be that—then he was succeeding. She was a puppet to his puppeteer. For the wanting him brought with it no pleasure, no longing to be in his company, but only a distress and a horror. Almost a fear.

Amy closed her arm more tightly about Kate and reached up for the strap by her shoulder. Rupert let out a whoop and bounced in his seat. The carriage was turning from the roadway onto a driveway and stopping outside a solid square lodge house for directions. But the coachman's guess appeared to have been right. The carriage continued on its way along a dark, tree-lined driveway that seemed to go on forever.

"Oh," Amy said, peering from her window eventually. "How very splendid indeed. This is no manor, Judith. This is a mansion. But then I suppose we might have expected it of a marquess. And then, Denbigh Park is always mentioned whenever the great showpieces of England are listed. Is that a temple among the trees? It looks ruined."

"I daresay it is a folly," Judith said.

The house—the mansion—must have been built within the past century, she thought. Or rebuilt, perhaps. It was a classical structure of perfect symmetry, built of gray stone. Even the gardens and grounds must be of recent design. There were no formal gardens, no parterres, but only rolling lawns and shrubberies, showing by their apparent artlessness the hand of a master landscaper.

Their approach had been noted. The front doors opened as the carriage rumbled over the cobbles before them, and two footmen ran down the steps. The marquess himself stood for a moment at the top of the steps and then descended them.

And if she had had any doubt, Judith thought, tying the ribbons of her bonnet beneath her chin and drawing on her gloves and cautioning Rupert to stay back from the door, then surely she must have realized the truth at this very moment. Something inside her—her heart, her stomach, perhaps both—turned completely over, leaving her breathless and discomposed.

And angry. Very angry. With both him and herself. He looked as if he had just stepped out of his tailor's shop on Bond Street, and there was that dark hair, those harsh features, those thin lips, the piercing eyes and indolent eyelids. And she was feeling travel-weary and rumpled. She was feeling at a decided disadvantage.

The carriage door was opened and the steps set down and the marquess stepped forward. Rupert launched himself into his arms—just as if he were a long-lost uncle, Judith thought—and launched into speech, too. The marquess set the boy's feet down on the ground, rumpled his hair, and told him to hurry inside where it was warm. And he reached up a hand to help Judith down.

"Ma'am?" he said. "Welcome to Denbigh Park. I hope your journey has not been too chill a one."

She was more travel-weary than she thought, she realized in utter dismay and mortification a moment later. She stepped on the hem of her cloak as she descended the steps so that she fell heavily and clumsily into his hastily outstretched arms.

A footman made a choking sound and turned quickly away to lift down some baggage.

"I do beg your pardon," Judith said. "How very clumsy of me." There was probably not one square inch on her body that was not poppy red, or that was not tingling with awareness, she thought, pushing away from his strongly muscled chest.

"No harm done," he said quietly, "except perhaps to your pride. Is the little one sleeping?" He turned tactfully away to look up at Amy, who was still inside the carriage. "Hand her down to me, ma'am, if you will."

Judith watched as he took Kate into his arms and looked down at her. The child was fussing, half asleep, half awake.

"Sleeping Beauty," the marquess said, "there will be warm milk waiting for you in the nursery upstairs, not to mention a roaring fire and a rocking horse. But I daresay you are not interested."

Kate opened her eyes and stared blankly at him for a few moments. Then she smiled slowly and broadly up at him while Judith felt her teeth clamping together. A long-lost uncle again. How did he do it?

"Do let me take her, my lord," she said, and felt his eyes steady on her as she relieved him of his burden.

He turned to help Amy down to the cobbles.

"What a very splendid home you have, my lord," Amy said. "It has taken our breath quite away, has it not, Judith? Are we not all fortunate that there has been no more snow in the past week? Though of course it is cold enough to keep the ice on the lakes and rivers. I do declare, it must be the coldest winter in living memory. And it is only December yet."

"I have snow on order for tomorrow or Christmas Eve," Lord Denbigh said. "And plenty of it, too. It cannot fail, ma'am, now that all my guests have arrived.

And it has been trying so hard for the past two weeks or more that it surely will succeed soon."

He had taken one lady on each arm and was leading them up the front steps and into the tiled and marbled great hall with its fluted pillars and marbled galleries. And if the approach to the house had not taken one's breath away, Judith thought, then this surely would. The hall was two stories high and dwarfed any person standing in it.

And yet it was unexpectedly warm. Fires blazed in two large marble fireplaces facing each other at either side of the hall.

The Marquess of Denbigh presented his housekeeper, who was standing in the middle of the hall curtsying to them and smiling warmly from a face that must boast a thousand wrinkles, Judith thought, and turned them over to her care. Mrs. Hines smiled with motherly warmth at Rupert, clucked over Kate, and led them all upstairs to their rooms.

Tea would be served in the drawing room, she told them, after they had refreshed themselves. She would return to conduct them there in half an hour's time.

The children had been put into the care of a very competent nurse, who had been provided by the marquess. Judith sank down onto a small daybed at the foot of the high four-poster bed in her room and blew out two cheekfuls of air.

So it had begun. A week's stay at Denbigh. The final week of her punishment, doubtless. There was a week to live through before she could make arrangements to return to her own home in Lincolnshire and try to begin normal life again.

A week was not an eternity. It was a shame that it had to be the week of Christmas so that her first Christmas free of Andrew's family was to be ruined after all. In fact, it was more than a shame, it was infuriating. But nonetheless it was only a week. She must fortify herself constantly with that thought.

She frowned suddenly. All his guests had arrived, he had said. Where, then, were all the children he had promised Rupert and Kate? Had he lied to them on top of everything else?

She straightened her shoulders suddenly as there was a tap on her door and Amy's head appeared around it.

"Are you going to change your frock, Judith?" she asked. "Or are you just going to wash your hands and face?"

"Oh, let us change by all means," Judith said, getting briskly to her feet. She had already made a disaster of an opening scene—her mind touched on her clumsy stumble and the firm security of his arms and chest, and veered away again. At least she would face the next one in a clean and fresh dress and with combed hair. "There is a maid in my dressing room, unpacking my things already."

"Yes, and in mine, too," Amy said. "I shall see you shortly, then, Judith." She withdrew her head and closed the door again.

Yes, shortly, Judith thought, drawing a deep breath and walking through into the dressing room.

"WE WERE FACING that much-dreaded experience," Lady Clancy was telling Judith during tea in the drawing room, "a Christmas alone. Why is it, I wonder, that no one would dream of pitying a married couple for having to spend any other day of the year alone in each other's company whereas any number of people would consider it a dreadful fate on that one particular day?"

"Perhaps because Christmas is for families and sharing," Judith said.

"Oh, undoubtedly," Lady Clancy agreed. "Clement

and I have been assuring each other since November that it will be delightful to spend one quiet holiday free of our daughter and her family. But of course it was mere bravado, and Max saw that in a moment. He always does. His home is always filled with lonely persons at Christmas—first at his other home and now here. Not that I am for a moment suggesting that you are one of that number, Mrs. Easton. Your two children are upstairs? They must be weary after the journey. Carriages and children usually do not go well together."

Filled his home with lonely persons? Judith thought as she answered Lady Clancy's questions. That did not sound at all like the Marquess of Denbigh as she knew him.

"He used to fill his house to overflowing," Lady Clancy said. "But last year and this there have been fewer invited guests because he has been taking in the children for the holiday. I daresay it will be very noisy once they arrive. I am not sure whether to look forward to it or to plan my escape tomorrow. But we have had plenty of warning, of course. And I like the idea. I really do admire Max more than I can say for actually doing it instead of merely talking about the problems as most of us do. Are you in any way apprehensive about your children's mingling with them, Mrs. Easton?"

Judith looked at her companion, mystified. "Lord Denbigh mentioned that there would be children here," she said. "But where are they? And who are they?"

"He has not told you?" Lady Clancy laughed. "How naughty of him. They are children from the streets of London, Mrs. Easton, children who had no homes and no prospects for the future except perhaps a noose to swing from eventually. They are housed in the village and fed and clothed and taught. The older ones will be trained eventually to a trade and I am sure Max will see to it that they find suitable positions. From what I have heard, they also enjoy a great deal of recreation and merriment. They will be here, staying at the house, for Christmas."

"Ten boys and ten girls," the marquess's voice said from behind Judith's shoulder. She had not heard him come up. "And a more boisterous score of youngsters you would not wish to meet, ma'am. Did I neglect to explain to you in London who the children were? I did mention the children, did I not?"

He seated himself close to Judith and Lady Clancy and proceeded to engage them both in conversation. His manner was amiable, Judith found. He seemed at ease, relaxed. The country and his home apparently suited him.

Lonely persons? She had been introduced to everyone in the drawing room. Lord and Lady Clancy were without their daughter and her family that year and would have spent Christmas alone. The Misses Hannibal, his aunts, were elderly ladies, both spinsters, who would perhaps not have been invited anywhere else. Sir William and Lady Tushingham she did not know. But she remembered Mr. Rockford. She had been slightly acquainted with him during her come-out Season. Andrew and his friends had used to make ruthless fun of the man because no one could listen to him talk without falling soundly asleep after three minutes if they suffered from insomnia, they had used to say.

Was Mr. Rockford a lonely person, too? Did he have no family? Or friends? Somehow it seemed unlikely that the Marquess of Denbigh was his friend. And yet he had invited the man to his home.

And Amy and the children and she. They would have been alone, too, lonely despite the fact that there were four of them. Was that why he had invited them? But no, she knew that was not the reason. Besides, she did not like to think of its being the reason for any of the invitations to his guests. The Marquess of Denbigh compassionate? She did not like the image at all.

But what about those children? The ones he had taken from lives of desperation in London and brought here. But she knew only Lady Clancy's version of that story.

The marquess and Lady Clancy had been left to talk alone, she realized suddenly. She was being ill-mannered and not doing her part to sustain the conversation.

Lord Denbigh was looking at her, his keen gray eyes holding hers. "Your children are contentedly settled in the nursery, Mrs. Easton?" he asked. "Mrs. Webber will make them feel quite at home. She was my nurse many years ago and was quite delighted to come out of retirement for the occasion."

"Thank you," Judith said. "Kate had eyes for nothing but the rocking horse before I left, and Rupert had spotted the books."

"But you must not feel that they are being confined to the nursery," he said. "You must allow them downstairs as often as you wish. I have never subscribed to the theory that children should remain invisible until they have grown as sober and dull as the rest of us. And at Christmastime especially children should always be allowed to run wild—or almost so, anyway."

"Thank you," Judith said again.

And she stared, fascinated, as he smiled at her. A smile that only just touched the corners of his mouth and brightened his eyes, but a smile nonetheless. And one that transformed his face for the moment from harshness to handsomeness.

Judith felt that growingly familiar somersaulting feeling within and concentrated on keeping her breathing even.

7

"JUDITH." AMY CAME BURSTING INTO HER SISTER-IN-law's dressing room the following morning after a quick knock. "Ah, you are up. His lordship is a magician or a prophet, I do declare. Have you seen?"

Judith had indeed seen and had had much the same thought. And also the thought that if it had only happened one day sooner, or better still, two, she might have been saved. *She*, not anyone else. Amy would have been disappointed and the children quite despondent.

"Yes," she said. "It must have been snowing in earnest all night for there to be such a thick covering already."

"And it is still coming down," Amy said. "Do you realize what this means, Judith? Snow for Christmas. It does not happen often, does it? Especially fresh white snow. It is going to be perfectly splendid for the children. Have you heard about the children? I do admire Lord Denbigh for doing such a thing. But will this snow impede their coming here tomorrow night, Judith? I do hope not, though of course it could be said that it is not at all the thing for such children to be brought into a house with guests. I think the idea quite charming, however. I hope you do not think it is in poor taste with Rupert and Kate here."

Amy was excited and enjoying herself already—Judith could see that. There was even a flush of color in her cheeks. The Misses Hannibal had taken her to their bosoms the evening before and Mr. Rockford had even tried flirting with her. Amy had never been made so much of in her own home.

"It will be a new experience," Judith said, swiveling about on the stool, her temporary maid having finished pinning up her hair. "I look forward to it. Shall we go down to breakfast?"

Amy's fears were put to rest very soon after breakfast. Rupert and Kate were very eager to be outside in the snow. Judith and Amy dressed themselves and the children warmly and descended the stairs. But when they emerged into the great hall, it was to find the front doors being opened and children of all sizes and descriptions pouring inside, all variously covered with snow, all seemingly talking at the same time. Two adults came in after them. The marquess was emerging from a downstairs room.

"Cor blimey," someone yelled, "it's three feet thick out there if it's an inch."

"Ow, luverly," someone else shrieked, "fires. Me fingers is froze off me 'ands." A thin girl detached herself from the mob and raced for one of the fires. Two others followed her.

"Ow, look," a tall and gangly boy said above the general hubbub of noise. "'Oo are the nippers, guv?"

The Marquess of Denbigh stood with his feet apart and his hands clasped behind his back. "The nippers, Daniel, my lad," he said, "are Master Rupert Easton and his sister, Miss Easton. Could you children not have left at least some of the snow outside? Did you have to drag it all inside with you?"

A chorus of voices explained with varying degrees of coherence that there had been snowball fights to accompany the walk from the village.

"And Val got shoved in the snow by Toby," one of the

larger girls said, "and Toby got shoved in by five of us girls and got 'is face washed in it, too."

"Ah," the marquess said. "That explains it, then. Now, left turn the lot of you and march smartly into the salon. Mrs. Hines is having warm chocolate sent up for you."

"And cake, too, guv?" Daniel asked, a cheeky grin on his face.

"Left turn," the gentleman who had arrived with the children said sternly. "And the 'guv' is 'my lord' to you, Daniel, as I have explained five thousand times at a conservatively low estimate."

As quickly as the hall had filled, it emptied again, leaving behind only the adults and Rupert and Kate.

"May I go, too, Mama?" Rupert asked hopefully.

"Me, too, Mama?" Kate tugged at her cloak.

"I shall take them in with me if you have no objection, ma'am," the lady who had come with the children said. She was plump and matronly and looked perfectly capable of dealing with the toughest urchin.

"Mrs. Easton," the marquess said, "Miss Easton, may I present Mrs. Harrison and Mr. Cornwell, the very capable and long-suffering guardians of the hurricanes who just passed through here?"

Mr. Cornwell was short and inclined to stoutness, though Judith guessed that there was a great deal more muscle than fat on his frame. Frost was melting from his sandy mustache and eyebrows. His fair hair was thinning.

"Ladies?" he said, bowing to them.

Mrs. Harrison curtsied. "Despite all the noise," she said to Judith, "the children are quite a harmless lot, ma'am. They will not gobble up your own children, I promise you." She smiled.

"I am afraid," Mr. Cornwell said, "that their elocution slips alarmingly whenever they get excited about something, Max. And this morning they are very excited." He turned and addressed himself to Amy. "One would hardly know that in the schoolroom they often speak something approximating to the English language, would you?"

"Go along, then," Judith said, relinquishing Kate's hand to the outstretched one of Mrs. Harrison.

The two children disappeared inside the salon. A moment later two maids followed them, each with a tray laden with steaming cups. A third maid was carrying a tray of cakes and muffins.

"Come into the library, Spence," the marquess said, "and breathe in some sanity for a few minutes. Ladies, will you join us? You are dressed for the outdoors, I see. I was about to send up to invite you and the children to accompany us once the party arrived from the village. This is the morning when we are to haul in the Yule log and gather the greenery for decorating the house. The task is now to be made more difficult and infinitely more exciting by the presence of the snow. Rockford should be down soon, too."

Amy clasped her hands tightly and beamed. "Oh," she said, "this is so much more pleasurable than being in town, shopping at a market. We would be delighted to come, would we not, Judith?"

Lord Denbigh ushered them all into a large and cozy library. Looking about, Judith guessed that he spent a great deal of his time there. There was an open book on a table beside a leather chair, she noticed. The desk was strewn with papers. It was obviously a room that was used, not just a showpiece.

Both gentlemen had a drink. The ladies refused.

Amy had been a little divided in her feelings about the invitation to spend Christmas at Denbigh Park. The lure of a country home was strong and she liked the marquess and looked with hope on what appeared to be a budding romance between him and Judith. But there was also the fact that they must leave London so soon after she had finally gone there.

She no longer had any misgivings. From the moment of her arrival the afternoon before, she had felt like a person. Judith had always made her feel that way, of course, and the marquess in the past few weeks had been very civil. But now she was in a country home with several other guests and she was being treated with respect. That silly Mr. Rockford had even tried flirting with her the evening before.

Amy realized in full just how much less than a person she had always been considered at home.

She was enjoying herself immensely. And she was enchanted by the story of all the children and by her first sight of them. She was almost envious of Mrs. Harrison and was admiring of Mr. Cornwell.

"I do think it a splendid job you are doing, sir," she said to him now. "But what gave you the idea? Or was it his lordship's?"

He looked at her and smiled. He was quite as willing as the marquess and the other guests to take her seriously, she thought in some surprise. He had a pleasant face. It was not at all handsome, but it was good-natured. It was the kind of face that would inspire trust in troubled children, she thought. Just as his rather solid frame would inspire respect and a sense of security.

"It was a joint brainchild, actually, ma'am," he said. "We dreamed up the idea one night, thought at the time that we must both have taken leave of our senses, and are even more convinced of the fact two and a half years later." He chuckled. "I have never been happier in my life."

"How wonderful it must be," she said somewhat wistfully, "to be able to devote one's life to children."

"Are you sure you wish to come gathering greenery,

ma'am?" he asked. "It is a longish walk to the trees and there is bound to be a great deal of noise and foolery. I cannot assure you in all confidence either that the language will all be suitable for a lady's ears."

"I would not miss it for worlds," Amy said. "This is what Christmas is all about, sir—children and decorations and trudges in the snow. And company."

He actually winked at her as he set his empty glass down. "Never say I did not warn you, ma'am," he said.

Amy felt herself turn pink, reminded herself that she was thirty-six years old, and told herself not to be silly.

"I would imagine," the marquess said to Judith, "that by the time these children have finished gathering and decorating there will be more greenery inside the house than out. And a great deal more noise and chaos. I hope you will not mind. I was a little afraid last year that my aunts might have an apoplectic fit apiece. But they smiled and nodded and were enchanted—and horrified the boys by kissing all the girls. The boys thought that they would surely be next. Fortunately, my aunts had more sense of decorum."

Judith laughed, finding the situation and his humor amusing despite herself.

"I should have told you about the children," he said. His eyes were looking very directly into hers, a hint of a smile in them again. "But I was afraid that you would cry off if you knew. It was shameful of me, was it not?"

Judith felt a twinge of alarm. If she had not known him eight years before and again in the past few weeks, she might well be gaining a totally different impression of him than the true one, she thought. He seemed quite human suddenly. More than human. And there was a warmth in his look.

Yet there was something else, too, something quite intangible and unexplainable.

"I have a feeling," she said, "that Rupert and Kate are

going to be talking with nostalgia about this Christmas for a long time to come."

"I hope so," he said. "And their mother, too."

She was saved from having to reply, though she felt shivers all along the length of her spine, by the appearance of the butler at the door to announce that Mrs. Harrison, Mr. Rockford, and the children were ready to leave.

"We had better not keep them waiting a single moment then, Max," Mr. Cornwell said. "If the children are ready to leave, that means right now at this very moment if not five minutes ago."

CHRISTMAS HAD BEEN a lonely time when he was a child and a boy. His father had sometimes had house guests and had frequently invited neighbors to various entertainments, but he had never felt the necessity of seeing to it that there were other children to play with his son.

Now he loved Christmas and loved to surround himself with people who might be lonely if he paid no attention to them—and with children. His and Spence's decision to open children's homes in the village had been an inspired if a somewhat mad one.

He had done this before—gone out with the children and Spence and Mrs. Harrison to gather the decorations for the house. And it had always been a merry occasion. But there had never before been the added festive detail of snow.

And there had never been Judith Easton on his arm. She had taken it with some hesitation when they had stepped out of the house. But there had been no excuse not to do so. The boys and Spence and Rockford were pulling the heavy sleds. Rupert was walking along with two older boys, Daniel and Joe, and gazing up at them somewhat worshipfully. Kate was holding Mrs.

Harrison's hand—at least she was until Daniel stopped, made some comment about the nipper's boots, and hoisted her up onto his thin shoulder. Kate made no protest but sat with quiet contentment on her new perch. Judith drew in a deep breath and then chuckled.

Amy was walking between the two newest girls, sisters, talking cheerfully to them before taking them both by the hand. No, Judith Easton had no excuse for not taking his arm.

"They have been with Mrs. Harrison for only four or five months," Lord Denbigh said, nodding in the direction of the two little girls with Amy. "The mother was stabbed by a lover and both girls were dependent upon gin as a large part of their diet. Their first two months here were very difficult for Mrs. Harrison and a nightmare for them. They are still quieter than the other children, but they are coming around. If you had seen them four months ago, Judith, you would not believe the difference in them now."

"Poor little girls," she said, gazing ahead at them. "They must have known more suffering in their few years than most people can expect in a lifetime. Imagine all the countless thousands who never know even such a reasonably happy ending as this one. I hate driving into London past the poorer quarters. Though that is a very cowardly attitude. The poverty and the suffering exist whether I can block them from my consciousness or not."

She was unbelievably beautiful, he thought, looking down at her. Far more so than she had been eight years before. He could not look at her without feeling the churning of old desires. Touching her was enough to catch at his breathing.

There was a sense of unreality about the moment. He was walking with her, talking with her on his own land—with Judith. And he was to have her with him over Christmas, for a full week. And while his main purpose had nothing to do with the peace and joy of the season, he had decided to allow himself some pleasure from her presence, too. For despite his basic dislike of her, his opinion of her character, and his intention of breaking her heart as she had broken his, she was also the most desirable woman he had ever known.

He desired her. He wanted her. And since it did not at all contradict his purpose to do so, he would do nothing to quell the feeling.

"I believe that the mistake many people make," he said, "is looking at the whole vast problem of poverty and social inequality and feeling helpless and guilty. For there is nothing the average man or woman can do to solve a universal social problem. But all of us can do something on a very small scale. There are thousands of children in England suffering untold hardships at this very moment. But twenty children who would have swelled those numbers by only an infinitesimal amount are well fed and well loved, have their futures secured, and are at the moment having a boisterous good time."

The unfortunate Toby was having his face rubbed in the snow again by four screeching girls.

"That lad," the marquess said, "is going to have to learn something about diplomacy. Or something about running fast."

"Why did you do it?" she asked, looking up at him, frowning. "Just because your friend needed the financial backing?"

"Partly, I suppose," he said. "And partly because I was a lonely child."

"Were you?" Her frown had deepened.

"An only child," he said. "It was a terrible fate. Perhaps it was not my parents' fault, since my mother died when I was an infant. But I have always vowed that when I married I would have either no children at all or half a dozen."

Her flush was noticeable even against the rosiness that the cold was whipping into her cheeks. *Those children might have been yours, too,* he told her very deliberately with his eyes. *Ours.*

"It would be dreadful to have no children," she said. "Mine have been the light of my life for several years."

"Even before your husband died?" he asked her quietly.

Her eyes wavered from his and fell for a moment to his lips.

"Was it all worth it, Judith?" he asked her. "Were you happy?"

She looked ahead of her again. He heard her swallow. "It was my choice," she said at last. "I chose my course and I remained committed to it."

"Yes," he said, "I believe you did. It is a pity sometimes, is it not, that it takes two to make a good marriage."

Her arm had stiffened on his. Perhaps he had gone too far, he thought. Perhaps he was moving too fast. Perhaps he should not have started calling her by her given name, though she had made no open objection to his doing so. Perhaps he should not have started yet caressing her with his eyes. And perhaps he should not have made any reference to the past or to her marriage, which was, after all, none of his business.

However, he was saved from the present situation when a soft, wet snowball collided with the back of his hat, tipping it forward over his brow, and he turned sharply to detect the culprit. One moment later he was darting after seven-year-old Benjamin, whose flesh had been so deeply ingrained with soot two years before when he had dropped down the wrong chimney in the marquess's town house to land in the study hearth when his lordship was occupying the room that it had been impossible to know even what color his hair was.

"Attack an enemy from behind, would you, Ben?" Lord Denbigh roared, grabbing the child about the middle. "There is only one fitting punishment for that: to be strung up by the heels and forced to contemplate the world upside down."

He dangled the shrieking and giggling child by the ankles while all the other children cheered and jeered and advised his lordship to drop Ben head first into the nearest snow drift.

Ben was hoisted onto the marquess's shoulders for the remaining distance to the trees. Judith had joined Mrs. Harrison.

Mr. Rockford volunteered to take the largest sled and the three largest boys to find and load a suitable Yule log. Kate, who was still on Daniel's shoulder, and Rupert went with them. Mrs. Harrison took some of the girls to find mistletoe. Mr. Cornwell took several boys and a few of the girls to gather holly. He needed people who would not squeal too loudly at pricking their fingers once or twice, he said.

"That excludes you, Val," he said cheerfully and winked at the girl.

"Violet, Lily, and I will come, too," Amy said. "Holly has always been my very favorite decoration. There could not possibly be a Christmas without holly."

"Pine boughs for the rest of us, then," the marquess said. "Toby and Ben, haul a sled apiece, if you please. Mrs. Easton, if you would care to stay here, we should not be long. The snow is very deep among the trees."

"And miss the fun?" she said, smiling at him. "Never."

And they waded off through the deeper snow toward a grove of pine trees. Half an hour later their sleds were laden and their arms, too, and they were at leisure to look about them for signs of the other groups.

Judith gasped suddenly. "Fire!" she cried. "Something is on fire. Rupert! Kate!" There was panic in her voice. She started forward.

The marquess laid a firm hand on her arm and chuckled. "A cozy fire inside a gamekeeper's cottage," he said. "The children all know about it and visit it as often as they may. It is Rockford's group at a guess. I don't believe either Mrs. Harrison or Cornwell would allow the children to indulge themselves when there is work to be done. But one group is enjoying some warmth and some indolence."

Two young boys in their group whooped with delight and made off through the deep snow in the direction of the line of smoke.

"Kate and Rupert among them," she said, relaxing beneath his grip. "They are with Mr. Rockford's group."

"They will all be punished," he said. "They will miss the fight and be as furious as a pack of devils."

"Fight?" Judith asked.

"Snowball fight," he said. "We cannot expect all work and no play from such a large number of children, now can we? A good fight is what everyone needs as a reward before we start back to the house."

"Oh, dear," she said.

But everyone else, emerging from the trees at about the same time, greeted the idea with wild enthusiasm.

"Men and girls against ladies and boys," the marquess announced. "Five minutes to prepare and then battle in earnest."

He grinned as the two teams lined up a suitable distance apart and began feverish preparations. The boys on the other side were building impressive ramparts and snowbanks, which would be largely useless as they would all be unable to resist coming out in front of them to fight when the action started, anyway. His girls were busy making a reserve supply of snowballs.

The missing party, newly warmed from their rest at the gamekeeper's cottage, arrived before the five minutes were at an end and joined in the preparations with enthusiasm.

"Time up!" the marquess yelled when the five minutes were over, and the air rained snowballs. There were squeals and yells and bellows and giggles, and sure enough, his girls had the early advantage as the boys abandoned their fortifications and were forced to make their weapons while defending themselves against continuous attack.

Miss Easton, he saw, flanked by two of the larger boys, who were certainly as large as she, was engaged in a duel with Spence. Mrs. Harrison was defending herself against attack from a group of her girls. Rockford, laughing and clearly enjoying himself, was allowing a group of little boys, including Rupert, to score unanswered hits on his person.

And then a large snowball shattered directly against the marquess's face.

"Oh, no," Judith Easton yelled as his eyes locked on her. She was laughing helplessly. "I have lamentably poor aim. I was throwing at that little boy who just hit me." She pointed at Trevor.

He bent and scooped up a large handful of snow, not taking his eyes from her despite the fact that two more snowballs hit him one on the shoulder and one on the knee. He molded his snowball very deliberately.

"You would not," she called to him as he strode toward her, and she stooped down to scoop snow harmlessly in his direction and then turned to dart behind the snow hills thrown up by her boys.

He followed her there. She was still laughing. And looking damned beautiful, he thought. He would not allow himself for the moment to think anything else. He was enjoying himself.

"Don't, please," she said, setting her hands palm out in front of her. She could not stop laughing. "Please don't."

He reached out with one booted foot, caught her smartly behind the ankles, jerked forward, and sent her sprawling back into the snowbank. Beyond the bank there was a great deal of noise and a great barrage of snowballs still flying in both directions.

"How clumsy of you," he said, stretching down his free hand for one of hers. "Do allow me to help you up, ma'am."

"Oh, most unfair," she said. "I am going to be caked with snow."

"In future," he said, drawing her to her feet when she set her hand in his, "you must be careful about allowing your feet to skid on the snow." He drew her all the way against him and held her there with one arm about her. "You could easily break a leg, you know."

The laughter was dying from her face, only inches from his. A great awareness was taking its place in her eyes. He could feel his heart beating in his throat and in his ears. He moved his head an inch closer to hers, his eyes straying down to her mouth. Her lips were parted, he saw.

The temptation was great. Almost overpowering. One taste while everyone's attention was distracted and they were partially shielded anyway by the snowbank. One taste, though it was far too early for such familiarity. But he had a plan to follow. A plan that called for greater patience and caution.

"Revenge can be very sweet sometimes," he told her in a low voice, keeping his eyes on her mouth as he brought his hand from behind her and pressed his snowball very firmly against her face.

"Argh!" she said, sputtering snow.

He laughed and turned away. "Time up!" he yelled. "I

have penetrated the enemy defenses, as you can all see, and declare the men and girls to be the winners."

Shrieks of delight from the girls and high-pitched insults hurled at the boys in place of snow. Loud protests and bloodcurdling threats from the boys.

"Back to the house," the marquess said. "If we cannot have luncheon and rehearse for the Christmas pageant soon enough, there will be no time for skating on the lake afterward."

Skating! The word was like a magic wand to set everyone scurrying in the direction of home. Most of the children had skated the year before during a cold spell and remembered their bruises and their triumphs with an eagerness to have them renewed.

"I can skate like the wind," Rupert Easton told the marquess, falling into step beside him and reaching up a hand to be held, forgetting for the moment that he was six years old and a big boy.

"Then I will have to see proof this afternoon," Lord Denbigh said, taking the hand in his. Judith, he could see, was walking with Rockford. He, inevitably, was doing all the talking.

The marquess was still regretting that he had not after all kissed her before making use of his snowball.

8

GATHERING THE CHRISTMAS GREENERY HAD NOT taken as long as expected. There was still time when they returned to the house to decorate the drawing room and the ballroom, though the marquess did suggest that perhaps the children would welcome a rest before beginning work again.

"Of course," he added to Mr. Cornwell, who was taking a bundle of holly very carefully from Amy's arms, "I might have saved my breath as you obviously have not taught the meaning of the word *rest* in that school of yours yet, Spence. What do you teach, anyway?"

Judith hoped fervently that the outing would have tired Kate even if not Rupert. She hoped that at least her daughter would be willing to be taken back to the nursery. But Kate had attached herself to Daniel, and Daniel had promised that he would lift her onto his shoulders so that she could hang some of the greenery over the mantel and perhaps over some of the pictures.

"Though I think you'd 'ave to sprout arms ten feet long to reach the pictures, nipper," he added. "P'raps I'll stand on a chair."

Judith closed her eyes briefly.

She longed to escape, but there was no excuse to do so. Lord and Lady Clancy and Sir William and Lady Tushingham had also appeared to help, and even the marquess's aunts had come downstairs from their rooms to exclaim at the enormous piles of holly and mistletoe and pine boughs and at the size of the Yule log.

Mr. Cornwell, Amy, Mr. Rockford, and the Tushinghams would help supervise the decorating of the drawing room, it was decided. The rest of the adults would move on to the ballroom.

She longed to escape, Judith thought, and yet there was that old seductive excitement about the sights and smells of Christmas in the house. The smell of the pine boughs was already teasing her nostrils. At Ammanlea the servants had always done the decorating. At her home they had always done it themselves. It was good to be back to those days, and good to see so many children happy and excited and working with a will.

She shook off the mental image of Daniel standing on a delicate chair in the drawing room with Kate on his shoulders reaching up to a picture. One of the adults would doubtless see to it that no unnecessary risks were taken.

Several large boxes had been set in the middle of the ballroom and soon the children were into them, unpacking bells and ribbons and bows and stars—several large, shining stars.

"To hang from the chandeliers," the marquess explained. "No, Toby, it would be far too dangerous. I would hate to see you with a broken head for Christmas. I shall do it myself."

And Judith, gingerly separating piles of holly into individual sprigs so that the children could rush about the room placing them in suitable and unsuitable spots, also watched the marquess remove his coat and roll up his shirt sleeves to the elbows. She watched him climb a tall ladder held by Lord Clancy and two of the biggest boys in order to attach the stars to the chandeliers.

She held her breath.

And then looked away sharply to resume her task and suck briefly on one pricked finger. She did not want this to be happening, she thought fiercely. She did not want this feeling of Christmas, this growing feeling of warmth and elation, to be associated in any way with him.

But how could she help herself? Ever since her arrival the afternoon before, and especially this morning, she had been fighting the realization that perhaps he was not at all as she had always thought him to be. She remembered her impressions of him eight years before, impressions gathered over a two-month period. He had seemed cold, morose, harsh, silent. She had been afraid of him. And there had been nothing in London this time to change that impression.

Oh, there had been, of course. There had been his civility to Amy, his kindness to her children and even to her. But her fear of him had not lessened. She had suspected his motives, had assumed that somehow it was all being done to punish her, since he knew that the worst he could do to her was inflict his company on her and ingratiate himself with her family.

But here? Could she really cling to her old impressions here? He was mingling with twenty children from the lowest classes, teasing them, playing with them, making them as happy as any children anywhere at Christmastime. And it could not even be said that it was just a financial commitment to him, that he provided the money while Mr. Cornwell and Mrs. Harrison did all the work and all the caring. That would not be true. He so clearly loved all the children and enjoyed spending time with them.

She recalled the contempt she had felt for him in London when he had remarked on one occasion that he had a fondness for children. He had not lied—that was becoming increasingly obvious. Rupert had tripped along at his side all the way back to the house, his hand in the marquess's, talking without ceasing.

"There," she said to Violet, smiling, "that is the last of it."

Mrs. Harrison and two of the girls were just coming in with armloads of ivy, she saw.

She did not want this to be happening. Lord Denbigh, still in his shirt sleeves, was standing in the middle of the ballroom, his hand on Benjamin's shoulder, pointing across the room at something. Ben went racing away.

He was not at all thin, Judith thought. His waist and hips were slender, but his shoulders and upper arms were well muscled beneath the shirt and his thighs, too. She caught the direction of her thoughts and swallowed.

He had waited almost eight years for a second chance with her, he had told her in London. And this morning he had asked her if it had all been worth it, if she had been happy. And he had held her against him—she turned weak again at the knees with the memory—and had almost kissed her.

And the shameful thing was that she had wanted it in a horrified, fascinated sort of way. She would have done nothing to stop it. She had a curiosity to know what his mouth would feel like on hers.

She shuddered.

"I must confess," Lady Clancy said, coming to stand beside her and gazing about at the ballroom, which had suddenly become a room full of Christmas, "that Clement and I were not at all sure that we were doing the right thing in accepting our invitation. But I am already beginning to enjoy myself more than I have done for years. Max and Mr. Cornwell and Mrs. Harrison have done wonders with those children, have they not?"

The decorating having largely being completed, the children were having noisy good fun, mostly with a few sprigs of mobile mistletoe. There was a loud burst of merriment from the far side of the room, accompanied by catcalls and loudly hurled insults, when Val soundly slapped Joe's face after he had stolen a kiss.

"Keep yer 'ands to yerself," she said before letting loose with rather more colorful language.

"But I got mistletoe," Joe protested. "It's allowed."

"I don't care if you got a certificate all decorated up wiv gold lettering from the Archbishop of Canterbury," Val said. "Keep yer 'ands to yerself or I'll chop 'em off at the wrists."

The other boys all gave an exaggerated gasp of horror.

"It is Christmas," the marquess said, "and mistletoe does excuse a great deal of familiarity, but a gentleman is a gentleman for all that, Joe. A simple 'May I' would solve the problem. No lady would be so rag-mannered as to refuse."

"Yeh, Val," someone yelled, and there was another loud outburst of laughter.

"Max is taking them all skating this afternoon," Lady Clancy said to Judith. "I do believe I may go out myself. I used to fancy myself a skater."

"I never could stay upright," Judith said. "I gave up even trying years ago."

"Well, you know," Lady Clancy said, "the secret is to keep your weight over your skates. So many people pull back out of fear and then, of course, lose their balance."

There was still a great deal of laughter from the children, especially from one group of them behind Judith and Lady Clancy, but they continued to converse with each other and did not look to see what was happening.

" 'Ere, guv," someone yelled. There were smothered giggles from some girls.

"I can still feel some of my bruises," Judith said. The marquess was striding toward them. She could feel the familiar breathlessness and tried to continue the conversation, her face expressionless, her voice cool.

But she turned her head with sudden suspicion as he drew closer. One tall boy, grinning wickedly, was standing directly behind her, a sprig of mistletoe waving above her head. But it was too late to duck out of the way. Lord Denbigh, she saw, was standing directly in front of her.

"May I?" he asked.

What could she do? Give in to a fit of the vapors and swoon at his feet? Say no? With all the children and the adults, too, either smiling at her or convulsed with merriment? She nodded almost imperceptibly.

And then his hands came to rest lightly on either side of her waist and as she drew breath his lips touched her own.

Briefly. Only for the merest moment. But she felt as if she had been struck by a lightning bolt. Sensation sizzled through her. And she felt as if it would be quite impossible to expel the air she had just drawn into her lungs.

"Aw, guv," the boy who was standing behind her said, and she became aware at the same moment of jeering voices about the ballroom, "carn't yer do better than that?"

"Certainly," the marquess said, and Judith stared into his heavy-lidded eyes and felt that she would surely die. "I merely raised my head because I remembered that I had forgotten to wish Mrs. Easton a happy Christmas."

Somewhere, youthful voices were cheering. Lady Clancy was chuckling close by. Someone behind her whooped and whistled. Judith's fingertips came to rest against a muscled chest, warm beneath the silk of his shirt, and she fought desperately to detach her mind from what was happening.

It was not an indecorous kiss under the circumstances. She told herself that. He touched her only at the waist, holding her body a few inches from his own. And his mouth was light on hers. His mouth. Not his lips. He had parted them slightly over hers so that she was aware of warmth and softness and moistness.

Andrew had never kissed her so, she told herself, deliberately keeping up the flow of an interior monologue. There had been only an increased pressure to show his heightened passion. After the first year he had rarely kissed her at all.

She had never been kissed just so.

It lasted only a few seconds. Ten at the longest, she guessed. An eternity. The world had turned right about. The stars had turned, the universe. She was being indescribably foolish.

"Happy Christmas, my lord," she said coolly.

"You see, Joe?" Lord Denbigh said, turning his head and raising his voice. "No slaps, and the lady even wished me the compliments of the season. That is the way to do it, my lad."

He released her waist finally and turned away to organize a tidy-up.

"Little rascals," Lady Clancy said with a laugh. "Max is a better sport than I would have expected. And you, too, my dear. I must say that both Clement and I were disappointed when you married Mr. Easton instead of Max. He was always a favorite with us, shy though he was—and still is to a certain degree. He disappeared for a whole year after your marriage. No one seemed to know where he was. He went walking in the Lake District and Scotland, apparently—all alone. But that is old history and I do not wish to embarrass you. I am glad that you have been able to bury your differences. I wonder if luncheon is ready. It must be very late already."

"Yes," Judith said. "I imagine all these children must be ravenous. They have done a good day's work already."

* * *

AFTER LUNCHEON, MRS. Harrison and Mr. Cornwell took the children into the drawing room for a rehearsal of their pageant. Amy had been invited to go with them. She took Rupert with her while Judith took Kate upstairs to the nursery for a sleep.

All the children had parts, Mrs. Harrison explained to Amy. There were no scripts.

"Most of our children cannot read well yet," she explained. "We have merely told them the story and allowed them to improvise their lines—sometimes with hair-raising results, though I have great faith that they will all perform beautifully on Christmas evening and be perfect angels."

"Would you like to be a shepherd, lad?" Mr. Cornwell asked Rupert, laying a hand on his shoulder. "We can always use more shepherds."

Amy smiled gratefully at Mr. Cornwell as Rupert raced off to join a small group of boys.

"You do not by any chance have some skill at playing the pianoforte, ma'am, do you?" he asked her. "Mrs. Harrison declares that she is all thumbs, but I am afraid that even my thumbs would be useless. Our angel choir cannot possibly sing without accompaniment. They would go so flat that we would have to go belowstairs to find them."

Amy laughed and flushed. "I do," she said, "and would gladly relieve Mrs. Harrison if she wishes it."

"If she wishes it?" He took her by the arm. "Eve, come here. Christmas has come early for you."

Amy was soon seated on the pianoforte bench surrounded by the angel choir.

"Cor," one of them said, "you got a luverly voice, missus."

"Thank you," she said. "Maureen, is it? And so do all of you if you will just not be afraid to sing out. Sing from down here." She patted her stomach.

Mr. Cornwell came and stood behind the bench when the full rehearsal started. He chuckled.

"Can we keep you, ma'am?" he asked. "What would you ask as a salary? That sounded almost like music."

"This is such fun," Amy declared a moment before clapping a hand over her mouth as the innkeeper's wife beat the innkeeper over the head for suggesting that they turn Mary and Joseph away.

"Not the head, if you please, Peg," Mr. Cornwell said firmly. "The shoulder maybe? And not too hard. Remember that you are just acting." He added in a lower voice, for Amy's ears only, "The angel did not wait for the glory of the Lord to shine around about the shepherds during our first rehearsal. She kicked them awake."

Amy stifled her mirth.

And she remembered suddenly a dark tent on the River Thames and the prediction about children. Lots of children. And about a comfortable gentleman of middle years whom she would soon meet.

But how foolish, she thought, giving herself a mental shake. How very foolish. Mr. Cornwell would surely run a million miles if he could just read her mind. Poor Mr. Cornwell.

And her father would have forty fits if she ever decided to fix her choice on a gentleman who worked for his living caring for and educating a houseful of raga-muffins from the London slums.

It sounded like rather a blissful life to Amy.

Silly! she told herself.

THE MARQUESS JOINED his aunts and Sir William in a game of cards in one of the smaller salons.

Soon enough it would be time to skate. The children, Lord Denbigh thought, would not allow him to forget that promise despite the fact that they had had a busy day and faced the walk home at the end of it.

There was a large box of skates he would have taken out to the lake. No one who needed a pair would find himself without, though he remembered from the previous year that many of the children preferred to slide around on the ice with their boots. He had already had a portion of the lake cleared of snow.

"What a delightful child little Kate Easton is," Aunt Edith said.

"And very prettily behaved," Aunt Frieda added.

The marquess and Sir William concentrated on their cards.

"Maxwell, dear," Aunt Edith said, "Frieda and I were wondering—it was so long ago that neither of us can be sure—but it seems to us, if we are remembering correctly, that is . . . Of course, dear, we never went up to town and our brother did not keep us informed as much as perhaps he might. Though of course, he was a busy man. But we were wondering, dear . . ."

"Yes," the marquess said. He had grown accustomed to his aunts during several visits in the past few years. "You are quite right, Aunt Edith. And you, too, Aunt Frieda. Mrs. Easton and I were betrothed for almost two months eight years ago."

"We thought so, Maxwell," Aunt Frieda said. "How sad for you, dear, that she married Mr. Easton instead. And how sad for her to have lost him at so young an age. He must have had auburn hair, I believe. The children both have auburn hair, but Mrs. Easton's is fair."

"Yes," Lord Denbigh said, "he had auburn hair."

"How very kind of you, Maxwell, dear, to invite her and her children to Denbigh Park for Christmas," Aunt Edith said. "Some men might have borne a grudge, since she is the one who ended the betrothal if we heard the right of the story. And I daresay we did as it would not have been at all the thing for you to have done so, would it?"

The marquess pointedly returned his attention to the game of cards. He had been in danger of forgetting during the morning. But he had a vivid image now of Easton as he had been—handsome, laughing, charming, a great favorite with the ladies, and with another class of females, too.

Lord Denbigh had never suspected that a romance was growing between Easton and Judith, though he had seen them together more than once and Easton had almost always danced with her at balls. He had not seen the writing on the wall, the marquess thought, poor innocent fool that he had been.

And he remembered again as he and Aunt Edith lost the hand quite ignominiously, entirely through his fault, how he had tortured himself after she had run away with Easton with images of the two of them together, of the two of them intimate together. He had walked and walked during that year, constantly trying to outstrip his thoughts and imaginings.

And then the news almost as soon as he finally returned to town that she was with child.

He had been in danger of forgetting during the morning. He had forgotten when he kissed her in the ballroom. He had forgotten everything except his fierce hunger for her and his awareness that he was kissing her for the first time and that she was warm and soft and fragrant and utterly feminine.

Well, he remembered now. He would not forget again. And he was not sorry that young Simon had maneuvered him into kissing her, for there had been a look in her eyes and a slight trembling in her lips. She was not indifferent to him. It was not by any means an impossible task he had set for himself.

"Ah," Aunt Edith said with satisfaction as they won

the hand, "that is better, Maxwell dear. I thought a while ago that you had quite lost your touch."

"And I hoped the same thing," Sir William said with a hearty laugh. "One more hand to decide the winner, Denbigh?"

"JUDITH," AMY SAID, letting herself into her sister-in-law's dressing room after knocking, "do you think this bonnet becoming? Would my green one look better?"

Judith looked up in surprise. Amy had worn her brown fur-trimmed bonnet through most of the winter without once asking anyone's opinion.

"It will be a great deal warmer than your green one," she said. "How was the rehearsal?"

Amy came right into the room and laughed. "Quite hilarious," she said. "Those children flare up at the slightest provocation, Judith. Val, who plays the part of Mary, is the fiercest of all. She thumped poor Joseph in the stomach when he was not paying attention to some of Mrs. Harrison's instructions. And yet there is a warmth about their presentation that will be quite affecting, I believe. Mr. Cornwell says they have come a long way since they started three weeks ago."

Judith smiled at her sister-in-law's enthusiasm.

"Rupert is a shepherd," Amy said. "Mr. Cornwell suggested it and Mrs. Harrison said it would be all right."

"Oh dear," Judith said, "I hope he was not making a nuisance of himself."

Amy laughed. "Mr. Cornwell said that there are so many shepherds anyway that one more will be neither here nor there."

Mr. Cornwell. Judith looked at the bright spots of color in her sister-in-law's cheeks.

"Are you ready?" Amy asked eagerly. "I would hate to find that everyone has left without us."

But everyone had not, of course. They were all gathered in a noisy group in the great hall.

"Where's that nipper?" someone demanded loudly, and Kate chuckled and left Judith's side to be borne away on Daniel's shoulder.

The lake was only a few hundred yards to the west of the house, not a long walk. Judith walked there with Mr. Rockford and watched with interest as Amy took Mr. Cornwell's arm and chattered brightly to him. She did not even look unduly short in his company. Her head reached to his chin.

Amy had never had a beau. Judith's heart ached suddenly. She hoped that her sister-in-law was not about to conceive a hopeless and quite ineligible passion.

"Mama." Rupert rushed at her as soon as she reached the lake, a pair of skates clutched in his hands. "Help me put them on. I want to show you how I can skate. I can skate like the wind. Papa said, remember?"

Andrew had done so little with his children. But it was good, Judith thought, that her son remembered at least one thing and one occasion when his father had been kind to him and shown him some affection. He must have loved Rupert, she thought. He had been ecstatic with pride at his birth. He had been far less so at Kate's. He had wanted another son.

"Yes, I remember," she said. "And Papa knew what he was talking about. He was a splendid skater himself. But it has been a long time, Rupert. You must not be surprised if you need to find your skating legs before you can compete with the wind again."

She was down on one knee in the snow lacing the skates over Rupert's boots. People all about her were doing the same thing, though some of the children were already on the ice without skates, sliding and sprawling and laughing. Daniel, she saw with some amusement, was strapping a small pair of skates onto Kate's feet and leading her by the hand to the edge of the lake. He was not himself wearing skates.

"I think your daughter has a champion," the Marquess of Denbigh said from behind her. "You cannot know how fortunate she is to have won his protection. All the other children live in mortal terror of his fists."

"Oh dear," Judith said.

"Watch me, Mama," Rupert called as he reached the edge of the ice and prepared to step onto it. "Watch me, sir."

"I am watching," Judith called. "Oh dear," she said again as her son landed flat on his back even before his second skate had touched the ice.

"Give him an hour," the marquess said. "He will improve. And he does not have far to fall. That is the advantage of skating when one is a child. You are not skating?"

"No," she said. "I came to watch. I never could get a feel for skating. My feet always would move at twice the speed of the rest of my body."

"Ah yes," he said. "Painful."

He left her without another word and skated onto the ice. He did so quite effortlessly, Judith noted with some admiration and envy. And he took Rupert by the hand and one of the little girls and patiently slowed his pace to accommodate their wobbling ankles and stiff legs.

Amy and Mr. Cornwell, she saw, had organized a line of children, all holding hands, Amy between two of them and Mr. Cornwell between two others. The children were moving gingerly forward. Judith could hear Amy's laughter. Skating was something she had always been good at.

Some of the boys and a few of the girls were darting recklessly about on their skates. Others were still skidding about on their boots. Lady Clancy was gliding gracefully about the perimeter of the skating area with Mr. Rockford.

9

IT WAS A LOVELY SIGHT, JUDITH THOUGHT, WAVING at a beaming Kate and glancing at Rupert, who was so intent on frowning at his feet that he did not see her. It was so rare in England and so precious. Snow was still clustered on the branches of some of the more sheltered trees and was banked high about the area that had been cleared for the skating. Scarves and hats and mittens were bright against the white and the gray. And then there were the shrieks of merriment coming from the ice.

Rupert was skating alone finally, his arms outstretched. His pace was slow but he was beaming with triumph and risked one glance at the bank to make sure that she was watching him. She smiled and waved.

And then she was aware of Lord Denbigh stepping off the ice. She thought for one moment that he was coming to speak with her, but he stopped at the box of skates and rummaged among its contents. And then he really did come toward her, a pair of skates in one hand.

"These should fit you," he said. "Let me help you on with them."

"I don't skate," she said. "I told you that."

"I understand," he said. "You cannot skate alone, or at least you think you cannot. You will not be skating alone. You will be with me and I will undertake not to let you fall." He was down on one knee, one hand out-stretched, waiting for her to lift a foot.

"No," she said indignantly. "I cannot, and I do not wish to."

"Afraid, Judith?" he asked, looking up into her face.

"Oh," she said, and she could hear the slight shaking in her voice, "I wish you would not."

"Call you Judith?" he said. "I would prefer it to Mrs. Easton. Quite frankly, I do not wish to be reminded of that name. Will you call me Max? Then we will be equal."

"No," she said, "it would not be seemly. Besides, I do not want to."

She realized suddenly that she must have lifted one foot. A skate was already strapped to it and he was waiting for her to lift the other foot.

"Set your hand on my shoulder," he said, "so that you will not lose your balance."

"I wish I knew," she said as she obeyed, "why you are doing all this."

He said nothing until he had finished his task. Then he straightened up and looked down at her. "But you do know," he said. "I told you in London—at the foot of the stairs in your own home."

She frowned. "But why would you want a second chance with me, as you put it?" she said. "You did not care the first time, did you? It was an arranged match."

She flushed. She had not intended to make such an unguarded reference to the past.

"On your part perhaps," he said. "Take my arm, Judith. When we reach the ice, I am going to set my arm about your waist. Put your own up about my shoulders. And don't even think of falling. You are not going to do so."

For the first minute or so he might as well have carried her, Judith thought with a great deal of embarrassment.

Her skates certainly felt quite beyond her own control. Amy went by with Mr. Cornwell and waved at her, and Rupert called to her to watch him. No one seemed to be paying any particular attention to her, she realized finally, with some relief, though she did not believe she had ever felt so foolish in her life.

But someone was taking notice of her. The Marquess of Denbigh was laughing and when she looked up it was to find his face alight with amusement. She had never noticed until that moment what very white and even teeth he had.

"I am too tall for you," he said, bringing them to a halt. "You are quite unbalanced by the position of your arm. Let us try something different."

He kept his one arm firmly about her waist while he took her nearer hand in his free one. And she did indeed find it easier to maintain her balance.

"Oh," she said without thinking, "this is fun." And she heard herself laughing.

"I have the utmost confidence in you," he said. "I daresay that by this time next year, provided we have at least two months of cold weather both this year and next and you practice diligently every day, you will almost be able to skate alone."

"Oh," she said, laughing again. "I don't believe that was a compliment, was it? How lowering."

"Relax," he said. "You are tensing again. You cannot skate when you are tense."

"Oh," she said, looking up at him. And the laughter died. She was aware suddenly of his closeness, of his one arm tight about her, the upper part of it pressed against her shoulder.

He was staring back down at her, the amusement gone from his face, too. His eyes were intent, steely gray beneath drooped lids. It was the look that had always terrified her when she was a girl. A look that she had not at all understood at the time, though she believed that she understood it very well now.

"You are not sorry you came, Judith?" he asked. "I did trick you into coming. You realized that. You would not have come if I had asked you alone, would you?"

"No," she said.

"And are you still sorry?" he asked. "Would you return home tonight if you could?"

She swallowed and looked sharply away from him. "The children are having a wonderful time," she said. "And so is Amy."

"You know," he said, "that that is not what I am asking you, Judith."

"I don't know," she said, and she looked back up into his eyes again. "I don't know. There is something about you I do not trust."

"Is there?" he asked. "Or is it something about yourself? Do you not trust yourself to keep on believing that you did the right thing eight years ago?"

She drew in a sharp breath. "I must believe that," she said fiercely. "There are Rupert and Kate."

"Yes," he said. "You are right there, Judith. There are your children. But that was then. This is now. It is not the same thing at all. We are both older."

"Yes," she said.

And she wondered if he was right. Was it herself she did not trust? But it was not that. There was something about him. There was still that something.

But perhaps she was wrong. Surely she must be wrong. He had come very close to declaring an affection for her, to demonstrating to her that he was indeed trying to fix his interest with her.

Was it possible? Was it possible that after all this time and all the humiliation she had dealt him he was considering renewing his offer for her?

The idea was absurd when put into words in her mind. And yet there were his looks and his words.

But then there was that something else, too.

"Can we go to see the dogs, guv?" someone yelled across the ice.

"Oh, yes, can we?" There was a chorus of voices.

"I fear the house is about to be invaded by the canine kingdom," the marquess said. "I had all the dogs confined to the stables out of respect to my guests. But these children know very well that several of the animals normally live in the house. I hope no one has a fit of the vapors when they take up residence again. Will you?"

"We have dogs at home," she said.

"Ah, yes," he said. "You mentioned that once before." He raised his voice. "Off to the stables, then. But no biting the dogs, mind."

There was a burst of raucous laughter as the children scrambled off the ice and tore impatiently at skate straps.

"I get Rambler," Daniel announced loudly. "Come on, nipper. Up you come."

Judith watched her daughter being borne away toward the stables.

"Your grooms will have forty fits apiece, Max," Mr. Cornwell said. "I had better go after them. Would you like to come, Miss Easton?"

"I shall be along, too," the marquess said. He looked down at Judith. "But I cannot leave you stranded in the middle of the ice, can I? Do you wish to see the dogs, too?"

She was being given a chance to shorten this encounter with him? A chance to return to the house alone or with Mr. Rockford and Lady Clancy?

She put up her chin. "Yes," she said, "I do."

* * *

CHRISTMAS EVE. IT was snowing again, the flakes drifting lazily down without the aid of wind. There was enough to freshen up what had already fallen, Lord Clancy announced after a morning walk, but not enough to bury the house to the eaves.

Miss Edith Hannibal was afraid that the carriages would not be able to take them to church that evening.

"And it never quite seems to be Christmas without church," she said. "Indeed, I cannot remember a year when we did not go to church. Was there ever such a time, Frieda? But of course there was the year Mama was so sick. Indeed, she died the day after Christmas. We did not go to church that year, but then it did not seem at all like Christmas that year anyway."

The marquess assured his aunts that most of them would enjoy the walk since the church was only a mile away. There were two sleighs to convey those who would prefer to ride.

No one was quite as busy as on the day before. Except the servants, that was. By midmorning, tantalizing smells were already escaping from belowstairs and those people who were still in the house were invited down to the kitchen to stir the Christmas pudding in its large bowl.

Judith clasped her hands over Kate's and they stirred together, both laughing. Rupert took a turn alone.

Amy had left the house soon after breakfast, declining the marquess's offer to call out one of the sleighs, choosing to walk to the village instead.

"I have offered to play the pianoforte for the angel choir," she had told Judith the night before. "Mrs. Harrison plays only indifferently and was most grateful for my offer. And Mr. Cornwell says that the children will cheer when they know I am willing to join their caroling party. They are always delighted to have someone among them who can hold a tune, he says." She laughed merrily. "We will be going all about the village as soon as darkness falls, coming to the house here last. It all sounds quite perfectly splendid."

Mr. Cornwell had also been talking with Amy about his future plans for the homes. And Amy had apparently suggested to him that in future it might be a good idea to have a home in which there were both boys and girls.

"It will be more like a real family, I told him," Amy said. "There would be problems, of course, which Mr. Cornwell was quick to point out to me, but it would be a lovely idea, would it not, Judith? What it would need, of course, is a married couple to oversee it. A couple whose own children are grown up, perhaps, or who have been unfortunate enough never to have had children of their own. Then it would be a splendid experience for them, too."

Amy was very obviously enjoying herself. The lure of a great house on the eve of Christmas could not hold her from a day spent in the village with her new friends.

Lord Clancy and Sir William retired to the billiard room after luncheon. The ladies sat in a salon with their needlepoint and embroidery while Mr. Rockford entertained them with stories of a recent visit to Paris and a not so recent one to Wales. The marquess's aunts, seated one each side of the fire, soon nodded off to sleep, lulled by the heat and the particular drowsiness that afternoon brings—and perhaps by the droning voice of the lone gentleman in the room, too.

Judith was upstairs in the nursery, reading a story to Rupert and hoping that Kate would have a sleep since she was likely to have a late night. Rupert sat still at her feet and listened, playing with the ears of the collie stretched out before him as he did so, though all morning he had been restless and had demanded a dozen times at the very least to know when the children would be arriving to stay.

The Marquess of Denbigh had some errands to run,

he had announced at luncheon. He always delivered a basket of food to all the cottagers on his estate each Christmas Eve and always put a personal gift of a few gold coins inside each. This year the task of delivering the baskets was complicated by the snow, but it could be done nevertheless. He would not delegate the task to his servants, knowing that his people set great store by his visits. Besides, he would deprive himself of some pleasure if he neglected to go.

He set out in one of the sleighs, delivering baskets to the closest of the cottages first. It was not a fast job. He did not refuse a single invitation to step inside the cottage to take refreshments. He grinned to himself as he turned the horses' heads for home again and another load of Christmas offerings. There was always the danger on the afternoon of Christmas Eve that he would become too drunk to attend church in the evening. Everywhere he went he was offered either ale or cider, and always a generous mugful because he was the marquess and must be suitably impressed.

Two footmen carefully loaded the sleigh for his second run. But he hesitated before taking his place again, and glanced with indecision at the house. It would not really do, he thought. He was enjoying his afternoon, enjoying the smiles on the faces of his cottagers and their somewhat flustered conversation. He was enjoying the widening eyes of all the children as he handed each a coin.

He should not spoil the atmosphere of Christmas. He should not bring darkness to his mood.

He frowned, something fluttering at the edge of his memory. And then he remembered the fortune-teller out on the ice of the River Thames. He remembered her telling him that there was darkness in him as well as a great deal of light and that Christmas might save him from being swamped by the darkness. He shrugged. He had never given heed to such nonsense. But he remembered that afternoon with some pleasure.

And he found himself running up the steps to the house, peering into the salon, and then taking the stairs two at a time to the nursery floor. He knocked at the door and let himself in.

She was sitting in a rocking chair by the window, wearing the simple blue wool dress that she had been wearing that morning. Her daughter was asleep in her arms, one small hand spread on her bosom. Her son was on his stomach on the floor at her feet, his legs bent at the knees, his feet waving back and forth. He was tickling the collie's stomach.

The marquess felt a stab of some indefinable longing. It was such a very quiet, contented domestic scene.

Rupert jumped to his feet and ran toward the marquess. The collie tore after him, barking at this promise of a new game. "Are they here?" the boy asked.

Lord Denbigh rumpled his hair. "I heard your mama tell you earlier that they would be coming for the caroling this evening and then walking to church with us," he said. "Does the day seem quite interminable? How would you like a sleigh ride?"

"Ye-es!" Rupert jumped up and down. "Super! May I, Mama?"

"The invitation is for your mama, too," the marquess said. "Would you like some fresh air, ma'am? I am delivering baskets to my cottagers."

Her face brightened. "Are you?" she said. "Oh, I always used to enjoy doing that at home with Mama and Papa. It was always the beginning of Christmas, the start of that wonderful feeling that only Christmas can bring."

"The little one has just fallen asleep?" he asked.

"Yes," she said, getting carefully to her feet. "I shall put her to bed."

And there. He had done it. He had ruined his afternoon, brought darkness into it. Except that he would
not think of the ultimate revenge, he decided as he offered his arm to lead her down the stairs and out to the
waiting sleigh. He would not think about how such encounters as this would all be used to contribute gradually to the final denouement.

He would pretend that he had no other purpose than
to enjoy her company. He had very little time left in
which to do so. He had been without her for almost
eight years. He would be without her for the rest of his
life. Surely he could allow himself a few days in which to
feast his eyes on her beauty. Besides, all time spent with
her would contribute to his ultimate purpose.

She was wearing a fur hat rather than a bonnet, one
that completely covered her hair and her ears. She
tucked her hands inside a matching muff. Her face, he
noticed, did not owe its beauty to her hair. It was a clas-
sically beautiful face in its own right.

They sat side by side in the sleigh, Rupert squashed
between them, surrounded by cloth-covered baskets.
The collie had been left curled at the foot of Kate's bed.

"Mm," Rupert said. "They smell good."

"At least we will not starve if we get stuck in a snowbank," the marquess said, and the boy giggled.

They did not talk a great deal. But the air felt fresher
with her sitting beside him, and the crunching of the
horses' hooves on the snow and the jingling of the harness bells and the squeaking of the sleigh runners were
more intimate and more festive sounds.

"This is the most beautiful weather there could possibly be," she said, lifting her face to the high broken
clouds above and drawing in a deep breath. "It makes of
the world a fairytale place."

And Lord Denbigh knew that she shared his mood.

They paid eight visits in all and were invited inside

each of the eight cottages. Lord Denbigh found himself living out an unplanned fantasy. What if she had not broken off their engagement? They would have been married now for eight years. They would be paying these calls together as man and wife, the ease of years of acquaintance and intimacy between them. And they would be going home together afterward to their guests and their children and a shared Christmas. And when it was all over they would stand together on the steps of Denbigh and wave good-bye to their departing guests. And they would be alone together again, with their family. Perhaps she would be with child again.

Mrs. Richards had delivered her fourth child less than two weeks before. The child was awake and fussing, though Mrs. Richards insisted that they come inside for refreshments. The baby had been fed already, she assured them.

"Oh, may I?" Judith asked, smiling at Mrs. Richards and leaning over the baby's crude cradle.

Mrs. Richards was flustered, but she assured Mrs. Easton that the baby had had a clean nappy only a few minutes before.

And Judith lifted the child from the cradle and held it gently to her shoulder. The fussing stopped and the baby wriggled its head into a comfortable position and sucked loudly on a fist. Judith closed her eyes, smiling, and rubbed a cheek against the soft down on the baby's head.

"Oh," she said, "one forgets so quickly how tiny new-born babies are. How I envy you."

Lord Denbigh turned his head away sharply and addressed a remark to Mr. Richards. He felt as if he had a leaden weight in his stomach. For some reason he felt almost as if he were about to cry. Steady, he told himself. Steady. He should not have let down his guard for even a moment. Had he not learned his lesson long ago?

"Was that the last one, sir?" Rupert asked when they emerged from the Richardses' cottage and took their places in the sleigh again. "Are we going home now? Will the carolers be coming soon?"

The marquess laughed. "Not for several hours yet," he said. "But I tell you what we will do, with your mother's permission, of course. We are close to the village, and your aunt is with Mrs. Harrison and Mr. Cornwell and the children. Doubtless they have all sung carols until they are blue in the face. We will take you there and leave you in your aunt's charge. How does that sound?"

Rupert shouted out a hurrah.

"Is that all right with you, ma'am?" the marquess asked. "This lad could well drive you to insanity within the next few hours if we do not rid ourselves of him."

Judith laughed. "They will probably make you sing, Rupert," she warned.

"I can sing," Rupert said indignantly.

Five minutes later he was admitted to the house where all the children and adults were gathered and swallowed up into the noise and cheerful chaos.

"Amazingly," Mr. Cornwell told them, "we have had not a single casualty all day even though Mary tried to box the ears of all the kings for setting down their gifts closer to Joseph than to her. The heavenly host are beginning to sound almost like a choir with Miss Easton to provide the accompaniment and to sing along to keep them in tune. And sometime within the next few hours we will have to decide how twelve volunteers are to carry five lanterns—a minor problem. I can confidently predict, Mrs. Easton, that we will be able to deliver your son to you this evening all in one piece."

And so, Lord Denbigh discovered, quite without planning to be, he was alone with Judith Easton, a mile-long drive between them and home. He drove his team in silence, and decided on the spur of the moment to take a long route home. He turned along a little-used lane that led uphill until it was above a grove of trees and looking down on the house from behind. He had always loved the view from up there. He eased his horses to a halt.

"I used to come up here a great deal as a boy," he said, "and imagine that I was lord of all I surveyed."

"And now you are," she said.

"And now I am."

The silence between them was companionable. Strangely so, considering what had happened between them in the past, considering his reason for having her at Denbigh Park, and considering the fact that she did not trust him—she had told him so the day before.

"You are very different from what I have always thought you to be," she said quietly.

"Am I?" He turned to look at her.

"You care," she said. "All your house guests are people who would have spent a lonely Christmas without your invitation, are they not? And you are generous to your people. I expected that you would wait outside each cottage until someone came outside to take a basket from your hands. But you visited and made conversation. And there are the children in the village. You have far more than just a financial commitment to them."

"Perhaps it is all selfishness after all," he said. "I have found that I can secure my own happiness by trying to bring some to other people. Perhaps I am not so very different from what you thought, Judith."

She frowned. "You used to be different," she said. "You used to be cold, unfeeling. But then, of course, our betrothal was forced on you. Perhaps I was unfair to judge you just on that short acquaintance."

Cold? Unfeeling? Had she not known? Had she not realized? Cold? He remembered how he had used to toss and turn in his bed, living for the next time he would see her, wondering if he would have the opportunity to touch her, perhaps to kiss her hand. Unfeeling? He remembered the pain of his love for her even before she left him and his fear that he would not be able to give her all she desired from life.

A forced betrothal? He had gone to his father the morning after his first meeting with her and begged to have the marriage with her arranged as soon as possible. Although he had been apprehensive at the prospect of allowing his father to choose his bride, he had forgotten his misgivings as soon as he had met her. The betrothal, the wedding could not be soon enough for him.

Poor naive fool that he had been. Twenty-six years old and entrusting his heart, his dreams, all his future hopes to a young girl he did not even know. A young girl who had preferred charm and flirtation and the apparent glamor of a near elopement. A young girl who had broken his heart without one thought to his feelings—because she had believed him cold and unfeeling. Had she ever tried to see beyond his shyness? Had she ever tried to get to know him?

And now she sat calmly beside him telling him that that was the way he had been. She still did not understand.

But she would. *Oh, yes, my lady,* he told her silently and bitterly, *you will know what it feels like.*

10

THE MARQUESS OF DENBIGH TURNED SIDEWAYS, rested one arm on the back of the seat behind her, and slid his free hand inside her muff to rest on top of her hand.

"Perhaps," he said. "It is always difficult to know what goes on in another's mind. I thought you were content with our betrothal, Judith, but apparently you wanted something different. Well, you had it—for a while. And you have your children."

She was looking down at her muff. Her hand was warm and still beneath his own.

"Yes," she said.

There was a silence between them again, not so comfortable as before. There was an awareness, a tension between them. Her hand stirred. He looked at her, his face hardening.

"Did you love him?" he asked.

"Yes." She answered him without hesitation.

"Always?" he asked. "To the end?"

"He was my husband," she said, "and the father of my children."

"In other words," he said, "it was loyalty, not love, after the honeymoon was over. Did you not know about him, Judith, before you married him?"

He thought she would not answer. She stared downward for a long time. "I was eighteen," she said. "I was still young enough to believe that one person can change another through the power of love. He was very handsome and very charming. And very persuasive. Did you know why he married me?"

He had often wondered, since though she had been beautiful and well-born, she had not been particularly wealthy. He had wondered why Easton had saddled himself with a wife when his subsequent actions had seemed to prove that it was not for love.

"He loved you, I suppose," he said.

"You did not know," she said. "I thought these things quickly became general knowledge in the gentlemen's clubs."

He felt a pulse beat in his throat. Had Easton raped her?

"Tell me," he said.

She turned to look at him and smiled ruefully before looking away down the hill. "It was a wager," she said. "It seemed that there were enough gentlemen willing to wager a great deal of money on the belief that Andrew could not snatch me away from a wealthy viscount and heir to the Marquess of Denbigh."

The pulse was hammering against his temples.

"He told me," she said, "after we had been married for about a year. He thought it a huge joke. He thought the story would amuse me."

There was one thing the marquess wished fervently. He wished that Easton were still alive so that he could kill him.

"I thought you would have known," she said.

"No."

He withdrew his hand from her muff and turned in his seat. He picked up the horses' ribbons and gave them the signal to start down the slope that would bring them around the east side of the house. He did it all mechanically, without thought. Her words were pounding in his head.

He thought of a shy and beautiful eighteen-year-old, fresh from the schoolroom, fresh from the country, pitted against the practiced charms of a handsome and accomplished flirt and rake. She had been married because of a wager. He had suffered those months and even years of agony because of a wager.

"Your daughter must be awake by now," he said as the sleigh drew to a halt before the front doors. "Bring her downstairs for tea, Judith, will you? My aunts dote on her, if you had not noticed."

"Yes, I had," she said. "And I will bring her down. Thank you."

He watched her ascend the stairs to the house and disappear into the warmth of the great hall before taking the sleigh and the horses to the stable block.

Did this change everything? he wondered. Did this mean that she had been as much of a victim as he? But she was still guilty of not having said anything to him. She had still behaved dishonorably, running away without a word or even a note. But she had been eighteen years old and in the clutches of an unprincipled rake.

He needed to think, he knew. But he had no time to think. He would be expected indoors for tea. Besides, he did not want to think.

If there was one place in hell hotter than any other, he thought viciously as he strode back to the house, he hoped that it was occupied by Andrew Easton. It was not a Christmas wish or even a Christian one, but he wished it anyway.

THE CAROLING HAD always been one of Amy's favorite parts of Christmas. This year it was even more special with almost all of the singers being children. They went from house to house, singing lustily and not always quite on key. Several of the children pushed close to her when it came time to sing.

"You got a lovely voice, mum," Joe told her. "The rest of us sounds like rusty nails."

"Speak for yerself," Val yelled at him.

Amy laughed and felt warmed and wanted and very happy. Mr. Cornwell always stood behind her shoulder, sharing the music with her.

At each house they were offered refreshments, always welcome after the cold walk. Where some of the children put all the cakes they took Amy could not fathom. For none had bulging pockets.

"There will be a few stomachaches tomorrow or the next day," Mr. Cornwell said when she mentioned her concern to him. "But it is Christmas."

Some of the smaller children showed signs of weariness before they had finished making their calls. Amy, feeling a slight dragging at her cloak, found little Henry clinging to her.

"Are you tired, sweetheart?" she asked him, and when he nodded she picked him up and carried him. How wonderful, wonderful, she thought as he nestled his head on her shoulder. She knew what the psalmist had meant when he had written of a cup running over. But Henry was no featherweight.

"Here," Mr. Cornwell said, appearing beside her, "let me take him, ma'am. Henry, is it? He is our youngest." He lifted the child gently into his own arms. "We cannot have you out of breath when we arrive at Denbigh Park, now, can we? You sing better than any angel I have ever heard."

Amy laughed. "And how many angels have you heard, Mr. Cornwell?" she asked.

"In the last little while?" He grinned at her. "None,

actually, ma'am, except you. And my friends call me Spencer or Spence. I consider you my friend."

"Spencer," Amy said, and flushed. She had never called any man by his given name except her brothers. "Then you must call me Amy."

"Amy," he said, smiling. "A little name for a little lady. You live all the time with Mrs. Easton?"

Yes, Amy thought, as Peg ran up beside her and took her hand, my cup runneth over.

IT WAS ALMOST ten o'clock when the carolers finally arrived at Denbigh Park, bringing a draft of cold air with them through the front doors and a great deal of noise and merriment. Cheeks and noses were red and eyes were shining. Stomachs were full. Five of the smallest children clutched the lanterns and hoisted them high when it came time to sing, though they were largely for effect; the hall was well lit. The smallest child of all was asleep against Mr. Cornwell's shoulder.

The marquess and his guests came down from the drawing room to listen to the carols, quite content to have their own singsong to Miss Frieda Hannibal's accompaniment interrupted. Kate, her cheeks bright with color, her eyes wide with the lateness of the hour, clung to Judith's neck and waved across a sea of heads at Daniel.

Mr. Cornwell had a hand on Amy's shoulder and watched the music she held in her hands.

The carolers made up in volume and enthusiasm what they lacked in musical talent, Judith thought after they had sung "Hark the Herald Angels Sing" as if they were summoning all listeners to the nearest tavern and "Lully Lulla Thou Little Tiny Child" as if they intended their rendition to be heard in Bethlehem.

It did not matter that the choir was unskilled. It did

not matter at all. For there they all were, crowded into the great hall of Denbigh Park, a roaring log fire burning at either side of it, sharing with one another and their listeners all the joy of Christmas.

There was nothing quite like the magic of those few days, Judith thought. And every year it was the same. Even during those years with Andrew's family, though she had not enjoyed them on the whole, there had always been some of the magic.

Or perhaps magic was the wrong word. Holiness was perhaps a better one. Love. Joy. Well-being. Goodwill. All the old clichés. Clichés did not matter at Christmastime. They were simply true.

Everyone was smiling. Mr. Rockford, whose conversation was never of the most interesting because he did not know when to stop once he had started, had one of the marquess's aunts on each arm and was beaming goodwill, as were they. Sir William and Lady Tushingham, who had regaled them at dinner with stories of their nephews' and nieces' accomplishments and triumphs, were flanked by Lord and Lady Clancy and looked rather as if they were about to burst with geniality.

The Marquess of Denbigh was standing with folded arms, his feet set apart, smiling benignly at all the children. Just a week before, Judith thought, she would not have thought him capable of such an expression.

And Amy was smiling up over her shoulder at Mr. Cornwell, the singing at an end and the hubbub of excited children's voices being in the process of building to a new crescendo. And he was pointing upward to a limp spray of mistletoe that some wag had suspended from the gallery above and lowering his head to give her a smacking kiss on the lips.

Judith, watching his beaming face and Amy's glowing expression, felt as if warmth was creeping upward from her toes to envelop her. If anyone on this earth deserved happiness, she thought, it was Amy. And there would be nothing at all wrong with that match. Nothing.

"Mama!" Rupert was patting her leg and talking quite as loudly and excitedly as any of the children. "Did you hear me? I got to carry the lantern for part of the way. And I am going to walk to church with Ben and Stephen. They said I may."

"'Ow's my nipper?" Daniel was demanding loudly, and Kate wriggled to be set down from her mother's arms.

There were more refreshments and a great deal more noise in the half hour that remained before it was time to go to church. The marquess's aunts and Sir William and Lady Tushingham would ride to church in the sleighs, it had been decided. Lord and Lady Clancy would walk, though the marquess offered to have one of the sleighs return for a second trip.

Three of the smaller children, including Henry, gave in to the lateness of the hour and the long excitement of the day and the novelty of having the big house to sleep in and agreed to stay with Mrs. Webber and be put to bed. Kate, after several huge yawns, was persuaded to stay with them.

And so they set out into the crisp night air, the distant sound of the church bells ringing out their glad tidings of the birth of a baby in Bethlehem and the coming into the world of a savior.

"It is so easy to forget," Judith said, finding herself walking beside the marquess and taking his offered arm. "There is so much to do and so much to enjoy that sometimes we forget what the season is all about."

"Yes," he said. "Going to church on Christmas Eve is rather like walking into the peace at the heart of it all, is it not? But we will be reminded again tomorrow. The children will be performing their pageant between dinner and the start of the ball."

"Yes," she said, smiling.

She liked him. She admitted the amazing truth to herself at last—not only that she liked him but that he was a likable person. And she wondered if he had always been so or if he had changed in eight years. If he had always been like this, she thought, then . . .

She stopped her thoughts. She did not want to be sad on Christmas Eve. She did not want to look back in regret on all that she might have missed. Besides, there were Rupert and Kate. Her years with Andrew had not been all bad. She had not wasted those years of her life. There were her children.

The sounds of the church bells pealing out their invitation grew louder as they stepped onto the village street. People were flocking to church, many of them on foot, some by sleigh.

THE MARQUESS OF Denbigh smiled to himself. The singing at the village church was not usually noted for its volume or enthusiasm. And yet tonight, with the familiar Christmas hymns, the whole congregation seemed infected by the spirited singing of the children. And the rector, no longer rendering a virtual solo, as he was usually forced to do, lifted up his rich baritone voice and led his people in welcoming a newborn child into the world once more.

There was no time like Christmas, the marquess thought, to make one feel at peace with the world. He could not for the moment think of one enemy whom he could not forgive or one enmity that was worth holding onto. The one spot of darkness on his soul he pushed from his mind. It was unbecoming to the occasion. And he was filled with that unrealistic dream that infects all of the Christian world at that particular season of the year that love was enough, that all the problems of the world and of humanity would be solved if only the spirit of Christmas could persist throughout the year.

He smiled inwardly again. He knew that it was a foolish dream, but he allowed himself to be borne along by it nevertheless.

Judith shared his pew to the right, his aunts and Rockford to his left. His other guests sat in the pew behind, the children behind them again. His neighbors packed the rest of the church. It was a good feeling of wellbeing. He turned his eyes to the right as the congregation sat for the sermon and watched Judith clasp her hands loosely in her lap.

And he indulged in his other dream for a moment before turning his attention to what the rector was saying. She was his wife and had been for several years. Their children were at home in the nursery or sitting behind them with the other children. They were celebrating Christmas together.

He knew that there was something about her, about his relationship to her and his plans for her, that he needed to think through. There were perhaps some adjustments to make in light of new evidence. But not at present. Later he would think.

Judith, sitting beside him, was trying to remember a Christmas when she had felt happier. There had been the Christmases of her childhood and girlhood, of course. They had always been happy times. But since then? Surely the first year or two after her marriage had brought pleasant Christmases. Certainly Ammanlea had always been full of family members and children. There had been all the ingredients for joy.

But she remembered that first Christmas, when she had still been in love with Andrew. He and his brothers and male cousins had spent the afternoon and evening of Christmas Eve going from house to house wassailing and using the occasion as an excuse to get themselves thoroughly foxed. Andrew had fallen asleep several times during church while she had prodded him with her elbow with increasing embarrassment. And all the next day at home they had continued to drink.

And that had been the pattern for all the Christmases of her marriage and for the first of her widowhood.

It was little wonder, she thought, that she was feeling so happy this year. So unexpectedly happy. She had been horrified when Lord Denbigh had trapped her into coming to Denbigh Park. She had still been convinced that he was a harsh and unfeeling man and that he had issued the invitation only to punish her for humiliating him eight years before.

She had never dreamed that she could come to like him, and more than that, to admire him. She had never dreamed that she would stop fighting the strong physical attraction she felt for him.

She had stopped fighting, she realized. She had stopped that afternoon, if not before. She could still feel the warmth of his hand on hers beneath her muff—the hand that was now spread on one of his thighs. She glanced at it. It was a slim, long-fingered hand, which nevertheless looked strong.

It was strange to realize that for a two-month period eight years before she had been betrothed to him. They had been within one month of their wedding when she had run off with Andrew. What would marriage to him have been like? she wondered. Performing those intimacies of marriage with him. Bearing his children. Sharing a home with him in the familiarity of everyday living.

She shivered and turned her attention to the rector.

Halfway through the lengthy sermon there was a slight rustling from the pews where the children sat. A few moments later Rupert wriggled his way between his mother and the marquess, yawned widely, and tried to find a comfortable spot for his head against her arm.

She smiled down at him and marveled at how well all the other children were behaving. It was a long and a late service after a busy day.

Rupert's head fell forward and Judith lifted it gently back against her arm. Her son looked up at her with sleepy eyes. He should have stayed at the house with Kate, she thought. But of course he would have been mortally offended had she suggested any such thing.

And then the marquess's arm came about the boy's shoulders, drawing him away from her, and his other slid beneath Rupert's knees and he lifted him onto his lap and drew his head against his chest. Rupert was asleep almost instantly, his auburn curls bright against the dark green of Lord Denbigh's coat.

Andrew's child, Judith thought. Her husband's child cradled in the arms of the man she had jilted and never faced with either explanation or apology. The man who might have been her husband, the father of her children. She felt an almost overwhelming longing to move closer and to close her eyes and rest her head against his shoulder.

She was falling in love with him, she realized with sudden shock. No, perhaps it was already too late. She had fallen in love with him. With the Marquess of Denbigh. It was incredible. But it was true.

There was no longer any thought in her mind of the suspicions that had troubled her in London and again here at Denbigh.

"THE DEAR LITTLE boy," Miss Edith Hannibal said to the marquess as the congregation spilled out of the church after the service and exchanged cheerful Christmas greetings while the church bells pealed again. "He is fast asleep."

The marquess was carrying Rupert, the child's head resting heavily on his shoulder.

"You must give him to me," Miss Hannibal said. "I shall take him home in the sleigh, Mrs. Easton, and his nurse will have him tucked up in bed in no time at all."

"Thank you, ma'am," Judith said, smiling.

"And I shall take that little one on my lap," Miss Frieda Hannibal said. "It was a very long service for children, was it not, Mr. Cornwell? But they behaved quite beautifully. They could teach a lesson to several of the children of our parish, who are allowed to fidget and whisper aloud in church. Edith and I find it most distracting."

"Thank you, ma'am," Mr. Cornwell said, and he waited for the marquess's aunt to seat herself in the sleigh before laying in her lap the little girl who was sleeping in his arms. "This is Lily, ma'am. If she should wake up, you may assure her that her sister is quite safe with Mrs. Harrison and will be home in no time at all. Lily becomes agitated when separated from her sister."

"Then we must squeeze her sister in between us," Miss Edith Hannibal said. "There is plenty of room, I do assure you, Mr. Cornwell. Come along, dear."

Violet climbed gratefully into the sleigh.

In the meantime, Sir William and Lady Tushingham had singled out two little boys whose eyes were large with fatigue and who, Lady Tushingham declared, reminded her very much of two of her dear nephews, now twenty-two and twenty-four years old, and had taken them on their laps in the other sleigh.

Mrs. Harrison arranged the remaining children into pairs and led the way home. There was loud excitement over the fact that they were to spend the night and all the next day and night at Denbigh Park.

"It's the feather pillows wot tickles me," Toby told a

younger child. "Your 'ead sinks right through 'em to the bed."

"Last year we all 'ad gifts," Val said. "But I daresay the guv spent all 'is money last year."

"I remember the mince pies," Daniel said. "I ate 'leven."

"Ten," Joe said. "I counted. It was ten."

"It was 'leven, I betcha," Daniel said, bristling. "You want to make somethin' out of it, Joe?"

"It was ten," Joe said.

"Someone is going to be hanging by ten toes over the nearest snowbank in a moment," Mr. Cornwell called sternly.

"I tell you what," Mr. Rockford said, walking among the children and sweeping up into his arms one little boy who was yawning loudly. "Tomorrow whenever you eat a mince pie, Daniel, you let me know and I will keep count. We will see if you can stuff ten or eleven into yourself."

"Twelve," Daniel said loudly. "I 'ave to beat last year's count, sir."

"His lordship's cook may well be in tears," Mr. Rockford said. "No mince pies left by the end of Christmas morning. Yes, lad, rest your head on my shoulder if you wish. Now I could tell you a story about mince pies that would have your hair standing on end. . . ."

Amy took Mr. Cornwell's offered arm and walked behind the children with him.

"You must be tired, Amy," he said. "You have had a busy day and have done more walking than anyone else."

"Yes, I am," she said. "But I do not believe I have ever lived through a happier day, Spencer."

"Really?" he said. "You do not find it intolerable to be surrounded by children all day long, listening to their silliness and exasperated by their petty quarrels?"

"But I think of what their lives were like and what they would be like without your efforts and those of his lordship and Mrs. Harrison," she said, "and I could hug them all until their bones break."

"Impossible!" He chuckled. "You are just a little bird, Amy. You would not have the strength to crack a single bone."

"I have always hated even thinking of the poor," she said. "Their plight has always seemed so hopeless, the problem too vast. And I could cry even now when I think of all the thousands of children who might be with us here but are not. But there are twenty very happy children here, Spencer, and that is better than nothing."

"You like children," he said, patting her hand. "I have watched you today talking with them. That is sometimes the most neglected part of our job. There is always so much to do and so much talking to be done to them as a group. I do not always find as much time as I would like to talk with them individually."

"They have such fascinating stories to tell," she said.

He looked down at her. "And all of them quite unfit for a lady's ears, I have no doubt," he said. "I should not have encouraged you to spend a day with us."

"A lady's ears are altogether underused," she said, provoking another chuckle from him. "Perhaps we should be told more of these stories by our governesses or at school and spend a little less time dancing or sketching or learning how to converse in polite society."

"My dear Amy," he said, patting her hand again, "we will be making a radical out of you and scandalizing your family."

"Is caring about children being radical?" she asked.

"When the children are from the slums of London, yes," he said.

"Well, then," she said briskly, "I must be a radical."

"All in one tiny little package," he said. "But of

course," he added, grinning at her when she looked up at him, "diamonds are small, too, and pearls and rubies and other precious gems."

"Flatterer!" she said. She looked back over her shoulder suddenly. "Where are Judith and Lord Denbigh?"

"Lagging a significant distance behind," he said. "I have been in the habit of thinking that Max is as confirmed a bachelor as I have always been. It seems I have been wrong. It is intriguing, though, that Mrs. Easton is the lady who was once betrothed to him. Most intriguing."

"Judith will not have it that he is trying to fix his interest with her," Amy said. "But it is as plain as the nose on her face, and has been since we were in London. I am glad you have noticed it, too. I was sure I was not imagining things."

"And what will you do if she remarries?" he asked.

She was silent for a while. "I have my parents' home to go back to," she said.

"You do not sound enthusiastic about the prospect," he said.

"I will think of it when the time comes," she said.

"A wise thought," he said, curling his fingers about hers as they rested on his arm.

11

IT DID NOT FEEL PARTICULARLY COLD. THERE WAS no wind and the sky was clear and star-studded. They strolled rather than walked, by tacit consent letting everyone else outstrip them before they were even halfway home.

"Aunt Edith and Mrs. Webber will see to it that your son is put to bed," he said. "He will probably not even wake up."

"They very rarely have late nights," she said, "and the past two days have been unusually active and exciting ones for them."

They strolled on in silence.

"It is Christmas Day," she said. "It always feels quite different from any other day, does it not?"

"Yes." He breathed in deeply. "Even when one cannot smell the goose and the mince pies and the pudding. Happy Christmas, Judith."

"Happy Christmas, my lord," she said.

"Still not Max?" he asked.

She said nothing.

He was close to reaching his goal, he thought. He could sense it. She would not call him by his given name, perhaps, but there was none of the stiffness of manner, the anger even, that he had felt in her in London. She had accepted his escort to and from church without question, and he had not had to use any effort of will to force her to slow her steps on the return walk. The others had disappeared already around a distant bend in the tree-lined driveway.

Perhaps he would not even need the full week. There was triumph in the thought. She had resisted him eight years before, but then of course he had been a great deal more shy and inexperienced with women in those days. She would not resist him now. His revenge, he sensed, could be quite total and very sweet.

Sweet? Would it be? Satisfying, perhaps. But sweet? His triumph was tempered by the fact that he had just come from church on Christmas Eve and been filled with the holiness and joy of the season. He had wished the rector and all his neighbors a happy Christmas. He had just wished Judith a happy Christmas.

He wished suddenly that it were not Christmas. And he wished that his thoughts had not been confused by what he had heard that afternoon. He was so close to putting right a wrong that had haunted him for eight years. So close to getting even.

And another thought kept intruding. If he was so close to reaching his goal, then surely it would be possible to use his triumph in another way. It would be possible to secure a lifetime of happiness for himself.

For he had made a discovery that afternoon—or rather he had admitted something that had been nagging at his consciousness for some time, perhaps ever since he had set eyes on her at Nora's soirée: He was still in love with her. The love that he had converted to hatred so long ago was still love at its core.

And yet the hatred was still there, too. And the hurt. And the inability to trust again. He had trusted utterly before and been hurt almost beyond bearing. He would be a fool to trust her again—the same woman. He would be a fool.

* * *

AROUND THE NEXT bend in the driveway the house would come into sight.

Through all the years of her gradually deteriorating marriage, Judith thought, only one conviction had sustained her. Sometimes it had been almost unbearable to have Andrew at home, frequently drunk, often abusive, though he had never struck her. And yet it had been equally unbearable to be without him for weeks or months at a time, knowing that he was living a life of debauchery, that he would be coming back to her after being with she knew not how many other women.

Only one thought had consoled her. If she had not married Andrew, she had thought, she would have been forced to marry the Viscount Evendon, later the Marquess of Denbigh. And that would have been a thousand times worse.

She walked beside him along the driveway to his house, their boots crunching the snow beneath them, their breath clouds of vapor ahead of them, and held to his arm. And she was aware of him with every ounce of her being. And aware of the fact that they were alone, that they had allowed everyone else to get so far ahead that they were out of sight and earshot already.

If she had not been so naive at the age of eighteen, she thought, and had not misunderstood her physical reaction to him; if there had not been that stupid wager and Andrew had not turned his practiced charm on her; if several things had been different, would she have fallen in love with the viscount then? Or would she at least have accepted the marriage that her parents had arranged, prepared to like her husband and to grow to love him?

They were foolish questions. Things had happened as

they had and there was no point in indulging in what-ifs.

His footsteps lagged even further as they approached the bend in the driveway and hers followed suit. She could feel the blood pulsing through her whole body, even her hands.

She turned to him when he stopped walking and fixed her eyes on the top button of his greatcoat as his gloved hands cupped her face. She lifted her hands and rested her palms against his chest. And she lifted her eyes to his and then closed them as his mouth came down to cover hers.

He was kissing her as he had the day before beneath the mistletoe, his lips slightly parted, the pressure light. And the wonder of it filled her. He was the man she had feared for so many years. She tried to remember the impression she had always had of his face until recent days—narrow, harsh-featured, the eyes steel-gray, the lips thin. It was he who was kissing her, she told herself.

The moan she heard must have come from her, she realized, startled. And then one of his arms came about her shoulders and the other about her waist, and he drew her against him. She sucked in her breath.

He must not overdo it, he told himself. He must not move too fast, must not frighten her. He must be patient, take it gradually. He wanted total victory, not a partial one. His motives might be confused, but he knew that he wanted victory.

And yet she tasted so sweet. And so warm. He set his arms about her and drew her against him and fought to keep his control. She was soft and yielding and shapely even through the thicknesses of his greatcoat and her cloak.

He had waited so long. So very long. An eternity. And here she was at last in his arms. He could not force his mind past the wonder of it. She was in his arms after an eternity of emptiness.

He lifted his head and looked down into her eyes in the darkness. They looked directly back into his and he read nothing there but acceptance and surrender. He was not going too far. She wanted this, too. And in the faint light of the moon and stars through the branches of the trees she looked more beautiful than ever.

"Judith," he said.

"Yes," she whispered.

He did not know what his hands were doing until he looked down to see them undoing the buttons on her cloak. He left only the top one closed. And then he was undoing the buttons of his greatcoat, opening it, opening her cloak, and drawing her against him, wrapping his coat about the two of them.

And he brought his mouth down to hers again, open, demanding response, pushing at her lips with his tongue, exploring the warm soft flesh behind them when they trembled apart, demanding more, and sliding his tongue deep inside when she opened her mouth.

He wanted her. God, he wanted her. He loved her. He slid one hand down her back, drew her hard against him, chafed at the barrier of clothing between them, wanted to be inside her.

He wanted her. He had always wanted her. And he had waited so long. Judith.

"Judith."

She had never felt physical desire before. She realized that now. She had been in love before, had had stars in her eyes, had been eager for the intimacy of marriage, had tolerated it while she had been in love. But she had never felt desire.

Never this bone-weakening need to be possessed. Never this aching desire to give herself. Her hands must have unbuttoned his evening coat and waistcoat, she thought dimly. They were at his back, beneath both, against the heat of his silk shirt.

She heard her name as his mouth moved from hers to her throat. He was holding her to him so that she could be in no doubt that his desire matched her own.

"Yes," she said. "Yes."

And then the side of her face was against the folds of his neckcloth, one of his hands holding it there, his fingers threaded in her hair. Where was her bonnet? she wondered vaguely. His other arm was about her waist and he was rocking her against him. She could hear the thumping of his heart. And she could feel him drawing deep and even breaths, imposing calm on himself. She closed her eyes and allowed herself to relax.

God, he thought, it was not easy. It was not easy to love the woman one hated. He held her, his eyes closed, and rested one cheek against the top of her head.

Judith. Perhaps he should not blame her. Not after what he had learned that afternoon. She had been very young, just a green girl in the hands of a rake intent on winning a wager. Perhaps he should forget, let go of all the hatred that had been in him so long that it was almost a part of him.

But how would he ever be able to trust her again? Even at the age of eighteen she should have behaved better than she had. She should not have sent her father. She should have told him herself. He did not believe he could ever forgive her for that even if he could excuse her for the rest.

"You should know better than to walk alone with a man on a dark driveway at night," he said.

"Yes." Her voice was low. She did not sound worried or sorry.

"You never know what might happen to you," he said.

"No."

"Judith." He rubbed his cheek against her hair. "Call me by name. Just once. Please?"

"Max," she said softly. She lifted her head and smiled up at him a little uncertainly.

He set his hands at her waist and took a step back from her. He bent down and picked up her bonnet from the driveway, shook the snow from it, and handed it to her. And he buttoned up his greatcoat and drew his gloves from his pockets—he could not remember removing them or putting them there.

"I have been wanting to do that for a long time," he said.

She finished doing up her cloak and looked up at him. "I have wanted it, too," she said. A smile touched her lips. "Max."

He leaned down and kissed her softly on the lips once more. "My aunts will be imagining that we have been caught and devoured by wolves if we do not appear soon," he said, and he held out a hand for hers.

A minute later they had rounded the bend in the driveway and were in sight of the house. They both chuckled at the surprising sight of a few of the older children with Spencer Cornwell, and Amy, too, engaged in a fierce snowball fight close to the front doors.

LATE NIGHTS SEEMED to make no difference to children on Christmas morning. There was always far too much excitement ahead to allow them to sleep until a decent hour.

Judith tried to pretend that she was dreaming and burrowed her head beneath the blankets and pillows. But the chill little body that wormed its way beneath the covers next to her and laid cold feet against her thighs and encircled her neck with little arms was too persistent a dream. And the larger body that launched itself on top of her refused to be ignored.

"Wake up, Mama!" Rupert demanded.

"Are you awake, Mama!" Kate asked, kissing Judith's cheek.

She did not want to be awake. Having lain awake through much of the night reliving the evening, marveling at the wonder of it, dreaming about the consequences of it, she had finally fallen asleep very late. And she had been having dreams that she wanted to cling to, dreams of strong arms about her and a warm mouth open over hers.

"I am now," she said with a sigh, and turned to wrap one arm about each child and pull them into a close hug. "What day is it? I have forgotten."

She laughed as they both answered her question, one in each ear. Of course it was. How could it be any day other than Christmas Day? There was a special feel about the day, as she had said on the way home from church the night before, something that made it different from any other day of the year.

"Oh, so it is," she said. "How silly of me to forget. What shall we do now? Go back to sleep for a while? Or shall we wash and dress and go in search of breakfast?"

She chuckled again at the chorus of protests that greeted her. Even Kate at the age of three knew very well that that was not the routine for Christmas morning.

"Presents first, Mama," Kate said, kissing her on the cheek again and looking at her with wide, pleading eyes.

"Please," Rupert added.

"Presents?" Judith frowned. "Ah, yes, presents. Now let me see, I believe there are a few here somewhere."

Rupert bounced on the bed.

"I tell you what," Judith said. "You two run along and wake Aunt Amy—gently, please—and bring her here while I see if I can find any presents."

"Silly Mama," Kate said, scrambling down from the bed. "You know where the presents are."

Judith reached out to ruffle her hair.

In truth, she thought—and felt guilty at the thought— she would have liked nothing better than to rush through washing and dressing and brushing and all the other tasks that would have to be completed before she could go downstairs to breakfast. She wanted to see him again.

She pushed her feet into a pair of slippers and drew on a dressing gown over her nightgown, then went in pursuit of the pile of parcels that were hidden at the bottom of a wardrobe in her dressing room.

She still felt as if she were in something of a daze. She was a woman of twenty-six years, a widow, the mother of two children. And yet she was wildly, exuberantly, head over ears in love. Far more so, she thought with another stab of guilt, than she had ever been with Andrew.

And yet the object of her feelings was none other than the man she had jilted in order to marry Andrew. The man she had feared and disliked at the time and during all the years since until just a few days ago. Not even as long. Even as recently as two days before she had been wary of him, suspicious of his motives. There had been something about him that had made her uneasy.

She smiled to herself as she carried the parcels through to the bedroom and piled them beside the bed. It was herself she had been wary of. It had seemed just too strange to be true that she was attracted to him, that she was growing to like him and admire him, and that she was falling in love with him.

Amy had been right all along, she thought. He had been trying to fix his interest with her from the start. That was why he had arranged all those meetings and outings with her in London, and that was why he had invited her to Denbigh Park for Christmas.

He was in love with her, too. If she had had any doubt, then it had been swept away the night before when he had kissed her. And afterward he had led her home, her hand in his, until they had come up to the others, and then liberally pounded her with snowballs as they joined in the battle that the others had started. He had laughed the whole time.

She loved to hear him laugh, to see his harsh features softened and made handsome.

When would he declare himself? she wondered. Today? It seemed likely. It was Christmas Day. And would she accept? She had two children whose security and happiness she must put first in her life. But he knew all about her children and was fond of them, she was sure. And they liked him and his home.

Was it possible that after all she was to be his wife? Eight years after she should have married him?

Her thoughts were interrupted by the return of the children, bringing Amy along with them.

"Ooh!" Kate said as she caught sight of the brightly wrapped gifts.

Rupert ran across the room and dived headlong onto the bed.

"How kind of you to invite me in," Amy said. "I have not been a part of a family gift opening for years."

Judith stared at her sister-in-law. Oh, yes, that must be true, she thought. It had always been the custom at Ammanlea for each family group to open gifts privately. But Amy had belonged to no family group. How cruel they had all been never to think of that.

"But you are an essential part of our family," Judith said. "We could not possibly begin without you."

There was a special glow about Amy, Judith thought as she handed the first parcel to Kate. And she was not convinced that Christmas morning and the gift opening could account for all of it. Amy and Mr. Cornwell had given up the snowball fight before everyone else the night before and had stood together on the steps of the house, watching the battle and laughing. His arm had been loosely about her shoulders.

Judith wondered if her sister-in-law was feeling as she was feeling that morning.

Was he at breakfast already? she wondered. Would he have left before they arrived there?

THE MORNING WAS taken up almost entirely with gift giving. First the children were presented with their gifts in the morning room—books from Mrs. Harrison, balls from Mr. Cornwell, and watches from the marquess. The marquess's aunts, too, had something for each of them: hand-knitted caps for the boys and mittens for the girls. The other guests all gave them some coins each so that Daniel declared loudly that they were all rich enough to join the ranks of the nobs.

Kate pulled at Rupert's hand until he went from the room and upstairs with her to drag down the box of Christmas bows they had made in London but not used after all. She gave one to each of the children. The two that remained she gave to the Misses Hannibal, each of whom insisted on hugging and kissing her.

"Come an' sit 'ere, nipper," Daniel said to her, "an' I'll let yer listen to my watch ticking."

The marquess smiled. If Kate were growing up in the same neighborhood as Daniel, she would have a powerful protector against all harm. The boy would probably grow into her devoted servant.

Lord Denbigh had small gifts to distribute to each of his guests after the children's excitement had begun to subside a little. He had given his aunts more precious gifts in private earlier that morning.

And after that there were the servants to call in and

present with their gifts and Christmas bonuses and to serve with tea and dainties left in the kitchen by the cook and brought up by him and Nora and Judith and Miss Easton. That part of the day's ceremony had always used to be an unbearably embarrassing one for the servants as they had attempted to make conversation with their employers. Since the coming of the children, however, that had all changed.

Lily and Violet, awed to silence by their own gifts, sat on either side of Annie, one of the scullery maids, as she unwrapped hers and she smiled at them and appeared to feel quite at home even though she was in his lordship's morning room with his lordship present, standing in the middle of the room with a large silver tray in his hands.

The gift-opening was always, the marquess thought, one of the loveliest parts of Christmas. But then, every part of Christmas seemed the loveliest as it happened.

She was looking exceptionally lovely that morning, he thought, his eyes straying to Judith. She was wearing a simple wool dress of deep rose pink. Wool was flattering to a slender figure, he decided, his eyes passing over her. Slender, but very shapely, too. He remembered again the feel of her in his arms the night before, when he had pushed back her cloak and drawn her inside his greatcoat and she had opened his evening coat and his waistcoat and put herself against the silk of his shirt.

Slender and shapely, warm, yielding, arched against him, making no resistance even when he had brought the lower half of her body intimately against him.

"Listen." It was Lily, looking shyly up at him, her watch held up toward him. Her eyes, gin-drugged but a few months before, were wide with Christmas.

He stooped down, put his ear obediently to the watch, and listened for a few seconds. "It ticks as loudly as your heart," he said. "You must not forget to wind it up each night."

"Never," she whispered fervently. "Thank you."

He smiled and kissed her cheek. "Your smile is thanks enough, Lily," he said.

She turned abruptly away, suddenly anxious because she had left Violet's side for a moment.

He glanced to Judith again and caught her eye. She half smiled at him and returned her attention to his housekeeper, with whom she was conversing. It was hard to know what she was feeling. She looked remote, serene, as she had always looked when they were betrothed. Perhaps she was deliberately hiding her feelings?

As she had done then?

And what had those feelings been then? She had jilted him in order to marry a rake. She must have had no feelings for him at all. Or else her feelings must have been negative ones. Perhaps she had actively disliked him.

And now? She had responded to him with hunger the night before. But that might mean nothing. She had been a widow for longer than a year. Perhaps she was just ripe for a man's attentions. Any man's.

It was impossible to know. But her behavior this morning was warning enough of one thing. He might be in love with her again—or still in love with her—but he must never trust her again, never allow himself to hope for a future with her. For even if she was responding to his lovemaking now and would perhaps accept an offer of marriage from him, he would not be sure that it was not just loneliness for any man that drove her to accept. He would find out only after they were married, when it was too late.

She had broken his heart once. He was not going to allow it to happen again. He did not think he would be able to survive its happening again.

But for all that, he hoped that he was more to her than just any man. If he was to break her heart as she had broken his, and cause her even one fraction of the pain he had suffered, then it was important that she at least fancy herself in love with him.

Last night he had been sure. This morning he was uncertain again. But then he supposed he would always feel unsure of himself with Judith Easton.

"No, no," he said to his flustered cook. "I shall return the tea tray to the kitchen."

The children had eaten most of the food from the trays even though they had had a large breakfast. Judith took the three trays in a pile and followed the marquess with the tea tray from the room and down the back stairs to the kitchen.

She looked up at him as they set their trays down on the wide kitchen table. "The lace handkerchief is beautiful," she said. "I am sorry that I do not have a gift for you."

"Your presence here in my house is gift enough," he said and watched her cheeks glow with color. He laid the backs of two fingers against her jaw.

She smiled at him and he was sure again. There was a certain look in her eyes, an open and an unguarded look.

"Save some dances for me tonight," he said. "The opening set and at least one waltz?"

"Yes," she said.

There was no time to say anything else. The servants were coming back down the stairs.

But he was sure of her again and ready to move on to the final stages of his revenge, and he was wishing once more that it was not Christmas. He wanted to be happy, yet it was impossible to feel quite happy when plotting the misery of another human being. Even if it was right and just to do so. Even if she deserved it. Even if he owed it to himself to get even.

He wished he was not still in love with her. And he wished she had not told him what she had the afternoon before to shake his resolve and make him wonder if she had been quite as much to blame as he had always thought. He wished he could stop thinking. He wished that humans were not always plagued by thoughts. And by conscience.

He wished it was possible simply to love her. Simply to trust her.

12

THE MARQUESS OF DENBIGH DISMISSED HIS VALET and glanced once more at his image in the full-length pier glass in his dressing room. Yes, he decided, he looked quite presentable enough to greet his neighbors and to host his Christmas ball. He felt as if he should look somewhat like a scarecrow.

His guests had found various amusements during the afternoon. His aunts had slept and gossiped with Lady Tushingham in one of the salons, Nora and Clement had gone out walking, taking three of the girls with them, Rockford had gone skating with some of the boys, Sir William had retired to the billiard room with Spence and a few more of the boys, Mrs. Harrison had taken several other children out to a distant hill to sled, Judith and Miss Easton had played games in the nursery with several of the younger children.

Everyone had seemed accounted for until, passing through the hall to join the billiard players, he had received a message from one of the grooms that some of the dogs who were not allowed in the house had been set loose and were causing something of a commotion in the stableyard. There he had discovered four guilty urchins who had been trying to make a dog sled until all six of the dogs had burst from their harness, flatly refusing to cooperate, and scattered to the four corners of the earth.

The marquess grinned at the memory. And sobered again at the memory of Ben, who had cowered and thrown both arms defensively over his head when he had seen the marquess approaching. It was hard to persuade the children to shake off old habits and expectations. He had once held Ben in his arms, soot and all, and promised him that never again would he be flogged for any wrongdoing, real or imagined.

He had taken all four boys out of the stableyard while his grooms gathered up stray dogs, and engaged them all in a wrestling match in the snow. Ben had soon been giggling helplessly.

They had eaten their Christmas dinner early and stuffed themselves with goose and all the good foods that went along with it. And they had all declared that they had not left even one spare corner for the pudding but had eaten it anyway.

The children's party had come next, a riot of games in the ballroom, which all his guests had attended though there was dinner to recover from and a ball to get ready for. He grinned afresh at memories of Aunt Frieda blindfolded in a game of blindman's buff and quite unable to catch anyone while the children had shrieked with laughter about her.

Rockford had caught Aunt Edith beneath a sprig of mistletoe and pleased her enormously by giving her a smacking kiss. Spence had kissed Miss Easton a little less smackingly and a little more lingeringly later beneath the same sprig. Lord Denbigh wondered if a romance was blossoming in that direction.

Judith had joined in one of the relay races and had raced the length of the ballroom and back, her skirt held above very trim ankles, her face glowing with the fun of it. His heart had somersaulted.

And now it was almost time for the outside guests to arrive, earlier than usual so that they could watch the children's pageant before the ball began and the children were herded off to bed.

It was no wonder he was feeling like a scarecrow, the marquess thought, turning to leave the room so that he could be sure of being downstairs before the first arrival.

NO ONE HAD played a single hand of cards all day. And except for the wine at dinner, she had not noticed anyone drinking any alcohol. What a difference from Christmas at Ammanlea, Judith thought, taking a chair in the marquess's ballroom, nodding to neighbors she had noticed at church the night before, and waiting for the pageant to begin.

This Christmas had been wonderful. If there were not one more moment of it to come, it would be the best Christmas she had ever known. But there was more to come. There was the pageant that the children had worked so hard to prepare and Rupert's excitement at being a shepherd.

"I am the one who cannot wake up, Mama," he had explained to her in some excitement. "I miss what the angel says and have to be told by Stephen and dragged off to Bethlehem. I have to yawn the whole time until I see the baby."

Judith smiled at the memory of Rupert practicing his yawns.

"It is hard to yawn, Mama," he had said, "when you are not tired."

"I am sure you will do quite splendidly when the time comes," she had assured him.

Kate climbed onto her lap and stared expectantly at the empty stage area.

And there was the ball to come. The dancing. She had

always loved dancing. And he had asked her to save the opening set and at least one waltz for him.

There was a growing glow of excitement in her. There had been little time all day to exchange more than the occasional glance and word with him. But his looks had been warm, full of an awareness of what had happened between them the evening before. During the ball they would touch again and talk again. Perhaps he would find the chance to take her aside and declare his feelings.

He loved her. She knew he did. She could see it in his eyes whenever she looked into them. He loved her as she loved him.

She wanted him to kiss her again as he had kissed her the night before. She wanted him to hold her. She wanted to hold him. She wanted more than those kisses. She wanted everything. Her cheeks grew warm at the thought.

"There is Aunt Amy," Kate said, pointing across the ballroom to where Amy was taking her place at the pianoforte.

Conversation about them was dying away as attention turned expectantly to the empty half of the ballroom. Judith smiled and rubbed a cheek against Kate's curls and caught the marquess's eye across the room.

AMY SAT DOWN on the bench behind the pianoforte and looked about the ballroom at all the splendidly dressed ladies and gentlemen who had come for his lordship's ball. And she made sure that her music was in proper order on the music rest. She set her hands in her lap and waited for Mary and Joseph to trudge through the ballroom doors on their weary way to Bethlehem.

She had always loved Christmas because of church and the caroling and the decorating and because it always brought her nieces and nephews to a house that was usually quiet and lonely. And she had always liked to have her brothers and their wives close to her again, reminding her that she was part of a family. But she had never experienced a Christmas as wonderful as this one.

There was Lord Denbigh and the courteous, kindly manner in which he tried to see to it that all his guests were comfortable and entertained. And his interest in Judith, which would surely blossom into a splendid match for her sister-in-law, who deserved more happiness than she could have known with Andrew. And there were the other guests, all amiable, even the unfortunately tedious Mr. Rockford, and willing to accept her as an equal.

And there were the children. All the wonderful children with their exuberance and mischief, their fun and their wrangling, their sad and funny stories from their past, and their capacity to bring joy into any adult's heart.

And the snow and the food and the decorating and skating and snowball fights and . . . oh, and everything.

And Spencer. Amy could feel her heart thumping faster. She had never had a gentleman friend. Never anyone to call her by name and to talk with her and laugh with her and throw snowballs at her and set a careless arm about her shoulders. No one had ever kissed her beneath the mistletoe except her brothers.

Spencer had kissed her twice under the mistletoe and once without. He had kissed her outside the ballroom doors a few minutes before. The children had been ready in their dressing room, though a few of them had still been dashing about in near hysteria. Mrs. Harrison had told Amy that she might take her place and they would try not to keep her waiting longer than half an hour or so—those last words spoken with a harassed look tossed at the ceiling.

Spencer had accompanied her from the dressing room

and through the great hall to the ballroom doors, one arm about her shoulders.

"You are a real sport, Amy," he had said. "I do not know what we would have done without you."

"It is not over yet," she had said. "Perhaps I will suffer from a massive dose of stage fright and suddenly find myself with ten thumbs."

He had bent his head and kissed her firmly on the lips. "You could not let us down if you tried, Amy," he had said. "There is far too much love in you for the children. And far too much common sense, too."

He had opened the ballroom door for her and winked at her as she passed through.

Friendly kisses all? she wondered, lifting a hand to touch her lips. Or had there been more to them? A real affection, perhaps. Her eyes grew dreamy. She wished . . . Oh, she wished she were fifteen years younger and six inches taller and beautiful. Or pretty at least. She wished . . .

The ballroom door opened again and Amy could see two frightened faces beyond it with Spencer beaming down at them. Mary and Joseph were approaching Bethlehem.

MARY AND JOSEPH were approaching Bethlehem. She was tired and brave and cross and not always careful in her choice of words. And he was strong and tender and reassuring—and could not resist returning one insult rather sharply. They were a loving and weary and very human couple.

The innkeeper, harassed by an unusually packed house and bad-tempered and demanding guests, would have turned away the couple from faraway Galilee without a qualm of conscience, but his wife fiercely defended the right of a woman just about to give birth to be given some place other than the street. Hands on hips, she browbeat the poor man until he suggested the stable, his voice heavy with sarcasm. And then she drove him out with a broom to clean a manger ready for the baby.

The Bible story, though beautifully written, the Marquess of Denbigh thought, somehow took the humanity out of the players. His ragamuffins from the slums of London put the humanity right back in and made a strangely touching, almost a moving, experience out of it.

The wise men called one another all kinds of idiot as they argued over which route would take them in the direction of the star, but all of them gave the impression that they would have followed it through quicksand if that was the way it pointed. The shepherds, except for the one who remained snoring and whistling on the ground, cursed the air blue in their terror at the appearance of the unknown but soon dropped their jaws in wonder and awe. The angel told them to shut up and pay attention. The choir sang like angels only slightly off-key.

And then Mary in the stable was bending protectively over the manger, warning the shepherds to stay back because she did not want them passing any sickness on to her baby. And she shushed one of the kings, who spoke too loudly for her liking. And she beamed down at the manger and reached down with a tickling finger just as if it were a real baby lying there and not just a doll from the nursery.

Joseph folded his arms, frowned about at the whole gathering, including the angel, and tried to look tough. Anyone who had it in his mind to harm the baby was obviously going to have to go through him first.

Rupert Easton was certainly never going to be able to earn a living as an actor, the marquess thought with amusement, watching the boy yawn and stretch with exaggerated gestures until he gasped at the sight of the baby and fell to his knees.

The marquess glanced across the room at Judith. She was leaning forward in her chair, one arm about her daughter, smiling broadly and watching her son intently. He would be prepared to wager that there were tears in her eyes.

And indeed, he thought, there were probably several eyes in the room that were not quite dry. For all the occasional irreverence of their language, these children were bringing alive a story so familiar that sometimes it lost its wonder. Into a very human world, a world full of darkness and imperfection and violence, a savior was being born. And despite everything, despite all the human darkness of the world, he was being welcomed and loved and protected—and worshiped.

There was a sudden and unexpected ache in Lord Denbigh's heart. And a reminder of something that had eluded his conscious mind for the moment. So much darkness. And so much light. Especially at Christmas. Light to dispel the darkness. A single candle to put the darkness to flight. A Christmas candle.

Unless the darkness fought against it too stubbornly and snuffed it forever.

He joined in the loud and appreciative applause that greeted the ending of the pageant, and found that he had to blink his own eyes several times.

SHE WAS LATE for the ball. It had taken a long time to quiet Rupert's excitement after the success of the pageant. All of the children had been made much of by the assembled adults before being finally herded off to the dining room for refreshments before bed. All of them had been in a mood to swing from the chandeliers, as Mr. Cornwell had put it.

Long after Kate had been tucked into bed, Judith had sat in the nursery with Rupert on her lap, reading a story to him, assuring him that yes indeed, she had heard him snoring, and that yes, certainly his yawns had been very convincing, and finally singing lullabies to him just as if he were an infant again, her fingers running through his soft auburn curls.

She wondered if Mrs. Harrison and Mr. Cornwell were having a similarly hard time getting the other children settled down. And gracious, they had twenty to cope with, not just one. She suspected that Amy was helping them, too, and probably Mrs. Webber.

Her son was growing up already, she thought as she got to her feet eventually and carried him to his bed. He was getting heavy. She looked down at his sleeping face with love and a little regret. She wished she could have kept him as a baby for a little longer. She thought of Mrs. Richards's newborn and of how it had felt in her arms. She wished she could have another child. Kate was three years old already.

A dark-haired baby . . . Would he ask her that night? she wondered. Had she refined too much on a kiss? They had after all been walking alone along a dark driveway. They would have had to be almost inhuman not to have given in to the temptation of the moment. Perhaps he had no intention of making her an offer. Perhaps he did not love her.

But he did. She had seen it in his eyes, those keen heavy-lidded eyes that had used to disturb her, frighten her. She had seen it in his eyes. He did love her.

She was late. The dancing had already started when she reached the ballroom. But she was not the last, she saw, looking about her. Mr. Cornwell, Mrs. Harrison, and Amy had still not come down. The marquess was dancing with an older lady. He was dressed with all the formality of a London ball, and was all gold and white,

his silk knee breeches, embroidered waistcoat, and bro-
caded evening coat all varying shades of gold, his stockings and linen of gleaming white.

Had she ever thought that he was not a handsome
man? she wondered. She could hear her heart pounding
in her ears.

"I thought you had deserted me completely when you
did not appear for our dance," he said with a smile,
coming to her as soon as the set ended. "Did you finally
get your children to sleep?"

"Yes," she said. "Rupert was very excited."

"I suppose," he said, "that deciding to have them perform their pageant just before bedtime was not a great
idea. I have too little experience with children, I am
afraid."

"But they have taken a wonderful feeling to bed with
them," she said. "They did very well and were well
praised for it."

"One thing I have learned about children in the past
two years," he said. "They will respond to one word of
praise faster than to ten of criticism. They need to feel
good about themselves, as we all do. Good comes out of
love and evil out of hatred. And here I am mouthing
platitudes. Come and dance with me."

She smiled and remembered the very stiff and formal
and unsmiling gentleman to whom she had been
betrothed for two months a long time ago. And the
harsh, morose gentleman whom she had met again in
London just a few weeks before. She looked up at the
man who had just said with easy informality, "Come
and dance with me."

It was a very intricate country dance, which she
remembered only with difficulty and great concentration. Some people who attempted it did not know it at
all. There was a great deal of laughter in the room as
couples or individuals occasionally went spinning off in

quite the wrong direction. Both the marquess and Judith were laughing as he spun her down the set after they had been separated for some of the patterns.

"There you are again at last," he said. "Did you promise to save a waltz for me, Judith? If not, promise now."

"I promise," she said, and they were separated again. She was dancing with a very large gentleman who was wheezing rather alarmingly from his exertions.

It was quite the most wonderful ball she had ever attended, she decided, looking about her at the twirling dancers and the berry-laden holly and up to the stars that twisted and glinted with the lights of dozens of candles above them in the chandeliers. By London standards it would not have been described as a great squeeze by any stretch of the imagination, but still to her it was wonderful beyond words.

She was back with Lord Denbigh again. "What a wonderful ball this is," she told him.

"You are not trying to flatter the host are you, Mrs. Easton?" he asked her.

"Yes, I am," she said. "I also mean it."

He smiled at her before they parted company yet again.

She would have been looking forward to their waltz with some impatience if she had not also wanted to live through and savor every moment of the evening.

"I HAVE NEVER seen them so excited or so puffed up with their own worth," Mr. Cornwell said.

"They had every right to be," Mrs. Harrison said. "They did quite splendidly even if in the final performance they disregarded or forgot every suggestion we had made to them about their use of the English language. My only consolation is that half the audience probably had never even heard some of the words before. Perhaps they assumed they were Latin or Greek."

Amy laughed. "I could have hugged every one of them," she said.

"I believe you did," Mr. Cornwell said.

The three of them were standing in the doorway of the ballroom, watching the vigorous country dance that had already been in progress by the time they arrived. Mrs. Harrison was being beckoned by the marquess's aunts and made her way to the empty chair beside them.

"Well, dear," Mr. Cornwell said, "Christmas is almost over."

Amy looked sharply up at him. "Yes," she said. "But it has been wonderful, and the glow of it will carry us all forward for some time to come."

"I sometimes worry about my boys," he said with a sigh. "And about the girls, too. Shall we stroll? It seems that this set is not nearly finished yet." She set her arm through his and they began to stroll out into the great hall. "I worry about what will happen to them when we finally have to let them out into the world to fend for themselves."

"But you will not let that happen until they have been well prepared for some employment, will you?" she said. "And I believe that his lordship will help them find positions."

"Yes," he said. "But will they forget everything else they have learned? Love and sharing and respect and courtesy toward others and belief in themselves and everything else?"

Amy chuckled. "I do believe, Spencer," she said, "that you are sounding like any father anywhere. You are busy giving your charges wings but are afraid to let them fly. If they are loved, they will love. And they will carry with them everything else you have taught them and shown them and been to them."

He patted her hand. "You are a beautiful little person, Amy Easton," he said. "Where have you been hiding all my life?"

She laughed. "That is the first time I have ever been called beautiful," she said. "My family hid me at home. They were afraid I would be hurt if I went out into the world. They clipped my wings, you see."

"Was it smallpox?" he asked her.

She nodded. "Only me," she said. "It afflicted no one else in the family. For which I can only be thankful, of course."

"If they had only allowed you from home," he said, "you would have been called beautiful many times, Amy. Your beauty fairly bursts out from inside you."

"Oh," she said.

He worked his arm free of hers and set it about her shoulders. "And the exterior is not unpleasing either," he said. "Have you allowed a few pockmarks to influence your image of yourself?"

"Oh," she said, "I stopped even thinking about my appearance years ago. We have to accept ourselves as we are, do we not, or live with eternal misery."

"I wish . . ." he said, and stopped. He smiled at her. "I wish I had met you ten years ago, Amy, and had a fortune as large as Max's."

She swallowed. "I have never believed that wealth necessarily brings happiness," she told him. "And age makes no difference to anything." She looked up at him, liking and affection and hope in her eyes.

He stopped and drew her loosely into his arms. "Ah, Amy," he said, resting his cheek against the top of her head, "these are foolish ramblings. Forgive me. It has been a lovely Christmas, has it not?"

"Yes." There was an aching pain stabbing downward from her throat to her chest. And an inability to say more because she was a woman and because she had no experience whatsoever with such situations. "It has been the loveliest."

She drew her head back to smile at him and he lowered his to kiss her warmly on the lips.

"Come," he said, "I had better take you back to the ballroom while you still have some shreds of your reputation left. Will you dance the next set with me?"

"I have never danced in public," she said.

He frowned at her. "Clipped your wings?" he said. "Did they cut them off completely, Amy?"

She smiled.

"But in private?" he asked. "You danced in private?"

She nodded.

"Then we will see and hear no one else in the ballroom," he said. "You will dance for me—in private. Will you?"

"I would like to try," she said.

He drew her arm through his again and curled his fingers about her hand.

13

His Aunt Frieda was flustered and tittering, protesting to Mr. Rockford that she had never seen the waltz performed and indeed had not even danced at an assembly for more years than she cared to remember.

Mr. Rockford was insistent and Aunt Edith nodding and simpering. Judith was close by and enjoying the moment.

"It is a very easy dance to learn, ma'am," she said. "All you have to do is move to counts of three and allow the gentleman to lead you."

Aunt Frieda threw up her hands, tittered again, and looked alarmed. The Marquess of Denbigh grinned as he walked up to the group.

"My dance, Judith?" he said, extending a hand to her. "Why do you not watch us for a minute, Aunt Frieda?"

"Oh, yes," his aunt said gratefully as Judith placed a hand in his. "That would be best, Maxwell."

"And I am quite sure," Aunt Edith said, "that Maxwell and Mrs. Easton will waltz quite splendidly, Frieda, since they have both recently been in town and the waltz is all the crack there."

Judith was smiling up at him as he led her onto the floor and set one hand on her waist. "It was rather rash of Mr. Rockford to ask your aunt," she said. "She will probably have a fit of the vapors when she sees what a very improper dance it is."

"I believe my aunts are made of sterner stuff," he said. "And improper, Judith? Merely because one faces the same partner for the whole dance and can carry on a decent conversation?"

She continued to smile as the music began.

Both of his aunts were watching them intently. He was very aware of that and kept his steps simple. And he held her at arm's length, her spine arched back slightly from the waist, her hand light on his shoulder.

Improper? Hardly. There was distance between them. He touched her only at the waist, her other hand clasped in his. And yet there was something intimate about the waltz. There was something created within the circle of bodies and arms, some awareness, some tension. Not always, it was true. But with some partners. With Judith it was an intimate dance.

He kept his distance, kept his steps simple, kept conversing lightly with her. His aunts were still watching them, though Rockford was talking to Aunt Frieda and bowing.

It had been an intimate dance in London at the Mumford ball. Almost unbearably intimate. And tense. He had deliberately fostered the tension on that occasion, keeping his eyes fixed on her face the whole time, neglecting to converse with her. He had hated her at that time. Hatred and the desire for revenge had outweighed the renewed attraction he had felt toward her.

And now? But he did not want to spoil the evening or Christmas by thinking and analyzing.

"You were quite right," she said. "Your aunt is ready to try."

They both watched Aunt Frieda take her first dance steps in years.

"I would almost be prepared to say that a romance is

in the making," the marquess said, grinning, "if Aunt Frieda were not at the very least twenty years older than her partner. I believe Rockford has taken a liking to my aunts because they are always willing to listen to his stories—even if they do frequently fall asleep before he has finished."

"I think he is enjoying Christmas," she said. "You have made at least one of your lonely persons happy."

"Lonely persons?" He looked at her with raised eyebrows.

"Lady Clancy's name for your guests," she said.

"Lonely persons." He smiled and shook his head. "You, too, Judith?"

Her smile faded slightly. She searched his eyes. "Why did you invite me?"

He twirled her about a corner of the ballroom now that there was no longer the necessity of keeping his steps simple. "You do not know?" he asked her.

"Because we would have spent Christmas alone in town without your invitation?" she said.

"Four of you?" he said. "Alone? It could have been a very cozy Christmas."

"Yes," she said. He held her eyes as he whirled her to the music. "I thought you were bringing me here to punish me."

"To punish?" he said.

She nodded. "You knew I was uncomfortable with you in London," she said. "You knew that I did not wish to be in your company. I thought you had devised this as the ultimate punishment. A week in your country home at Christmastime."

He smiled at her. "But you have changed your opinion?"

She continued to search his eyes. And then she nodded slightly again. "It is a Christmas that has been made wonderful by your kindness to many people," she said.

"I do not believe you could spoil it all by bringing one person here out of hatred. I misjudged you in London. Perhaps I have always misjudged you. I am sorry."

Her eyes wavered to his mouth and then returned to his. And he gazed back at her. So beautiful. So slender and warm. And so very, very beautiful. And he held his mind blank. He had to do so, for he knew that a fierce war would rage in his mind if he but opened up his thoughts. His desire for her, his love for her at war with his determination to complete what he had begun. And it was so close to completion. It could be completed within a few minutes if he so chose.

"You are making me uncomfortable," she said. Her cheeks were flushed. "Why are you looking at me like that?"

"Because I can think of no other way of looking at you," he said.

They were close to the doors leading out into the great hall. He waltzed her toward them and through them and continued to dance with her on the tiles. He looked keenly at each of the two footmen standing there, and they both hurried away as if they had remembered pressing business elsewhere.

"My only alternative," he said, "is not to look at you at all." He set the hand he held flat over his heart and held it there with his own. He tightened his arm about her waist, drawing her against him until she slid her own hand from his shoulder up about his neck and rested her forehead against his shoulder.

He continued to waltz with her, her body moving in perfect time with his own. He rested one cheek against the smooth hair at her temple.

"I have guests I must return to when this set is at an end," he murmured into her ear after a few minutes had passed. "There is no time for what we both wish to do, Judith."

She raised her head and looked up at him, shocked. And yet there was knowledge in her eyes, too, and the admission that he was right, that what was between them was no idle or innocent flirtation.

"Tomorrow," he said. "Arrange to have the afternoon free. Will you?"

She gazed into his eyes for a long time and he could see the conflict of emotions in hers. "Yes," she said at last.

He stopped dancing, closed the distance between their mouths, and kissed her. She responded instantly, molding her body to his, opening her mouth even without persuasion, moaning as he licked hungrily at her lips.

"Max," she said when he moved his mouth to her chin and down to her throat.

But he had not forgotten where they were: in the middle of the great hall, the doors to the ballroom open beyond it.

"Tomorrow," he said, straightening up, cupping one hand lightly against her cheek. "Tomorrow we will settle everything between us, Judith." He was not even sure himself what he meant by those words. He held his thoughts blank. He did not want to know.

"Yes," she said, and she raised a hand to cover his.

He kissed her softly on the lips once more.

FIRST THE MEREST suggestion of light on the eastern horizon. Then a gradual lifting of the blackness of the world to gray. A brighter line of light turning from white to pale gold to brighter gold, to pink, to orange-gold. And then all the glory of the dawn sky before the sun came up.

Judith watched it all from the windowseat in her

room, where she sat warmly wrapped in a blanket from the bed, her knees drawn up against her, her arms tight about them.

It looked as if it was going to be a glorious day. Cold but glorious. Even as she watched she saw him—Max—emerging from the stable block on horseback, a large bundle tied behind his saddle. He rode beneath her window, picking his way carefully, not pressing any speed on his horse because of the snow. Why was he up so early after such a late night?

But it was midwinter. She had no idea what time it was, but it was probably not as early as the coming of dawn made it seem. He was up for some morning fresh air and exercise. She wished she were with him.

She looked back into the room. It was a pretty and a cozy room despite the fact that the fire had died down long ago and the air was chill. It looked familiar already, even after just a few days. It looked like home.

Would it be home? she wondered. Would Denbigh Park be her home? After this afternoon she supposed she would know the answer to her question. She knew it now. But it seemed just too wonderful to be true. Could she really be finding such happiness so soon after the ending of a bad marriage, in which she had expected to be trapped for the rest of her life? And with Max of all people?

It was hard to believe in such happiness. And so, even though she was almost certain of it and would be certain before this day was over, she was anxious, too. What if she had misinterpreted all the signs?

She had expected to have her answer on Christmas Day. She had fully expected it at the ball, when he had waltzed with her, when he had danced her out into the great hall. She had expected him to declare his love for her, to make his offer for her. It had been all there in his eyes and in his mouth when he had kissed her.

Instead, he had said something that had taken her by surprise. "There is no time for what we both wish to do, Judith," he had said.

She had been shocked. For what they both wished to do? Make love? He wanted to make love to her? But of course it was there in his face. And it was what she wanted, too. It had not taken her many moments to admit that to herself.

If she had been in any doubt of his meaning, there had been his next words. He wanted her to be free for the whole of tomorrow afternoon. For the whole of *this* afternoon. Why? So that he might ask her to marry him? A few minutes would suffice for that. A whole afternoon?

He was going to make love to her. Her breath caught in her throat and she set her head back against the wood paneling behind her. That very day. He was going to make love to her. And she had not noticed any resistance in herself, though she had been awake for more than an hour already and had lain awake for an hour after the ball before sleeping. She was going to allow it. She was going to allow him to take a husband's privilege with her. But not as a passive experience, she knew. She was going to make love to him, too. They were going to make love to each other.

"Tomorrow we will settle everything between us, Judith," he had said.

She closed her eyes. They would make love and he would ask her to marry him and she would say yes. And they would live happily ever after. Except that it would not be as simple as that, of course. She knew from experience that it would not. Every day for the rest of their lives they would have to work hard on their marriage. But it would be worth it.

Oh, it would be worth it.

Judith shivered and pulled the blanket more closely

about her. Was she being a fool? Why had he not declared himself the night before? He might have done so and still asked her to be free for him this afternoon. They might have made love as a betrothed couple.

She thought for one moment of the uneasiness she had felt before coming to Denbigh Park and for a day or so after arriving. The feeling that there was something a little frightening about him. Perhaps . . . but no. She had seen into his eyes. His eyes could not lie. Oh, his eyes could perhaps, but not what was behind his eyes. And she had seen what was behind them.

How many hours until the afternoon? she wondered. How many interminable hours?

Christmas was over, she realized suddenly.

THE CHILDREN WERE up early. They breakfasted as fast as they could and scurried from the room in order to cram into the morning hours a whole day's worth of entertainment. They were to return to the village after luncheon. They skated and sledded and made snowmen and chased and played with the dogs. Some of them took their new balls into the ballroom and got under the feet of the servants who were clearing up after the night's ball. A few of the younger ones went to the nursery to play with Kate and ride the rocking horse.

"You must be longing for the sanity that the next few hours are going to restore to you, Max," Mr. Cornwell said, having abandoned his charges to the care of other willing adults for half an hour. He was sitting in his friend's library, one leg hooked casually over the arm of the chair on which he sat.

The marquess handed him a glass of brandy. "It will be quiet," he said. "My guests may find it unbearably so. The children have been general favorites, I believe."

Mr. Cornwell twirled the brandy in his glass and

sipped on it. "We could not quite have foreseen all this two years ago, could we?" he said. "I must confess, Max, that I really did not expect to succeed. Did you?"

The marquess slumped into the chair opposite his friend's. "Yes," he said. "I expected that we would successfully set up homes, Spence. We were both too determined to allow the scheme to fail utterly, I think. What I did wonder about was whether the homes would become almost like other foundling homes with time—impersonal places where the children's basic physical needs would be cared for but nothing else. I wondered if the life would really suit you."

"I cannot imagine one that would suit me more," Mr. Cornwell said.

The marquess smiled. "You are like an experienced and indulgent father, Spence," he said. "You do not sometimes feel the need for a wife to make the illusion of family life more of a reality?"

His friend looked at him warily and lowered his glass. "Good Lord," he said. "What a strange question to ask, Max. I am almost forty years old."

The marquess shrugged. "I thought perhaps Miss Easton . . ." he said.

Mr. Cornwell set his glass down and got to his feet. "Miss Easton is a lady, Max," he said.

"And you are a gentleman," Lord Denbigh said.

Mr. Cornwell scratched his head. "And father to ten lads who are anything but," he said. "Use your head, Max. I would not give up my boys, and even if I did, I would have almost nothing to offer a lady. It is true that I have enough blunt that you do not have to pay me a salary, but that is because my needs are modest. I would not dream of inflicting my situation on Amy."

"A pity," the marquess said. "I like the lady."

"And so do I," Mr. Cornwell said fervently. "Good Lord, Max."

The marquess smiled. "Sit down and relax while you have the chance," he said. "And finish your brandy. She is going to walk back to the village with you after luncheon?"

"Violet and Lily have asked her," Mr. Cornwell said, "and half a dozen other children, too. We are all going to have tea together at the girls' house to celebrate the success of the pageant."

"Ah," the marquess said, "then young Easton will want to go, too."

Mr. Cornwell chuckled. "It is quite a challenge to have to find a wholly new part in a play at the very last moment," he said. "And I hated to have the boy be a shepherd and just stand about quite mute. I am afraid he almost stole the scene. I fully expected our angel to tell him to pipe down when he was snoring so loudly. Yes, he will be coming to tea, of course."

"His sister will feel left out," the marquess said.

"Oh, she can come, too," Mr. Cornwell said. "One extra child here or there really does not make much difference. And her aunt will be there to watch her. Young Daniel will be pleased. I think she reminds him of a little sister he left behind—which reminds me, Max. We might try to mount a search for her and include her with our next batch. Amy thinks it would be a good idea to have a home with boys and girls together and perhaps a married couple to care for them. What do you think?"

"An admirable idea," the marquess said, looking keenly at his friend.

The morning seemed interminable. He should not have risen so early, he supposed. But he had been unable to sleep. He had got up before dawn and taken blankets out to the gamekeeper's cottage in the woods, though there were bedcovers already there. And he had spent half an hour there gathering firewood, preparing a fire so that all that needed to be done was to light it.

He wondered if she would come with him there. He had made his intentions very clear to her the night before. He had left her in no doubt. He had seen the shock in her eyes, a virtuous lady being so openly propositioned by a gentleman who was not even her betrothed. But he had seen the desire, too, the temptation, and the acceptance. And she had said yes.

That had been last night, of course. During the night and now in the cold light of day she might well have changed her mind. And she knew very well what was going to happen between them if she came with him.

He had wanted her to know that. He did not want either her or his own conscience to be able to tell him afterward that it had been rape. She knew that if she came with him that afternoon he was going to take her. The only thing she did not know was his motive.

But then, did he?

She had her chance. Her chance to avoid his revenge despite the care with which he had set it up. He would get even with her if he could. But he could never force anything on her. He could not ravish her.

If she was the virtuous lady she appeared to be, he thought, watching the brandy swirling slowly in his glass, his jaw hardening, then she would find some excuse for not accompanying him that afternoon. She would save herself. And if she did so, if she refused to come, then he would let her go at the end of the week. Perhaps she would feel regret. Perhaps she already expected a declaration from him. Perhaps she would be disappointed—severely so maybe. It would be a sort of revenge. Not as satisfactory as he had originally planned, but good enough.

Truth to tell, he was becoming somewhat sickened by the whole thing. He wished her husband had not died or that he had never heard of it. He wished he had not heard that she was in London or that he had ignored the knowledge. He wished to God that he had never seen her again.

"Perhaps her mother will want to come with her," Mr. Cornwell said.

The marquess looked up blankly. "Judith?" he said. "She has promised to come walking with me."

Mr. Cornwell raised his eyebrows and pursed his lips. "Has she, now?" he said. "In that case, Max, I shall have to assure the lady that the girls' house will be quite full enough with twenty-two children and three adults."

"Thank you," the marquess said. "I would appreciate that, Spence."

"I am not surprised, of course," Mr. Cornwell said. "It would have been pretty obvious to a blind man in the past couple of days. Your aunts have been nodding and looking very smug behind your back."

Lord Denbigh got abruptly to his feet and set his half-empty glass on the tray. He put the stopper back in the decanter. "It is not quite what you think, Spence," he said. "We had better go and see if any of my servants or dogs have been worried to death yet."

His friend chuckled and set an empty glass down beside his.

"YOU ARE QUITE sure you want to go?" Judith was stooped down tying the strings of Kate's hood beneath her chin.

Two large dark eyes looked back up at her and the child nodded.

"You want to be with the other children?" Judith smiled.

"Daniel is going to carry me on his shoulder," Kate said.

"You like Daniel?" Judith asked.

Kate nodded again.

"And you do not mind if Mama does not come with you?"

Kate put her arms around her mother's neck and kissed her cheek. "I'll tell you about it when I come home," she said.

"Well," Judith said, "Aunt Amy will be with you." She need not feel guilty, she thought, or as if she were neglecting her children. Rupert had already raced from the room and downstairs. And Mrs. Harrison, Mr. Cornwell, and Amy had all asked—separately—if Kate might be taken along, too, so that she would not be the only child left alone.

"Of course you must not feel obliged to come," Amy had said when Judith had expressed her concern. "Goodness, Judith, do you not believe that I will guard the children with my life? Besides . . ." she had added, but she had looked uncomfortable and had not finished the sentence.

Besides, she wished for some time alone with Mr. Cornwell? Amy had not been looking very happy all morning. Or rather, she had been looking too determinedly happy. Judith had seen her looking so once or twice when her father and her brothers had persuaded her to forgo some expected outing that might take her into too close a communication with strangers.

Had things not gone well for Amy at last night's ball? Judith wondered. Amy had been so very excited at the prospect of attending a ball. And she had danced several sets, two of them with Mr. Cornwell.

But there had been no announcement or private confidence during the evening—or this morning. Had Amy, too, been expecting, or hoping for, a declaration and not received it?

Kate reached up a hand to take hers and they left the nursery almost to collide with Amy, who was coming to meet them.

"Are you ready, Kate?" she asked. "Oh, and all nice and warmly dressed. Are you going to hold Aunt Amy's hand?"

"Ride on Daniel's shoulder," Kate said.

"Ah, of course," Amy said. "Daniel." She smiled brightly at Judith.

There was noisy chaos in the great hall. Mr. Rockford was solemnly shaking hands with all the children while the Misses Hannibal were kissing them. Two balls had escaped from their owners' hands. Someone was demanding to know what time it was since he had forgotten to wind his watch. A chorus of voices answered him. Mrs. Harrison and Mr. Cornwell were organizing the children into twos for the walk to the village. The marquess was standing cheerfully in the middle of it all.

"All right," Mr. Cornwell said in the voice that always drew everyone's attention, "before we quick march, what do you have to say to his lordship?"

"Thank you," twenty voices chorused. "Guv," someone added.

"Hip hip," Mr. Cornwell said unwisely.

"Hooray!" everyone shrieked, and caps and mittens and balls flew upward and then rained down on the great hall.

"Hip hip."

"Hooray."

"Hip hip."

"Hooray."

The marquess grinned as everyone broke ranks to retrieve lost possessions.

"We may be out of here before nightfall, Max," Mr. Cornwell shouted over the hubbub.

"I shall send the carriage for you and the children, ma'am," the marquess said to Amy.

"Oh, please do not," she said to him earnestly. "We will enjoy the walk."

"As you will," he said, glancing from her to Mr. Cornwell and back again.

And then they were on their way, more or less in twos and more or less at a brisk march. Kate and one of the smallest boys rode sedately on other children's shoulders. Mr. Rockford had already gone in search of Sir William in the billiard room. The Misses Hannibal assured each other that they must not catch a chill from the opened front doors and retreated to a warm salon.

The hall was suddenly very quiet.

"You will come walking with me, Judith?" the marquess asked.

Walking? She looked up into his eyes. "That would be pleasant, my lord," she said, noticing how foolish her formality sounded after the night before.

"Go and dress warmly, then," he said. "I shall meet you down here in—ten minutes' time?"

"Yes," she said.

He looked stiff and cold, his face harsh, his eyes hooded. Almost as he had always used to look, she thought, with a quickening of her breath and a sudden strange stabbing of alarm. But then he smiled, and he was Max again.

She smiled in return and turned to hurry from the great hall to the staircase.

14

THERE WAS A CHILLY WIND BLOWING SO THAT EVEN though the sky was clear and the sun shining, it was less pleasant outside than it had been for the past two days. She held the hood of her cloak together beneath her chin and clung to his arm.

She had thought that he must have changed his mind or that perhaps she had misunderstood all the time. Perhaps he really had just wanted to spend an afternoon with her. But she knew soon after they had left the house just where he was taking her. And she was not sure whether to be glad or sorry.

"You are cold?" he asked her, and he unlinked his arm from hers, set it about her shoulders, and drew her firmly against his side. They walked on through the snow. "Soon you will be warm."

It was a promise that made her knees feel weak. She rested her head against his shoulder since that seemed the most sensible place to set it.

"Max," she said at last when they had trudged through the snow for a while in silence, retracing their steps of a few days before, when they had come with the children to gather the greenery for decorating the house, "where are we going?" She was talking for the sake of talking.

"You know where," he said, stopping and turning her

to face him. "You did understand me last night, Judith? You do not wish to go back?"

There was something. His voice was low. He was looking down at her lips. She could feel the warmth of him through his greatcoat. But there was something intangible. Her own conscience? Could she be quite so coolly doing what she was doing?

She shook her head and he brushed his lips briefly over hers before they walked on.

She had made no protest at all. Only the question whose answer she must have known. And only the slightly troubled look when he had given her the chance, even at that late moment, to go back, to be free of him. He held her protectively against his side, feeling her slenderness through the thickness of their clothing.

But she had shaken her head and looked at him with such a look of—nakedness in her eyes that he almost wished that he could turn back himself or direct their steps somewhere else and pretend that all along his intention had only been to walk out with her. There had been desire in her eyes, as he had intended. And there had been that other in her eyes, too—as he had also intended. Except that seeing it there he had been terrified. Terrified of his power over another human being. The same power as she had exerted over him eight years before.

To be used as cruelly.

"Max," she said, and her voice was breathless even though they had not been walking fast or into the teeth of the wind. They were turning to take the path through the trees that Rockford and the bigger boys had taken a few days before, the one he had taken that morning. "Are you going to make love to me?"

"What do you think?" he asked.

"I think you are." Her voice was shaking.

"Do you want to go back?" he asked.

"No."

He wanted to. He wanted to turn and run and run and never stop running.

She would not have been at all surprised if her legs had buckled under her. They felt not quite like her own legs, but like wooden ones she was unaccustomed to. There was something wrong about what was happening, something sordid, something calculated. Except that his arm was about her and her head was on his shoulder. And she loved him more than she had ever thought it possible to love. And she wanted to give him something to make up for what she had done to him all those years ago. She wanted to give him herself.

And it was good that the giving would come before his offer, she thought. It would be a free and unconditional gift. The cottage was in sight, a real cottage, though very small. Not the rude hut she had expected. It was in a little clearing by itself.

There was not a great deal of light inside the cottage. The two windows were very small, and the clearing was surrounded by trees. He lit a candle with the tinderbox on the mantel and set it on the small table. And then he stooped down to hold a light to the fire he had set that morning.

"Keep your cloak on," he said, straightening up and turning to her. She was standing quite still just inside the door. He watched her eyes stray to the newly made up bed in one corner of the room. She licked her lips. "This is a small room. It will be warm in here in no time at all."

"Yes," she said, and raised her eyes to his. They were full of that nakedness again. There were no defenses behind her eyes. She was totally at his mercy. And he was intending to show her none. "Max."

There was something about his eyes, something about the set of his jaw. Was he having second thoughts? Was he feeling that he had gone quite wrongly about this whole business of courtship? She was having no such misgivings. Since the door had closed behind them a couple of minutes before, she had put behind her all her doubts and all her guilt. She was where she wanted to be and with the man she wanted to be with and she would think no more. She reached up a hand and set it lightly against his cheek.

He took the hand in his and turned his head to kiss her palm. When he looked back to her, something had lifted behind his eyes and they smiled at each other.

"This is where I want to be," she whispered to him.

"Is it?" he asked. "It should not be, Judith. You should turn and run through that door and keep on running and not look back."

He was giving her a last chance. He begged her with his eyes to take it. He should reach behind her, he thought, and open the door and push her out and bar the door behind her. He turned his head to kiss her palm again.

"I am where I want to be," she said again, and her free hand was on his shoulder and she was his for the taking.

"Judith." He bent his head half toward her and stopped. Her eyes and her lips were smiling at him, but the eyes were growing dreamy.

He was afraid. She could see the uncertainty in his eyes, the pleading for something. Reassurance? Was he afraid of bringing ruin on her? Afraid that she would weep afterward and blame him?

"Max," she said, and she closed the distance between their lips until hers touched his. "I love you."

And then she gasped and clung to him with both hands as he made a sound that was more like a growl than anything else and wrapped her about with arms like iron bands and kissed her with an almost savage hunger.

He could not draw her close enough. He wanted her against him, inside his own body, part of him. He had wanted her for so long. Always. He had always wanted her. And he had always wanted to hear those words. Always. All his life. In her voice. Spoken to him. He wanted her. Now. Sooner than now.

There was heat against his back. He was shielding her from the warmth of the fire. He turned her in his arms, not taking his mouth from hers, fumbled with the strings of her hood, tore at the buttons of her cloak, threw it from her, gathered her against him again, and thrust his tongue into her mouth.

But he did not want her like this. He did not want to take her. He did not want to master her. He wanted to love her. He wanted her to love him. He had waited so long. So very long. His arms gentled. His mouth moved to brush her cheek, to kiss her below the ear.

"Judith," he said into her ear, "I have waited so long for this."

"Yes," she said, and her hands began to work at the buttons on his greatcoat and she was lifting it away from his shoulders and sliding it down his arms. It fell to the floor. "Are you warm enough?" She was undoing the buttons of his coat.

"Am I warm enough!" He tightened his arms about her, imprisoning her hands against his chest, and laughed down at her. "Have you ever asked a more foolish question in your life, Judith?"

She laughed back at him, the sound low and seductive and carefree. "Probably not," she said. "But you know what I meant."

"Let's take our time, shall we?" he asked her, brushing his lips across hers. "We have all afternoon. Let me kiss you silly before we undress each other. Will you?"

She laughed again. "Kiss me silly!" she said. "I like the sound of it. Let me kiss you silly, too."

She did not need to. Just holding her like this, the heat from the fire warm on his arms about her, her face turned up to his, laughing, made him want to shout with joy. He wanted to pick her up and spin her about and about until they both collapsed from dizziness. But the room was very small. And as like as not they would collapse onto the fire.

He laughed down at her. "Proceed then," he said. "No quarter given or asked?"

"Never," she said, and she put her arms up about his neck and lifted her mouth for his kiss.

The tone of the afternoon had changed. The sexual tension, the total concentration on the physical deed that was to be performed between them, had been replaced by something else. Judith did not even try to put that something into words in her mind, but she felt it and responded to it. There was warmth, affection, love between them.

She smoothed her fingers through his hair as they kissed each other lightly, warmly, exploring almost lazily with lips and tongues and teeth and withdrew from each other occasionally just to smile and murmur words that they would never afterward remember. Passion was there, held in check for the moment, to build to fierceness and even frenzy later, but for the time there was the warmth of love.

His hair, she discovered, was thick and soft to the touch. His lips, which she had always described to herself as thin, were warm and firm and very masculine. And his eyes—those steel-gray eyes with the heavy lids—held her enslaved. Bedroom eyes.

"Bedroom eyes," she murmured to him and watched those eyes soften into an amused smile.

"A between-the-sheets body," he said against her mouth, and they both chuckled before he deepened the kiss.

He had withdrawn all the pins from her hair, slowly, one at a time, dropping them carelessly to the floor about her. She shook her hair when he had pulled free the last one and he ran his fingers through it—full-bodied silky hair the color of ripe corn.

His hands explored her lightly, unhurriedly, through the wool of her dress. Breasts as full and as firm as they looked, hard-tipped for him, a small waist, shapely hips, flat stomach, firm buttocks. And warm, all warm and delicious and inviting from the proximity of the fire.

He could not remember a time when he had felt happier.

"Judith," he murmured to her, lifting his head to look down into dreamy eyes and at a mouth that looked thoroughly kissed.

"Max."

"Profound conversation," he said, rubbing his nose across hers.

"Yes."

"I think the room is warm enough," he said, and he found the buttons at the back of her dress and began to undo them.

"Yes."

Her eyes wandered over his face as he continued his task and then drew the dress over her shoulders and down her arms with the straps of her chemise. She closed her eyes when he had her naked to the waist and held her a little away from him so that he could look at her. He lowered his head to kiss one shoulder and one breast.

Beautiful. More than beautiful. Need began to burn in him.

He slid his fingers down inside all her clothing so that his palms lay flat against her back, and he lowered it all over hips and buttocks until it fell to her feet. And she kicked free of the clinging fabrics and boots and stockings.

She marveled at the fact that she was not for a moment embarrassed even though there was a bright fire behind her and a candle burning on the table and daylight peering in at the windows, and even though he was looking at her and touching her and kissing her. And even though he was fully clothed. She had always been embarrassed with Andrew when he had raised her nightgown, even when she had still loved him. But the thought of her husband did not form itself fully in her mind.

She was undressing him. He stood still and watched her, her eyes lowered to the task of undoing buttons. He had never had a woman undress him before. It was a far more erotic experience than having a valet do it. The thought made him smile. She looked up and saw it.

"Are you trying to put my valet out of a job?" he asked.

She smiled and shook her head and he kissed her deeply, tasting the heat of her mouth with his tongue, allowing passion to build in him.

"Coward," he whispered to her. She had stopped with the removal of his coat and waistcoat. He reached up and removed his neckcloth and undid the top button of his shirt. But her hands pushed his aside and continued the task.

Dark hair curled on his chest, and it was a well-muscled chest despite his lean physique. She leaned forward, her face against his chest, her eyes closed, and breathed in the smell of him. Cologne, sweat, pure maleness. A throbbing low in her womb was threatening the steadiness of her legs again.

Her feet were cold, bare against the packed earth of the floor. She raised the left one to warm against the right.

"Cold feet?" he asked.

She lifted her head and smiled fully at him. "Yes and no," she said. "Mainly no." And she watched the laughter gather in his eyes again as he leaned down and swung her up into his arms.

The bed was soft and comfortable against her back. Surprisingly so. He had put a down-filled cover beneath the sheet, she realized. She watched him pull his shirt free of his waistband and remove it entirely. And she watched as he pulled off his Hessian boots and undid the buttons at his waist.

He watched her the whole time, watching him, unashamed, uncovered, waiting for him. He watched her glance at him as he removed his pantaloons, and swallow.

The bed had never been meant to hold two. But soon enough they would take up no more space than one. He lay carefully on his side beside her, propped on one elbow.

"Feet warmer?" he asked her.

She set one against his leg. It was cold.

"I have a cold woman in bed with me?" he asked, lowering his head, pecking at her lips.

"No," she said. "The woman is warm enough from the ankles up."

"Is she?"

"Yes." There was a catch in her voice. He deepened the kiss. And he feathered one hand over her breast, his thumb circling the tip before touching it, brushing over it. He felt her draw in breath.

The slow languorous time of love was past. The heat of passion was back, but with it an intimacy that went beyond the mere physical. She could feel it in his hands, in his mouth, his body. And it was with the love at the core of her, not just with her hands and her mouth, that she touched him.

She let her hands roam over him, touching leanness and hardness and muscle. And warmth and dampness and desire. She explored him and touched him as she had never dreamed of touching Andrew. And she wanted him. She wanted him with a fierce ache. She wanted him at the core of her. She wanted to give and receive everything. All that there was.

"Max."

It was an ache that he was building to an almost unbearable tension. He was touching her where she had never been touched with a hand, with fingers, stroking, parting, feathering, tickling. Pushing inside. Deeper inside. She felt her muscles clench around him.

"Max."

"I want to be there," he said. His voice was low against her ear.

"Yes."

"Do you want me, Judith?"

Foolish words. Her body and her voice were crying out for him. "Yes."

"There?"

"Yes."

"Here?"

His weight was on her, his blessed weight, bearing her down into the softness of the bed, and her thighs were being opened against the hardness of his legs, and he was there, pressing where his fingers had been, holding, waiting.

"Yes."

He was watching her, her eyes tightly closed, her face tense. Beautiful. And he savored the moment. The moment for which he had waited all his life. This was not something he would do in quick frenzy. He was going to love her as he had dreamed countless times of doing it. In a moment he would be inside her and she would be his. And he would be hers. She opened her eyes.

"Like this," he said. "Like this, Judith." And he held her eyes with his as he entered her, feeling himself gradually sheathed in heat and moistness and contracting muscles.

"Yes," she said. Her voice was almost a sob.

He had to lower his head and close his eyes for a moment so that he would not lose control.

It had always been a purely physical thing. Not quite unpleasant except toward the end when she disliked and despised Andrew. But not quite pleasant either. Something a little embarrassing, a little distasteful. A duty. Something she had always wanted to be over and done with quickly. She had never, even in the early days of her marriage, really enjoyed the sexual act.

There could be nothing more physical than what was happening to her now. An act performed slowly and in nakedness. Heat. Depth. Wetness. The sound of wetness. A slow deep rhythm.

And yet there could be nothing more beautiful on this earth. His body. Hers. Himself. Herself. Their love meeting and entwining and expressing itself inside her. Both of them inside her, exchanging love, exchanging selves in the slow rhythm of the early stages of the love act. One body. The phrase suddenly made perfect sense to her.

"Max?"

"Mmm." He lowered his head to hers, kissed her warmly.

"Max, it hurts."

"Does it?" He continued to kiss her, felt her hips move against his, felt the stirrings of climax in her, and speeded his rhythm.

He could not wait much longer. He wanted the closeness, the intimacy, never to end. He wanted never to let her go, never to allow her to be free of him. But the physical act must end. It was time for the ultimate giving and receiving. He wanted to feel her final surrender, the final opening to him, the final pushing beyond the barrier of her tension. And he wanted to give himself, his seed, his future to his woman.

And she was coming to him, lifting to him, tensing against him, whimpering, and then opening and stilling with the wonder and shock of her surrender, and shuddering and reaching for him and crying out his name.

And his seed sprang in her and he held her to him, feeling all his strength, all his tension drain out of him and into the woman he had loved all his life, for all eternity. He heard the sound of her name.

WHEN SHE WOKE up, she was lying on her side pressed warmly against him, her head on his shoulder, his arm about her, the blankets up around them both. She could not remember ever feeling quite so comfortable.

The room was warm, the fire crackling in the hearth. He had got up some time after their first loving and built it up again before returning to the bed to love her again.

She could not see the room because she had her back to it. But she could picture it in her mind, small and snug. An idyllic cottage in the woods. She wished they could spend the rest of their lives there, and smiled at the thought. The two of them and Rupert and Kate all together in the one-roomed cottage for the rest of their lives. And perhaps . . . well, she had made the calculations last night. She had known even before leaving the house with him that this was quite the most dangerous part of her month. And he had loved her twice.

The two of them and Rupert and Kate and a black-haired baby. She smiled again at the absurdity of her own thoughts and tipped her head to look up at him. He was awake and gazing back at her, his face quite serious.

"What are you thinking?" She raised a hand and laid the backs of her fingers against his jaw.

He shook his head slightly.

"I was thinking about our living here in this cottage for the rest of our lives," she said. "Silly, is it not?"

"Yes," he said.

"How long have we slept?" she asked. "It is still daylight outside, but we will have to be going back soon, won't we?"

"Yes," he said.

"Mmm." She sighed. "I wish we did not have to. Don't you?"

"We have to," he said. He was still not smiling.

"Max." She rubbed her face against his chest, kissed him there, and tipped her head back again. "I love you."

He looked back at her and said nothing.

She rested her fingertips against his cheek and gazed into his eyes. There was something there, something far back in them. "What is it?"

"I am embarrassed," he said.

"Embarrassed?" She laughed, but he did not smile. She sobered again.

"I thought you understood," he said. "You did understand, did you not, Judith? That this is just a Christmas flirtation?"

Her hand stilled against his cheek. She frowned slightly. "No," she said. "No, Max. Don't do this. It is not funny. Don't look at me like that."

"It was understood from the start, was it not?" he said. "You are a widow and young and it is Christmas. I thought . . . but perhaps I did not make myself clear."

"Max." She withdrew her hand from his cheek and pounded the edge of her fist once against his chest. "Don't be silly. Do you think to frighten me only so that you can laugh at me? Do you think to make me doubt what this has been? Don't be silly. And don't spoil it. Tell me you love me. Tell me."

He set the back of one hand over his eyes. "Judith,"

he said. "I am so sorry. I had no idea that your feelings were involved. I had no idea. I thought you felt as I did."

She lay very still, looking into his face, though his eyes were still covered by the back of his hand. And it was as if a giant hand had lifted the cottage up and off its foundations and they had been exposed to all the chill of a winter's day and the cutting force of the wind. She felt cold to the very heart.

And she knew—she had known from his first word though she had fought against the knowledge—that he was not teasing, that he would not the next moment reach out to pull her to him and laugh away her fears. She knew that she had been right about him from the start. She knew that she had been made his victim, that she had made herself his victim.

For it was not a Christmas flirtation. And it was certainly not Christmas love. It was vengeance from hell and had nothing to do with Christmas at all. She understood it all at last in a blinding flash.

He had not changed. He had never changed. And she had been right about him eight years before. He was cold to the very core. She had shamed him publicly and she had had to be punished. She had been punished.

She got up quietly from the bed and dressed silently and quickly. She found as many hairpins as she could on the floor and pinned up her hair without benefit of mirror or comb. She drew on her boots and her cloak and pulled up the hood over her head. She tightened the strings beneath her chin.

And she left the cottage without once glancing at the bed. She closed the door quietly behind her and began the long trudge back to the house through the snow.

He lay still, his hand over his eyes, until he heard the door close behind her.

He had had no idea as he had lain awake, holding her to him, waiting in dread for the moment when she would stir and look up at him, exactly what he would say to her when the moment for talking came. He had had no idea which side of his warring nature would finally win.

He had listened to himself almost as if he were standing beside the bed observing himself. Observing both of them. "I love you," she had said, and the words had come straight from the depths of her being. Her body pressed to his had uttered the same words. And her eyes had told him the truth of them. She loved him.

Triumph. Total victory beyond his best expectations. Revenge complete. She would suffer from rejection and humiliation as he had suffered. She would suffer from unrequited love as he had suffered. She would suffer from an uncontrollable hatred as he had suffered.

She would know darkness. Darkness that fought and fought against the light and threatened always to put it out.

He turned his head sharply and looked at the candle on the table. It was out although it had not completely burned down. A single candle snuffed. The fire was dying down and dusk was beginning to settle beyond the windows.

He set both hands over his face. After a few minutes he rolled over onto his stomach and buried his face and hands in the pillows.

15

IT WAS THE DAY AFTER CHRISTMAS. NOT AT ALL THE time to think of work. Several of the villagers called at the homes as soon as they knew that the children had returned, bringing food offerings and stories of Christmas, and bringing with them ears to be filled with the children's own accounts of the holiday.

She was not to think that they lived normally in such chaos and in such decadent luxury, Mr. Cornwell told Amy with a smile. The following day they would be back to work, the boys spending the morning with the rector having a Bible lesson, the girls stitching with Mrs. Harrison.

"And you must not believe that my boys will run straight to perdition while I walk home with you," he told her. "There are plenty of adults to keep a friendly eye on them, and a few who will keep a firm hand on them if necessary."

"It is very kind of you," Amy said. "But I did not intend to give you an extra two-mile walk."

He patted his rather round middle. "After the rich foods of the past two or three days," he said, "I think perhaps I should have a two-mile walk every hour, Amy."

She laughed. The children walked ahead of them, Kate holding Rupert's hand and looking up occasionally to show interest in the long story he appeared to be telling her.

"Lovely children," Mr. Cornwell said. "Nicely behaved. It is a pity they lost their father so young."

"Yes," she said. "They look very like my brother. He was a handsome man."

"But Mrs. Easton is young," he said. "Doubtless they will have another papa soon. Will you mind?"

"No," she said. "I love Judith as if she were my real sister."

"You will still live with her when she remarries?" he asked. "Have you made a final decision?"

"No." She spoke quite firmly. "But not with Judith. That would not be fair."

"But not with your family again," he said. He patted her hand as it rested on his arm. "They overprotected you, Amy."

"I am afraid they did," she said. "Since I have been away from them, I have found people to be very kind. I am not treated like some sort of monster after all."

He clucked his tongue. "Did you expect to be?" he asked. "Did you really expect to be?"

She smiled. "All three of my brothers are unusually handsome men," she said. "I believe all my family acted out of the wish to protect me. I suppose I came to believe that some terrible disaster would befall me if I left the nest. I am glad that Judith persuaded me to do so."

"But you may go back to them?" he asked.

"I don't know," she said. "I have made no definite plans for the future."

They were halfway along the driveway already. Soon they would be at the house. The next day his boys and he would be back at work again and unlikely to come near Denbigh Park. And she would have no further excuse to visit them. Time passed so quickly, she thought, and remembered a time not so long in the past when she had believed just the opposite.

"I wish . . ." he said, and stopped. "I wish you would meet some gentleman you could be fond of, Amy. Someone with a comfortable home and fortune. Someone with whom you could spend your remaining years in contentment."

Her throat ached as if she had just run for a mile without stopping. "I once dreamed of it," she said, "of a home and children of my own and a modest place in society. I no longer care much for the home and it is too late for the children. But I would still like to belong somewhere, to feel wanted and needed. To feel useful. But I count my blessings every day of my life."

"Ah," he said. "To feel useful. I can understand that need, Amy. It is the way I felt before Max and I dreamed up our plan for our children's homes."

"Yes," she said, "and you found your dream. How I envy you."

They had reached the house. Rupert and Kate turned to look at them and Mr. Cornwell waved them on toward the doors.

"Run inside and get warm," he said.

"Will you come in and warm yourself before returning?" she asked.

"No." He patted her hand. "If I do that, Max will insist on calling out a sleigh or a carriage, as like as not, and I will not get the exercise I need."

"Thank you for walking with me," she said as he took her hand in both of his and held it. "It has been a wonderful Christmas, has it not? The best I can ever remember."

"And for me, too," he said, raising her hand to his lips. "You will be here for a few more days, Amy? Perhaps I will see you again before you leave. If I do not, have a safe journey home. I shall always hope that you find what you deserve in life. I'll never forget you."

She bit her lip. "Or I you," she said. And in a rush, "You are the first friend I have ever had outside the family."

"Am I?" He smiled at her. "Then I am deeply honored. And I shall hope always to be your friend. Perhaps if your sister-in-law and Max . . ." He smiled and shrugged. "Then perhaps we would meet again."

She nodded.

"Amy," he said softly, "it would not work. Believe me, it would not. You are a lady and brought up to the life of a lady."

An empty, empty, empty life, she thought, concentrating on their clasped hands. She nodded.

"I think maybe I should not come here in the next few days," he said.

She nodded again.

"Good-bye, then, my dear," he said after a pause. "For the first time in more than two years I wish things could be a little different, but they cannot."

She looked up into his face. "I wish it, too," she said. "I wish other people did not always, *always* know what is best for me. Is it my size, I wonder? Is it because I look so much like a child to be protected?" She withdrew her hand from his. "Good-bye, Spencer. Thank you for these few days. I cannot tell you all they have meant to me."

And she turned about and was gone up the steps and into the house before he could even return his arms to his sides. He stood for a long time frowning after her.

THE MARQUESS OF Denbigh was standing in the great hall when the two children came inside alone. He raised his eyebrows and looked at them.

"We just came home from the village," Rupert explained to him. "Aunt Amy is outside with Mr. Cornwell. Mr. and Mrs. Rundle came visiting and Mr. Rundle said he once met my papa. He said that papa liked to watch all the mills outside town, but Mrs. Rundle would not let him tell me about them. I think it was because ladies do not like to watch mills. Do they?"

"It is not considered a genteel sport for ladies," the marquess said, noticing that the little girl looked tired. She clung to her brother's hand and gazed upward at him with those dark eyes, which were going to fell a large number of young bucks when she was fifteen or sixteen years older. He smiled at her. "They do not derive much enjoyment from watching noses get bloodied. Don't ask me why."

The little girl had detached herself from her brother's side and was standing in front of the marquess, her arms raised. He picked her up and she set her arms about his neck and rested her cheek against his.

"Tired?" he asked.

She yawned loudly.

"Do you want me to carry you up to the nursery?" he asked.

She nodded. "Daniel lost his ball," she told him.

"Did he?"

"But he found it again."

"I am glad to hear that," he said.

"They all play cricket in the summer," Rupert said. He was trotting up the stairs at the marquess's side. "Cricket is a super game. I am going to play on the first eleven when I go to Eton, just like my papa did. Uncle Maurice told me."

"So did I," the marquess said, ruffling the boy's hair. "It is a noble ambition."

"Did you?" Rupert said, looking up at his host with renewed respect. "But I would like to play with the boys here. They all say that Joe is the best bowler. Perhaps if we come back in the summer I will be allowed to play with them. I will be almost seven by the summer."

The boy's hand was in his, Lord Denbigh noticed.

"I want to play with the dogs when we come back," Kate said.

The marquess allowed Rupert to open the nursery door since he did not have a free hand himself. Judith turned from the window at the far side of the room as they entered. She had obviously been awaiting the return of her children. Her face looked as if it had been carved out of marble.

"Mama." Her son raced toward her. "There was a gentleman at the house in the village who used to know Papa. He said I look just like him. He said he would have known me anywhere."

She rested a hand on his curls.

The marquess bent down to set Kate's feet on the floor. But she squeezed his neck tightly and kissed his cheek before scurrying across to her mother with some other pressing piece of news.

Judith was bending down to listen to her daughter's prattling as he turned to leave the room.

CHRISTMAS WAS NOT quite over, it seemed. The decorations still made the house look festive, and there were still all the rich foods of the season at dinner. And it appeared that the marquess's aunts had busied themselves during the afternoon organizing a concert for the evening.

"Everyone is to do something, Maxwell," Aunt Edith told him when they were all at table. "Miss Easton was not here, of course, when we made the plans. She was in the village with the dear children. But I am sure she will favor us with a selection on the pianoforte." She smiled at Amy. "And you and Mrs. Easton were out walking." Her smile, echoed by Aunt Frieda and Lady Tushingham, was almost a smirk.

"I shall read 'The Rape of the Lock,'" Lord Denbigh said. "It always shocks the ladies."

"But I am sure it cannot be quite improper despite its title if you are willing to read it aloud with ladies present, dear Maxwell," Aunt Frieda said.

Judith supposed she would sing. Amy would be willing to play for her. She had deliberately seated herself beside Mr. Rockford at dinner, knowing that a few carefully selected questions would keep him talking the whole time. She excused herself as soon as Lady Clancy got to her feet to signal the ladies to leave the gentlemen to their port, promising to return to the drawing room in time for the concert.

Kate and Rupert were both fast asleep, she found when she looked in at the nursery. She went to her own room. Her heart plummeted when there was a tap on the door almost immediately and Amy came inside. She so desperately wanted some time alone. But she needed to talk with her sister-in-law, too.

"Amy," she said, "I have been meaning to tell you that we must . . ."

But Amy did not wait to hear what she had to say. "Judith," she said, her voice agitated, "is it possible that we can leave here tomorrow? Or that I can, perhaps? Is it possible that you can come with someone else later or else that you will not wish to leave at all?"

Judith had been wondering how her sister-in-law would react to having to leave Denbigh Park a few days earlier than they had planned. She frowned and watched aghast as Amy burst into tears and hurried across the room to gaze out of the window onto the dark world beyond.

"Amy?" she said. "What is it?"

"Oh, nothing." Amy blew her nose. "Just homesickness. This was not such a good idea after all, Judith. I have never been away from home at Christmas."

"Mr. Cornwell?" Judith asked softly.

Amy blew her nose again. "What a foolish, pathetic creature I am," she said. "I am thirty-six years old and from home for the first time in my life, and I fall stupidly in love with almost the first gentleman I meet."

"And he with you, if my eyes have not deceived me," Judith said. "He seems very fond of you, Amy. Did something happen this afternoon?"

"Only good-bye," Amy said. "And the assurance that 'it' would never work—whatever 'it' is. I am a lady, you see, and have been brought up to the life of a lady."

"Have you ever told him," Judith asked, "how lonely that life was, Amy, and how sheltered from the world you have always been? And have you ever told him how you surrounded yourself with the children and happiness whenever all your family came to visit?"

Amy did not answer. She sniffed and Judith knew that she was crying again.

"Oh, Amy." Judith crossed the room and set firm hands on her sister-in-law's thin shoulders. "We live in a cruel world. We women have to wait for the men to make all the moves, don't we? And if they decide not to do something, there is almost nothing we can do about it."

"Perhaps he does not even want me," Amy said. "Why should he? Look at me, Judith. And I am too old to be starting to bear children—or almost too old anyway. He must have guessed my feelings. It must have been embarrassing to him. I am fortunate that he is a kind man."

Judith clucked her tongue impatiently. "These things can be sensed, Amy," she said. "If you have felt that he cares for you, then you are probably right."

Amy straightened her shoulders and blew her nose

once more. "I cannot bear to stay here even one more day," she said. "Will you mind if I leave, Judith? Will Lord Denbigh be offended, do you think?"

"My things are already packed in the dressing room," Judith said. "I have already sent word that the carriage is to be got ready for the morning."

Amy turned and looked up at her with reddened eyes. Judith's smile was a little twisted.

"It seems that it was something of a mistake for both of us," she said. "I just wish it were possible to leave tonight, Amy. No!" She held up her hands sharply as her sister-in-law took a step toward her. "Please don't say anything, or ask any questions. Not yet. My control can be very easily broken and there is this wretched concert to be lived through. Perhaps on the journey home I will tell you all about it."

"But has he not made you an offer?" Amy asked. "I thought . . . It seemed so obvious that . . ."

"No," Judith said. "It was just a Christmas flirtation, Amy, nothing more."

"Oh, no." Amy frowned. "It was definitely more than that, Judith. He . . ."

"I think we should go down to join the ladies," Judith said. "Shall we?"

Amy sighed. "It was all so perfect until this afternoon, was it not?" she said. "In time, Judith, we will remember that and judge it after all to have been one of the best Christmases ever, perhaps *the* best."

"Yes," Judith said. "Perhaps in time."

THERE WAS MUCH sleeplessness in Denbigh Park that night. Amy stood at her window long after everyone had gone to bed, staring sightlessly out, thinking of Judith's words. It was something that could be sensed, Judith had said from an experience of life that was more extensive than Amy's. If Amy thought he had cared, then he probably had.

He had cared. She was sure of it. He had wished things could be different. He had wished he were ten years younger and wealthy. He had wished she could find someone who would make her comfortable for the rest of her life.

He cared.

Life was cruel, Judith had said. Women had to wait around for men to speak, and if the man never spoke, then the woman remained disappointed. Unfulfilled. Unhappy. Life a dreary waste.

Tomorrow she would go away with Judith. And she would never see him again, or all those children. In time, Judith would marry again. It was inevitable even if for some strange reason she did not marry Lord Denbigh. And then she, Amy, would go home again. And that would be the end of life until the time, some unknown number of years in the future, when she breathed her last.

Because she was a woman. Because he was a gentleman and did not believe his way of life suitable for a lady. And because she was a woman and unable to speak up against him.

She was thirty-six years old. Perhaps she would live for thirty or forty more years. Years of dreariness and uselessness and humiliation—because she was a woman and unable to speak her piece.

It was a stupid reason. Because she was a woman!

Well, she thought finally, and the thought sent her to bed at last, if she allowed such a stupid reason to spoil the rest of her life, perhaps she deserved the future that was yawning ahead of her.

She was going to persuade Judith to put off calling the carriage until noon. If she did not lose her courage with the light of day, she was going to use the morning to speak her piece. If she did not lose her courage . . .

She scrambled into bed.

JUDITH LAY IN bed staring up into the darkness. She could still feel the physical effects of that afternoon's happenings. Her breasts were still tender. There was still an ache where they had coupled. And if she closed her eyes, she could still feel him. And smell him.

She did not close her eyes.

The anger, the hatred that had sustained her during the walk home that afternoon, during that brief and un-expected meeting with him in the nursery, and during the interminable evening of cheerful Christmas enter-tainment, had faded. She was no longer either angry or filled with hatred. She was empty, blessedly free of any violent feelings.

And she began to live again through the events of eight years before. The very correct, very harsh-looking man who had been her betrothed, who had escorted her to the various *ton* events of the Season, conversing with her stiffly, never touching more than her hand. Her own frightening awareness of him, which she had naively interpreted as revulsion. And Andrew, handsome, charming, smiling, easy and familiar in his manners.

And her own dreadful behavior. Unthinkable. Unfor-givable.

And his revenge. He had planned it all, moment by moment. She could clearly see that now. Everything, from that first encounter in Lady Clancy's drawing room, had been directed toward achieving his revenge.

But why? That was the question that had revolved and revolved in her brain since the afternoon. Wounded pride and consequence? Would that account for all he had done? Would not some public humiliation have been more appropriate to a revenge from that motive? This revenge would surely not be public enough for such a man, even though there were undoubtedly several people who were expecting them to marry. She did not believe that he would make public the fact that she had given herself to him and declared her love for him.

But if not that motive, then what?

If he had not changed radically in the past eight years, if he had been then in character what he was now, then what must he have been like beneath the harsh exterior? She had never tried to find out at the time. How must he have felt about his betrothal? About her? He was a man now who loved to give happiness, a man who loved children. He loved her own children even though they were hers—and Andrew's.

She had not thought him quite human eight years before. And yet even if he had changed in that time, he had still been human then. He had been a man engaged to be married and within one month of his wedding. A man who had since proved himself to be fond of children . . .

Judith dashed a tear from her cheek impatiently and continued to stare upward into the darkness.

THE MARQUESS OF Denbigh sat in his library for a long time after his guests had gone to bed. He was not really thinking. He was just allowing sensation to wash over him and felt too lethargic to drag himself off to bed.

"I love you," she had told him when they had first arrived at the cottage. And during the following couple of hours she had loved him indeed with all of herself, with her body and with the part of herself that had looked at him through her eyes.

"I love you," she had told him again, lying warm and relaxed in his arms beneath the bedcovers, smiling at him with love and trust and the full expectation that he would return her words.

A Christmas flirtation! I thought you understood. Judith, I am so sorry.

And this was what sweet revenge felt like. He had waited eight years for this. This was what it felt like. So empty, so very very empty that there was pain.

She had smiled at him almost throughout their second loving and teased him about having to watch her. Was he afraid she would run away if he did not keep an eye on her? And she had told him what she liked and had gasped and bitten her lip and smiled again when he had done it.

"Tell me what else you like," he had told her, "and I will do it."

"I like all of it," she had said. "All of it. All."

He had given her all and they had both laughed until passion had taken away the laughter and replaced it with ecstasy.

He had filled her with his seed—twice. Perhaps even now there was new life beginning in her. His life. Hers. Theirs. A new life. She was going away in the morning. He would be as greedy for news of her as he had ever been. He would want to know, he would need to know if she showed signs of swelling with child.

And if the news of such came back to him, then what would he do?

And if no such news ever came, then what would he do?

He had brought a single candle with him from the drawing room. But he had not lit the candles in the branched candlestick on the mantel with it as he had intended. It stood on his desk, the berry-laden sprig of holly twined around its base giving it a festive glow.

A Christmas candle. All that was left of Christmas. A single frail light in a dark room. He could snuff it with one movement of his fingers. And then there would be total darkness. No Christmas left at all. Nothing left at all.

He jerked to his feet and wondered belatedly and in some surprise why he had not touched the brandy decanter.

He was not the only person in the house still awake, he discovered as he reached the landing at the top of the stairs, holding his single Christmas candle. There was a little figure in a long white nightgown standing there, obviously frightened to stillness by the sight of the approaching light.

"You cannot sleep?" he asked.

"I was on my way to Mama," Rupert said. "To see if she was all right."

"She has probably been asleep for hours," the marquess said. "Will I do instead?"

"I could not find Papa," the child said.

"Couldn't you?" The marquess stooped down and picked up the little boy, who wrapped his arms about his neck and shivered.

"He kept going through doors," Rupert said. "But when I went through them, he was not there. And they all said they had not seen him. Some of them said they had never heard of him. But I could see him going through another door."

The marquess let himself quietly into the nursery. The doors into Kate's and Mrs. Webber's bedchambers were open. Mrs. Webber was snoring loudly. Obviously, she was too elderly a lady to have the night charge of two young children. He went into the boy's bedchamber, pulled a blanket from the bed, and seated the two of them in the nursery again. He wrapped the blanket warmly about the child.

"I knew your papa," he said. "I saw him many times."

Rupert looked up at him hopefully. "They said they had never heard of him," he said.

The marquess smiled. "That was because they were dream people," he said. "Dream people are always re-markably stupid. How could anyone with any sense not have heard of a man who was once on the first eleven at Eton?"

"Uncle Maurice said he once hit three sixes in one in-ning," Rupert said.

"Did he?" The marquess shook his head. "Then he was a greater champion than I ever was. The best I ever hit was one six and two fours."

"Was I dreaming?" Rupert asked.

"You were," Lord Denbigh said. "The next time you meet those foolish people in a dream, you can tell them that the Marquess of Denbigh knew your papa very well and envies his record at cricket. And he could skate like the wind, too, could he not? I am afraid I can skate only as fast as the breeze."

The boy chuckled. "Tell me about Papa," he said.

"Your papa?" The marquess looked up and thought. "Let me see. Did anyone ever tell you how he charmed all the ladies? How he charmed your mama and whisked her away to marry him when I fancied her myself?"

"Did he?" Rupert asked. "Tell me."

Lord Denbigh told a tale of a handsome, charming young gentleman who could dance the night away long after everyone else had collapsed from exhaustion and drive a team with such skill that he was known as the best whip in London and spar with any partner at Gen-tleman Jackson's without once coming away with a bloodied nose.

Andrew Easton's son was sleeping before the mar-quess had finished.

16

AMY WAS HURRYING DOWN THE DRIVEWAY, WON-
dering whether she had the courage to do what
she had planned to do or whether when she reached the
village she would merely step into the shop to purchase
some imagined need. There had been no problem with
Judith. She, too, apparently had something she wanted
to do before the carriage was called.

Amy rounded the bend, head down against the wind.
It was a chilly morning. There was no sign yet of the
cold spell breaking. She lifted her scarf up over her
mouth and nose.

"Good morning," someone called. "You are up and
out very early."

Her head snapped up and there he was, walking toward her, his chin buried inside the neck of his coat, his
cheeks reddened by the cold, his mustache whitened by
the frost. And everything she had rehearsed fled from
her mind.

"We are leaving," she said. "At noon. I was walking
into the village to—to buy something."

"Leaving?" He stopped beside her and hunched his
shoulders. "All of you? So soon?"

"Yes," she said. "We need to be back. We have en-
gagements, you know. And Judith's parents will be returning from Scotland soon. She is eager to hear news of

her sister from them. And I love town. There is so much yet to see there."

"We are going out to collect firewood this afternoon," he said. "We always make a festive occasion out of it. I thought that perhaps you would care to come with us. But I said good-bye yesterday, did I not? It would have been better to have left it at that, I suppose."

"Yes," she said.

He offered her his arm. "May I escort you to the village shop?" he asked.

"Thank you." She took his arm and they began walking toward the village, exchanging opinions on the weather and guesses about when it would begin to warm up and predictions on whether it would snow again.

"I was not on my way to the shop," she said in a rush all of a sudden. "I was on my way to call on you. I remembered that the rector would be busy with the boys this morning."

"Yes," he said quietly. "That was why I was free to walk to the house."

She drew a deep breath. "I have had material comforts and a large home and a protective family all my life," she said, fixing her eyes on the roadway ahead. "And though I have always counted my blessings, I have been unhappy, Spencer. There has been nothing to give my life purpose. Nothing to warm my heart."

He was patting her hand.

"The only bright moments in my life have been the times when my brothers and some cousins came with their children," she said. "I always loved to play with them and talk with them. I used to think that I would give up every last thing, every last brick of the house and rag of clothing just to extend those times. It was foolish, of course. One cannot in reality live without even the basic necessities of life. But I felt it and believed it and still believe it in part."

"Amy," he said. They had stopped walking and he had turned to her.

"You were wrong," she said, her voice agitated. "You said that it would not work. Perhaps it could not from your point of view. But you were wrong about me, I . . ."

He laid two gloved fingers against her lips. "Don't," he said. "Don't say any more."

But she pulled back her head. "Yes," she said, "I will. It is not fair that just because I am a woman . . ."

"Sh," he said, and he set his hands on her shoulders and pulled her against him. "Don't say any more, Amy."

"I came to say it." She looked earnestly up into his face. "I will be sorry forever after if I do not. For once in my life . . ."

"Sh," he said, and he kissed her briefly on the lips. "You are a woman, Amy, like it or not, and we live in a society which would make you feel ashamed of having to say such a thing. And you do not need to say it when I can just as easily say it myself and propriety will not be outraged. Will you marry me, my dear?"

She gazed mutely back into his eyes.

"I do not need to explain that it will not be a brilliant or even a very eligible match for you. You know that already," he said. "I have an independence, Amy, in the sense that Max does not pay me a salary, only all the expenses of the home. But I cannot offer a wife any sort of luxury. And I cannot give up this work I have begun. I am too selfishly happy doing it. But you would not want me to, I know. I can only feel sorry that I cannot offer you a better life. But the decision must be yours. I am offering myself and my life to you for what they are worth."

"Only because I was going to ask?" she said wistfully. "Only because you are a gentleman, Spencer?"

He chuckled. "I have avoided matrimony for almost forty years," he said. "I do not think I would consider entering it now just to be gentlemanly. I am not much of a romantic, am I? It should have been the first thing I said. It will have to be the last. But it is the most important. I love you, dear."

"Do you?" She put her arms up about his neck and looked earnestly into his face. "Oh, but you can't, Spencer. Look at me."

"A little bird," he said. "A cheerful little singing bird. Will you give me your answer? If it is no, I shall escort you back to the house without further delay. If it is yes, we had better go and break the news to the boys—if you are prepared for a great deal of noise and commotion. But it is dashed cold standing here. A foolish place for a marriage proposal, is it not?"

"Yes," she said.

He raised his eyebrows.

"Now we can go to tell the boys," she said.

"Ah." He threw back his head and laughed. "It was yes to the first question, was it? And would you care to tell me why you are accepting?"

She looked somewhat taken aback for a moment. And then she smiled brightly. "Because I love you, of course," she said.

Mr. Cornwell seemed to forget that it was far too cold a place for such a scene. He caught her up into a tight hug and swung her once around. And then he kissed her soundly and quite unhurriedly.

"Perhaps we can think about taking on that home of boys and girls together," he said.

"Yes," she said. "An instant and large family, Spencer. I would like that."

"And a large bundle of problems to come with them, I warn you," he said.

"Something to challenge the mind and give a reason for living," she said.

"How old are you?" he asked her.

"Thirty-six," she said.

"Quite young enough still to have what you most want out of life, then," he said, and watched her flush quite outshine the glow of coldness in her cheeks. "Perhaps a child or two of our own, Amy."

"Oh." She hid her face against his broad shoulder. "I'll not be greedy. I already have the promise of heaven."

"Heaven!" He chuckled. "Are your feet numb yet? Excuse me, but I am going to have to look down to make sure that mine are still there. Here, let me tuck my arm about you like this. You will be warmer and you fit very snugly there, do you not?"

"Yes," she said. "Oh, yes. Oh, Spencer, has this not been the most wonderful Christmas?"

FORTUNATELY, HE HAD not been at breakfast with his guests. He had ridden out on some errand, Lord Clancy explained, but he would be back soon. And they had all been invited to a neighbor's home later for dinner and an evening of cards.

"What a shame it is that you have to leave today, my dear Mrs. Easton," Miss Edith Hannibal said. "You will be missed, and your dear little children, too."

"Thank you," Judith said. "But I am eager for news of my sister. I have not seen her for an age."

"And the bond between sisters is a close one," Miss Frieda Hannibal said.

No one seemed to have thought to question the fact that Lord and Lady Blakeford were expected back from Scotland so soon after Christmas, far too soon for them to have celebrated the holiday there, in fact.

"Maxwell must be disappointed," Aunt Edith said. "It seemed . . . We thought . . ."

"Doubtless he will go up to town for the Season and

meet Mrs. Easton there again," Lady Clancy said. "And talking about the Season . . ."

Judith returned her attention gratefully to her breakfast and excused herself soon afterward to go to the children in the nursery. They were not at all pleased at the prospect of going home that day. But children were resilient. They would be happy again once they were back in London.

"Papa was the best whip in London," Rupert told her. "And everybody at Gentleman Jackson's was afraid to spar with him because he was so handy with his fives."

Judith smiled. "Mr. Rundle told you a great deal yesterday," she said.

"No," he said, "it was not Mr. Rundle who told me. It was Lord Denbigh."

Judith gave him her full attention.

"Last night," he said. "He was in here. I was having that dream about Papa. But I won't be afraid of it anymore, Mama. He says I am to tell those people that the Marquess of Denbigh knew Papa very well indeed and wishes he could have knocked sixes like Papa did. He said you would be asleep."

"Did he?" Judith said. "And you did not dream anymore afterward?"

Rupert shook his head. "I don't remember his going," he said.

Judith had been relieved to find that he was not at breakfast. But she hoped he would not be gone all morning. She wanted to be on her way. She wanted to start on the rest of her life. She hoped that Amy would not be gone long. Or else she hoped that Amy would be gone forever. She had guessed her sister-in-law's errand from the set look on her face that morning.

If only Amy could come to an understanding with Mr. Cornwell, then something good would have come out of this Christmas after all. And Amy deserved happiness more than anyone else in the world. More than Judith did. Far more than she did.

She went into her bedchamber and summoned a maid. She sent the girl with a message requesting a private word with his lordship at his convenience. And she sat down in the windowseat, heart thumping, to wait.

OVER AN HOUR passed before the summons came. It was amazing, Judith thought as she descended the staircase, shoulders held firmly back, chin high, how resolution could falter in the course of an hour and how knees could weaken and heartbeat accelerate. She had not exchanged a word directly with him since before getting out of his bed at the cottage the afternoon before.

She stepped inside the library and stood still while the footman who had admitted her closed the doors behind her. And her resolution almost fled entirely. He was the Viscount Evendon as she had known him eight years before and the Marquess of Denbigh as she had known him in London a few weeks before. He stood before the fire, one elbow propped on the high mantel, one Hessian boot crossed over the other. His face was harsh, thin-lipped. He looked at her steadily from keen and hooded eyes.

I have summoned the carriage for noon. Her mouth opened to speak the unplanned words and closed again, the words unsaid.

"It was not a Christmas flirtation," she said. "It was revenge."

He said nothing.

"I have asked myself," she said, "why you would wish to take revenge. Because you were the Viscount Evendon and heir to the Marquess of Denbigh and very high in the instep? But such a man would plan some public humiliation, would he not? You will not be able to boast of this particular triumph. So your plan for revenge must have had a more personal motive."

He turned his head sideways to look across the room away from her.

"I think," she said, "that I must have hurt you. Did I?"

His jaw hardened. He said nothing, though she waited for several silent seconds.

"Whether I did or not," she said, "I behaved very badly. And that understates the case. I behaved abominably. I could not bring myself to face you at the time because I feared you and because—oh, because everyone under such circumstances, I suppose, is tempted to play the coward and I gave in to the temptation. And I have never been able to face you since over that particular matter, though the guilt has always gnawed at me. I suppose I have persuaded myself that what happened was of no great significance to you."

She found herself being regarded suddenly by those steel-gray eyes again.

"After yesterday," she said, "I know that I was wrong. I have come to beg your pardon, inadequate as the words are."

He laughed, though there was no amusement in the sound. "You still have the power to amaze me," he said. "I expected that you were coming here to rave at me and accuse, perhaps to demand that I do the decent thing. You ask my forgiveness after what I did to you yesterday?"

"I am right, am I not?" she said. "I did hurt you?"

"I loved you," he said. "Does it surprise you that a man who had none of the charm or easy manner of an Andrew Easton could love? And feel the pain of rejection? And try for a whole year literally to outrun his pain?"

She swallowed and closed her eyes. "I did not know, Max," she said. "I had no idea."

"You are forgiven," he said shortly. "There, does that make you feel better? Now what must I do to win *your* forgiveness? Marry you? I owe you that after yesterday. Is there a chance that you are with child? Should I summon the rector here to speak with both of us? Or should I ride in to the village alone after luncheon?"

"Max," she said, "don't."

"My apologies," he said. "You are a romantic, I suppose. You want sweet words and bended knee? Well, you can have them if you wish, Judith."

She took several steps toward him across the room. "I did not sleep last night," she said. "I don't think you did either. Certainly you were awake and not even in your room when Rupert awoke with his usual dream. I did a great deal of thinking last night."

"You need not have worried," he said. "I am giving in, you see, without even a fight."

"I hated you when I left you yesterday afternoon," she said. "I thought it had all been a plot of revenge. I thought it had all been cold calculation. I thought I had been right about you from the start. But I was wrong. You still love me, don't you?" She could feel herself flushing, but he was not looking at her. He had turned his head away again and set his forefinger against his mouth.

"Perhaps you did not hear my words," he said, "or fully comprehend their true meaning."

"Oh, yes," she said. "Loud and clear. But they were just words, spoken at the end of it all. I think perhaps they were what you had planned to say and so you said them. But what happened before you spoke those words was not part of your plan, Max."

He laughed again. "That good, was it?" he said.

"You know it was," she said. "And thinking about it last night and remembering, I knew that I could not have been mistaken. I could not have been. Even if I had

had no experience with such matters I would know beyond any doubt that I was not mistaken. But I have had experience. I was married for almost seven years. I have been made love to many times. But yesterday you were not making love to me or I to you. We were making love with each other. That has never happened to me before, and I could not possibly be mistaken. It was no game you were playing, Max. It was love. I know it."

"So." He turned his head to look at her, and his eyes were weary, bleak. "What do you want me to do about it?"

"I don't know." She shrugged her shoulders. "Forgive me in your heart as well as with your mouth. Forgive yourself. Let go of all the bitterness. Move on into the future. There is so much goodness in your life. I will be gone within the hour. Let me go—right out of your life. Start again."

He stared at her, nodding his head slowly. "And you?" he said. "You will move on, too?"

"Yes," she said.

"And if you are with child?"

"I will know," she said. "Whatever you may say, I will know that the child was begotten and conceived out of love. That is all that will matter. I do love you, you know, and it will always hurt me to know that I was pain and shadow and darkness in your life for eight years. But you can be free of me now, partly because you got even, but more importantly because you have forgiven me. And I you."

"Judith," he said. "We have given each other so much pain. That can have nothing to do with love, surely?"

She shrugged. "I don't know," she said. "It obviously has a great deal to do with life."

He reached out his free hand toward her and she took a few steps closer to him until she could set her own in it. He drew her closer until she was against him, and his arms closed loosely about her and hers about him. She turned her head to lay against his chest and closed her eyes.

They stood thus for many minutes, comforting each other wordlessly for pain and guilt and for all that might have been.

"And so," he said finally, "in one hour's time you will be gone and we can both start to reconstruct our lives."

"Forgiven and forgiving," she said.

"Pardon and peace," he said.

"Yes."

His cheek rested against the top of her head briefly. "It cannot be done together, Judith? Is it too late for us?"

She heard a gulp of a sob suddenly and realized in some horror that it had come from her. "I don't know," she said, and she tried to push away from him.

But she was pulled back against him by arms that were suddenly as hard as steel bands and when she raised her face to avoid suffocation against his neckcloth it was to look into eyes that were themselves brimming with tears. He lowered his head and kissed her fiercely, a wet and breathless kiss.

"Let us do it, Judith," he said. "Let us give life and love and peace a chance together, shall we? I cannot contemplate any of the three of them without you. Not again. I don't have the strength to do it again. I love you. Is that what I told you with my body yesterday? Did you recognize the language? I am telling you with words now. I love you. I always have."

He took one of her hands and held the palm to his mouth. She stood smiling up at him until gradually he relaxed and smiled back.

"I think we had better get married and be done with it," he said. "Don't you?"

Her smile deepened.

"You are holding out for the poetic speech and the down-on-one-knee business, aren't you?" he said.

But before her smile could give place to laughter they were interrupted. One of the doors opened slightly and two little figures appeared around it.

"Mama," Rupert said, "Aunt Amy is not back yet and it is beginning to snow again and Mr. Rockford said he would take us sledding if we had nothing else to do. May we stay?"

"The dog was sick all over the floor," Kate said.

"Oh, dear," the marquess said, keeping his arms firmly about Judith when she would have pulled away. "You must have been feeding him muffins again, were you?"

"And toast," Kate said.

"May we, Mama?" Rupert asked.

"How would you like to stay forever and a day?" the marquess asked. "If your mama would just consent to marry me, you know, you could do so. And go sledding and skating and have plenty of company from the children in the village. And I could teach you to ride a real horse, Rupert, and to play cricket as well as your papa. And Kate could see the puppies when they are born in the spring and train one to sleep on her bed all night without once wetting the blankets or being sick all over the floor."

"Ye-es!" Rupert yelled. "Famous. Will you, Mama?"

Kate had crossed the room and was clinging to a tassel of the marquess's Hessian. "A black puppy?" she asked. "All black?"

"I shall see what I can arrange," he said.

"Will you, Mama?" Dark and pleading eyes gazed up at her from beneath soft auburn curls.

"Will you, Judith?" Lord Denbigh's eyes smiled into hers. "Will you make it unanimous? It is already three against one."

"One thing I have noticed about you from the start,"

she said, "is that you will quite unscrupulously get to me through my children."

"Guilty," he said.

"And it works every time," she said.

"Does it?"

"Yes."

"This time, too?"

"Yes."

"You will marry me?"

She smiled broadly at him.

He sighed. "Kate," he said. "Stand back if you will. And watch carefully. This is going to happen to you one day. And you watch, too, Rupert, my lad. You are going to have to do this one of these fine days. I am about to get down on one knee to propose to your mama."

"My Christmas beau," Judith said fondly, smiling down at him as he suited action to words.

*Get ready to fall in love
with a brand-new series from Mary Balogh. . . .*

WELCOME TO THE SURVIVORS' CLUB.

*The members are six gentlemen and one lady,
all of whom carry wounds
from the Napoleonic Wars—some visible
and some not. These tight-knit friends have helped
one another survive through thick and thin.
Now, they all need the perfect companions
to teach them how to love again.
Learn how it all begins in:*

The Proposal

Featuring the beloved Lady Gwendoline Muir from
One Night for Love and *A Summer to Remember*.

Available from Delacorte in hardcover.

Turn the page for a sneak peek inside.

1

GWENDOLINE GRAYSON, LADY MUIR, HUNCHED HER shoulders and drew her cloak more snugly about her. It was a brisk, blustery March day, made chillier by the fact that she was standing down at the fishing harbor below the village where she was staying. It was low tide, and a number of fishing boats lay half keeled over on the wet sand, waiting for the water to return and float them upright again.

She should go back to the house. She had been out for longer than an hour, and part of her longed for the warmth of a fire and the comfort of a steaming cup of tea. Unfortunately, though, Vera Parkinson's home was not hers, only the house where she was staying for a month. And she and Vera had just quarreled—or at least, Vera had quarreled with *her* and upset her. She was not ready to go back yet. She would rather endure the elements.

She could not walk to her left. A jutting headland barred her way. To the right, though, a pebbled beach beneath high cliffs stretched into the distance. It would be several hours yet before the tide came up high enough to cover it.

Gwen usually avoided walking down by the water, even though she lived close to the sea herself at the dower house of Newbury Abbey in Dorsetshire. She found beaches too vast, cliffs too threatening, the sea too elemental. She preferred a smaller, more ordered world, over which she could exert some semblance of control— a carefully cultivated flower garden, for example.

But today she needed to be away from Vera for a while longer, and from the village and country lanes where she might run into Vera's neighbors and feel obliged to engage in cheerful conversation. She needed to be alone, and the pebbled beach was deserted for as far into the distance as she could see before it curved inland. She stepped down onto it.

She realized after a very short distance, however, why no one else was walking here. For though most of the pebbles were ancient and had been worn smooth and rounded by thousands of tides, a significant number of them were of more recent date, and they were larger, rougher, more jagged. Walking across them was not easy and would not have been even if she had had two sound legs. As it was, her right leg had never healed properly from a break eight years ago, when she had been thrown from her horse. She walked with a habitual limp even on level ground.

She did not turn back, though. She trudged stubbornly onward, careful where she set her feet. She was not in any great hurry to get anywhere, after all.

This had really been the most horrid day of a horrid fortnight. She had come for a month-long visit, entirely from impulse, when Vera had written to inform her of the sad passing a couple of months earlier of her husband, who had been ailing for several years. Vera had added the complaint that no one in either Mr. Parkinson's family or her own was paying any attention whatsoever to her suffering despite the fact that she was almost prostrate with grief and exhaustion after nursing him for so long. She was missing him dreadfully. Would Gwen care to come?

They had been friends of a sort for a brief few months during the whirlwind of their come-out Season in London, and had exchanged infrequent letters after Vera's marriage to Mr. Parkinson, a younger brother of Sir Roger Parkinson, and Gwen's to Viscount Muir. Vera had written a long letter of sympathy after Vernon's death, and had invited Gwen to come and stay with her and Mr. Parkinson for as long as she wished since Vera was neglected by almost everyone, including Mr. Parkinson himself, and would welcome her company. Gwen had declined the invitation then, but she had responded to Vera's plea on this occasion despite a few misgivings. She knew what grief and exhaustion and loneliness after the death of a spouse felt like.

It was a decision she had regretted almost from the first day. Vera, as her letters had suggested, was a moaner and a whiner, and while Gwen tried to make allowances for the fact that she had tended a sick husband for a few years and had just lost him, she soon came to the conclusion that the years since their come-out had soured Vera and made her permanently disagreeable. Most of her neighbors avoided her whenever possible. Her only friends were a group of ladies who much resembled her in character. Sitting and listening to their conversation felt very like being sucked into a black hole and deprived of enough air to breathe, Gwen had been finding. They knew how to see only what was wrong in their lives and in the world and never what was right.

And that was precisely what *she* was doing now when thinking of them, Gwen realized with a mental shake of the head. Negativity could be frighteningly contagious.

Even before this morning she had been wishing that she had not committed herself to such a long visit. Two weeks would have been quite sufficient—she would actually be going home by now. But she had agreed to a month, and a month it would have to be. This morning, however, her stoicism had been put to the test.

She had received a letter from her mother, who lived at the dower house with her, and in it her mother had recounted a few amusing anecdotes involving Sylvie and Leo, Neville and Lily's elder children—Neville, Earl of Kilbourne, was Gwen's brother, and lived at Newbury Abbey itself. Gwen read that part of the letter aloud to Vera at the breakfast table in the hope of coaxing a smile or a chuckle from her. Instead, she had found herself at the receiving end of a petulant tirade, the basic thrust of which was that it was very easy for Gwen to laugh at and make light of her suffering when Gwen's husband had died years ago and left her very comfortably well off, and when she had had a brother and mother both willing and eager to receive her back into the family fold, and when her sensibilities did not run very deep anyway. It was easy to be callous and cruel when she had married for money and status instead of love. Everyone had *known* that truth about her during the spring of their come-out, just as everyone had known that Vera had married beneath her because she and Mr. Parkinson had loved each other to distraction and nothing else had mattered.

Gwen had stared mutely back at her friend when she finally fell silent apart from some wrenching sobs into her handkerchief. She dared not open her mouth. She might have given the tirade right back and thereby have reduced herself to the level of Vera's own spitefulness. She would not be drawn into an unseemly scrap. But she almost vibrated with anger. And she was deeply hurt.

"I am going out for a walk, Vera," she had said at last, getting to her feet and pushing back her chair with the backs of her knees. "When I return, you may inform me whether you wish me to remain here for another two weeks, as planned, or whether you would prefer that I return to Newbury without further delay."

She would have to go by post or the public stagecoach. It would take the best part of a week for Neville's carriage to come for her if she wrote to inform him that she needed it earlier than planned.

Vera had wept harder and begged her not to be cruel, but Gwen had come out anyway.

She would be perfectly happy, she thought now, if she *never* returned to Vera's house. What a dreadful mistake it had been to come, and for a whole month, on the strength of a very brief and long-ago acquaintance.

Eventually she rounded the headland she had seen from the harbor and discovered that the beach, wider here, stretched onward, seemingly to infinity, and that in the near distance the stones gave way to sand, which would be far easier to walk along. However, she must not go *too* far. Although the tide was still out, she could see that it was definitely on the way in, and in some very flat places it could rush in far faster than one anticipated. She had lived close to the sea long enough to know that. Besides, she could not stay away from Vera's forever, though she wished she could. She must return soon.

Close by there was a gap in the cliffs, and it looked possible to get up onto the headland high above, if one was willing to climb a steep slope of pebbles and then a slightly more gradual slope of scrubby grass. If she could just get up there, she would be able to walk back to the village along the top instead of having to pick her way back across these very tricky stones.

Her weak leg was aching a bit, she realized. She had been foolish to come so far.

She stood still for a moment and looked out to the still-distant line of the incoming tide. And she was hit suddenly and quite unexpectedly, not by a wave of water, but by a tidal wave of loneliness, one that washed over her and deprived her of both breath and the will to resist.

Loneliness?

She never thought of herself as lonely. She had lived through a tumultuous marriage but, once the rawness of her grief over Vernon's death had receded, she had settled to a life of peace and contentment with her family. She had never felt any urge to remarry, though she was not a cynic about marriage. Her brother was happily married. So was Lauren, her cousin by marriage who felt really more like a sister, since they had grown up together at Newbury Abbey. Gwen, however, was perfectly contented to remain a widow and to define herself as a daughter, a sister, a sister-in-law, a cousin, an aunt. She had numerous other relatives, too, and friends. She was comfortable at the dower house, which was just a short walk from the abbey, where she was always welcome. She paid frequent visits to Lauren and Kit in Hampshire, and occasional ones to other relatives. She usually spent a month or two of the spring in London to enjoy part of the Season.

She had always considered that she lived a blessed life.

So where had this sudden loneliness come from? And such a tidal wave of it that her knees felt weak and it seemed as though she had been robbed of breath. Why could she feel the rawness of tears in her throat?

Loneliness?

She was not lonely, only depressed at being stuck here with Vera. And hurt at what Vera had said about her and her lack of sensibilities. She was feeling sorry for herself, that was all. She *never* felt sorry for herself. Well, almost never. And when she did, then she quickly did something about it. Life was too short to be moped away. There was always much over which to rejoice.

But *loneliness*. How long had it been lying in wait for

her, just waiting to pounce? Was her life really as empty as it seemed at this moment of almost frightening insight? As empty as this vast, bleak beach?

Ah, she *hated* beaches.

Gwen gave her head another mental shake and looked, first back the way she had come, and then up the beach to the steep path between the cliffs. Which should she take? She hesitated for a few moments and then decided upon the climb. It did not look quite steep enough to be dangerous, and once up it, she would surely be able to find an easy route back to the village.

The stones on the slope were no easier underfoot than those on the beach had been; in fact, they were more treacherous, for they shifted and slid beneath her feet as she climbed higher. By the time she was halfway up, she wished she had stayed on the beach, but it would be as difficult now to go back down as it was to continue upward. And she could see the grassy part of the slope not too far distant. She climbed doggedly onward.

And then disaster struck.

Her right foot pressed downward upon a sturdy looking stone, but it was loosely packed against those below it and her foot slid sharply downward until she landed rather painfully on her knee, while her hands spread to steady herself against the slope. For the fraction of a moment she felt only relief that she had saved herself from tumbling to the beach below. And then she felt the sharp, stabbing pain in her ankle.

Gingerly she raised herself to her left foot and tried to set the right foot down beside it. But she was engulfed in pain as soon as she tried to put some weight upon it— and even when she did not, for that matter. She exhaled a loud "Ohh!" of distress and turned carefully about so that she could sit on the stones, facing downward toward the beach. The slope looked far steeper from up here. Oh, she had been very foolish to try the climb.

She raised her knees, planted her left foot as firmly as she could, and grasped her right ankle in both hands. She tried rotating the foot slowly, her forehead coming to rest on her raised knee as she did so. It was a momentary sprain, she told herself, and would be fine in a moment. There was no need to panic.

But even without setting the foot down again, she knew she was deceiving herself. It was a bad sprain. Perhaps worse. She could not possibly walk.

And so panic came despite her effort to remain calm. However was she going to get back to the village? And no one knew where she was. The beach below her and the headland above were both deserted.

She drew a few steadying breaths. There was no point whatsoever in going to pieces. She would manage. Of course she would. She had no choice, did she?

It was at that moment that a voice spoke—a male voice from close by. It was not even raised.

"In my considered opinion," the voice said, "that ankle is either badly sprained or actually broken. Either way, it would be very unwise to try putting any weight on it."

Gwen's head jerked up, and she looked about to locate the source of the voice. To her right, a man rose into sight partway up the steep cliff face beside the slope. He climbed down onto the pebbles and strode across them toward her as if there were no danger whatsoever of slipping.

He was a great giant of a man with broad shoulders and chest and powerful thighs. His five-caped greatcoat gave the impression of even greater bulk. He looked quite menacingly large, in fact. He wore no hat. His brown hair was cropped close to his head. His features were strong and harsh, his eyes dark and fierce, his mouth a straight, severe line, his jaw hard set. And his expression did nothing to soften his looks. He was frowning—or scowling, perhaps.

His gloveless hands were huge.

Terror engulfed Gwen and made her almost forget her pain for a moment.

He must be the Duke of Stanbrook. She must have strayed onto his land, even though Vera had warned her to give both him and his estate a wide berth. According to Vera, he was a cruel monster, who had pushed his wife to her death over a high cliff on his estate a number of years ago and then claimed that she had jumped. What kind of woman would *jump* to her death in such a horrifying way, Vera had asked rhetorically. Especially when she was a *duchess* and had everything in the world she could possibly need.

The kind of woman, Gwen had thought at the time, though she had not said so aloud, *who had just lost her only child to a bullet in Portugal,* for that was precisely what had happened a short while before the duchess's demise. But Vera, along with the neighborhood ladies with whom she consorted, chose to believe the more titillating murder theory despite the fact that none of them, when pressed, could offer up any evidence whatsoever to corroborate it.

But though Gwen had been skeptical about the story when she heard it, she was not so sure now. He *looked* like a man who could be both ruthless and cruel. Even murderous.

And she had trespassed on his land. His very *deserted* land.

She was also helpless to run away.